P9-DDS-517

Praise for *New York Times* bestselling author
CELESTE BRADLEY
and her previous novels and series

DEVIL IN MY BED

"From its unconventional prologue to its superb conclusion, every page of the first in Bradley's Runaway Brides series is perfection and joy. Tinged with humor that never overshadows the poignancy and peopled with remarkable characters (especially the precocious Melody) who will steal your heart, this one's a keeper."
—*Romantic Times BOOKreviews*

"Laughter, tears, drama, suspense, and a heartily deserved happily-ever-after."
—*All About Romance*

THE DUKE MOST WANTED

"Passionate and utterly memorable. Witty dialogue and fantastic imagery round out a novel that is a must-have for any Celeste Bradley fan."
—*Romance Junkies*

"A marvelous, delightful, emotional conclusion to Bradley's trilogy. Readers have been eagerly waiting to see what happens next, and they've also been anticipating a nonstop, beautifully crafted story, which Bradley delivers in spades."
—*Romantic Times BOOKreviews*

MORE...

THE DUKE NEXT DOOR

"This spectacular, fast-paced, sexy romance will have you in laughter and tears. With delightful characters seeking love and a title, [this] heartfelt romance will make readers sigh with pleasure."   —*Romantic Times BOOKreviews*

"Not only fun and sexy but relentlessly pulls at the heart-strings. Ms. Bradley has set the bar quite high with this one!"   —*Romance Readers Connection*

DESPERATELY SEEKING A DUKE

"A humorous romp of marriage mayhem that's a love-and-laughter treat, tinged with heated sensuality and tender-ness. [A] winning combination."
                    —*Romantic Times BOOKreviews*

"A tale of lies and treachery where true love overcomes all."
                    —*Romance Junkies*

SEDUCING THE SPY

"Thrilling up to the last page, titillating from one sexually charged love scene to the next, and captivating from begin-ning to end, the last of the Royal Four series displays Brad-ley's ability to tell an involved, sexy story. If you haven't yet read a Bradley novel, let yourself be seduced by the mis-tress of the genre!"   —*Romantic Times BOOKreviews*

"Have you discovered the bawdy charms of Celeste Brad-ley? Laced with intrigue and adventure, she has quickly become a staff and reader favorite and with each book we

just fall further in love with her characters. This is the final book in the superb Royal Four quartet, with her most dangerous deception yet!"
—*Rendezvous*

THE ROGUE

"Once you've read a Liar's Club book, you crave the next in the series. Bradley knows how to hook a reader with wit, sensuality (this one has one of the hottest hands-off love scenes in years!) and a strong plot along with the madness and mayhem of a Regency-set novel."
—*Romantic Times BOOKreviews*

"Bradley continues her luscious Liar's Club series with another tale of danger and desire, and as always her clever prose is imbued with wicked wit."
—*Booklist*

"Celeste Bradley's The Liar's Club series scarcely needs an introduction, so popular it's become with readers since its inception . . . Altogether intriguing, exciting, and entertaining, this book is a sterling addition to the Liar's Club series."
—*Road to Romance*

TO WED A SCANDALOUS SPY

"Warm, witty, and wonderfully sexy."
—Teresa Medeiros, *New York Times* bestselling author

"Funny, adventurous, passionate, and especially poignant, this is a great beginning to a new series . . . Bradley mixes suspense and a sexy love story to perfection."
—*Romantic Times BOOKreviews*

ROGUE IN MY ARMS

Celeste Bradley

St. Martin's Paperbacks

"Greensleeves" credit to Henry VII

This is a work of fiction. All of the characters, organizations, and events portrayed in this novel are either products of the author's imagination or are used fictitiously.

ROGUE IN MY ARMS

Copyright © 2010 by Celeste Bradley.
Excerpt from *Scoundrel in My Dreams* copyright © 2010 by Celeste Bradley.

All rights reserved.

For information address St. Martin's Press, 175 Fifth Avenue, New York, NY 10010.

ISBN: 978-0-312-94309-7

Printed in the United States of America

St. Martin's Paperbacks edition / April 2010

St. Martin's Paperbacks are published by St. Martin's Press, 175 Fifth Avenue, New York, NY 10010.

10 9 8 7 6 5 4 3 2 1

This book is dedicated to everyone in America who has lost their home due to the financial crisis. Bless you all and best wishes for a hopeful and prosperous future for every single one of you. Don't let the bastards get you down!

ACKNOWLEDGMENTS

This book could not have been written without the help of Darbi Gill, Robyn Holiday, Cheryl Lewallen, Joanne Markis, and Cindy Tharp. The crew at St. Martin's Press deserve a lot of credit as well. Thanks especially to Monique Patterson, my editor, and to all the people who helped me get it done.

Once again I must thank little Frankie Jean Baca-Lucero for inspiring madness-monkey Melody. If you think Melody is incredible for her age, you should meet the real article!

To my own babies, who aren't babies anymore, I have to say thanks for putting up with me!

PROLOGUE

*The mony stopped coming from the mother. I can't keep her
no more. The father can take her now. Don't know his name.
He's a memmber of Brown's.*

Once upon a time, a little girl of no more than three years
of age was left upon the steps of a respectable if less
than fashionable gentleman's club in St. James Street of
London. Pinned to her tiny coat was a note, intended for her
father, who was allegedly a member of the aforementioned
establishment. Since most of the club's members were of the
fossilized—er, elderly—persuasion, she was assumed to be
the progeny of one of the three younger, randier members of
the club.

One of these three, Aidan de Quincy, Earl of Blankenship, was a sober and brooding fellow and was the first to assume responsibility for little Melody. In order to learn the
truth, he compelled himself to face his past and once again
face the only woman he'd ever loved.

The widow Madeleine Chandler had secrets indeed—but
furtively giving birth wasn't one of them. Still, her secrets
were dangerous enough for her to seek shelter with Aidan,
even if she had to lie.

After surviving the calamitous events which followed,
Aidan and Madeleine decided to be parents to Melody until
her true father was discovered.

Wilberforce, the head of staff of Brown's, then felt obligated to remind everyone that ladies could most definitely *not* visit the club. Upon the ensuing protest from members and staff alike, Wilberforce did observe that the rules said not a thing about ladies *living* at the club.

Aidan and Madeleine wed at once, but they both regretted the fact that little Melody was not their own.

Sir Colin Lambert, however, was beginning to hope—er, suspect—that Melody was actually his.

Twenty years later . . .

"Wait—that's not the end of the story, is it? That can't be the end! Don't stop there!"

Lady Melody sat up straight on the sofa, leaving the comforting circle of the storyteller's arm in order to look him in the eye. "Button, tell me the rest! What happened next?"

Her companion crinkled his eyes at her, laughing puckishly at her demand. "You sound as though you're three years of age, not two and twenty!"

Melody glanced warily at the wedding dress hanging expectantly nearby and then looked away, tucking her chilled bare feet up under her dressing gown to warm them. "I feel like a child." She dropped her face into her hands, hiding from the momentous day before her. "How can I get *married*? How can I possibly know if I'll love him forever?"

Button tilted his head and frowned at her fondly. "Hmm. Perhaps another story is in order. There's time left. Come, pet." He tucked her into his arm once more, like the surrogate grandfather he was to her, not the fabulous dressmaker the rest of the world knew.

She went willingly, eager to delay that walk down the aisle still further. Snuggling into his shoulder, she closed her eyes and sighed. "Tell me a story, Button."

She felt the chuckle in his chest more than heard it.

"Very well, two-and-twenty Melody who feels like a child."
He dropped a kiss upon her brow and went on.

"Once upon a time there was a scholarly fellow who
thought he knew everything . . ."

The woman onstage wasn't simply beautiful. She was incan-
descent. She glowed with the purity of the ingénue role she
played as she swayed gracefully across the boards, weaving a
spell over the breathless audience. Each gesture was a dance,
each word a song.

Colin Lambert, son of a prominent social scientist, was
so entranced by the pale, black-haired goddess onstage that
he trod upon the toes of his closest friend, Jack, as they made
their way through the crush of the theater pit.

He received a jovial shove for his trespass. "Ger'off, you
great ass." Then Jack realized what had captured his friend's
attention. "Good Lord, what a pretty bird," he said thoughtfully.

That particular tone was the only thing that could have
snagged Colin's attention away at that moment. He glared at
his friend. "I saw her first!"

Jack raised both hands in mock surrender. "She's all yours
then . . . if you can get her while wearing that suit. You dress
like an accountant."

"Better an accountant than a peacock." Colin glanced
down at his admittedly sober suit. "I could never be taken
seriously as a scholar in the rig you wear."

Jack grinned. "Yes, but peacocks have better . . . tail." He
straightened his own stylish cuffs smugly. "I'm engaged
anyway, if you recall."

Colin rolled his eyes. If he had to hear Jack trolling the
virtues of Miss Amaryllis Clarke one more time he was quite
certain he'd have to find a pair of boots to vomit into—
preferably boots belonging to his rival in everything, the high-
and-mighty Aidan de Quincy, Earl of Blankenship.

But for once Aidan wasn't tagging along soberly in Jack's wake, taking the gleeful edge off any interesting trouble they might find for themselves. No, tonight would be absolutely packed with peril if Colin had anything to say about it.

That is, after he bribed his way backstage and wangled an introduction to that radiant female. The playbill hanging outside had named her as Miss Chantal Marchant.

Chantal.

"Jack, do you believe in love at first sight?"

Jack didn't reply. Colin tore his gaze away from the entrancing vision onstage to turn to his friend. Jack's usual smile was gone as he gazed about the full theater.

"I'm leaving tomorrow, you know," Jack said, almost too softly to hear.

Colin's gut chilled. "You don't have to go to war. You're second in line for your uncle's title."

Jack turned to him then, the brief serious moment already in the past. "Let's find a way to get you backstage. The beauteous Chantal awaits!"

. . . And then there was war.

The sight before Colin's eyes terrified him beyond belief. Jack returned from war was not Jack at all. Colin saw a different Jack, sitting quietly, with that half-lost, half-sick expression on his face. It was the same expression he'd worn home from the war, the same he'd worn when he'd been jilted by the girl he'd survived the war for. Now Colin saw Jack, just Jack, sitting on the edge of the roof of Brown's Club for Distinguished Gentlemen, five stories from the cobbled street below.

"Shh. Don't startle him."

That was bloody Aidan de Quincy for you, always stating the obvious. Colin's shoulder twitched backward, creating a little distance from the hovering Aidan.

"I found him like this an hour ago," Aidan continued in a whisper. "I sent for you right away."

And dragged him from the elegant and astonishingly hedonistic embrace of Chantal. Again. Not that Colin wouldn't do anything for Jack, anything at all. For Jack, but not for Aidan.

He glanced over his shoulder. "How could you let him get drunk again?" His own whisper was furious. "You know perfectly well he gets worse when he drinks!"

"It isn't the whisky, it's his spirit." Aidan narrowed his eyes. "And I only lost sight of him for a quarter of an hour. Tonight was supposed to be your turn, at any rate."

"That's beside the point." Fifteen minutes was enough time to put away a great deal of whisky if you didn't care what happened to you after. And Jack didn't care, not in the slightest. Aidan was fortunate he'd found Jack before another brawl had broken out. Jack's guilt over not dying in battle instead of his beloved cousin Blakely—good-hearted but foolish Blakely—seemed to make him want to go down in some sort of fight.

With Blakely gone and Jack's uncle, the elderly marquis, soon to follow, Jack's only surviving bonds were to Colin and Aidan. Most men about to inherit a title and several grand estates would be drunk in celebration. Jack, however, had never wished the agonizing battleground death of Blakely, nor the subsequent heartbroken decline of the Marquis of Strickland. Therefore, Jack was simply hard, stinking, suicidal drunk.

Rumor had it that Blakely had lost his life saving Jack. As far as Colin was concerned, it was possibly the only worthwhile thing that poor fool had ever done.

So now here sat Jack, only ten feet away from Colin and Aidan, yet never more distant. Then Jack rose slowly to his feet, his toes at the very edge of the roof with only a knee-high decorative iron railing to keep him from ending his guilt forever. He gazed out into the foggy London night as if it held some sort of answer for him.

"I think he's really planning on doing it this time," Aidan whispered in horror.

Colin rubbed a hand across his face and turned to look at Aidan. "Right. You hit him high, I'll hit him low."

It was late morning before Colin could make his way back to Chantal. Although it had only been a few hours since Colin had climbed from Chantal's scented sheets, it felt like days. Jack was down off the roof and Aidan was sitting on him firmly, pouring coffee and common sense down his throat whether Jack liked it or not.

Colin and Aidan had hopefully managed to convince Jack that suicide was selfish—that too many people needed him to be a good master. He had responsibilities to the people of Strickland while his uncle was unwell. This seemed to stabilize the darkness for once, but Jack remained withdrawn and unhappy. Colin had stayed at his side, feeling awful about abandoning his friend for Chantal the night before. It wasn't until Jack had dropped into a deep, quiet sleep that Colin tore himself away to return to his lover.

Only to find himself turned away from Chantal's house. Weary beyond belief, Colin could only stare at the servant who blocked him from entry. "What do you mean, she's not at home? She always sleeps late on the morning of a performance!"

The servant gazed at him sourly. "I mean, sir, that my mistress is Not At Home . . . to *you*."

Bloody hell. Chantal meant to wreak a little vengeance for his abandonment last night. Colin rubbed the back of his neck. "Fine. Have it your way. When will your mistress be At Home to me?"

The man actually sneered. "I wouldn't count on it bein' anytime soon, guv'nor. Yer in the doghouse but proper."

Colin refused to acknowledge the tendril of worry twining through his belly. All he needed to do was make her smile. A gift, perhaps more pearls . . . or a sapphire pendant to match her lovely eyes! Or, as he considered the state of his accounts, perhaps a confection, wrapped up in gold paper. Something sweet, to bring out the sweetness in Chantal.

Later, when he approached the theater with thc gift, the manager sourly let him pass.

In her perfumed chamber, Chantal lay half reclined upon the ivory silk-covered fainting couch in the very center of her dressing room. The wickedly tempting curves of her perfect figure were demurely covered by an enormous silk shawl. It clung ever so gracefully to her body, betraying the luxurious fullness of her bountiful breasts as she gasped at his sudden entry. Her exquisite face was pale against her black hair as she gazed up at him, her enormous blue eyes shadowed beautifully in the faintest purple. They were the eyes of a woman who was sad beyond belief.

Colin's heart sank. "Chantal . . ."

A single perfect tear rolled down her perfect cheek. "You left me!"

Oh, no. Colin swallowed. "It was but a few hours—" Desperately, he thrust one hand out, the one that held his gift. The confections looked rather tatty surrounded by the sumptuous gifts given to Chantal by richer men.

Another perfect tear joined the first. "My dearest, my only, please understand. I need someone upon whom I can depend. To be deserted like last night—to be *abandoned*—"

He went cold inside. "No. No, Chantal, I promise, it shan't happen again! I vow, I shall never leave your side—"

She held up one delicate hand to halt his protest. "But my darling, that is not the only chasm between us."

He drew back. "What do you mean?" Jealousy heated his veins. "Is there someone else?"

Her bottom lip trembled as her lovely brows drew together.

"Are you accusing me—why, you know I could never—my love, you destroy me!"

He started forward as she melted into tears, her long, vulnerable neck bowed in despair. "No, of course not! Forgive me, Chantal. I am a fool!"

With a long shuddering breath, she lifted her face to gaze into his eyes with her own eyes dampened and perfectly hopeless. "You must leave me, my champion, my protector, my love—you must take yourself away from me at once!"

The blow rocked him back onto his heels. "What?"

She sat up very straight, her pose almost prim but for the marvelous swelling of her bosom framed by the shawl. "I must let you go, for your own good! You cannot continue to expend yourself thus on me. I know that you have reached the bottoms of your accounts. I cannot allow you to beggar yourself further. I could never live with myself if you did. No, you must go. You and I—we are a beautiful dream, a dream created by the angels, but one that was never meant to be!"

She shivered and pulled the rich silk shawl he'd bought for her more tightly about her fragile white shoulders. "I cannot bear to part from you, my love, but we must each make our own way in the world from this moment onward."

She made a motion with her hand, a subtle movement of her fingers, yet suddenly a dark shape loomed behind Colin. He blinked at the size of the usher who stepped up to take him by the arm.

"Yer business is done 'ere, sir."

Colin turned back to gaze at Chantal in confusion. "You're throwing me out?"

She dabbed at the corner of her eye with the expensive lawn handkerchief he'd given her, the one with her monogram embroidered in silk so fine that one could scarcely see the stitching. "It's for your own good, my dearest. I cannot abide a prolonged parting, you know that. I could not bear for you to see me prostrate with grief, as I will be in mere moments!"

She lifted her chin bravely. "I can hold out for a moment more, for your sake, but only a moment. You must go before your last memory of me is blemished by the sight of my most profound anguish."

The usher began to tow Colin from the dressing room. Not surprisingly, Colin's efforts to resist were met with stoic indifference. In less than a minute, he found himself in the alley behind the theater with an aching shoulder and a throbbing hole in his heart. *Chantal!*

The look in her beautiful, soulful eyes as she'd reminded him that his accounts were empty—damn, how had she known that? He'd taken care that his gifts were still exquisite, if somewhat less frequent.

How was he ever to live without her? How could he go on without the scent of her hair, the feel of her smooth skin in his hands, the way she whispered such filthy things to him in that breathless way when he was inside her?

Rocked to his core by the suddenness of it all, he stood in the reeking alleyway with his palms pressed to his aching chest. Chantal.

He would never love anyone else.

Chantal.

CHAPTER 1

Three and a half years later . . .

Sir Colin Lambert had thought nanny duty would be so simple.
After all, perfectly idiotic people raised children every day.
Well, except that his own father had made rather a muck of it,
and then had dumped him on the doorstep of his aunt, but
Colin had come out all right, hadn't he?

So it couldn't be so very difficult, could it? He was an
intelligent fellow, some might even say a brilliant scholar.
He'd been knighted for his work, after all. Furthermore, one
would think that having a platoon of younger cousins had
granted him some experience with children.

So why couldn't he manage to keep an eye on one tiny
little girl?

He'd had it easy before, he realized. When little Melody
had been left on the doorstep of Brown's Club for Distinguished Gentlemen, he and Aidan de Quincy, Earl of Blankenship, decided to take care of her until their friend Jack
returned. Since neither he nor Aidan wanted to believe that
they were the father, Jack had made a convenient suspect.
Then Aidan had brought in his former lover, Madeleine, and
things had gone quite smoothly from there—if one didn't
count the homicidal maniac kidnapper lurking in the attic.
Which, to be entirely truthful, hadn't been Melody's fault.
Not even a little bit.

This mess, however, was entirely of his own doing. When Aidan and Madeleine had left on their honeymoon, Colin had blithely decided to leave the safety of the club and all its convenient and tolerant staff behind and venture out into the world of fatherhood.

Where he now suffered on his own with dear little Baby Bedlam.

When he'd thought Aidan and Madeleine were going to take little Melody away with them, the pain had been unbearable. He'd been alone before, but it was worse now, with his father and his aunt gone, his cousins busy with their own broods, Aidan gone to Madeleine, and Jack . . . Jack so unreachable.

Colin had lost so much he could scarcely stand to lose Melody as well. It was more than fear of loneliness. He loved her like a father, not like an uncle.

She could be his. Her age was close enough to the timing of his affair with Chantal. Even the fact that Chantal had fostered her out with a nurse made sense. A well-known actress could hardly raise her bastard child in the spotlight of public scorn. Melody even somewhat resembled Chantal with her dark hair and blue eyes, although Chantal's features were more dramatic. Melody's obvious intelligence made it even more likely that she was his.

Naturally, he'd inquired at the theater in London where Chantal had performed four years ago. There he'd learned that not only had Chantal since left London for Brighton, but that only a few weeks after they'd parted ways, Chantal had taken several months away from the stage. "Rheumatic fever" he'd been told.

"Romantic fever" it was sometimes called, for such an excuse was often used when a girl of good family needed to be out of sight for, oh, say, nine months.

That had clinched it for Colin. Melody was clearly his.

Upon which followed the exhilarating possibility that Chantal might also soon be his!

It gave him such hope, picturing that new life—Melody was his, Chantal was his at last—seeing that future in his mind, the sort of life that Aidan and Madeleine could look forward to, with more children as well, a crowd of them, enough to fill the great empty house at Tamsinwood.

He could wake each day with Chantal beaming and happy. He could shower her with silk and lace now. He could drown her in jewels. He could sleep in her arms and wake with his face in her hair and her body aligned with his . . .

Being a man of logic and forethought—usually—he'd thrown caution to the wind and set out with a tiny child to Brighton in the hopes of finding the woman who might be Melody's long-lost mother.

First, however, he had to find Melody!

"Mellie! Mellie, I know you're hiding in there! Come out this instant!"

Of course she didn't come. Why should she? He was doing the same thing he'd thought so idiotic when he'd observed other adults dealing with children. Children weren't stupid. Calling them when one was angry was like a dog trying to coax a cat out of a tree.

Fine. Colin took a deep breath and sat down in the shade of the aforementioned tree. He listened for a moment and was rewarded by the slightest scuffling of little boots. Powdered bark sifted down through the moist spring air to ornament his dark green superfine surcoat. He brushed at it in resignation and then tilted his head back and closed his eyes against the leaf-dappled sunlight.

If one had to be stuck on the side of the road, unable to get one's possible offspring back into the vehicle after she'd been turned loose on yet another call of nature . . . well, this was most definitely the spot to do it. Even if a one-day journey had turned into two.

He opened his eyes to gaze fondly at his new two-wheeled Cabriolet parked on the roadside. It was the very latest model and marked the first time he'd indulged himself with his father's money, purchasing it for this journey. The gleaming, elegantly swept fantasy was the perfect vehicle for a very smart bloke-about-town. The modern lightweight frame of the one-horse chaise followed the sweet curve of a woman's body and the lacquered finish glowed red in the sunlight. The shine was echoed in his very fine gelding, Hector, whose excellent form and shimmering black coat set off the ebony trim and fine brass fittings to perfection.

It was a thing of beauty. Aidan would say it was hideously impractical.

Colin grinned at the thought. Aidan wasn't here.

Unfortunately, he and Melody were and they would remain here for the rest of the day if he couldn't coax her out of her tree.

"I was thinking about a bit of lunch, Mellie . . ." He let the sentence fade away unsaid. "Well, you probably don't want to hear about that." He picked at a bit of grass. "Or do you?"

Silence. She was undoubtedly hungry, but she was too stubborn to admit it.

You'll need better bait than that.

He nearly whimpered. *Not again.* He'd only been traveling with Melody for two days and already he'd told her more outlandish pirate tales than there had ever been outlandish pirates! If he had to review the gory details of keelhauling one more time he was definitely going to lose the last of his mind.

Ah, well. "You see . . . I was wondering what pirates had for lunch . . ."

"Fish."

Speaking of fish, his own little shiner had just taken the bait. He smiled. "Of course, how silly of me. I imagine they ate a great deal of fish." He hummed to himself for a moment. "What about breakfast? Too bad they didn't have any eggs."

"Fish eggs."

He stifled a laugh. "Ah, yes. Why not?"

More bark fell onto his jacket. The scuffling of little boots was closer now. He was tempted to jump up and reach for her but he'd learned his lesson well over the last hour and a half. Melody might be scarcely three years old, but she showed an early aptitude for altitude.

So he gave in with a sigh and began the litany that he must have repeated forty times over the last days. "Once upon a time on the high seas"—*damn the high seas!*—"there sailed a mighty pirate ship. Upon the prow were letters etched in the blood of honest men and they read—" He waited.

"Dishonor's Plunder!"

"Dishonor's Plunder," Colin affirmed wearily. And the story was on. Blood ran, gore oozed, and a horridly high body count mounted. At least three keelhaulings later, he realized that Melody had climbed down from the tree and was seated tailor-fashion on the grass beside him.

In her lap was Gordy Ann, the smeary wad of knotted cravat that Melody called a doll. Gordy Ann gazed at Colin with floppy tilted head and blank inky eyes. She looked a bit suspicious, as if he weren't to be trusted.

"Hullo," he said carefully.

Melody blinked big blue baby eyes at him. Her dark curls were decorated with leaves and bits of bark. "I'm hungry."

"I'm not." He was, in fact, ever so slightly nauseated by his own imagination. If anyone in the Bathgate Society of Scholars were to hear the dreck he spouted sometimes . . .

Well, that would never happen.

He stood and brushed at his clothing. "Right, then. The city of Brighton is only a few more miles down the road. Up you go, Cap'n Mellie." With that, he tossed her giggling onto his shoulders and strode back to where the still-harnessed Hector was manfully striving to mow the entire roadside, despite the bit in his mouth. Colin put Melody into the chaise and vaulted up into the driver's seat.

Hector, always ready for action, pulled his head out of the weeds and began to trot.

So convenient, Colin thought, just the two of them making this journey together. No servants, no nattering companions. No one telling them when to start and when to stop—

"Uncle Coliiiin! I gotta *go!*"

Prudence Filby threw her sewing bag down onto the dressing room floor in frustration. Damn Chantal! She put her hands over her face, trying very hard to quell the panic icing her veins.

"She isn't coming back?" she asked the manager of the Brighton Theater even though she knew his answer. "Are you sure?"

The stout man behind her made a regretful noise. "She's gone. Took off with that dandy, sayin' she was in love. Wouldn't take her back if she did return. Chantal Marchant might be the most beau'iful actress in England but she's also a towering b—" He cleared his throat. "She's a right pain in the arse, she is! The last ten shows, she's only finished two! Keeps saying she's too weary, too bored, too good for such a horrid play."

It was an accurate depiction of Chantal, except he'd left out "spiteful." Pru raised her eyes to see the dressing room's true disarray. It looked as though a tornado equipped with vindictive scissors had torn through it. Everything was ruined.

Damn you, Chantal.

The small room had been Pru's home for two years, this and the costume sewing room. Dark, grim, and cramped, but home. Most people who came to the theater saw the grand stage, the crimson velvet curtains, the bright foot lamps lighting the current fantasy on stage. The real world of the theater was here, backstage, in the chilled fingers that could scarcely sew, in the long hours bending over complicated seams, in the endless demands of the spoiled star.

Pru had spent more time here, attending to the demanding Chantal, than she had in the tiny rented chamber she shared with her younger brother, Evan. The destruction of this dressing room was a direct stab at her, she knew.

She looked over her shoulder at the manager and tried to smile. The man had managed to perfectly capture Chantal's petulant tones. "You should go on the stage yourself, sir. You've a right knack for playin' a towering b—"

He smiled, but shook his head regretfully. "It'll do ye no good to flatter me, Pru. I can't get ye another job. Ye can't sew a lick and all the cast knows it. The only reason ye lasted so long was that ye were the only one who could put up with Chantal's tantrums."

Pru nodded in resignation. "Not your fault, sir. You've got the right of it." There was no point in denying it. Not that she was a patient person in reality. She'd simply realized that if she could keep her temper through Chantal's rages and abuses and bouts of throwing breakable objects, she'd be able to keep feeding herself and twelve-year-old Evan. The other seamstresses and dressers had helped her with the more difficult stitching, grateful that they weren't called upon to personally serve the she-devil.

Now it was over. Chantal had left without paying her for her last month's work and there was nothing left in her pockets but bits of snipped thread and extra buttons.

She couldn't even sell the costumes, for Chantal had shredded them in a last fit of malice.

The manager left her to contemplate her short and miserable future. This was the only job she'd ever managed to keep here in Brighton. No one wanted a girl without useful skills or socially acceptable references—no one but the factories.

Her chest felt heavy with the cold undeniable truth. She

was going to have to go into the factories. She only hoped she would be one of the lucky few to someday come out.

All the dressers at the theater had horror stories to tell. Factory work was grueling and unhealthy. Girls froze at their machines in winter and fainted from the heat in summer. Cruel foremen made advances and refused to be refused. Machines lopped off fingers and slashed hands and there was no law that told the factory owners nay. Despite the grim conditions, as soon as one girl was abused past her ability to endure, another one would be begging for the work.

It was a last resort, but there were many who were forced to take it out of desperation.

Better she than Evan. The younger children in the factories scarcely ever saw their next birthday once they walked through those doors. She swallowed hard at the thought.

You could go back. At least that way Evan wouldn't starve.

No. She'd rather face the factories! She was stronger than her small frame and large eyes led people to believe. She was smart and careful. Besides, she told herself firmly, ignoring the cold ball of dread in her belly, if she could abide Chantal, she could tolerate anything!

Anything except going back.

CHAPTER 2

When Colin at last drove the chaise into Brighton, he was exhausted and frustrated. Nevertheless, he nearly turned around and drove back to London at the sight of the sticky seaside crowds with their ludicrous swimming costumes and their whining, sunburned children.

"May in Brighton. What was I thinking?"

He'd been thinking that he would see the exquisite Chantal again, that's what. Just the thought of her, so lovely, so sweet-tempered, so delicate, so very, very amorous when he had at last managed to worm his way past her modest and righteous morals—

He gave the distracted and weary Hector an easy touch of the whip. *Chantal awaits!*

Except, as it turned out, she did not.

At the Brighton Theater Colin blinked around him at the empty, shabby velvet seats and the peeling gilt of the stage border—not quite as magical during the day, was it?—then turned back to the stout fellow who claimed to be the theater manager. Melody stood between them, one arm wrapped around Colin's shin, gazing about her in awe.

Gordy Ann, dangling limply from one sticky fist, seemed somewhat less impressed.

"She isn't coming back?" Colin asked. "Are you sure?"

The man scowled. "Why do people keep saying that? She ain't comin' back, I don't want her back, and she ain't

welcome in any other theater in the city!" He threw up his
hands in an Italianate manner and strode away muttering
resentfully.

Colin's knees felt wobbly as he slowly lowered himself to
sit on the edge of the deserted stage. At least the theater was
dim and cool, a welcome respite from the dusty road. Melody
promptly deposited herself in his lap and rested her head on
his waistcoat. Colin curled one hand around her tummy and
dropped a kiss upon her curls.

"Uncle Colin, I'm tired. I wanna go back to Brown's. I
wanna see Maddie and Uncle Aidan and my room and the
garden and . . ." She went to sleep quickly, as she always did.
Melody only had two styles: "go" and "unconscious."

Colin rather wanted to crawl somewhere and sleep himself. All this for nothing? The hours and hours on the road,
the continuous stops to attend to Melody's infant bladder,
the hundreds of exhaustively detailed decapitations?

For a moment he fervently wished he were scarcely three
years old so he could fling himself down upon the stage and
kick and scream in frustration.

"*No!* I won't go and you can't bloody make me!"

Colin looked up at the furious voice, automatically covering Melody's ears from any further profanity. His action was
not so much to protect her innocence as to limit her by now
extensive vocabulary. There had already been a few embarrassing moments on their journey so far.

From around the back of the stage came a small figure,
stomping angrily in boots too large, swinging fists that were
none too clean, and scowling with a face that apparently had
only a passing acquaintance with soap. The person saw Colin
watching and glared back belligerently.

"What you starin' at, you posh bastard?"

Colin blinked at the miniature vulgarian in dismay. The
creature couldn't be more than twelve years of age, and a
poorly grown twelve years at that. However, his large gray

eyes showed the shadows of too many hardships and too few childish pleasures.

Colin shook off his fascination. When had he begun to pay so much attention to children?

"I'm looking for Chantal Marchant," he told the boy. *Why did I share that?* Really, to someone who didn't understand the past that Colin and Chantal shared, for him to come looking for her with the road dust still on his clothing . . . well, it might come across as just a tad—

"Pathetic, that's what!" The boy spat. Then he turned to face the direction he'd just come from. "There's another fancy blighter pantin' after Herself!" he yelled.

Colin turned to gaze at the shadows behind the half-drawn curtain. He saw a dark figure bend gracefully, deposit something on the floor of the stage, and then stretch her arms above her head like a dancer. Against the backlight, he could see that she was slightly built but there was no hiding the fact that her bosom was lush and full. What a lovely figure!

She lowered her arms and planted her hands on her hips. The pose only served to show off the narrow dimensions of her waist.

Really spectacular. Colin leaned sideways for a better view. *Chantal?*

A low, velvety voice came from that luscious shadow. "Leave the fancy blighter be, Evan. It ain't his fault he's an idiot."

Colin was so distracted by the sensual richness of that voice that it took a long moment for him to realize that he'd been slighted. In addition, the speech patterns were of an uneducated woman of no social stature, i.e., "not for him." He blinked wistfully at that momentary fantasy as it seeped away.

Still he couldn't help await her entrance into the light. If her face matched that body and that voice—! Well, he simply might have to reassess his standards a bit.

She stepped into the dusty daylight streaming in through

the great double doors that stood open to the sea air. Colin felt
a hit of disappointment. She wasn't precisely unattractive . . .
more like a bit plain. She had small, pointed features that did
not fit his usual idea of beauty—though her large gray eyes
were rather attractive.

They matched the boy's eyes, in fact. Her son?

She gazed back at him for a long moment with one eye-
brow raised. He suddenly had the uncomfortable sensation
that she somehow knew precisely what he'd been thinking
about her.

Then she tossed a bundle to the boy. "Evan, we got no
choice. Go ask the coach driver if he'll let us sit on top for a
shilling."

Evan smirked. "We ain't got a shilling."

She turned back to gaze speculatively at Colin. "We will."

Evan, defeated at last, stomped his way from the theater,
but not without a last resentful look at Colin.

The woman approached him and stood there, looking
down at Melody in his lap. "You're lucky there," she said,
indicating Melody with her chin. "That age is easy."

The very thought of it getting harder made Colin's spine
weaken just a bit. "Really?"

The woman gathered her full skirts and sat down next to
him, letting her worn boots dangle next to his costly calfskin
ones. "Oh, sure 'tis. Now she thinks you hung the moon.
You're her champion. When she gets a bit taller, she'll suss out
that you don't know what the hell you're doin' and she'll never
respect you again."

Colin gazed down at the top of Melody's head in alarm.
"But what if I do know what I'm doing?"

"Won't matter. You'll never convince her of it." She
shrugged. It did interesting things to the supple burden within
her bodice. Not that he was interested in her—but he breathed,
didn't he?

She swung her feet idly for a moment. "So . . ." Her tone was conversational. "You're lookin' for Chantal."

She was a bit too familiar for Colin's taste. "Don't you mean 'Miss Marchant'?"

Her fingers tightened on the edge of the stage but her response was respectful. "Sorry, guv'nor. I just thought you'd be wantin' to know where *Miss Marchant* took off to."

Ah. The gambit, at last. Well, he had shillings to spare if she had information. "What'll it cost me?"

She slid him a sideways glance. "Five bob."

He snorted. "Nice try."

"Three, then."

"Shillings or pounds?"

Her lips twisted in reluctant respect. "Shillings, then."

Colin shrugged. It was only money and she looked as though she needed it. "You have a bargain. Where is she?"

"Not till you fork over."

He reached into his waistcoat pocket and withdrew three shillings. He laid them out in his palm and showed them to her. "You can see I have them. I can see you have something to tell me. So tell me."

Her eyebrows rose and she scoffed. "What, an' let you walk away leavin' me empty-handed?"

"Fine. I get three questions, then. I pay as you answer."

She examined his face closely, then shrugged resentfully. "Right. May as well start cheatin' me then."

Colin nodded, amused. She was a peculiar little thing. "Why should I pay you for information? What makes you privy to Chantal's business?"

"Prudence Filby, seamstress and dresser to Miss Chantal Marchant, at your service." She smiled and dipped her head elegantly. Damn, she was graceful. Too bad she was so plain. And common. And had the boy . . . well, he was here for Chantal, anyway.

He dropped one shilling into her outstretched palm. "See, I am a gentleman. I pay my debts." She snorted at that. He went on. "Second question . . ." An image of the boy crossed his mind. He looked so much like his mother, it was hard to see the paternal contribution. "Who is Evan's father?"

Wait, that wasn't what he'd meant to ask!

She paled slightly and drew back. "Why'd you want to know?"

He cleared his throat and forced himself not to redden. "I'm asking the questions here. Who fathered your son?"

Her eyes narrowed. "He's dead."

"You're a widow, then?" Why couldn't he let this go? Perhaps it was Melody and how she'd been abandoned . . .

She gazed down at her very clean, very elderly boots. "I ain't never been wed."

An awkward silence stretched. "Right. None of my business."

She gave him a sideways glance, her lips twisting. "He's me younger brother, guv."

She was laughing at him. "Ah . . . my apologies." He dropped the shilling into her hand, feeling like a heel. That's what he got for prying.

"Third question . . . where is Chantal now?"

She shrugged. "Can't tell you that. She wouldn't tell anyone, would she, all the money she owes about town?"

Chantal had debts. Surprising, considering how she'd always been showered with luxury by every man she'd so much as smiled at.

Yet . . .

The money stopped coming.

Melody's nurse had turned her over to Brown's Club for Distinguished Gentlemen because she was no longer being paid. Debt, especially the must-flee-town sort of debt, would explain much about Melody's situation.

Even the timing of it all aligned.

Miss Filby was still talking. ". . . but I know who she run off with."

"She ran away with some . . . man?" Colin felt a jolt of jealousy. "Who?"

"Lord Bertram Ardmore. Him with the pink weskits."

"Lord Bertie?" Melody shifted in his lap so he dropped his tone to an outraged whisper. "That sniveling pup?"

She shrugged and held out her hand. "Chantal said they looked beau'iful together."

No longer interested in correcting her familiar manner, Colin seethed as he dropped the last shilling in her hand. "'Purty Bertie.' My God."

The clever miss climbed lightly to her feet and grinned down at him. "Don't take it so hard, guv'nor. I happen to know Chantal ain't really Lord Bertie's sort. Too womanly, if you take my meaning."

"I know." He closed his eyes and shuddered. "That's what makes it so mortifying!"

Miss Prudence Filby stiffened and her gaze turned cold. "Right. Off you go, then. You'd best hurry. She's set her sights on weddin' him straightaway."

Wedding? Chantal was actually considering marrying that . . .

Then the full implication struck Colin like a brick. If Chantal was Melody's mother—and he was becoming more convinced by the moment that she was!—then this was disastrous!

What if Chantal married another? The best possibility would be that she would allow him to keep Melody, to raise her as his acknowledged bastard. It would forever curtail Melody's future, that simple fact of illegitimacy. Even if he raised her in the grandest manner, Society would always be essentially closed to her.

The worst possibility, the one that took his breath away with the pain of it, was that Chantal would take Melody away to live with her and her new husband. Melody would grow up calling another man her father, and for the sake of her social standing Colin would have to let her go.

Forever.

His hold on Melody tightened and she protested limply, her nap disturbed by his tension.

If Chantal planned to wed another, then time was of the essence! Yet how could he continue to travel with Melody?

Well, he would not leave her behind, no matter what. Would not and could not!

Miss Filby turned away to pick up her other bundle. "I've a coach to catch, guv'nor. There's no work for me in Brighton. Evan and me are going to London."

He blinked, remembering what she'd told her brother. "You're going to ride all the way to London on top of a mail coach? In the changeable spring weather? You'll die!"

Gazing at the poor, small woman before him—a woman experienced with children, a woman who could help him find Chantal—Colin had a wonderful, marvelous, outstanding idea!

"Melody and I have to keep traveling in order to find Chantal, but we'll end up in London. Why don't you and your brother come with us?"

CHAPTER 3

Pru froze as Mr. Lambert gazed at her expectantly.

"I don't know how much child nurses are paid," he admitted. "How about that five pounds you mentioned earlier? Will that do?"

Five pounds. She couldn't believe it. *I'm going mad. I know I'm going mad because I'm going to accept this strange man's offer.*

She clenched her jaw shut against the words of agreement that threatened to leave her lips. She wrapped her fingers about the shillings in her pocket. Three shillings. If she were careful, it meant a ride to London and a week of plain food and safe shelter while she looked for work.

Work that she possibly would not get.

And even if she did, who could say if her employer would be any better than Chantal? Then the money would be gone.

Five pounds.

Riches. Bread and meat. A safe, quiet place to live with a real bed. *Heat.* Not for a day, not for a week, but for *months.* If she didn't eat any meat herself, she might be able to stretch it into a year or more.

Five pounds to keep an eye on one little child. Heavens, she'd been doing that for nothing.

She gazed up at the handsome man before her. Who was Mr. Lambert? Men like him didn't hire nurses. They had people who had people who did that. Men like him . . . well, she couldn't honestly say, for she didn't think she'd ever encountered a man quite like him before.

Wide shoulders that blocked the light from the open doors. Towering height. Green eyes that danced with humor, then flashed with something deeper, something darker. Even his hands, curled protectively around the tiny little girl, were broad and manly, tanned with neatly trimmed nails.

Very clean hands. That alone was something new in these environs. The tenderness in the way his fingertips came down to touch the little girl's curls, as if to reassure himself that she was still there, made her swallow hard and look away.

From somewhere inside her came the thought . . . *He makes the hairs on the back of my neck stand up.*

And that wasn't all. The tips of her breasts tingled at the way the corners of those green eyes crinkled when he almost smiled.

She crossed her arms over her chest. Men like him couldn't help having an effect on women. He likely didn't even know he was doing it. Sandy blond hair and crinkling green eyes were simply the weapons he'd been born with.

It was only too bad she'd had to come to battle without her armor.

Take off my armor. Please.

Now she was just being a ninnyhammer. He couldn't be trusted. She'd learned long ago that no one could be trusted. She and Evan were on their own, as always.

Furthermore, he was hiring a servant. He probably didn't even think of her as a person, much less a woman. She certainly shouldn't be thinking of him as a man!

She ought not to accept the job when he affected her this way. Then again, what did it matter if wages came from a handsome man? She was to be nurse, not mistress.

Ah, best be sure about that. "What would me duties be, exactly?"

He blinked. "Er . . . well, you would take care of Melody, and keep her out of mischief and . . ."

She narrowed her eyes. "And?"

He looked worried. "Can you climb trees?"

A laugh broke from her lips. It certainly didn't sound as if he were after a tumble, unless he fancied himself a carnival act. "Aye, I'm a fair climber, but Evan's better."

He brightened. "That's capital!" He gazed down at the pretty baby sleeping in his arms. "Melody is quite ambitious . . . er . . . vertically."

A wisp of dark curl swept over the round pink cheek. The little one didn't look much like Mr. Lambert. Of course, neither she nor Evan looked a bit like their father. They were their mother all over again.

"If I may ask, sir, where is her mother?" What was a man like Mr. Lambert doing toting a child across the country while he searched for Chantal Marchant?

He didn't frown but the smile slipped. "Does it matter?"

Right. None of her business. She cared nothing for idiot men and their idiot obsession with Chantal. Pru lifted her chin defiantly. She would tend his child and take his money with a smile, though it was five times too much. She quelled her conscience. Evidently he could spare it and Evan needed so much more than she'd been able to give him.

Five pounds and transport to London, albeit roundabout. Not to mention the possibility of finding Chantal and twisting her arm until she paid what she owed. Pru smiled grimly. That alone would make it worthwhile.

She stuck out her hand. "Then I think we're havin' a deal, sir."

Colin answered her grip automatically, though he was not in the habit of shaking hands with women. When her warm palm met his, he blinked in surprise as a jolt when through him. Her callused grip was firm but her hand was small in his larger one. The surprise came from the fact that he couldn't seem to let her go. For a long moment, they stayed like that, hand in hand, green gaze locked to gray.

Those eyes . . . like a cool rainy sky . . .

He suddenly had an overwhelming desire to stand in the rain.

Then she pulled her hand from his with just enough force to shock him back to himself. *Bloody idiot, what are you doing?*

"Oh. My apologies. I was merely thinking . . ."

She raised one brow at him suspiciously. He couldn't blame her. He must be more weary than he thought to have drifted away like that. He closed his hand around the trace of warmth left in his palm. "I was thinking that we had best get on if we want to get to an inn by dark."

She pursed her lips. "Or we could set out in the morning."

He shook his head. "I truly do need to find Chant—Miss Marchant. I'd like to make Lord Bertram's estate by tomorrow evening." He hoped she didn't realize that he was proposing a rather grueling pace, but he'd lost so much time on the way to Brighton. If Chantal wed another—

"Shall we go?"

She turned away from him and let out a small sigh that he was probably not meant to hear. "I'll just go and fetch Evan then, guv. We're already packed-like."

Colin shifted Melody to his other arm, where she lay limp and warm upon his shoulder. Damn, he'd forgotten about the boy already. Where were they all going to sit?

Well, it was ride crowded or ride alone with Melody— and he didn't think his nerves could take another two days of that!

Pru blinked away her weariness and set out to find Evan. She had the feeling he wasn't going to like this arrangement. Evan could be so stubborn sometimes. She really didn't know how a brother and sister could be so different.

* * *

A man stood in the odd daylight shadows of the theater and watched the manager supervise the props onstage.

The man did not move or call out to anyone but it wasn't long before the manager became aware of his presence. The heavyset theater man approached him where he stood at the back of the hall. He'd known it would not take much time. Being quiet could be more emphatic than being loud.

He eyed the burly manager for a long time before he spoke. "You haven't told her I'm here. Why not?"

The manager swallowed. "She ain't about, like."

The shadowed man drew in a long slow breath. "You mean she's flown."

The manager daubed a stained handkerchief to his brow. "Been gone near two days. Didn't leave a note nor nothin'."

The man said nothing for a long moment. "Those might be the facts but you're leavin' out the gossip."

The manager grimaced. "Gossip has her runnin' off with a bloke. Can't recall his name—"

"Yes you can." Oh, yes, he would know the name of this man. It wouldn't make him any harder to kill and it might just make him easier to find.

"All I heard was Bertie." The manager averted his gaze. "Just Bertie."

It was a start. This Bertie would be a wealthy man, no doubt, or else his lovely Chantal would not have turned to him. A man of rank, possibly. That world was a small one, even smaller than the tightly bound world of crime. Small worlds were quite easy to search, if one had a name.

"Bertie."

Far away in bustling London, on a street that was just beginning to fill with gentlemen of Society who sought the masculine refuge of their clubs, there stood a stuffy, slightly archaic institution by the name of Brown's Club for Distinguished Gentlemen. Like a stout, balding uncle who lived on the edges of the family income, Brown's stood several doors down from such glittering establishments as White's and Boodle's. Where those lively card tables and dining rooms were only beginning to reach capacity for the evening, the chambers of Brown's echoed only the faint sounds of the club's septuagenarian population retiring to their well-deserved beds.

Belowstairs, there could only be heard the brisk footfalls of Wilberforce, the club's rather excellent head of staff. With the efficiency of years of practice, Wilberforce settled the club and his charges in for an early night. If he inwardly longed for the sound of lighter footsteps than his own, or even paused a moment thinking he heard the peal of childish laughter on a floor far above, he made no outward sign of such dissatisfaction.

As he turned the corner into the main kitchens, he caught sight of his youngest footman, Bailiwick, who was gloomily polishing off the last of his youthfully enormous dinner at the heavy wooden table where the servants took their meals.

Bailiwick looked up at his entrance and sighed gustily. "Will they be back soon, d'ye think, sir?"

Since Wilberforce had fielded this question from Bailiwick, the cook, the scullery boy, and every single elderly member of Brown's several times that day, he might be excused the slight shoulder twitch of irritation that resulted. Bailiwick wilted further, however, and turned his mournful gaze back to his nearly clean plate where a crust of bread and a small pile of peas remained.

"See? I've lost me appetite, I 'ave, sir."

Wilberforce eyed the nineteen-year-old eating machine dourly. "Pray, tell me it isn't so," he murmured.

Yet there was no denying that the light had gone out of the days this past week. With Lord and Lady Blankenship away on their honeymoon and Sir Colin's decision to take little Melody on a sea holiday to Brighton, the passing hours at Brown's felt somewhat dry and papery, like the husks of a sweet fruit long eaten.

After the adventures of the previous weeks, even Wilberforce had to admit that the return to the drowsy daily routine of old left one rather edgy and restless. Still, it was not his place to be restless. It was his place to provide perfect service to his charges, even if it meant answering that same petulant query all day long.

"When will they be back?"

Colin had them all in the chaise and on their way with blinding speed. It was a bit of a task to fit the new passengers' sparse luggage into the small trunk fitted behind the seat of the Cabriolet and the seat was none too wide for three, but before long the noisy streets of Brighton were behind them and they were on the northwest road to Basingstoke. City gave way gradually to town gave way to country.

"Sir, did you and the little miss come all the way from London in this rig?"

"Yes." Colin patted the dash fondly. "Isn't it a beauty?"

No answer. He looked at her. "Don't you think so?"

Miss Filby pursed her lips. "Not for me to say, sir. Just . . ."

"Just what? If you have something to say, say it."

Her gray eyes sparked at the challenge. "It's a bit flash for a family man, don't you think?"

He straightened. "No. It's perfectly serviceable."

Her chin lifted. "If you say so, guv. It bein' your rig and all."

The light caught the shadows beneath her eyes. She was very pale for someone who'd spent years at the seaside. "What about you? Did you originally come from Brighton?"

She gazed outward at the passing fields. "Me and Evan were born there. Never been anywhere else."

"Ah." He thought of all the world that he'd seen. "This must be exciting for you then."

She looked at him then with delicate russet brows raised. Right.

He grinned. "Exciting sheep? Exciting fields?"

Her lips twitched. "I'm beside meself, I am," she said tonelessly.

He laughed out loud. She smiled back, a quick flash of white teeth. For an instant her pallor and plainness disappeared. Her gray eyes laughed into his and he found himself held there, captured easily and willingly by her smile and her quick wit and the way she rode next to him with Melody in her lap, as if she belonged there—

The wheel of the Cabriolet struck a deep pothole and the entire curricle lurched heavily. For an instant she was thrust hard against him. He flung out a hand to keep her and Melody on the seat. "Steady on!"

Unfortunately, his palm caught nothing but a rich handful of soft breast. She gasped and jerked backward, but that only worsened matters. Her hand slid down into his lap to push off from him. His traitorous lap really enjoyed the entire experience.

They jerked apart and froze there.

"Sorry!" Colin swallowed. Oh, God. How embarrassing. The weight and fullness of her breast lingered in his palm. He closed his fist around it.

What a magnificent handful.

"Sorry, sir!" Pru was mortified. She shrank into her seat, juggling Melody protectively in front of her. The child giggled.

"Gordy Ann wants to do that again!"

Gordy Ann wasn't the only one. Pru hid her blush in Melody's curls. She could still feel the heat of his groin held in her palm.

What a magnificent handful.

There was no more cheerful banter, no more easy companionship. They both sat in careful silence, rigidly resisting every sway and jolt of the curricle. There wasn't a sound but the clop of the pretty black horse's hooves and the creaking springs of the curricle.

Trying not to let her body brush up against her employer's, Pru held little Miss Melody tightly on her lap in the center of the seat. The child didn't seem to mind. Anything that would get her closer to Evan, upon whom she'd immediately bestowed her worship—whether Evan wished it or not!

It was surprisingly familiar, the feeling of a small, squirming body in Pru's arms. She'd adored Evan from the moment he was born and had carried him about endlessly, her very own living doll. Mama could hardly get her to let go long enough to do her own maternal part!

Well, she wouldn't allow herself to feel that way about Melody, no matter how charming the child was. This was a paying job, not an adoption, and the last thing she needed was another person depending upon her for love and support.

No, she must remain brisk, efficient, kind but not loving. She was not Melody's mother.

Yet, who was? Mr. Lambert had called her his "ward." This was a loose description, indeed. It could mean Melody might be anything from the orphaned child of a distant relative to the "natural" child of the man himself, born out of wedlock.

Neither of which is your business. Watch the child. Make the five pounds. Go to London and survive a little longer.

Well, mystery or no, little Melody was a very nice child. Despite being a bit energetic, she was bright and voluble. One might say precocious. When Evan had been that age he'd been more of the point-and-howl variety. Sometimes he still was.

Pru smiled wearily as she looked sideways at Evan, seated next to her with the usual black cloud of resentment etched upon his brow. The poor boy had been through so much betrayal that it wasn't surprising he hadn't taken immediately to the situation. It was a risky one, leaving familiar territory with a man they didn't know. Still, what else was to be done?

She sighed. Somewhere inside Evan was the sweet boy who'd lived his life with a clever curiosity and a boisterous affection for everyone he'd met. She saw it still, sometimes, when they were alone. Less and less every day, it seemed.

Melody bounced brightly and leaned out of the circle of Pru's arms to peer into Evan's face, an inviting smile upon her chubby little features. Evan only shot a scornful look at the flirtatious baby and turned his gray eyes to the view of the surrounding countryside.

Then Pru noticed something that made her smirk. Evan might be disdainful of the little girl and wary around Mr. Lambert, but he was also currently mimicking Mr. Lambert's manly bearing perfectly—straight in the seat, shoulders square, hands on knees. Pru stifled her smile at once, but Evan must have realized what she was looking at, for he slumped back in the seat with his arms crossed resentfully.

Mr. Lambert hadn't noticed, of course. Pru couldn't resist letting her gaze slide curiously over him, her lashes lowered. There was something about him that didn't quite fit. He was no peacock—in fact, she found his attire a bit mature and somber, considering that he was young and handsome.

So very handsome. Could a man be so good-looking that one could feel his handsomeness radiating from him, even when one wasn't looking directly at him?

For all that, Pru couldn't imagine that Chantal would have been interested in him for long—not enough flash, not enough status. Handsome only held Chantal's attention for so long. Money and power held it longer. No wonder he lost her favor.

Best thing that could have happened to him, in Pru's opinion.

The chaise hit another pothole and Pru was tossed hard against Mr. Lambert's shoulder. He glanced at her, brow raised.

"All right?"

She jerked away and settled herself again with an apologetic nod, though heaven knew what she should apologize for. She wasn't driving, after all!

Unfortunately, the road continued to batter at her. Her body ached and her head was beginning to swim a bit. It was too bad she hadn't had time to spend a little of her new coin on some bread and cheese before setting out on the way. Typical disregard of the gentry. Mr. Lambert wasn't hungry—so no one else must be, either.

Swallowing grimly, Pru gritted her jaw and tried very hard to think of something else.

Her mind drifted back, before Chantal and the theater, before the years of hard work and little pay. She'd ridden like this in her father's curricle, her mother at her side and Evan in her lap. Sunday drives in the park, visits to the museum, to shop in the High Street.

Then, of course, her mind inevitably turned to that terrible day and those four terrible words. "Your parents have perished."

CHAPTER 4

In a single moment everything changed. Pru and Evan were taken to the home of their new guardians, Mr. and Mrs. Trotter. Mr. Trotter had been Papa's business partner and most trusted friend.

Prudence had been comforted by the Trotters' presence. She'd spent little time with them in the past but she'd known them all her life. When she'd woken that first night in tears she'd found Evan's little body tucked next to her in bed. She'd taken him by the hand and led him downstairs, certain that their new parents would reassure them.

The sight of them sitting by the fire in their parlor, Mrs. Trotter knitting and Mr. Trotter smoking his pipe, had made Prudence pause at the door. She simply wanted to fix the moment in her mind, for she'd missed so many opportunities to pay attention to the little moments with her parents.

As they watched, Mrs. Trotter looked up from her knitting and peered at her husband over her spectacles. "Why can't we get the money now?" Her tone was petulant, unlike her kindly voice earlier.

Mr. Trotter blew a casual smoke ring. "Not until he's eighteen, my dear."

"But then he'll keep it! He'll never simply give it to us."

Mr. Trotter grunted and smiled. It was not a nice smile. "He will when I get through with him. He'll be too terrified to do anything else. By the time ten years have passed he will be entirely my creature."

Mrs. Trotter sniffed. "Prudence will object if you abuse him."

"Prudence will find herself shipped off to a school if she gets in my way. That or an asylum. Those places are full of ungrateful girls who overstep themselves."

Mrs. Trotter narrowed her eyes. "Send her away now," she challenged her husband.

"Why?"

"Because I've seen your eyes on her."

He glanced away and sucked on his pipe. "Nonsense."

"Do it. Do it at once! Tomorrow!" Her knuckles were white with fury, her knitting trembling in her hands. "You'll do as I say! Don't you forget that it is my money that buys your cigars and brandy!"

Another long pull on the pipe. He snapped his paper open. "Very well, my dear. She'll be gone tomorrow. An asylum, do you think? She might be able to break away from a school."

Mrs. Trotter smiled and her needles clicked rhythmically once more. "That'll do nicely."

The scene was so tranquil, so domestic, that standing outside the door in the darkened hallway, Prudence could scarcely credit what she'd just heard.

They weren't simply greedy, they were evil.

And her parents had left them to this horrible fate, Evan beaten into submission and Prudence a Bedlamite! For the first time in her fifteen years, Prudence understood the meaning of rage.

Standing next to her, little eight-year-old Evan shrank back, pulling Pru into the darkness. "I'm scared, Pru," he whispered.

Yes, rage . . . and terror. Swiftly, Prudence returned them to their rooms, dressed them both, and managed to slip out the back door with no one the wiser. It took them hours to reach the home of the only other person Prudence trusted, her father's solicitor, Mr. Henry.

Mr. Henry listened carefully to her tale, then he ordered his carriage. Sure that the hand of justice was about to land upon the evil Trotters, Prudence and Evan accompanied him back to the house.

When Mr. Henry merely stood there in the parlor and turned them over to their guardians, Prudence was open-mouthed with shock. "But—but I told you! They are going to beat Evan! They want his inheritance!"

She gazed at the ring of adults around her, the regretful Mr. Henry and the Trotters, who projected nothing but kindly confusion.

"Her parents' deaths have unhinged her," Mr. Henry noted sadly.

"Such delusions." Mrs. Trotter made worried noises.

"I worry about her influence on her brother," Mr. Trotter pointed out.

Prudence backed away, her hand tight around Evan's. "No . . ."

"What if her madness affects him?" Mrs. Trotter was the picture of motherly concern.

Mr. Henry sighed. "Perhaps she ought to be separated from him."

Mrs. Trotter narrowed her eyes, but not before Prudence saw the flash of triumph in them. "Well . . ." the woman said, her tone reluctant, "if you think that's best."

Prudence tightened her grip on Evan and they ran. Through the house, as fast as his short little legs could carry him. The adults clattered behind them, but the Trotters were not small people and there was some confusion over who should pass through narrow doorways first. Prudence had the presence of mind to make a grab at a silver vase and a mother-ofpearl box on the hall table before they flung themselves out the front door at a run to disappear into the morning crowds.

Selling the trinkets had bought them a little time, enough for Pru to realize that no one wanted to hire an educated young lady, but would possibly take on a common girl who could read and count.

Pru felt sometimes that they were still running. They ran from betrayal, they ran from hunger, they ran from the day that she couldn't manage it anymore and she would be forced to give Evan back for the sake of his own survival.

The chaise jolted again and again as her memories of the past swirled and twisted inside her, mingling with her terror of the future.

One more mistake and they would not survive. One more mistake and she would lose Evan forever.

As the Cabriolet jostled down the road away from Brighton, Colin began to have the feeling he'd made a colossal mistake.

For one thing, the chaise was made to seat two adults comfortably. The addition of two squirming children made more of a difference than one might expect. The advantage of having another pair of eyes watching over Melody was outweighed by the added complication of young Evan, whose mere presence sent Melody into raptures of excessive behavior as she sought to capture the boy's attention.

Evan himself mostly sat scrunched in the far corner of the seat, arms crossed, with an expression of profound displeasure etched onto his thin features. Every so often Colin caught the boy giving him a darkly suspicious glare. Melody seemed not to notice the lad's sour disposition. She clearly saw him only as another child after being deprived of such company for most of her short life.

"Evan, Evan, Evan, look at meeee!"

Miss Filby caught Melody before she came to disaster again and again, but Colin could see that the strain was beginning to wear on the strange young woman.

Not that she was odd in her speech or manner, precisely. As he drove with one part of his mind, Colin the scholar began to toy with the puzzle that was this perfectly unremarkable girl whom he likely would never see again after this journey . . . but who kept snaring his attention with her every gesture, or sultry-voiced word, or husky resigned sigh.

Taking on more dependents didn't bother him, for he kept a full staff of fifty at Tamsinwood when he was in residence, however rarely that occurred.

No, it wasn't the addition of another employee that disturbed him. She seemed agreeable enough and the theater manager had confirmed that she was a dependable, steady sort. In fact, the man had seemed quite fond of Miss Filby.

Yet not of Chantal. That was odd, for Chantal was all that was sweet and compliant and good. Well, perhaps the fellow resented being left just as the theater season was beginning.

Colin could sympathize. Losing Chantal had been one of the most difficult obstacles he'd ever had to face—that and losing his mother. Odd that it was due to his father, whom he had once hated, that he might now have a chance to win Chantal back forever.

When he'd lost her, he'd been no one. Merely the son of his father, a wealthy scholar who had refused his defiant son more than the barest allowance. When Chantal saw him next, she would see a new man. Sir Colin Lambert, a man with a knighthood and a vast property. A very rich fellow indeed. Eagerly, he snapped the reins, ready for the moment when he saw Chantal with something significant to offer her.

Melody was chattering now, retelling fragments of pirate tales to Gordy Ann, whom she held like an infant in her folded arms. Young Evan tried to look immensely bored, but Colin could tell he was listening.

Colin shot another glance at his seatmate, who held the squirming child gently but firmly in her lap and gazed out over the southern landscape in silence despite the jolting of the wheels on the rough road.

Truly he wasn't distracted by what the motion of the curricle did to her figure. He was much too gentlemanly to stare at the way her bosom jiggled and swayed or how Melody's little monkey fist sometimes grabbed at the neckline of her plain gown, stretching it enticingly to one side for a brief moment.

No, he wasn't one to stare—not when judicious glances from the corner of his eye would suffice.

Although her figure was most diverting, he did sometimes sneak a glance at her face as well. Those eyes . . . large and gray and thick of lash, so stunning in her plain, pale little face.

A pale little face that had abruptly turned a sickly green!

Colin halted the horse in the middle of the empty road and snatched Melody from Miss Filby's lap. "Go!"

Pru scrambled over Evan and out of the chaise to stumble to the grassy edge of the road, where she dropped to her knees and heaved. Nothing came of it, for her stomach was empty and had been for a day and a half.

For the second morning in a row when she'd left breakfast for Evan before going down to the theater, she'd also left a falsely dirtied plate by the basin so he wouldn't realize that she'd given him the last of the dry bread and cheese they had.

Damn you, Chantal!

She heaved again, helpless against the waves of dizziness and nausea caused by her hunger and her fear and the jolting motion of the curricle. She felt a hand on her shoulder, patting awkwardly. Poor Evan. She must pull herself together before she frightened him.

Her body rebelled once more. *Goodness, Pru, don't be such a weakling!*

"Cor Blimey, Pru," Evan said in dismay.

"Cor Blimey, Pru!" piped a baby voice.

"You are not to say 'Cor Blimey,' Melody." Mr. Lambert's tone was gentle but distracted.

"I didn't! Gordy Ann did."

A fine lawn handkerchief appeared before Pru's streaming eyes. She took it with a shaking hand and forced herself to sit up on her heels. That was enough crawling about in the weeds! She mustn't let Mr. Lambert think he'd made a mistake in hiring her. After dabbing at her eyes and carefully wiping her mouth, she looked up at the three concerned faces gazing down at her and forced a smile.

"Sorry 'bout that, guv'nor. It's just been a while since I been usin' anything but me feet."

Mr. Lambert gazed down at her with his green eyes narrowed. "You are ill. Are you sure it is only the jolting of the road?"

"O' course it is!" She forced a bright tone. "Why, I'll have a sip of water and be right as rain in a minute."

He seemed reassured—until she made the fatal mistake of trying to stand. As the bright day swirled into gray dizziness she felt strong arms come about her, lifting her to rest against a broad, hard chest as if she weighed no more than little Melody.

Weak as she was, she found herself unable to resist laying her cheek against the silk of his waistcoat. So good to rest, just for a moment . . . so lovely to let someone else take charge . . .

As if finally allowed to let go the reins at last, her consciousness faded away to the sounds of Evan's worried voice.

"Leave 'er be, you great posh bastard!"

CHAPTER 5

The grim-faced landlord of the inn that Colin found just down the road didn't seem to think there was anything odd about a gentleman bursting through his doors with an unconscious servant girl in his arms and demanding a room. If Colin had had time to think about it, he might have wondered what sort of dastardly doings the innkeeper was accustomed to.

However, his entire attention was absorbed by getting Miss Prudence Filby into bed.

Young Evan was no help at all. The child vacillated between abject worry and aggressive resistance. When one of the innkeeper's daughters attempted to get Miss Filby out of her clothing, it was Evan who insisted that Colin leave the room. Colin compromised by turning his back on the process and staring out of the window.

When the other daughter brought the steaming bowl of broth that Colin had ordered, Evan tried to manage that as well, but eventually was forced to allow Colin to take over. The lateness of the hour stole the rest of the boy's ferocity and soon both he and Melody were asleep on the small upholstered settee before the fire.

Now in the quiet room, with only the glow of the coals to guide him, Colin sat on the edge of the mattress and lifted Miss Filby into his arms. She weighed nothing at all.

"Wake up, Miss Filby. Miss Filby?" He gazed down at her pale face with concern. She was so limp.

"Pru!" he whispered sharply. "Wake up, Pru!"

She stirred and her eyelids fluttered a few times but did not open. Good enough. He propped her against his chest and lifted the bowl of broth to her lips.

"Drink up, Pru," he urged. She obediently took a tiny sip, but immediately sagged against his chest once she'd swallowed. Colin kept at it, coaxing sip after sip into her semiconscious lips, all the while whispering encouraging words to "Pru." Damn, he was going to have trouble going back to the usual formality after this.

After half the bowl had disappeared, she curled up against his chest and refused to drink another drop. "No, Papa," she'd whispered. "No more."

"Papa?" Colin grunted. "Is it the suit?" he muttered. "That does it. One new suit, coming up."

Her response was to snuggle more comfortably against him and begin a gentle snoring. Still, her color was much improved and the very feeling of her body against his had changed from alarming limpness to the resilience of natural sleep.

He pushed a strand of hair back from her brow. When her mobcap had been removed, her hair had been revealed to be a deep auburn that now looked astonishingly red in the firelight. The silken strands caught at his fingers, warm and clinging.

Colin gazed intently into her face. Yes, the tight lines of weariness had left her eyes and the corners of her mouth. In fact, she looked quite young with her features relaxed in healing sleep. Young and a bit . . . pretty.

Narrowing his eyes, he studied the hollows of her cheeks and the way her collarbone protruded. He ran one hand down her arm and lifted her wrist, noting the curiously vulnerable thinness.

The old nightdress which Evan had found in her valise was too large for her spare frame and the neckline, though diligently tied, dropped over one bare shoulder. Feeling odd, Colin tugged it back up, trying to ignore the warmth of her skin on the backs of his fingers. It was an intimate gesture, one he'd only ever made with a lover. Yet what was he to do, sit here and watch it slip lower and lower until the upper swell of her breast was revealed?

Something animal in him stirred at that thought.

Yes, all right. Let's do that.

As if in response to his flare of awareness, the girl in his arms turned and wriggled closer to him, pressing her bosom into his chest and draping a limp arm around his torso, tucking her hand into the warmth of his weskit.

He could feel her touch on the flat planes of his stomach, with only the thin linen of his shirt between the heat of her palm and his skin.

"S'warm," she murmured.

Was he "Papa" still? Or did she dream she curled her body into that of a lover? Had she ever had a lover?

What do you care? She started it.

There was a scent rising from her, as she lay warm and pliant in his arms. It teased at his senses, worming its way into his consciousness until he itched with the need to know. With a glance at the sleeping children, Colin dropped his head and breathed it in, trying to decipher it. She smelled of clean, fresh . . . what was it? It was a little green and a little wild, yet a comforting, familiar scent all the same.

It made him think of the gardens of his childhood home, of running over the beds, a sharp spicy scent rising from underfoot, where his shoes crushed the . . .

Mint? Yes, she smelled of fresh crushed mint leaves and something else. He inhaled more deeply, closing his eyes. Something warm and female and . . .

Mint . . . and *her.*

His body reacted. The pulse in his cock increased, swelling his trousers and fogging his mind. He quelled the response almost instantly.

A long time had passed since he'd been this close to a woman. Years, in fact. Not since just before he'd stood in that damp alley in the gray morning and called out Chantal's name.

No. Miss Filby was Off Limits.

Off Limits, as in she was common, which meant she was unfairly susceptible to his rank. As in he was her employer, and he'd never been one to tupp the chambermaid. As in they were not alone.

He glanced over to where the children were sleeping by the fire. He'd have to take Melody into his room tonight again, when he'd been hoping to have his bed to himself and sleep without benefit of pointy little elbows and kicking little feet.

Sliding the surprising Miss Filby down his chest and onto her pillows proved difficult. She seemed unwilling to let go of his body heat. It was beyond tempting to let her pull him into the warm sheets with her, if only because he was so bloody tired after two nights of child-disturbed sleep that any horizontal position seemed to weight his eyelids closed.

At last he untangled himself without waking her. Tugging his weskit straight again, he tried to ignore that his belly felt cold without the heat of her hand upon it. Crossing the room to the hearth, he gazed down at the two small persons slumbering on the settee.

Melody was curled on her side with her head upon a pillow and Gordy Ann's "arm" in her mouth, wet from sucking. Evan sprawled faceup on the other end, one arm flung over his eyes, booted feet pointing in different directions. He was working on a man-sized snore to match the man-sized feet.

What was he to do with young Evan? Leave him alone here with his sister? With Miss Filby practically unconscious, the boy would hardly be properly supervised.

Resignedly, Colin rubbed the back of his neck and hoped his bed would be very, very large.

It wasn't.

Three weeks earlier, in a cramped cabin on a schooner in the Indian sea, a thin, dark-haired man bent over a sheet of paper, trying to think of something to write.

His friends were waiting for him to come home. He knew that. He'd left England as often as possible over the last three years, using his uncle's foreign plantations and holdings as his excuse. He felt their concern stretching out over the miles, reaching for him like tendrils of light in the fog.

Unfortunately for them, he preferred to remain alone, hidden away in the vast, blank fog that he'd walked in for the past three and a half years. Or had it been four? Somewhere in between, probably, and not worth figuring anyway. The event that had cut his last ties to the world was not precisely an anniversary to celebrate.

He glanced away from his empty page to rest his gaze upon the small stack of letters on one side of the desk, held there by a giant conch shell he'd found on a beach on some tropical island. He blinked at it, idly trying to remember where. His ships had taken him to so many lands on this headlong flight of his, he couldn't recall them all.

Flight?

That's what Colin had called it, in one of the letters pinioned by the conch shell. "Stop running away," his friend had urged. "No matter where you go, your cousin will still be dead and you'll still be the heir to Strickland. You might as well be so in England, with us."

In a different, much more tersely written letter, his friend Aidan had said much the same thing. "Come home. Blakely is dead. You're alive. Sailing away won't change that."

The ship wallowed drunkenly, but Jack's hand was steady, if still. It had been more than three years since he had taken a drink. He dared not go to that empty black place again. He hurt people, did things . . .

Drinking didn't keep the war away, it only set it free within him.

What did he have to fight for, in any case? He no longer believed in anything, not honor, not nobility, not even the land he'd nearly died for. This lack of belief wasn't bitterness, or even cynicism.

He simply couldn't remember why he should care.

He pulled the paper closer, dipped his pen into the inkwell held fixed to his nautical desk, and wrote a single line.

"I will come back to Brown's."

He didn't write why, because he didn't know. He simply had nowhere left to run to.

The next morning, Pru stretched her arms wide beneath the covers. Her hands didn't run out of bed, nor did they move across a stiff straw pallet covered by a rough blanket. Real linen met her touch, buoyed by deep, luxurious goose down within.

A real bed. With a deep sleepy sigh, she rolled over onto her belly and buried her face into the real pillow. It must be getting quite late. Mama would be short with her if she did not rise and help little Evan dress . . .

It didn't take long to remember that Mama would never be short with her again, or that little Evan wasn't very little anymore. The brief moment of living in the past was so sweet, so achingly real, that Pru felt her hands try to close about it as it slipped away. She tightened her fists as she woke fully.

She was in a room, a very nice room compared to what she was used to, but the sort of blank featureless room one might find in an inn.

She remembered accepting Mr. Lambert's offer. She remembered the jolting curricle and the way his body had felt under her hand. She remembered the endless bumping and the way her weariness had made the world seem a little stark, full of contrasting light and jerky motions.

Squeezing her eyes shut, she remembered the humiliating bout of nausea. Everything else was a sort of haze interrupted by flickering images. Evan's worried little face. Mr. Lambert ordering someone about. Papa feeding her little sips of broth, just as he had when she'd caught the influenza as a child.

Well, that must have been a dream. Easily dismissed until she saw the crockery bowl on the table next to the bed, an inch of cold broth remaining on the bottom.

Warm arms about her. A broad chest to lean upon. Mr. Lambert's voice, gruffly gentle. "Pru. One more sip. Just for me."

A touch, the barest caress, across the top of her breast.

Hm. That was a thought best not lingered upon.

Completely disregarding her state of mind, her belly reminded her that the smell of sausage and fresh baking wafted up from somewhere in the inn.

Pru sat up and rolled over in one motion, her moment of discomfiture swept away by the thought of breakfast. She never allowed distress to come between her and her meals.

Marvelous. A true night's sleep and now food. She hadn't felt so good in ages.

Colin gingerly descended the inn stairs. He hadn't felt so horrible since his wild, youthful drinking days. His eyes burned from weariness, his back ached from having held himself poised at the edge of the bed, and he'd swear that Melody's pointy little elbows and kicking little feet had left bruises all over him. Furthermore, he'd spent half the night tugging for his share of the covers and the other half with no covers at all, thanks to Evan, who was stronger than he looked.

The little sleep he'd managed had been disturbed by dreams of Chantal, whose hair had become inexplicably red.

The morning sun through the windows was too bright

and the clatter of dishes in the dining room was too loud. And Miss Filby seated at the far end of the room with her breakfast before her was too complicated a problem by half.

He couldn't allow anything more to slow him down. Melody's future was at stake. He needed to see Chantal now, before Bertie convinced her to wed him, before he lost all track of her whatsoever! He would not allow Melody to go through life as a bastard when it was in his power to make it all right.

And poor Chantal! Guilt tugged at him. She must have been so desperate.

The money stopped coming from the mother.

Chantal had likely worked herself into collapse, trying to support his child! This momentary fixation on Purty Bertie might even be no more than a frantic attempt to gain the resources to get her child back!

No, the distracting Miss Filby and her brother were not his problem, not when his plate was full of them already.

CHAPTER 6

When Mr. Lambert found her, Pru was seated in the dining room, digging into a steaming pile of eggs and buttered toast. Evan had long since wolfed his down, grunting appreciatively in his usual fashion, then bolting from the inn to romp in the stables. Melody had wanted to follow the boy, but Pru had settled her by the fire with her little rag doll and a spoon and told her to feed the baby.

Meanwhile, Pru ate slowly, savoring every delicious bite, knowing that even if she ate until her belly sat in her lap, she wouldn't want to stop.

She was fed and warm. Heaven.

Only the crisp footsteps of her employer could have brought her from her gluttonous reverie. He appeared before her attired in a crisp green surcoat and perfectly tied cravat. His eyes, however, looked rather more worn. In fact, he looked like absolute hell.

She blinked at him and smiled. "Good mornin', sir! Did you not sleep well?"

His lips twisted and irritation flashed in his green eyes. "No, Miss Filby, I did not."

Pru wasn't quite sure why this was her fault. She looked back down at her eggs rather than give in to the impulse to apologize for nothing.

He cleared his throat harshly. "Miss Filby, I regret to inform you that I will no longer be needing your services on this journey. You are in no condition to travel, so I have paid the innkeeper and his wife to look after you and Evan for a week as you recover."

Pru gazed up at Mr. Lambert with the delicious eggs turning to stone in her throat. She choked them down. "You're leaving us."

Her tone was flat, without emotion. What good would emotion do her? This man had swept her out of Brighton, where she might at least have hoped for some grueling factory work, and the moment she faltered the slightest bit he was eager to desert Evan and her in this remote inn!

His kindness in sheltering and feeding them aside—and why not, when he'd promised as much in the first place!—he was leaving her in far worse straits than he'd found her.

Of course he is. You know the Quality care about no one but themselves.

She shut her eyes for a moment against that insidious voice. *I am the Quality.*

Except that she wasn't. Not at the moment. At the moment, she was a poor servant girl with no employer and none in sight for the future.

Damn you, Mr. Lambert.

He had the grace to look slightly embarrassed and apparently the arrogance to resent it, for he scowled thunderously. "I cannot wait for you to recover, Miss Filby. I have most urgent business with Miss Marchant and you are hardly able to care for Melody in your condition."

Pru couldn't resist the urge to argue, though she knew it would do no good. "I'm fit. I am. I were only hungry, anyway. What sort of woman are you used to, guv'nor, that be needin' a week to recover from missing a meal or two?"

He gazed at her severely. "Miss Filby, you know perfectly well that you have missed more than two meals. What were you thinking to neglect yourself so?"

Oh, that was too much. Pru stood abruptly, sending her

bench backward with a screech on the bare wood floor. "Neglect meself? What, like one o' your fine ladies throwin' her dinner in the dustbin for wantin' to fit into her gowns?" She glared at Mr. Lambert, refusing to be cowed by his great height and mind-bending good looks. "It's folks like your fine Miss Marchant that 'neglect' themselves—and everyone they owe! It ain't me!"

It was strange, the way that her ill-bred vowels sounded wrong to Colin's ears, as if he constantly expected something better to fall from her lips. He shouldn't judge. It wasn't her fault she was uneducated and common, after all.

However, she didn't look common, not at that moment. Something flashed in those eyes, something proud and haughty and indignant.

Then it was gone and Colin decided it was a trick of the light.

He remained silent, staring her down. After a long moment, she looked away and shrugged. "Evan needed it more'n me."

Evan. Huge gray eyes in a face pinched by hunger, not ill humor. Colin felt a little ill. Good God, he was an idiot not to see it immediately. The two of them were wasting away!

This was definitely more than he'd bargained for. He clenched his jaw and glared at Miss Prudence Filby, walking, talking complication times two.

As if she could tell he wavered, she stepped forward then, lips parted to protest. He held up a hand sharply, furious at himself for being so unobservant that he'd saddled himself with hindrances, not helpers.

Bowing stiffly, he said, "Good-bye, Miss Filby. I wish you and Evan well."

Left behind in the public room of the inn, Pru stood frozen. What had just happened?

Blinking, she let her knees give out and sat abruptly back down on the bench. Her gaze fixed on her plate of eggs gone cold, the edges already congealing on the white-glazed pottery.

He'd left them. The rotter had just driven off and left them! What was she to do now?

Pull yourself together. There's no need to feel so betrayed. Who were you to him, anyway? Just the help, that's what.

She forced herself to draw a breath. Then another. She brought the tankard of water to her lips and made herself swallow.

You have a brain. Use it!

Yes. Right. Push the ache down. Cover it. Move onward.

Mr. Lambert had left the price of a week's stay with the innkeeper. If she could cajole part of that out of the man and leave at once, she could get passage on the next coach for her and Evan. She still had the three shillings from yesterday—

Her hand flew to her pocket, only to find nothing within, not even a spare button. Someone had undressed her last evening, someone who had helped themselves to her entire fortune.

A heavy step sounded before her and she raised her gaze to the florid face of the burly innkeeper. By his breath, he'd already started making a dent in his profits for the day. His narrowed gaze bore her no good.

All hope of wheedling a bit of Mr. Lambert's coin from the man died.

"Get up!" The man sneered. "This table's for payin' guests!"

"But—"

Her protest died as the man raised his hand high. She scrambled from the bench, her tankard still in her hand.

She backed up a step. "My employer left you with money for my stay."

The innkeeper's lip curled. "Did he now?"

Pru gaped. "You know he did!"

"I know ye owe me for a night and two meals, ye and the boy. I know there's a dozen tankards need scrubbin' and then ye can get on them chamber pots!" He leered at her bosom.

"Might take months to work it off, unless yer fond o' workin' on yer back."

Pru stood completely still, her blood pounding in her ears, drowning out the man's foul words. She saw the bleak future. She'd be a slave to the cruel man, paying off a debt that would never die. Evan would grow up underfoot at an inn with no chance to fulfill his birthright.

The throb of her own pulse increased.

She'd been abused by Chantal, deserted by Mr. Lambert, and now this wicked man meant to make her his scullery slave and whore. She'd worked her fingers to the bone serving and serving and serving and all it brought her was more drudgery!

Her hand tightened on her tankard until her knuckles whitened from the strain.

Enough, by God, was enough!

Surprisingly, when Colin swept Melody up from her play with Gordy Ann on the floor and toted her out to the waiting chaise, she made no protest at all at leaving Miss Filby and her son behind. A hundred yards down the road, however, realization struck.

He felt a tugging at his coat.

"Where's Evan, Uncle Colin? Uncle Colin, we lost Pru! Go back!"

Colin drove on, eyes on the road, jaw tight against the ache caused by her worried cries. It was for the best. He knew from experience that Melody needed her mother, her true mother, not a hired substitute. Especially not one so frail and undependable as Miss Prudence Filby. God, the way she'd looked at him, those stormy eyes flashing with indignation and betrayal and tinted with astonishing but undeniable hurt!

Melody began to wail, wrapping her arms about his bicep and stomping on the seat with both feet. "Go back, go back, go back—"

She was in danger of toppling right over the dashboard and into the road beneath Hector's hooves. Colin swept her into his lap with one arm, keeping a tight hold on the reins. Her banshee wails were beginning to spook the horse.

He tucked her face into his weskit and spoke softly but firmly. "We must go on and Miss Filby and Evan must stay at the inn, Mellie. Miss Filby is much too ill to ride with us today. Quiet now, Melody. Quiet."

She wrapped sticky hands up behind his neck, pressing Gordy Ann into his left ear, and wept into his lapel as if her heart were breaking. Her raw cries tore into him, making him ache with guilt. Colin's chest stayed tight until she finally slithered down his weskit to curl into his lap, her thumb in her mouth and her scrap of a doll held close. Wet lashes drooped and she dozed limply, as if her tears had emptied her entirely.

She'd had one day with Miss Filby and the boy! How could she care so deeply if she rode away from them?

Then again, she'd lost so many people in her short life. Her mother, her nurse, even Aidan and Madeleine and the staff of Brown's. Of course, she'd see the lot at Brown's again soon, but Colin didn't know if Melody truly believed that. How could she, poor wee mousie? No one who'd left her had ever come back.

She must feel like people were water she was trying to catch with open fingers!

And now he'd caused her to gain and lose two more.

He'd been selfish, hiring someone to ease his burden without thinking what the temporary arrangement might do to a tiny child. It was becoming very obvious to him that although he'd known a few children, he knew absolutely nothing about being a father.

Well, he would learn. He was a man of intelligence, after all. He was a knighted scholar, for pity's sake! If anyone could learn the ropes, so to speak, it would be he.

Cuddling the limp pile of heartbroken mousie on his lap

with one arm, he only hoped he could learn fast enough, before he did any permanent damage.

"He left?"

In her bedchamber at her grand family estate, Melody drew back against the cushions of the sofa where they sat before the fire and stared at Button, her jaw dropped in shock. "Did he go back for them?"

Button blinked. "Why, no. As a matter of fact, he never did."

"He simply left them there?" She flung herself to her feet and began to pace on the carpet before him, twisting her hands together until the whites of her knuckles showed. "*Men!* That's what I've been trying to tell you, Button! Just when you think you've done it, you've found the one man who will never fail you—why, he gets up and walks out of the inn, never to be heard from again!"

Button gazed sympathetically at her. "Oh, he does, does he? And who is telling this story, Mellie-my-love?"

Melody slowed her wild pacing and slid her gaze toward him, dismay on her face. "I interrupted you, didn't I?"

Button lifted a brow. "Ever so slightly, my dear."

She cleared her throat and lifted her chin, visibly trying to compose herself. "My apologies." She sat down next to him, a study in poise and self-control. "Please continue."

Button tilted his head and smiled at her fondly. "I will if you'll kindly remember who we are telling a story about? Prudence was capable of taking care of herself in any situation, I should think." He opened his arm. "Come and snuggle close, pet, and hear what happened next."

Melody relaxed into his embrace once more. "Poor Prudence," she said, sighing.

Button grunted. "Poor Sir Colin, you mean . . ."

CHAPTER 7

Colin needn't have worried that Melody would cry all the way to Basingstoke. She was never one to allow sadness to interrupt her habitual joie de vivre for long. And when Melody was enjoying life, there was usually hell to pay.

This, she most assuredly did *not* get from him.

"Look at me, Uncle Colin!"

Melody hung upside down by her little monkey fists from the overhanging edge of the seat, her little booted feet kicking the air in mingled fear and excitement. As he had done several times in the past days, Colin shifted the reins into one hand, made a long arm, swept her to safety, and deposited her right side up onto her seat without another word. Melody chortled with glee.

"Look at me, Uncle Colin!"

She lay on her belly on the upwardly sloped splash guard at his feet with her upper body out in space between the dangerously whirring wheels, reaching both arms out as if to fly. As Colin pulled back on the reins to slow Hector to a safer speed, he planted a foot on her bottom to keep her from slithering all the way out. Melody found this hilarious, of course.

Five minutes of blessed peace followed. Colin began to think about what he might find at his journey's end . . . and who.

Chantal.

"Look at me, Uncle—"

He looked. She was nowhere to be seen. Not on the seat, not on the floor, not dangling from the retractable roof. "Melody?" In terror, he stood to force the horse to a halt by brute strength. Hector, beautifully trained as he was, did his very best to stop in his tracks.

Unfortunately, carriages were not meant to stop in their tracks, not even lightweight racing gigs. When the weight of the forward-moving vehicle hit the wooden spar that held the harness shafts in place, the spar snapped with a dry, splintering shot that made the already alarmed horse jolt sideways in fear. Leather harness straps, twisted out of their purpose by the broken spar, gave way under the force of a large healthy animal moving in the wrong direction.

"Melody!"

The carriage jerked to a hard, forceful stop at last.

"Eeeeeee!"

Melody plopped into Colin's outstretched arms. He dropped the reins and caught her tightly to his chest.

"I flied."

Colin looked behind him to realize that Melody must have somehow climbed into the small "tiger" seat at the back of the curricle. At the impact, she had flown forward. What if he hadn't caught her? What if she'd fallen beneath the hooves of the anxious Hector? The thought of what might have happened to her made his gut twist. He closed his eyes and held her even more tightly, grappling with his patience. *Inhale. Exhale.* He blew out a long breath.

"Stop, Mellie. Please, just *stop*."

She blinked up at him with her wide, blue, innocent eyes. "You already stoppeded, Uncle Colin."

He sat down on his seat with her safely in his lap and surveyed the damage. The harness was a ruin. Hector was hopelessly tangled and stood there with white-edged eyes and twitching skin. Even if Colin could somehow harness him with the remains of the leather straps, the curricle itself was too damaged for him to pull.

Melody craned her neck to survey the tangle. "You mucked it, Uncle Colin."

Colin sighed, too weary to correct her vulgarity. "Indeed."

She thrust her rag doll into his view, inches from his nose. "Gordy Ann says 'Cor Blimey!', Uncle Colin."

"Ah." Gordy Ann's "head" flopped to one side. She indeed looked dismayed. Or dead. Colin closed his eyes momentarily. "Of course she does."

Having dispensed commentary to her satisfaction, Melody tucked Gordy Ann into her armpit and wiggled to a more comfortable position in his lap. "Can we go back to Brown's now, Uncle Colin?"

Brown's. Hell. When Melody recalled all this havoc to Aidan and Madeleine—and she would, he was sure, with great excitement—then he, Colin, was going to have to find a very deep hole to hide in.

"Er, mousie?" He couldn't ask her to lie, of course. That would be unthinkable. However, he was rather desperately not above bribing her to keep quiet.

"It sinkeded," Melody said thoughtfully, considering the forward-tipped gig.

"What, mousie?"

She pointed a chubby finger. "It sinkeded, like the bad pirate ship."

Colin cast an appraising look at the remains of the lovely but decidedly deceased Cabriolet. It did possess some of the curve of the bowsprit of a ship. Hmm. Desperate times . . .

"Yes, Mellie. When you get back to Brown's, you can tell Uncle Aidan and Aunt Maddie all about how our ship . . . er, sinkeded."

She snuggled deeper into his lap, angling for a story. "And Billy-wick?"

"Yes, you can tell Bailiwick."

"And Wibbly-force, too?"

God help him. If Wilberforce ever learned what a muck he'd made of this journey—it didn't bear thinking about. Colin smiled tightly. "And Wibbly-force, too."

In the elegant if somewhat old-fashioned foyer of Brown's Club for Distinguished Gentlemen, Wilberforce, the illustrious head of staff, gazed down at the silver tray of letters in his hand. The post included something most interesting this morning.

In a scrawling hand, a thick envelope that had seen better days was addressed to *Sir Colin Lambert, Brown's Club, St. James Street, London*. The heavy paper was stained and scuffed and marked with water, but the lettering was clear. The sender's identity was indicated by a single looping *R*.

R for Redgrave. Lord John Redgrave, the heir to the ailing Marquis of Strickland. Or, as he was known to his friends in London, simply "Jack."

Wilberforce was growing very weary of matters not being quite right. His very existence depended upon his ability to make things right.

Well, then. Without lifting his head, or taking his gaze from the post, Wilberforce called for assistance.

"Bailiwick!"

Immediately his ears were assaulted by the galloping strides of his youngest and largest—and most enthusiastic—footman. He didn't flinch, despite the racket and what those giant shoes were probably doing to the freshly waxed floors.

"Yes, sir, Mr. Wilberforce?"

Wilberforce raised his gaze—and raised it some more—to meet Bailiwick's eager one. "I have a most important task for you. This letter must be brought to Sir Colin's attention at once."

Impressed, Bailiwick leaned forward to gaze at the envelope. "Is it that important, then?"

Wilberforce scowled. "Do you have some reason to think it is not 'that important,' Mr. Bailiwick?"

Bailiwick straightened and swallowed. "No, sir, Mr. Wilberforce."

Wilberforce narrowed his eyes at his underling. "Right. Therefore, since we have no way of forwarding this very likely vital communiqué, I can think of no alternative but for you to personally follow Sir Colin's trail and hand-deliver it to him."

"Ah." Bailiwick brightened with understanding. "Yes, sir! To Sir Colin and Lady Mellie!"

"You'll need a horse."

The brightness faded slightly. "A . . . horse, sir?"

"Certainly. You cannot count on being able to find a coach going the same path as Sir Colin in his chaise. No, a horse is necessary. You do ride, do you not, Mr. Bailiwick?"

"Well, yes . . . a bit."

"Excellent. Pack a small bag. You'll set out at once." He made as if to hand the letter to Bailiwick, then drew it back at the last moment. "It is imperative that you do not fail to find Sir Colin, lad. I have the feeling that he has bitten off a bit more than he can chew."

Bailiwick nodded meaningfully. "Aye, sir. Lady Mellie can be a right handful sometimes."

CHAPTER 8

By the time Cap'n Jack had defeated the enemy (a prolonged and bloody skirmish with a horrifying body count), squelched the mutiny (by dint of three keelhaulings), and the rival ship had surrendered (sending four sailors down the plank), Colin was ready to take a stroll down the plank himself. Melody had apparently found the entire gory tale relaxing, for she was fast asleep in his lap with her bottom lip pooched out and her little belly rising and falling with each breath.

Colin sat in the shade of a tangled hedge on the side of the road with Melody curled in his lap and Gordy Ann flopped faceup on his knee. The once elegant and fashionable Cabriolet had been hauled to the side of the road like an abandoned farm cart and Hector, having recovered his high-bred nerves like the valiant steed that he was, cropped the high grass on the roadside with relish, tied to the wrong end of the wreckage.

"We look like Gypsies," muttered Colin. At the moment, he would be glad of even that company, for no one had passed in the hour since the accident. "I don't understand it," he said conversationally to Gordy Ann. "I didn't think we were so very far out of Brighton."

Gordy Ann made no reply, which showed her opinion of his statement of the obvious. They were going to have to abandon the gig and walk it soon.

Then Hector raised his head and gazed down the road in

the direction from which they had come. His ears perked and he gave a soft snort.

A moment later Colin heard the clopping of hooves and jingling of harness and mingled voices of people. Another moment after that, a procession of three wagons and several smaller carts came over the nearest rise.

Colin squinted. They looked like Gypsies at first glance, but they were dressed like ordinary common folk for the most part—with the exception of one grand fellow who led the party on a fine but elderly bay horse. This man was dressed like a cross between an English courtier of the last century and a garishly painted peacock.

First the eye was blinded by a truly brilliant purple coat— velvet, of course. Why wear purple unless one wore it in velvet? Beneath this was a heavily ruffled shirt of the sort fashionable two decades past, all above a pair of parrot-green breeches. The aforementioned did not clash so very nauseatingly until one took in the brilliant orange tricorne hat complete with white plumes sported upon said individual's bewigged head.

"I didn't know hats came in that color," Colin said in wonder. Gordy Ann did not comment.

The entire parade was becoming quite loud now and Melody stirred in Colin's lap. When the outrageous leader came even with Colin and Melody and pulled his horse to a stop with a broad hand signal to his followers, the subsequent cacophony of squeaking axles, questions, and equine snorts of relief managed to penetrate even Melody's famously deep sleep.

She sat up and rubbed her eyes. Her baby-blue gaze went wide. "Pirates!"

The leader bowed regally from horseback, sweeping his hat from his head and bending low. "Only on occasion, milady. I am Pomme." Then he raised his gaze to meet Colin's. "Methinks you broke your chariot, sir."

"He mucked it!" Melody scrambled up from Colin's lap,

eager to report events. Gordy Ann went along, upside down, knot head dragging on the ground. "He mucked it and then he sinkeded it!"

The fellow nodded most seriously. "Verily, little milady."

"Your hat! I like feathers!"

Colin stood. "That's enough, Melody. Go sit in the shade while I speak to the gentleman."

Melody went very willingly for once. Colin breathed a sigh of relief and turned to the leader of the group. "Sir, I am S—Mr. Lambert. My young ward and I have indeed had an accident. Is it possible that someone in your group could ride back to the inn there and have them send aid?"

Pomme shook his head sadly. "No, Mr. Lambert. It is not possible. We never look back." He turned his head to address his people. "Do we, lads and lassies?"

"Never look back!" The words came in a hearty chorus, out of dozens of throats.

Colin blinked. "But . . . you must help us!"

The man tilted his head. His feathers tilted with it. "Must we? Must we help a man who would desert one of us on the road after promising employment?" He turned his head again. "Must we?"

"No!" came the chorus again.

Colin stepped back under the weight of all that disapproval. He gazed at the party in disbelief. "But . . . I didn't—"

Then he saw her. Sitting on the side of one of the flat carts, with her booted feet swinging beneath the hem of her skirts and her auburn hair gleaming in the sun, was Miss Prudence Filby, watching the proceedings with a slight smile on her face.

The vindictive little wench!

On the other hand, she looked exceedingly well, even better than she had that morning. In fact, to be truthful, at the moment she was in far better form than he was.

Colin dragged his gaze back to Pomme, who was watching

him with narrowed eyes. Colin cleared his throat. "She was ill."

Pomme only continued to gaze at him.

"She really wasn't up to the journey." Which was a stupid thing to say, considering that she was journeying even now, in obvious good health. "I—I left money with the innkeeper—"

Pru hopped lithely down from the cart and sauntered forward. "He pocketed it and ordered me to wash tankards for me keep." She smiled sweetly at Colin. "I told him where to put his tankards."

"Pru!" Melody barreled past Colin and collided with Miss Filby's legs. "Where's Evan? Where? Where?"

Pru knelt and hugged the tiny girl. Then she turned her and pointed at her cart. "There, you see him?"

"Evan!" Melody took off, Gordy Ann flapping wildly. "Evan, Evan, Evan!"

Damn. Colin scowled. Deserted by his own troops.

Pomme smiled beneficently. "Prudence, my lovely, tell your Mr. Lambert who we are. The curiosity is killing him, I can see it."

"He ain't my Mr. Lambert," she pointed out, then turned to Colin and indicated the group with a toss of her head. "This here's the Montgomery Aloysius Pomme Theatrical Troupe."

Colin gazed at the motley crew. "Actors?"

"Indeed." Pomme bowed his plumed head graciously. "Players all, from the tots to the dotards. Lovely Prudence caught our attention with her sauce and spine and we soon realized we had many acquaintances in common."

Colin had the feeling that Pomme was using the royal "we." He could simply hear it in Pomme's tone.

"Whereupon she related the sad tale of your desertion—"

Colin bridled. "I didn't—"

Pomme held up one hand. Colin subsided in spite of himself.

"The sad tale of your desertion. We welcomed our sister

with open arms, for we would never desert one of our own in such a culturally arid locale." He raised his gaze upward. "And we've dire need of a seamstress."

Pru frowned. "I told you, Monty, I ain't the best w' needle—"

Pomme waved his hand. "Prudence, you are a professional theatrical seamstress, assistant to the great Chantal Marchant. No false modesty is needed."

Colin waved his fingers. "Pardon me, but can we get back to my broken gig and how you can possibly justify leaving a man with a small child on the roadside?"

Pomme narrowed his eyes at Colin once more. "It is not our way to pass judgment on anyone, sir. But when the offended party is one of us and the offender is not, we usually go upon our way with a small but significant act of vengeance. Agreed?"

"Ah—" That did not sound good. "I don't think I—"

"Agreed, then! Prudence, what say you to Mr. Lambert? Will we aid him or leave him in the mess he's made for himself?"

Colin held his tongue but sent a white-hot glare at Miss Filby that promised certain vengeance of his own.

Miss Filby smiled sweetly. Oh, hell. Colin knew what that meant.

"We must aid him—"

Colin let his breath out in a whoosh.

"—but he must sing for his supper!"

Jeers and laughter erupted from the carts and wagons behind her. Colin looked desperately from Pomme to Miss Filby. "I don't understand. Sing? Sing what?" Not literally, surely!

Pomme waved a hand. "Oh, we'll sort that out later," he said airily. "Are we agreed then, Mr. Lambert?"

Colin ran his gaze over the smiling troupe, the flamboyant Pomme and Miss Filby, with that triumphant gleam in her eye—and his poor, beautiful, broken Cabriolet.

His shoulders sagged. "Agreed." God help him, he hoped he hadn't gotten himself into something horrible.

Unfortunately, by the nasty twist to Miss Filby's smile, he was fairly certain that he had!

Once the Troupe de Pomme had laughingly cobbled themselves back together, having hefted the Cabriolet atop the performance wagon and tied a bemused Hector to the back of it, the entire company settled into their places and the caravan began to roll once more. Colin climbed cautiously aboard the same cart that Miss Filby rode on, braving young Evan's poisonous glare.

Melody had no idea that their welcome was anything but heartfelt. She immediately snuggled next to Evan on his packing crate and began to relate a long adventure involving broken ships and sinking carriages. Or was it sinking horses and broken drivers?

Evan rolled his eyes with the affected disinterest of a twelve-year-old, but Colin noticed that the lad didn't move away or otherwise discourage Melody in the slightest.

Noticing Miss Filby watching the two, Colin smiled at her. "She didn't want to leave you two behind."

Miss Filby slid him an expressionless look. "Imagine that."

Colin cleared his throat. "I am grateful, you know, for the help and—"

"You're not gettin' out of it," she said flatly. "You'll sing."

Colin rubbed his neck. "Well, that's just it, you see . . . I can't. Not a note. I'm hopeless."

Miss Filby smiled. "Then you'll juggle fire."

"What?"

She motioned with her chin. Near her on the cart rode a young man with heavily bandaged hands. "Cam here says he fumbled a burnin' axe a few days ago."

Young Cam saluted him with a white-wrapped paw. Colin gulped. "A burning axe, you say?"

Miss Filby smiled serenely. "Oh, you'll catch on straightaway. Nothin' like a bit o' fire to teach you quick-like."

"I do know one song," Colin said quickly. "A drinking song, from my younger days." It was a shouted chant more than a song. He might be able to carry it off.

Miss Filby shook her head. "This is a family act. Folks won't like you singin' that."

The way she said it made Colin think of angry farmers with pitchforks and irate wives swinging ladles! He shuddered. Perhaps he could manage a small, smoldering hatchet . . .

Pru could hardly contain her laughter at the look on Mr. Lambert's face. He deserved it, the betraying blackguard! The moment when he'd walked away had been one of the worst moments of Pru's life. To be abandoned in the country with no means of supporting herself and Evan—why, it was her worst nightmare come to life!

When that innkeeper had told her to scrub tankards, she'd snapped and behaved rather madly. Fortunately for her, the innkeeper had ducked those tankards very deftly. Even more fortunately, Pomme had been in the public room and had stolen her away when the landlord had threatened to call the law down on her.

None of which would have happened if Mr. Lambert had kept his side of the bargain. So no sympathy for him!

Still, her gaze slid to the worried frown on his brow again and again. Poor man. One would think she'd told him he was going to have to face his doom!

Melody spent the next hours crawling from one lap to the next, charming her way through the occupants of the cart like a pint-sized politician. Colin watched her with a smile, realizing that although he might be persona non grata among the players, they had no intention of holding that against Melody.

As if anyone could.

At the moment, she was being dandled on the knee of

Young Cam—was there a Cam the Elder somewhere?—examining his bandaged hands and peppering him with questions about being on fire.

Several of Cam's answers brought Miss Filby to laughter, which dampened some of Colin's burgeoning sympathy for the handsome young giant. Cam seemed to think that Miss Prudence Filby was a delight for the eyes and Colin had to admit that a night of rest and a few good meals had done wonders for her. She was bright-eyed and animated in the company of the players as she had not been with him.

Of course, he was the Evil Employer, Dastardly Colin the Deserter, the man who had kidnapped her from the sunny shores of Brighton and tossed her aside in the backwater of the Sussex countryside.

He felt rather sick at the thought himself. Of course, he knew the true circumstances and he knew his own reasons for his decision . . . yet he doubted that if he had the chance he would make the same one again.

It was Chantal. The thought of finding her again had him in a whirl. She had always been able to spin him about, to make him dizzy and forgetful and lost in thoughts of her.

Well, that was love . . . wasn't it?

His gaze had been absently following Melody's progress around the cart and now he noticed that she'd settled back into her tiny space next to Evan. The boy sat with his thin arms around his pointy knees, his oversized boots slightly pigeon-toed. He studiously ignored her girlish invasion into his manly brood, of course.

Melody seemed not to care. She simply snuggled into his side and began to talk to Gordy Ann. The wad of knotted cravat that was the doll was beginning to look pretty dire. Colin wondered idly if he would ever be able to pry it out of her hands long enough to wash it.

Or perhaps boil it.

Then he realized that Evan's gray gaze was fixed upon

him. There was a silent storm of resentment and fury in those expressive eyes, though the thin face showed none of it.

Colin took it as his due. He could see that he had become the perpetrator of all that was unfair in the boy's world. Sympathy made him smile into the wave of antipathy. He knew what it was like to have one's world changed drastically at such an age. When his own mother had died, he'd been fostered out to his aunt. Dumped, really.

His aunt was kind but busy with her own brood, and he'd felt the loss of his gentle mother fiercely. His father he'd professed not to miss at all, and had continued in that pretense well into adulthood.

For Evan, to be torn from his home in Brighton and dragged along on the road with a stranger—well, the lad was entitled to a few foul looks and a bit of temper, in Colin's opinion.

It did not occur to Colin to wonder why he had suddenly begun to see little Evan as anything but another piece of Miss Filby's baggage.

CHAPTER 9

When the caravan stopped in the early afternoon, there were no orders shouted or commands given. Everyone simply set about their business in a purposeful yet unhurried manner. In no time, the carts were emptied and the wagons put into place. The women swept Miss Filby along in their endeavors and Colin soon realized that the area behind the semicircle of wagons was going to be a sort of camp for the troupe.

Outside the circle, the area before the largest, most centrally placed wagon was left clear until Young Cam came along with a pile of tall wooden stakes laid across his forearms.

"Oy, Mr. Lambert! If yer takin' on me jugglin', then ye get to take on me hammerin', as well!"

Laughter rang out at that and Colin realized that all the men had gathered about them. He was being closely observed, it seemed. Hard work had never frightened him, so he stepped up to Cam and took the pile of stakes easily into his own arms. "Where would you like them?"

Cam grinned. "Oh, just watch a moment. I think ye'll figure it out right enough."

Colin nodded, his expression wry. "You're not going to give me an inch, are you?"

"Right enough, Mr. Lambert." Cam lifted his chin. "Our Miss Prudence wouldn't be wantin' us to, now would she?"

Colin bit back a sigh. He was determined to carry his weight. In addition to easing his own gentlemanly sense of debt, it might convince the lot of them that he'd earned his keep and no longer needed to sing for his supper.

So he followed directions without a murmur and pounded stake after stake into the hard lime soil. When he noticed the other men stripping off their shirts in the spring sunshine, he glanced about him in surprise. Not a woman in sight? Excellent. His own weskit and shirt joined the others on the shrubbery and he grinned at the welcome feeling of the sun and the breeze on his sweating skin.

The other men laughed at his eagerness. "Oy, if ye don't like them posh rags, I'll take 'em off yer hands for ye!"

Colin smiled easily. "You might want to wash them first. You wouldn't want to smell of toff."

That brought on a bit of ribald commentary but Colin could tell that he wasn't being treated quite as standoffishly as he had been. When he tossed back a few choice rejoinders, his jests met with just as much laughter as the ones he was the butt of.

On the other side of the wagons, Pru had quickly accomplished the tasks set out for her and was now going over the crates of costumes. They'd been set up at a suitable distance behind the main wagon, convenient for quick changes. With relief, she soon saw that most of what was needed was simple mending, something that even she could accomplish—at least well enough not to be noticed from the distance of the audience. Though she loathed sewing, it was ever so much nicer to do it in the sunshine of a fine spring day than in the dank cellar of the Brighton Theater.

At one point, a spate of girlish giggling disturbed her concentration. She looked up to see three of the younger ladies peering around the main wagon, their backs to her. Curious, she set down her sewing with relief and joined them.

"What are we looking at?" she whispered with a smile.

The three women, hardly more than girls really, turned to Pru with a smile. "We're just admirin' the fresh view, Miss

Prudence." It was the one Pomme called Fiona, a dark beauty with bold eyes.

"Oh?" Curious, Pru moved to the front and peered around the edge of the wagon. "What view is th—"

Oh, heavens. Naked, gleaming muscles. Broad shoulders. Hard, muscled arms swinging the sledgehammer in large, easy arcs. Wide, muscular chest. Tight, rippling abdomen. Slim hips and a firm, hard rear that the breeches clung to so damply that they may as well not have been there. Long, muscle-ridged legs rising from his boots and ending in a region that Pru's eyes could not avoid, not with the way the sweat-dampened arrow of hair on his bare belly directed her gaze to it again and again.

I touched him there. I know what happens to him.

Mr. Lambert, undressed and gleaming in the sun, was an absolute god.

"Would ye like to borrow me handkin, miss?" The giggles rose in volume.

Pru shut her mouth with a snap. And hoped that her chin was not, in fact, dripping with drool. She would not check. She refused.

She stepped back and inhaled, hoping her mind would clear once the scene before her was gone. "Just because Mr. Lambert has removed his coat—"

"And his weskit!"

"And his shirt!"

"Do ye think he'll remove anythin' else?"

"La, I hope so!"

Pru cleared her throat. "Now you're just being silly."

The women smiled at her knowingly. "It ain't silly to know a fine cut o' beef when ye see one," Fiona said with a cheeky grin.

Pru drew herself up tall. "Mr. Lambert is not a cut of beef!"

"Well, 'e ain't got chicken legs!"

"Not by 'alf, 'e don't!"

Pru turned and stalked away from their ribald teasing, knowing that her face was flaming and knowing that she was going to dream about Mr. Lambert's naked, gleaming chest tonight whether she liked it or not!

After the blood-heating view she'd just walked away from, it was a relief to sit down in the shade of the shrubbery. Melody had begged someone's brightly colored scarf to wrap Gordy Ann in and was apparently engaged in marrying the doll to a pinecone.

"And you, Lord Pinecone, take Gordy Ann to be your wedded life—"

Pru smiled. "That's very good. Have you been to a wedding, Melody?"

"Uh-huh." Melody walked the rag doll and the pinecone back down the aisle with great ceremony. "Gordy Ann got a new dress. You get a new dress when you get merry, just like Maddie."

Pru didn't laugh, quite. "And who is Maddie? Is she a friend of yours?"

"Maddie was my mummy. Except she wasn't my mummy, Uncle Aidan just thought she was my mummy, but Uncle Aidan thought he was my papa, too, only he wasn't."

Pru blinked. "I see." She didn't see at all. "Melody, who is your mummy?" If Melody's mother was still alive, she ought to be thrashed for letting Mr. Lambert traipse off with her child this way.

Melody was humming an off-key wedding march and didn't answer. Pru decided to drop the subject, for it truly wasn't her business.

Then Melody said, "Nanny Pruitt took me to Brown's to meet my papa."

"Oh?" Pru kept her tone casual. *Meet* her papa? "That sounds nice."

"Then Nanny Pruitt went away."

"After you met your papa?"

Melody began to dance the doll and pinecone in a sort of swirling waltz step. "I like Brown's."

"Who is Brown?"

"Brown's isn't a person. Wibbly-force is a person. Brown's is the place that Wibbly-force takes care of."

"What kind of place is Brown's?"

"Big. And quiet. I can play hide-and-seek all day. Billy-wick always finds me, though. He's really, really smart."

Pru was beginning to suspect that the cast of characters in Melody's imagination was larger than her live circle of friends. "If Billy-wick and Wibbly-force live in Brown's, then where do you live?"

"In Brown's."

Pru smiled and stretched out on her belly in the grass next to Melody with her chin planted on her hands. "Does Brown's have fairies and elves, too?"

The silence made Pru turn her head to look at Melody. The child was gazing at her with a tiny frown wrinkle between her barely there brows. She looked exactly like Mr. Lambert when she did that. Pru's smile faded slightly.

"Brown's isn't for fairies. Brown's is for Dis-squished Gentamens." Melody turned back to her play. "Like Uncle Aidan and Uncle Colin and Grampapa Aldrich and Lord Bartles and Sir James."

Pru went very still. Brown's. Distinguished Gentlemen. Lord Bartles?

"Brown's Club for Distinguished Gentlemen," she said slowly. Brighton was full of London travelers. One heard many things. She knew of White's and Boodle's . . . and Brown's. "In London?"

"Uh-huh."

"Melody, ladies do not say 'uh-huh,'" Pru said absently as her mind whirred. Melody lived at a gentlemen's club? Preposterous! "Ladies say 'yes.'"

Melody giggled. "You sound funny, Pru. You sound like Maddie."

Oops. Pru sat up, shaking off her strange thoughts. "Well, you ought to listen to your Maddie, then, Miss Melody. She sounds like a right lady."

"She is. She's Lady Blankenship."

Pru regarded Melody with stunned frustration. Who was this child who claimed to live in a gentlemen's club, yet knew exalted people like this Lady Blankenship well enough to call her "Maddie"?

Moreover, who was Mr. Lambert to tote this infant around the country roads of England in search of a promiscuous actress like Chantal?

And how could Chantal have borne to give up such a man once she'd seen him naked?

Pru stood abruptly. "Time for your nap, Miss Melody."

Colin let his sledgehammer drop at last and gazed about him at his work. After he had pounded in the stakes set out by the injured Cam, the others had come behind them using the stakes and the surrounding trees to string a complex array of ropes. Colin wasn't sure of the purpose of the ring of high ropes until someone rolled another cart around and began unloading rolls of canvas.

When they were hung, they made a wall of billowing white around the largest wagon, enclosing a space large enough for the wagon and . . . an audience?

"That's it, Mr. Lambert," Cam said when asked. "If we don't put a curtain up, we don't get the coin from them that wants a show. As it is, we got to go round and knock peepers out o' the trees once in a while." Cam shook his head. "Folks think we're doin' this for the joy of it."

There was joy in it, however. Colin could see that the troupe was like a family, full of personalities and melodrama and conflict, but also full of good fellowship and affection.

Except of course, for him.

"You done a right fine job of it, Mr. Lambert." Cam grinned at him. "But ye still 'ave to sing."

Colin's gut went cold. There was no help for it. He must seek out Miss Filby and make a formal apology for his decision to leave her behind.

He only hoped it would work.

It didn't.

Miss Filby put down her sewing and stood, planting her fists on her hips. "You made your deal. I know your word ain't as strong as it should be, but this time there's folk about who'll make you stick to it!"

Colin backed up a step, offended. "I was not trying to—" Except that he was. He really, truly was. He deflated, then straightened and gazed into those accusing gray eyes. "I'm sorry. I'm sorry I left you and Evan. I'm sorry I tried to get out of my commitment. I'm not at all sure I can do it but . . ." He swallowed. "I shall try."

Pru watched him walk away, her belly roiling with conflicting emotion. She wasn't normally vengeful, she truly wasn't, but this man had deserted her!

There was so much she wanted to say, words she wanted to shout at him, words that would never come out of a common little seamstress's mouth.

This from a man who has never soiled his hands with a good day's work! You have no inkling of my life, my past, my days as handmaiden to a tyrant who held the power of life and death, shelter and sustenance, over me! You think yourself too good to risk your dignity onstage. I think you too cowardly to try!

But Mr. Lambert was already walking away.

And no one knew that Prudence the gently raised lady still existed.

CHAPTER 10

In the end, Colin did try to follow through on his promise.

When the farthings had been pressed into the hands of the two boys who acted as ushers and the eager townspeople had filed in to take their places in the ring of billowing white, an expectant hum reached Colin's ears where he waited behind the stage wagon.

Oh, God.

He tried to focus his gaze upon the ingenious construction of the wagon. One side of it had folded out to make a level wooden stage and the interior had lifted into place, curtains already hung, to form the proscenium arch.

It truly was very clever. He could barely see it through the dizzying terror in his mind. Mr. Pomme moved past where he waited and clapped him on the shoulder in passing.

"It's only a song, lad."

I don't sing.

Ever.

But the words, which had been said already to no avail, would not come. Then Pomme was introducing "The Gentleman Minstrel" and a large palm—probably Cam's, damn him!—thrust into the center of Colin's back, propelling him onto the stage.

At a hiss from Cam, Pru turned from where she was fitting a stout boy into a tired velvet lady-in-waiting skirt. Cam waved her over.

" 'E's on, miss!"

Pru matched Cam's evil grin and bent to peer through the slit in the curtain that hid the backstage meadow from the audience. Mr. Lambert stood unmoving in the center of the stage, facing the restless audience.

Sing, man! Sing!

Pru bit her lip as she watched. Melody looked up from where she'd sat at Pru's feet, digging a hole with a spoon and burying Gordy Ann, who had recently met with some new and gory fate, apparently.

Seeing Pru's interest, she joined her and pressed her eye to the parting in the curtain. "What's Uncle Colin doing?"

"He's going to sing for us." *God, Mr. Lambert, sing! Please?*

Melody frowned. "Uncle Colin doesn't sing."

Pru was beginning to believe that. "He must sing a little," she whispered back desperately. "Doesn't he sing you to sleep at night?"

Melody looked at her as if she'd asked if elephants could fly. "No."

"No?" Pru's belly went cold. "Never?"

"Never-ever."

Onstage, Mr. Lambert opened his mouth. A croak issued forth. He swallowed and cleared his throat and tried again. "Alas, my love . . . you do me . . . wrong . . ."

It was awful. It was worse than awful. Mr. Lambert had the singing voice of . . . of . . .

Next to her, Pomme shuddered. "He sounds like a goose mating with a donkey," he breathed in horror. "I've never heard the like."

Apparently, neither had the audience. Dismay was etched on every upturned face, butcher and banker alike.

"To cast me off . . . discourteously . . ." Mr. Lambert stalled in his off-key braying and went silent. He seemed completely frozen onstage.

"God in heaven." Pomme's tone was laced with pity. "If I

had a real pistol instead of this prop, I would put him out of his misery."

Pru felt ill. What had she done?

And how was she supposed to fix it now?

Before she'd realized it, Melody slipped away from her and strolled easily onto the stage. With one finger in her mouth, the tiny girl looked at all the people curiously, but without any apparent fear. She sidled up to Mr. Lambert and tugged on his coattails. "Uncle Colin, tell me a story."

Colin couldn't answer because he hadn't any air in his lungs at all. In fact, the edges of his vision were beginning to gray just a bit. It occurred to him that if he passed out, he wouldn't have to sing anymore. He would, however, have to live the rest of his life knowing he was a coward. Hmm. Difficult choice, that.

He was dimly aware of Melody stepping in front of him and facing the dissatisfied crowd. If he was any kind of man at all he'd sweep his tiny daughter away from the maddened mob and take their chances running for their lives. And he would.

As soon as he found his knees. They must be around here somewhere.

Then he realized that Melody was speaking to the crowd. "Once 'pon a time on the high seas . . ." Melody's high piping voice rose above the grumble of the audience. They quieted at once. ". . . there sailed a mighty pirate ship."

She took a giant breath and continued. "'Pons the prow were letters retched in the blood of honest mens and they read—" She looked over her shoulder at Colin and waited.

"Dishonor's Plunder!" he croaked.

"Dishonor's Plunder," Melody affirmed. "And the wail-ly captain of this bicious maraubber was none other than the black-hearted outlaw himself—"

"Captain Jack!" Colin could breathe again!

Melody turned back to the crowd, who were beginning to

look truly interested. "And Captain Jack and his wail-ly crew sailed the ship . . . and . . . and . . ." She clutched Gordy Ann close and blinked her eyes rapidly.

Oh, no. She'd run out! Swallowing hugely, Colin stepped forward. "Captain Jack and his wily crew sailed the wide Atlantic looking for Spanish treasure ships that abounded there. And while they sailed looking for treasure, Captain Jack also kept his spyglass searching for the ship of his ruthless enemy . . ."

Backstage, Pomme stood next to a breathless Pru and nodded thoughtfully. "That's not bad." He turned and gestured to the other players. "Forget the Molière. Pirates up!" he whispered loudly.

With a silent flurry of practiced movements, the players pulled off powdered wigs and beauty patches and replaced them with brightly colored scarves and eye patches. The youngsters came running with swords and scabbards. Young Cam held out his arm while another player fitted him with a stuffed parrot on his shoulder, wired beneath his armpit.

In a flash, they'd changed from perfumed courtiers to merciless raiders. Pomme waved them onstage with Colin and Melody. "Go, go! Improvise, my players! Improvise!"

When the stage abruptly filled with real pirates, Melody clapped her hands with joy but Colin didn't miss a beat. He continued speaking even as he scooped up Melody and tossed her safely into Pomme's waiting arms. "Here before you, gentle audience, you see a great battle between the green-clad pirates of the *Dishonor's Plunder* and the black-clad pirates of the *Black Kraken*!"

The players each took a single glance down at their own sleeves, just to be sure, and then immediately set to fencing with one of their opposite number.

Backstage again with Melody, Pomme grunted in approval. "Now I'm glad we ran out 'o that black velvet."

Pru watched as Mr. Lambert, whose coat was a more

muted shade of green—which happened to match his eyes most attractively—took a sword from one of the "fallen" pirates and challenged Young Cam.

Cam's sword was awkwardly wedged into his bandaging, but he swaggered so convincingly and was so large and handsome as the villainous enemy captain that Pru doubted that the crowd noticed at all.

"They battled all the day and all the night because . . . because . . ." The crowd was enraptured.

Think, man, think!

"Because of the kidnapped princess!" shouted Melody through the curtain.

The battle onstage hesitated slightly as they all realized that there was no princess at hand.

Something lacy fluttered over Pru's head, getting in her view of the action onstage. She looked up to realize that Pomme had draped a Spanish head covering over her pinned hair. He smiled at her surprised expression as he pressed the comb rather painfully into place. "You're up, Prudence."

And then he shoved her through the curtain and onto the stage.

Out of the corner of his eye, Colin saw Miss Filby rather forcefully propelled from behind the curtain. She stumbled several steps as she struggled to unwind herself from the clutches of a tatty black lace mantilla.

Unfortunately, this put her directly into the confusion of the unrehearsed fray. Colin took a hit to his shoulder as he awkwardly dodged past Cam, but he was able to reach her side before she was impaled on anyone's dull tin saber.

"Careful," he whispered. He tucked her behind him.

Just as he did so, Cam performed an agile flip over them both, landing on his feet with his sword extended dramatically. "Unhand my prize, Captain Jack! She is mine, I tell you!"

Miss Filby shrieked in fear, shrinking conveniently toward stage left. "Oh, pray, save me, Captain Jack!" She wrung her hands. "Save me from the wicked pirate—er—"

"Black Pete shall not have you, my princess!" Colin mugged fiercely as he fenced with Cam. It was mostly a lot of dancing to and fro, with a great useless clanging of swords that mightily impressed the crowd. Colin enjoyed himself tremendously.

All around him, the body count grew. He saw that Melody now perched atop Pomme's shoulders, watching from the side of the stage. Colin winked at her and she waved gleefully. She obviously enjoyed seeing her bedtime story come to life.

Then Cam struck a wild blow. Colin felt the sword hit his diaphragm just wrong. It was too dull to do real damage but the wind went right out of him. He dropped to his knees.

"Sorry, mate," Cam muttered as he bent over him. "It's these bloody bandages." Then Cam stepped in front of Colin, hiding him from view while he swept the "princess" into his arms. "Yer mine now, my fine princess!" He cackled victoriously. "I've won ye, fair and square!"

"Woe is me!" Miss Filby lamented. "I shall perish in the grasp of such a blackguard! Will no one save me?"

The interesting thing about not being able to breathe, Colin found, was that he had a bit of time to notice things. Things like that Cam's legs looked like tree trunks wrapped in linen. Things like the boards of the stage had once been painted a rusty red.

Things like Miss Filby's voice sounded completely different. As the cultured, ladylike tones fell from her lips, he remembered his first impression of her in that darkened theater.

A beautiful voice. A husky, rich contralto filled with hints of sex and velvet. It made the hairs on the back of his neck stand up.

"I shall never surrender to you, you knave," she went on.

"I shall defend my virtue forever, or at least until someone rescues me!"

Lovely. Like fur on bare skin.

"And someone shall rescue me! Captain Jack is on his way—*even now*!"

Oh, right. That's me.

Colin sprang to his feet. To his shock, he saw that Cam had Miss Filby locked in his arms, his face planted in her neck as she struggled to push him off her, her pointy little boots kicking in protest.

Bloody hell! Forgetting the play, forgetting everything but the way that the young giant's hands were holding *his* Miss Filby, Colin let out a ferocious roar and raised his sword.

CHAPTER 11

With his vision fringed in red, Colin pulled Cam away from Miss Filby, spinning the man about and putting the point of his sword beneath the fellow's chin. Cam's eyes went wide.

"Erg!" Cam stumbled backward, away from Colin's ferocity. Colin followed slowly, menacingly.

"You are *done*. Is that understood?"

Cam nodded, his irises ringed in white. "Got it!" he choked out.

Colin planted one hand on that thick chest and shoved Cam away. Then he turned back to see Miss Filby standing at the edge of the stage, staring at him. The black lace had been flipped away from her face and her large gray eyes were filled with something entirely new. She gazed at him with bright spots of pink in her cheeks and her mouth softly open. Colin glowered at her as he slowly crossed the stage.

Mine, his gaze said.

Yours, hers replied.

When he reached her, he tossed his sword aside. Taking her face into his hands, he tipped her head back and lost himself in those storm-sky eyes.

Mine.

Then he swooped down upon those sweetly parted lips.

Mine.

The crowd went insane.

Colin didn't hear a thing but the great thudding of his

own heart and the tiny delicious sigh of surrender she uttered into his mouth. Hot, soft, melting, wet—

Mine.

Then he felt hands upon him, tugging at him, slapping his back. His mind snapped back to reality like a spring released.

What the hell am I doing?

He let go of the woman he'd been kissing and stared at her as if he'd never seen her before. His vision swam with shocked, clouded eyes and kiss-swollen lips. Then he felt himself being turned to face—

A roaring crowd. They were on their feet, stamping and shouting and whistling, farmers and squires alike. Melody bounced riotously on Pomme, waving Gordy Ann like a flag.

He'd forgotten the play completely.

He'd forgotten everything and everyone.

Everything but *her.*

He felt Cam's heavy arm drape across his shoulders.

"I think ye've got potential, Mr. Lambert."

Just then Evan appeared. He drove himself between Colin and Miss Filby with his own small wooden sword raised high. The look he gave Colin should have scorched his hair from his head.

Colin saw Miss Filby squeeze her brother's shoulder. "Don't fuss, Ev. It were just a play."

Right. Though Colin's throat was tight with desire and his lips still burned where her soft ones had pressed, to her it was simply a bit of theater.

He had to hand it to her. She was a bloody good actress.

They all took their bows to long, loud applause, then filed off stage. Colin made his bow and walked off just like everyone else. He just didn't remember doing it.

"Well," Pomme said as he clapped Colin on the back. "It wasn't *Voltaire,* but it wasn't bad, my son. Not bad at all."

* * *

That evening, after the very pleased audience went home and there was had a gleeful accounting of the day's take, all the players were in fine spirits.

At least, most of them were.

Gentle laughter came from those seated circling the fire. Pru sat with her back chilled and her cheeks warmed, arms tucked about her raised knees, finding it difficult to join in.

Even though she was there, in the center of it, she could feel the distance grow. There it was again, that feeling of being on the outside looking in. It didn't seem to matter if she were watching London families through the windows of their snug town houses or sitting among ragtag players about a bonfire. It was always the same. There was a family sharing warmth and laughter or even sorrow.

And she wasn't part of it.

It didn't matter. She'd had a family once. She had her memories. She laid her cheek upon her knees and closed her eyes, trying to pull the past into the present. It didn't work.

This happened more and more often now. Every year she had less to draw from. She remembered the trail of smoke from her father's pipe, but not the smell. She remembered the way her mother's blue silk gown rustled when she walked, but not her mother's voice.

There was no use in the mourning of such things. She had more memories left than Evan had, after all. And she had Evan himself. She had one person in the world, a family, a brother. One fractious boy who drove her mad with frustration one minute and broke her heart with tenderness the next.

She opened her eyes to look across the fire at Mr. Lambert. Who did Colin Lambert have? He spoke longingly of Chantal, of course, but Pru would never believe his love would be returned. At the moment, he held the child Melody on his lap, propping her sleepy form into the crook of his arm. With his other hand, he patted the little back soothingly. Pru doubted he was even aware he did so.

He was so good with the tiny girl. His ward, he'd called her. Melody called him Uncle Colin, but Mr. Lambert spoke of no sister or brother.

None of which is your business, Miss Filby, and don't you forget it.

He'd kissed her on stage. Her first kiss. For an instant she considered telling him so.

What purpose would it serve, other than to embarrass him and mock your own silly fancies?

It had been a shock, the way his lips had been so warm against hers, the way she could taste him after, the way he'd so easily swept her into his arms, lifting her onto her toes as if she'd weighed no more than her gown and a capful of air. The way the hardness of his chest had pressed the very breath from her body . . . the way her nipples had stiffened from the contact . . . the way her knees went soft and her thighs eased open . . .

The way he'd looked at her as if he owned her, heart and soul.

And body.

Her cheeks heated with no help from the fire. She ducked her head, hiding from the blush her own thoughts had caused her. Mr. Lambert had simply been caught up in his storytelling. He'd been putting on a show for the crowd. As far as he was concerned, he'd kissed a bit of stage scenery when he'd kissed her.

Such self-reproach did no good to ease the confusion in her body. She had to get away from the fire. The combination of heat and cold was making her feel feverish.

Colin looked up from his pint to see Miss Filby retreating from the golden circle of firelight into the blue chill of the shadows. Where was she going? To find her brother? He cast a glance around and spotted Evan nearby, rolling about in the dust with one of the troupe's lads, a boy twice his size whom he seemed to have no trouble thrashing. After pausing to make sure it was a friendly match, Colin stood to follow Miss Filby, Melody asleep on his shoulder.

"'Ere, let me take 'er, guv'nor." Pomme's stout wife, as practical as her husband was theatrical, plucked sleeping Melody from his arms as she passed him. "I'll put 'er to bed and that one, too." She indicated Evan with her chin. "You go talk to that young lady. You've got summat to say to 'er."

Colin blinked. "I—"

She slid him a knowing glance. "I been about long enough to know a kiss when I see one, guv'nor. 'Ave you?"

Clearing his throat, Colin decided to let that pass. Miss Filby was a mature, practical sort. She was no "young lady." She was a servant and a worldly theater seamstress at that. Surely she knew that he'd only done that particular act as part of the play.

However, it was the gentlemanly thing to do, to apologize when one had trespassed onto the person of a woman, no matter how lowborn. And trespass he had. Even now he could feel the way her full breasts had submitted to his chest when he'd pulled her close—

He halted abruptly. *Submitted?* What a strange choice of word . . .

Out of the corner of his eye he caught the sweep of gray wool skirts going behind the stage wagon. Right. He had a proper apology to make, the duty of a gentleman.

The spot where Melody had lain on his shoulder felt cold. He wished he still had her with him, as a sort of shield against . . .

Against what?

His thoughts were truly off point tonight. This quest was fair to making him as befuddled as one of the octogenarian fixtures at Brown's!

With a slow tread, Pru climbed the set of steps that led to the stage. The day's event seemed a distant moment now, a fantasy of pirates and swords and a roaring crowd. Nothing remained but the swelling sails of the canvas enclosure.

Safe in the darkness, Pru leaned one shoulder against the upright proscenium arch of the show wagon and ducked her head. Would she always be the wrong shape for the right space—too wellborn to live in the world below, too poor and misplaced to live in the world above?

Hearing a footstep close to her, she opened her eyes. In the dimness she saw a snowy handkerchief offered before her, resting in a large manicured hand. She turned away from it, from *him*.

"Pray, do not waste your gallantry on me, sir," she choked out, her throat tight. "I am surely in no need of it."

She felt his admiring chuckle vibrate through her.

"That is the damnedest bit of mimicry I've ever heard," he said. "Really marvelous."

Oh, God. Her true self was spilling out of her now and she hadn't even realized it. Soon she'd be doing needlepoint and pouring tea! When had Prudence the lady risen so close to the surface? Why wouldn't she stay dead and buried, like her past?

Reaching desperately for saucy Pru, pulling the insouciant seamstress about her like a suit of armor, she snapped her head up and gave Mr. Lambert a defiant glare. "Aye, the jolly pony tricks never end, do they? What would you like to see next? Would you like me t' stomp out a sum w' me foot?"

He didn't laugh and he didn't step back, as she'd expected him to. Absently, he pulled his hand and his handkerchief away with a furrow in his brow.

"I've offended you again, I see. I meant nothing of the kind." He gazed at her for a long moment. "You are a prickly thing sometimes."

Blast, now he was making her feel guilty for snapping at him. He'd only been polite, after all. He was quite the gentleman, to care about the feelings of a servant so.

Lord, she was growing as primitive as Evan. She straightened and faced him, her hands folded before her, her gaze somewhere about the middle button of his waistcoat. "I'm sorry, sir. I'm only in a mood, is all."

"I can see that. I fear that's my fault." He cleared his throat uncomfortably. "It seems I owe you an apology."

Pru blinked in alarm. Oh, no. He was going to mention *it,* wasn't he? Couldn't the man keep shut about anything? She backed away a step. "I must get back to Evan, sir. And Melody. It's time they went to—"

Colin caught her wrist as she tried to slip around him. "Mrs. Pomme has them both well in hand, Miss Filby. Stay. I need to speak to you privately for a moment."

He felt her pulse quicken against his fingertips. Her wrist was so delicate in his grip that he felt as if he were pawing her again. He would have let her go, but when she turned her startled gaze to face him at last, he saw the dampness still glazing those large, dark-lashed eyes, turning them moon silver in the dimness.

Don't let her go. She'll disappear into the night.

Truthfully, he couldn't have let go if he'd tried.

CHAPTER 12

Slowly, without taking his gaze from Miss Filby's, Colin raised her hand and pressed his handkerchief into it, folding her fingers about it. "Mood or no," he said, his voice low, "I have something I wish to say to you. Will you stand still a moment and hear it?"

She nodded slowly. Her heartbeat fluttered in his possession. He did not release it, but held her wrist gently in one hand and wrapped the other about her closed fingers, trapping her quite completely.

"I ought not to have left you behind," he said softly. "I see now that I was wrong to do so. I should have listened to you when you told me you were fit enough to travel or at the least I should have taken better care to ensure that the innkeeper would abide by his word."

"He was a greedy sort," she said, her tone grudging. "But you couldn't have known, sir."

He shook his head. "The point is that once I took responsibility for your employ, I should have made sure you went on to another dutiful employer."

Pru blinked. "D'you do that for all your servants?"

He smiled. "I don't know. I still have all my servants."

She thought about that for a long moment. It meant he was a good master, a rare thing in itself. A master who apologized when he was wrong? Unheard of.

My father was such a man.

She quelled that little voice. "Well, no matter. It started as a mess but it ended well. Pomme came along."

"Yes, well, about that . . ." Surprisingly, he seemed embarrassed. "Miss Filby, I know that Pomme has offered you transportation and work, but if you would consider continuing with me, I truly do need your help with Melody."

Stay with him? *Oh, yes, please.*

Not so fast. She narrowed her eyes as she gazed up into his face. "You left us. What prevents you from leaving us again?"

He thought about it for a moment, then shrugged. "I'd give you my word, but I doubt you'd take it." Then he brightened. "I could pay you half now and half when we reach London."

Please? Pretty please with a bonbon on top?

Shut it, I'm thinking.

Half now meant pounds in her pocket instead of pennies. It would be enough to get her and Evan out of any situation. The relief would be enormous.

Her street-taught suspicion warred with her inclination to trust him. He was rather fascinating, after all. He might be a fool for Chantal and he'd exhibited a certain unreliability, but he wasn't cruel and he wasn't dangerous.

Furthermore he'd apologized for his abandonment and in truth he had legitimately tried to see to her care. He'd even withstood her petty revenge in good humor.

What did she have to lose? Another low-paying sewing job with another theater troupe? Pomme was kind but the traveling life was hard and there was not a great deal to offer Evan here.

And . . . I don't want to go back to my life just yet.

Not until she untangled the mystery of this strange and beautiful man.

Who is still holding my hand. In the dark.

He'd waited patiently while she decided, so she rewarded him with a small smile. "All right then, guv. Evan and I will go on with you tomorrow."

He smiled then, a genuine smile of happiness that nearly took her breath away. "That's excellent news! Thank you, Miss Filby."

"T'weren't nothin', guv." She hoped he couldn't hear how breathless she was.

He'd been truly decent and she'd been a vindictive shrew. Thinking about her revenge, she bit her lip and looked away. "Sorry about the singin' bit. I didn't know."

He surprised her with a laugh. "More punishment for others than for myself, I expect."

She couldn't help a real smile at that. "That's for certain, guv."

Grinning as he gazed down at her, he squeezed her hand teasingly. "You made a splendid princess, however. I can't get over your gift for mimicry. Chantal herself could not have done better."

"Not at all, sir." For all her resentment of Chantal, Pru could not disregard the woman's talent. "Miss Marchant would have made 'em swoon."

He widened his eyes laughingly. "But *we* made them cheer."

"Oh, that." She shook her head. "Folks do love a kiss."

Oh, blast. Now she'd done it. She'd mentioned the bloody kiss!

Colin went still. The kiss.

"Right," he said slowly. "I should not have done that tonight, on the stage." His voice sounded rough, even to him. He softened it. "It was not right of me to manhandle you so. I don't know what came over me, to tell the truth."

She shook her head slightly. "It's all right, sir. It were only a bit o' playactin'." She tried to discreetly pull away from him, backing away. "You didn't mean nothin' by it."

He smiled but he did not release her. "Miss Filby, you are doing it again. This is *my* apology, is it not?"

She went still. "Yes, sir. Sorry, sir."

"Now where was I?" He absently pulled her trapped hand

closer as he gazed upward, pondering the stars. She stepped forward once, then again, pulled unwillingly. "Oh, yes." He smiled down at her. "I wish to apologize for grabbing you and kissing you briefly onstage. I am mortified by my behavior. I regret it completely. It shall never happen again."

In spite of her discomfort, the irrepressible Miss Filby couldn't resist a slight snort. "It weren't *that* brief," she muttered.

Colin frowned. "Of course it was. It was scarcely a peck. Hardly worth apologizing for."

She gazed at him cheekily, her lips quirked. "If you say so, guv. It bein' your apology and all."

"It was a very quick kiss," he insisted. "A mere brush of the lips. Hardly a kiss at all, really."

She tilted her head and raised one brow. "Of course, guv. Whatever you say, guv."

"It was! Here, I'll show you." He pulled her close and dropped the same quick firm kiss upon those impudent lips.

Only it turned out Miss Filby was right. It wasn't so quick after all.

Pru gasped when his hot mouth took hers. *Yes.* She'd teased him into it, unable to resist the temptation to see if he'd do it again. Now his lips were on hers, like fire and hunger, and her own longing exploded within her, a trap she'd laid for herself without knowing.

Yes. His lips were parted, his hot breath in her mouth, his tongue slipping inside, a welcomed intruder, greeting hers with the taste of him, strange and new yet familiar, as if she'd waited a lifetime to taste only him.

His big hands came up to frame her face, his long fingers driving into her hair, holding her in place while he slid his tongue in and out of her mouth, entering her, invading her, making her ache and shiver for something she'd only heard of.

Her cap slid free and her pins failed her, but she only felt released as her hair tumbled down warm over his wrists and hands.

His hot tongue took her again and again. The taste of him! Captive between his hands, her jaw opened, allowing him to delve deeply into her. She was stolen ground, conquered territory. Her borders surrendered and her knees dissolved. Somewhere in the shadows of her mind, she feared for herself. Then that cry faded away, forgotten in the heat and need and taste of him in her mouth.

Her heart galloped, fear and freedom and fantasy released within her like something wild. There was silk and warm linen in her hands. Her fingers slipped beneath his weskit, over his shirt. She needed to hold on, to hang on to something solid, to hold him as close as she could. Under his weskit, her hands traveled over his sides and up his hard back. Her mind recalled gleaming muscles rippling in the sun as she felt them play beneath her touch. Her mouth submitted to his invading tongue. Her thighs quivered and pressed together, the ache between them turning hot and wet and eager.

Yes. To hell with the past or the future. Right now she was here, in the dark, with this enigmatic man who apparently needed to kiss her as much as she needed to be kissed. The darkness covered them, sheltered them, barricaded them from the others.

From the world.

From their own doubts and fears.

Colin was unable to resist kissing her again and again. Her mouth was so sweet and soft and mysteriously giving. This was no play, no gambit to thrill an audience. She was open and vulnerable and madly enticing, all the more so for being rather endearingly awkward. Kissing her seemed as natural as breathing—as if he'd been kissing her for years yet as new as if he'd never kissed anyone before.

She clung to him ardently as he took her mouth with his

tongue and he reveled in her eagerness. The solid wall of the wagon supported them as he pressed her back, moving his body into hers as if he'd never lived anywhere else. She gave like sweet taffy, her stance widening as he stepped between her legs, trapping her against the wall. He slipped his hand behind her head, protecting her from the splintering wood as he marauded her mouth again and again.

His cock, already swollen, hardened further at the taste of her, at the sound of her breathless sighs, at the heat and softness of her full breasts against his chest. He couldn't help it. He pressed his rigid cock into her belly, the exquisite pleasure-pain of his trapped desire driving every thought from his mind but one.

Mine.

He needed to touch her, to be touched by her. He needed—

One hand slid from framing her face down her delicate neck. He paused as he felt her pulse throbbing as fast as his own. Then his touch passed over her collarbone and down. Her skin was warm and he knew its fairness would be flushed with desire.

He let his hand come to rest on the side of her breast. The rounded side filled his large palm and he gently pushed upward while his thumb found the point of her nipple.

It hardened in greeting, pressing ruby-hard through the barrier of her gown.

Stroke me, it said to his touch. *Squeeze me. Reveal me. Suck me.*

Who was he to refuse a lady?

He began to kiss his way down her neck. She shivered in his hands and he felt her hot panting breath on his hair as he bent over her. Her hands clutched at his back, those clever hands . . . he had plans for those hands, just as soon as he had her naked and begging for him.

His own hand behind her head slipped down the back of her neck and made short work of the tiny buttons at the top of her gown. He curled the fingers of his other hand over her neckline and pulled it lower, lower, following the path of it with his mouth. He kissed and sucked at her skin, marking the trail so he'd never lose it again.

At last, her nipple emerged from the snug neckline. *Suck me.*

Oh, yes.

He took that sweet point into his mouth and pulled gently at it, then released it to harden in the cool air. He felt her hands leave his back and dive into his hair, pulling his head close again.

Pru gasped and let her head fall back against the wagon. Hot, tugging, teasing pleasure swept her as he sucked her nipple to rigid hardness. She drove her fingers into his golden hair, pulling him close. Don't stop. Don't ever, ever . . .

His mouth left her breast and she let out a mewling sound she didn't even recognize as her own voice. No matter, for he was only moving to the other nipple, which he'd revealed without her realizing it. New hot sweet pleasure-pain as he sucked one nipple and teased the other with his fingertips, rolling and squeezing gently. Her hands fisted in his hair as she whimpered in pleasure, her lower body rocking toward his in a rhythm she'd never known before.

Kiss me. Suck me. Touch me.

His hand—where had he come up with all those hands?— slid down beneath her hem, lifting it to reveal her calf and knee. He pushed her skirts up and lifted her knee high. She wrapped her leg about him obediently, clinging to his neck as he slipped his hand higher, over her knee, up her thighs—oh, heavens, her thighs were damp, so damp!—past the negligent barrier of her pantalets with their convenient opening, until his large, warm palm cupped her gently.

Yes. No. Yes. Oh, sweet heaven, yes.

She heard the words as if from far away. Were they in her fevered mind or had she said them out loud? She scarcely cared, for the result was a long hard finger sliding between her slippery folds, invading her, claiming her heat and her wetness and her aching, throbbing want for its own.

He lifted his face and kissed her again, a deep moan rising in his throat, his tongue invading, matching the slow, gentle thrusting of the finger that impaled her most secret, innocent tunnel.

She balled up her innocence and threw it over her shoulder, choosing instead to grind her pelvis into that hand, reaching for something, aiming her newly awakened senses at some unknown, unreachable goal . . .

She wanted . . . wanted . . .

In the nearby encampment, a woman laughed, a high, hearty sound that impacted into their panting, heated bubble of silence like a boulder into a pond.

Through Colin's need-crazed haze, he heard Miss Filby squeak in alarm, felt her hands jerk out of his hair.

He flung himself away, stumbling backward, self-loathing throwing ice water onto the fire in his body. Bloody hell! What was wrong with him, assaulting the poor girl like some lust-crazed beast?

Bending over with his hands on his knees, he shook his head, desperate for clarity.

"I'm sorry, sir!"

Her words were noise, jumbled by his lust.

"I shouldn't of—it weren't—"

He held up one hand, begging for time. The roaring in his ears finally abated and he was able to straighten, though his cock still throbbed. He swallowed and prepared to apologize like he'd never before apologized in his life.

Miss Filby was gone.

CHAPTER 13

Her face flaming, her heart pounding, Pru rushed back to the central fire as if the pillaging pirates of the *Black Kraken* itself were after her. Unfortunately, when she reached it, her own outlaw thoughts were still skirmishing within her.

What had she done? What had *he* done? What sort of mad, impossible should-never-have-happened moment was that?

She'd never felt anything like his touch, his mouth, his body. She had the sneaking suspicion that until now, she'd never felt much of anything at all. She had an even larger suspicion that if she hadn't squeaked at just that moment, she would now be finding out just what it was that had bulged so prominently into her belly.

Not that she was completely ignorant. Chantal, she-cat that she was, was as indiscreet as she was wanton. Pru had listened to more explicit tales than she'd ever wanted to hear about men and their wants.

Except in her innocence, somehow she'd never truly believed any of it. After all, it was all rather ridiculous, wasn't it? The nakedness, the yelping, the ludicrous concept of . . . well . . . *impalement*.

Good heavens, it now appeared that Chantal had under-reported matters!

Shivering, feeling the aftershocks of unfulfilled desire jolting through her every time she tightened her thighs, Pru stood on the outskirts of the firelight, unable to continue into public view. It must show on her face. *I kissed Mr. Lambert!* The rest she frankly had no words for.

How could I let him do such things to me?

Let him? You would have begged for it if you hadn't been past speech entirely!

She covered her heated face with her hands. Licking her lips, she tasted him on her, in her mouth, felt him inside her body still, felt his hot demanding mouth and his large hot hands . . .

How could something so earthshaking, so astounding, not be written across her features like a brand?

All she wanted to do was to crawl into someplace small and warm and safe and hide her flaming cheeks from the world, even if she weren't able to hide her shocked and titillated thoughts from herself!

Her virtue had always been so precious to her, for it was the last single thing she had that she could cling to and say to herself, "I am a lady."

Now doubt crept in like a thief, stealing away her peace of mind. Did a lady want to feel a man's mouth on her breasts? Did a lady pine to know what roamed within his trousers?

"Ye must be right tired, pet." A kind, knowing voice came from the dimness nearby.

Pru lifted her face and peered carefully into the darkness, then sighed with relief. "Yes, Mrs. Pomme. It's been a full day, it has."

"The night seems to be brimmin' w' goings-on as well, eh?"

Swallowing, Pru tightened her folded arms across her bodice. "Is it?" Her attempt at a casual tone was a complete loss.

Mrs. Pomme's low chuckle was amused but without judgment. "I've got yer bairns tucked into the small wagon. There's a pallet there for ye and one for yer gentleman. I put the little ones between, so no one will speak nothin' of it. Folks all share when it gets cold-like."

"Yes, thanks," Pru said carefully. "That sounds right nice."

"Off t' bed w' ye then. Ye'll be able to fix yer silly little gig in town tomorrow and be back on yer way. Remember, the road don't take kindly to them what misses their rest."

Pru nodded and scurried off to the small wagon. When she crawled into her pallet next to Evan and Melody, she found that warm, quiet place she'd longed for. The warmth of the children and the soft, even sound of innocent childish snores were soothing and serene.

She only wished her own thoughts would be the same.

When Colin found his way to the wagon, directed by a very amused Mrs. Pomme, he climbed in to find that all three of the occupants were sound asleep. Relieved, he cast himself down on his own pile of blankets and threw his arm over his eyes.

Don't think of her. Don't remember the taste of her.

Don't remember how she kissed you back, as if she wanted to eat you alive. Don't remember how she parted for your hand, hot and ready and eager.

He'd experienced enough women to know that such intoxicating passion was extraordinary. She'd tossed aside every shred of her customary wariness and had responded to his mouth and his hands as if she wanted to do nothing else for the rest of her life.

Brilliant notion! Let's haul her out of this wagon and get on with it!

Nonsense.

It had simply been an indiscreet moment. A bit of play. It wouldn't happen again. It was simply that he'd still been drunk with the heady power of his public success, nonsense play such as it was. He did not desire Miss Filby.

Oh, really? Did you forget and leave that sledgehammer in your trousers, then?

Well, obviously he was overdue for some release. But he didn't desire Miss Filby *especially*.

He didn't dare. Not if he meant to marry Chantal. And he did mean to make Melody his rightful daughter, no matter what. He could not allow Miss Filby's earthy appeal to distract him from that mission! Tomorrow they must push on. The urgency of Melody's predicament allowed for no such diversion!

Even so, the weariness of his body and the warmth of the children seeped through him, melting such firm thoughts of resolve.

Sleepily, Colin rolled onto his side, away from her, away from the children. It had been a night full of surprises. He wasn't sure how he felt about some of them, but he was sure that right now, in this tiny, cramped wagon with an infant, a boy, and a maidservant, he was more content than he'd been in a very long time.

He closed his fist about that thought. He could still feel her heartbeat, he thought dreamily, like a trapped bird in his hand. It was the secret to her, he suspected. When he couldn't see past the sharp retorts and prickly demeanor, he need only touch her there to learn the truth.

In the smooth descent into sleep, he smiled to think he would ever need to understand the inner clockworks of a servant girl.

CHAPTER 14

The next morning, there was very little need for Pru to speak to Mr. Lambert at all, thankfully. Between the bustle of getting the children up and fed, and the loading of the shattered curricle onto one of the carts, the two of them were much too busy to converse. They made do with nods and throat clearings and Melody's bright chatter. All was managed very satisfactorily and they were soon on their way.

After many good-bye embraces and best wishes—surprisingly many of which were for Colin—the players waved them up the road.

Young Cam was to drive the cart to the next village, thankfully one large enough to have a smithy and a hostelry. After delivering their small party there, he would return to the encampment. Because of the success of the previous evening, the players had decided to wrest another night's pennies from the locals.

Pomme declared himself to be Mr. Lambert's natural successor in the part of Captain Jack. Fiona would play the Spanish princess. Fiona rode up front now, planted between Cam and Mr. Lambert. Pru was glad to see the bold-eyed Fiona paired off with the giant lad, until she heard Cam mention that Fiona was his sister.

After that, all Pru could do was sit in the back of the cart with the children and watch Fiona fling herself at Mr. Lambert.

Very well, perhaps there wasn't so much flinging as there was normal conversation, but Fiona made Mr. Lambert laugh and that twisted inside Pru for nearly a mile.

Fortunately for Pru's little-used sense of jealousy, it did not take long to reach the village and the blacksmith. Once the matter of transportation was dealt with, it was to be west to Basingstoke and the Ardmore estate.

Even farther from Fiona. Very satisfying.

With the trade of the expensive curricle and a bit of coin from his pocket, Colin had his choice of vehicles at the hostelry. Although he saw a sporting gig of a previous generation but much like his Cabriolet, he instead purchased a small but comfortable carriage and had the harness changed to fit a single large horse like Hector instead of two ponies.

Miss Filby and the children were shopping for necessities for the drive. When he drove the new vehicle up to where they waited, Miss Filby seemed very surprised by such a practical purchase. Colin gave her a wry look from his perch in the driver's seat. "Believe it or not, I can be taught."

She blushed slightly and had the grace to look a bit ashamed of herself, then nodded briskly and handed up the hamper of foodstuffs she'd purchased with the coin he'd given her. "Looks a sight more comfy, guv. Safer for the baby, as well."

Evan seemed disappointed as he walked around it appraisingly. "Liked the other one, I did. This one's a bit mumsy."

Mumsy, yes. Colin smiled to himself. He was a family man now, after all. "Shall we go then? Basingstoke is only a few hours from here."

Miss Filby rolled her eyes. Colin thought he detected a derisive mutter about "bloody Chantal" again but deigned not to hear it. Without thinking, he held out his hand to Miss Filby to help her in. She stopped in her tracks and frowned at it. "What's that for, then?"

Colin looked down at his hand. What was that for? That was for a lady, not a servant.

How very odd. He met Miss Filby's eyes, then quickly looked away. He wasn't quite up to meeting that stormy gaze, not when he could still taste her mouth and feel her heated dampness in the palm of his hand. "Will you hand me Melody's bag, please? I'll put it on top."

She handed it to him without a word, then clambered in to sit beside Melody. "Come here, miss. I've got one of Pomme's pretty feathers for you . . ."

Colin stowed the rest of their things on top with Evan's help, then sent the boy into the carriage.

"I want to drive Hector." The boy glanced away and softened his tone. "If you please, guv."

Colin smiled. "All right. You can sit up with me and learn the reins. If you can name all the harness parts by dinner, I'll let you drive."

Evan smiled then, a real smile, not an I've-seen-the-worst twist of his lips. His gray eyes brightened and his thin face lost its usual aged lines. "That'd be grand!"

Colin looked at the carriage to see Miss Filby watching him through the small window. She smiled too, though she looked away a bit too quickly, as well. Once again Colin was reminded of the stunning resemblance between her and Evan.

And of how rarely either of them truly smiled.

He and Miss Filby were very carefully not-talking, he knew. And what would he have to say for himself? He didn't dare ask for forgiveness again. He'd gone much too far for that. Furthermore, it was too dangerous, for apologizing seemed to cause compulsive kissing.

Pru settled back into her elderly but well-stuffed seat and smiled at little Melody. "Isn't this nice?"

Melody looked at her with pity. "It's not like Pomme's."

"No, that's true."

"Pomme said that riding in the open air was healthy.

Pomme said that closed carriages make people sour. Pomme said—"

Pru sighed. She had the feeling that she was going to become very sick of hearing about Pomme before the day was over. She felt the springs give when Mr. Lambert climbed aboard, then less so when Evan followed.

Evan must be in ecstasy. He'd formed quite a passion for horses, and for Hector in particular. Someday he would be able to buy a dozen horses like Hector if he wanted.

All they needed to do was survive six more years until Evan could finally claim his inheritance.

Six more years.

On their own.

The next time that Melody's diminutive bladder forced a stop, Mr. Lambert declared that it was fully time for a picnic lunch. Pru obeyed with alacrity, taking down the basket that had been purchased and pulling out the generous portions of cold ham, cheese, apples, and hearty brown bread. Mr. Lambert drank ale from a clay bottle while Pru and the children enjoyed the crisp, cool water from a nearby rivulet.

When Pru wasn't minding little Melody, or trying to keep Evan from depositing insects into Mr. Lambert's ale, she found she was enjoying the journey. It had been years since she'd seen anything but stone and cobbles. The spring day was warm and bright, the only clouds of the charming puffy variety.

A blue and gold day, Pru's mother would have called it, and dragged everyone from their occupations to go on a picnic. Pru's father would grumble good-naturedly that he ought to spend the day on his accounts or his papers or polishing his coin collection, just to make his wife turn her snapping gray gaze upon him, cheeks aglow with indignation. "A day like this is a gift, Atticus Filby, and one is never to ignore a gift!"

"You're the gift," he would retort, and he'd grab her about the waist and waltz her breathless while Pru and Evan giggled at their antics.

"Our picnics used to be just like this," Pru murmured to Evan. "Remember?"

But she could tell from the blank look he gave her that he didn't remember at all. She shook her head and smiled away the frown between his brows. "No matter, love." She ruffled his overlong hair. "Go catch me a butterfly, will you?"

That was all the prompting Evan needed. In seconds he was galloping across the meadow, little Melody scampering at his heels, caroling for him to wait for her.

Now, to see him running in the sunlight like an eager puppy, thin legs pumping, big feet stumbling, falling to roll unharmed in the meadow grass, Pru felt the loss of his childhood like a needle to her heart.

I ought to have made sure he played more. I ought to have tutored him more carefully. So much of what he deserved had been slighted in favor of cold, hungry survival.

Even with such regrets winding through her, she could not help but laugh when he tripped into a small brook and came up dripping, a rueful grin brightening his thin face. Melody was most impressed with his adventure and made sure to land rump first in the trickle as soon as possible.

Pru stood and brushed herself off, ready to assume her nanny duties once more. To her surprise, Mr. Lambert strode past her and swept the soaked, giggling tot into his own arms.

"You're a pretty sight, Mellie. Don't you know mermaids only live in the sea?"

Pru stepped forward. "I'll take her, sir."

Mr. Lambert grinned down at her as he continued to dangle Melody out at arm's length. "No need, Miss Filby. I am perfectly capable of changing a suit of clothing."

He whirled, swinging Melody, whose feet swished wildly

through the air as she shrieked with glee. He stopped and pretended to inspect the child. "Tsk-tsk," he muttered. "You're still wet. That won't do at all." Whereupon he spun her again with vigor, making her squeals echo out over the meadow.

When he finally staggered to a halt, Colin noticed that young Evan was watching with wary envy. After he plunked Melody down to stagger delightedly in circles in the grass, he gazed at the boy for a long moment.

He's not your problem. He's not your son.

He was no man's son, poor lad. What must it be like, to be a boy without education or connections? What would it be like to be so small and powerless? How could a good man—an admirable man—grow from such poor soil?

"Evan, I could use a man's help with Hector. A quick rubdown will make him shine like a piece of new coal."

Evan's eyes, those stormy gray windows, rose to meet his. "Don't know 'ow."

The boy's tone was sullen, but Colin could see the flush of eagerness rising up that scrawny neck. He gave the lad an unconcerned nod. "No man does, at first." He tossed his damp daughter onto his shoulders and began to stroll back to the carriage. Then he paused and looked back over his shoulder. "It's too bad, though. Someone needs to ride him to the stream."

The hook set then. Poor little fish never stood a chance. Evan worshipped the big gelding. As Colin turned back about and began to make his way through the meadow, he soon heard the swish-clomp-swish of oversized booted feet through the tall grass behind him.

He caught sight of Miss Filby as she carried the empty hamper back to the carriage. She strode through the grass, the waving strands of green no match for the forward progress of her sensible dark skirts. What an odd girl.

Our picnics used to be just like this.

Whose picnics? Hers and Evan's? Had there once been

another life where such things were common? Evan didn't seem to recall it, if there had been. Perhaps she had not always been so poor.

It bothered him to think of it. She'd had a very hard time of it. He wondered if there was something he could do about it.

He refused to wonder why, above all the other similar stories in the world, the problems he cared to solve were hers.

CHAPTER 15

"No! I don't wanna get back in the carriage!"

Melody's quick ascent into the nearest tree took Pru back for only a moment. Their picnic had been all too brief. Pru could hardly blame Melody for her reluctance, but Hector was refreshed and back in the harness and the day was passing. "Evan, go on. Keep 'er from goin' too high."

"Why do I have to do it?" Evan scowled convincingly.

Pru only lifted a brow. "You're dying to climb and you know it."

His scowl darkened but he sprang into the tree with a physical eagerness that belied that thunderous brow.

From behind her, Pru heard Mr. Lambert chuckle. She turned to meet his amused gaze.

"You are wonderful with him." He smiled. "He's fortunate to have you as a sister."

His approving smile stole her breath. She turned to the carriage and began to lift the hamper up.

Large competent hands took it away from her before she'd even wrested it to waist height. Startled, she turned to find herself nose to cravat with him. God, he was big! How could she have forgotten so quickly?

She'd managed to keep her distance from him all day, carefully not thinking about the night before. Now it all came back like a rush of fire through her veins.

His mouth on hers. His hands on her body. Her nipple hardening to his eager touch.

Flee at once.

She tried. Stepping away did her no good, for her back only contacted the side of the carriage with a hollow thud.

He gazed down at her with a frown, still standing much too close. "Are you unwell again?"

Unwell? Let's see, my heart is pounding, my palms are damp, and I think my knees have turned to water. All I can think of is how you felt pressed against me last night as you kissed me senseless. The way your big hands felt on my skin. Your mouth on me.

Does that sound well to you?

"I . . . I am very well, thank you," she muttered quickly. "You simply startled me."

He tilted his head. "What did you say?"

She'd slipped up again! *Remember who you are . . . and who you cannot be!*

Plunking a fist on one hip, she tossed her head to meet his gaze. "I said you made me leap a foot, you did! You'd best not be sneakin' up on a lass like that, you great lout!"

He blinked. "I'm a lout?"

The very idea was patently ridiculous. She couldn't keep back a snicker. "Well, you got the size for it, anyway. Could do with some practice but I think you'll pick it up in no time."

He laughed out loud then, a rumbling sound that went right through her belly and made her toes curl. Then he smiled down at her with his crooked grin and her toes tightened further.

"Thank you for the encouragement, but I think I'll pass on that particular challenge." He smiled at her with a gentlemanly little nod and turned away, still chuckling. "Lout?"

Once the sound of Mr. Lambert's amusement faded, Pru realized that she could hear the faint musical tinkling sound of the nearby rivulet. The sound alone made her wild with the need to cool her heated blood.

Looking about her, she realized that Mr. Lambert was busy with the horse and Melody and Evan were still enthusiastically climbing the nearest tree. No one would miss her for a few moments.

Following that liquid siren call, she pushed through fifty feet of bramble until the brush ended to reveal another branch of that lovely trickling stream rushing through a narrow green strip of meadow. Tiny wildflowers dotted the green, giving sweetness to the air. Birds fluttered languidly away, too soothed by the ease of their existence to care much about her presence. It was heavenly, like a painting that made one long for winter's end.

First she scouted the bank, hoping to find . . . yes, there it was! She plucked an herb she knew well, crushing it in her hands. Bending to the little stream, she filled her hands and splashed again and again, closing her eyes as it cooled her burning skin. Not enough, not nearly enough!

Pru cast a quick look about her, then lifted her skirts to kneel on a grassy bit of bank. It would only take a moment. No one would see her be so shameless.

Quickly, she reached behind her neck and nimbly undid the top buttons of her gown, then pulled her arms from the sleeves. Once the bodice was rolled about her waist, safe and dry, she bent to scoop the crystal water with her hands.

Heaven. She rinsed her arms and the back of her neck, cooling her blood, sending that confusing passion into memory where it belonged. Soon her chemise was soaked but she only enjoyed the respite of cool water upon her skin.

Dare she rinse her hair? She frowned at the stream. It was only a trickle, no deeper than a teacup. Perhaps if she lay on her back . . .

When Colin followed the sound of water through the overgrowth, it was only his thirst he wished to sate. When he stumbled upon Miss Filby, spread out upon the grassy bank like a pagan offering, a drenched naiad with her full breasts upthrust to the sky and her chill-hardened nipples pressing pink and rigid against the thin, wet cotton of her chemise and her sunset red hair flowing into the stream, rippling into the current like liquid fire . . . well, rather a different desire rushed to the fore.

Want her.

Want her *now.*

God, she was delicious. He stood, trapped by the sight of her, by the tumbling imaginings of her, of the cool feel of her skin, so ivory and perfect against the green grass. Of the heat of her mouth once he parted those pink lips with his thrusting tongue. Of the weight of those stunning breasts in his hands, of the taste of her nipples, of the way they would become diamond hard as he sucked them, of the resilience of her firm stomach as his mouth traveled down and as his hands moved up those shapely calves . . .

His cock hardened in seconds.

Colin forgot that he ought not to look. He forgot that he ought not to even want to look. There was no thought in his mind that did not involve Miss Prudence Filby, naked, panting, and impaled upon him, wrapping his cock in her wet heat, wrapping her firm thighs about his hips, sucking on his tongue as he took her hard and deep until she screamed aloud in animal ecstasy.

The scream that rang out over the pleasant grove wasn't precisely one of carnal climax. It was more of the "Oh my god, there's a pervert staring at my bosom!" variety.

Colin leaped back into the greenery as if a shot had rung out, but it was too late. He'd been hit.

"Mr. Lambert!"

Don't stand. Really. Now is not a good moment to stand. Think of something else. Something cold. Something cold and boring. Something cold and boring and painful.

"Mr. Lambert, I can see your boots sticking out of that bush!"

Closing his eyes against the humiliating inevitability of the coming scene, Colin rose from his brushy hiding place. "Miss Filby."

She stood before him with her arms folded protectively before her, dressed once more, pinned up right and tight, though her soaked hair tumbled over her shoulders and dripped a dark ring around the neckline of her gray gabardine gown.

He knew what that drab gown hid now, damn it. He could see right through it as if by magic, see directly through to the lavish opulence of her magnificent breasts, to the precise rose tint of her pointed, perfect nipples, to the way her navel dipped deeply into her taut, firm belly.

Hellfire, a sight like that would throw any fellow! Any man might forget he was a gentleman, just for a moment!

Or several, long, lecherous minutes.

Or a lifetime.

Dear God, he was in serious trouble with this woman!

"I'm sorry. I'm sorry again. And then, well, yet more."

Apologizing again. You know what happens when you apologize.

In two strides, he stood before her. Breathing hard, he gazed down into those thundercloud eyes. Curling red tendrils of damp hair surrounded her oddly appealing face. Not pretty, not exactly, though she was much improved from when he'd first met her. Delicate, yes. Otherworldly, absolutely. Almost elfin . . .

Changeling woman. Had she emerged from the shadows of that stage specifically to enchant him? Had his fate been written by some ancient hand, a destiny awaiting him, only to be woken when he'd walked into that theater with his child in his arms?

Silently he raised one hand and reached behind her to slowly coil the wet rope of her long hair around his fist, winding it round and round until she tilted her head back, bound in his trap.

His other hand he wrapped around her jaw, lifting and tilting her face. Her skin was cool and damp against the heat of his palm. Although her lips parted in surprise, she did not move, did not protest, as he slowly lowered his mouth onto hers.

This was no spontaneous stage kiss. This was no heated frenzy in the dark. He fitted his lips to her soft ones, tenderly but implacably. The tip of his tongue swept them, slipping ever so slightly between, just a brief taste, a stolen delight.

A sigh escaped her. He took it, as was his right, and used her hair to urge her body closer to his. She came, stepping so near that her feet moved between his own. His heart began to pound and hers pressed an echo against his chest.

She smelled of the water and the grass and the breeze. She smelled like spring.

She tasted of heaven.

When his groin swelled against her, he forced himself to lift his head, though he kept her close in his arms. He would not take, not again.

As the pounding in his head faded, he could hear Melody laughing nearby. "Evan, Evan, Evan!" she called.

Pru, Pru, Pru. The call came from inside, from a part of him he didn't recognize.

When she pressed her hands against his chest and slowly pushed him back, he let her. He had no right to be here, to hold her, to call for her in his heart.

Her gray gaze was somber and confused as she stepped back, tugging her wound hair from his grip. "What are you about, sir? What do you want from me?"

When he managed to find his voice, he said the very last thing he'd meant to say, but apparently it was the very first thing on his mind. "I covet you."

She blinked. "What did you say?"

He stood, too helpless in his need to even shrug in embarrassment. "I covet you. I cannot think of anything but touching you, of kissing you, of . . . being with you."

For a long moment she gazed at him, her lips softly parted, her gray eyes wide and surprised. The longer she stared, the more he began to hope that she would kiss him back.

Such hope was soon dashed. She stepped back with her arms folded before her and glared up at him.

"And what I am to do about it? Weep with gratitude? D'you think you're the first bloke to knock on this door?" Her lip lifted in an expression of disdain that told him he was lost. "Show a man a set of teats and he's just like all the others. Dogs, all o' you!"

She advanced on him then, her index finger poking him in the chest. "And what of the woman attached to the bosom? Has she nothing to say about it? Is she naught but a rack, standing there to hold your pleasure at the perfect height?"

With that, she whirled and stalked away, her very skirts twitching with fury.

Standing. Colin's mouth went dry at the thought of taking her standing, her skirts rucked to her waist, her legs about him as he pressed her to a wall with his deep thrusting cock—

Like a tuppence whore.

Shame washed through him, dousing his lust. She was right. She was a human being, not an object to be used. His temptation was his own problem, not hers.

Once she'd made it out of Mr. Lambert's sight, Pru felt the strength flow from her bones. She sagged back against the nearest tree trunk, weak-kneed and breathless.

God, that was close!

I covet you.

If it hadn't been for years of practice in the art of deflating the lust of every theater hand and delivery boy who imagined himself to be the answer to her womanly prayers, the outcome might have been entirely different.

She might have said, "Why, Mr. Lambert, how charming! I feel much the same myself."

Or worse, she might have said, "About bloody time, guv! There's a grassy spot. Let's go!"

No, it seemed she had been revealed to herself. It hadn't been her profound moral fiber which had protected her all these years. She simply never fancied anyone before, not the way she longed for Mr. Lambert— the way she dreamed of him—the way she grew hot at the thought of his large hands upon her fevered skin!

I covet you.

This was a pickle, indeed.

If it weren't for Evan, she could be Mr. Lambert's mistress. She could have a bit of passion and love for her own, something to keep her warm in the years of loneliness to come.

Not I. Not with Evan to care for. Someday she would find a way to return Evan to his proper level in Society and when that day came, she would become the old maid auntie, keeping house for her gentleman brother and his happy brood.

That portrait of the future usually brought her some measure of comfort. If she was not to have her own children, she would have the pleasure of Evan's. They would be a family again.

Now however, that formerly pretty scene, which seemed to have a large Mr. Lambert-shaped hole in it, did nothing to bring her comfort. It only seemed to draw the light from the day, making everything a little grayer, a little more faded, a little less like life and a little more like mere existence.

I covet you. She dropped her head into her hands. "Oh, Mr. Lambert," she whispered. "I covet you right back!"

CHAPTER 16

Colin walked slowly back to the carriage, his gaze on the ground. He'd done it now. Still, perhaps it was best that Miss Filby not trust him. He was beginning to realize that he wasn't quite as trustworthy as he'd once thought.

Perhaps he'd never been truly tested after all.

A damp sprig of green lay in his path. Something had fallen from Miss Filby's hair as she'd stalked furiously away. Colin followed and bent to pick it up from the ground. It was a mangled and crushed stem of . . .

He brought it to his nose. Mint.

"S'mint, you nitwit."

Colin manfully didn't cringe at being caught sniffing at Miss Filby's leavings in front of her brother. "Thank you, Evan. I'd figured that out myself."

Evan leaned against a nearby sapling with his arms crossed and a challenge etched upon his pinched face. "She washes in it. Summer and winter, even when she 'as to break the ice in the bowl. Steals it out o' window boxes in town or from the park. Dries it on the bedpost so she don't run out. Scrubs me with it too, when she can catch me."

"What's wrong with ordinary soap?"

Evan sneered. "Soap? When there's bread to be bought?" He pushed off from the tree and stalked after Miss Filby, muttering. "Soap, 'e says. Soap!"

Colin gazed down at the bent stem in his hand. When soap was too dear, she bathed in herbs. That habit was uncommon, in someone common. Most ordinary folk—and some of the gentry as well!—bathed only when absolutely necessary.

An alluring image sprang into his mind, an image of Miss Filby, stripped to the waist, full breasts damp and gleaming, nipples crinkled, sunset hair piled high and messy on her head, scrubbing her skin with mint and icy water in a glacial attic somewhere—

In his mind the image became not quite so enticing when she shivered.

The next hour or so to the Ardmore estate was strained. Pru sat quietly in the carriage with a sleepy Melody and a bored Evan. Her own thoughts were enough to keep her occupied, that was certain!

She had feelings for her employer. Inappropriate feelings. Admiration, of course. Curiosity, that was understandable. Desire . . . well, he was very handsome. And rather inclined to kiss her.

You are in grave danger, falling in love with a man like that.

Was it love? How should she know?

He, however, had confessed to nothing but covetous feelings. She was no acclaimed beauty but she'd been informed that her figure was something to covet. At least, men seemed to want to touch her rather more often than she'd like.

He wanted her body. Unfortunately, she was having difficulty remembering what was so wrong with that. Her loneliness swelled within her, the ache of it a constant companion—except when she was with him.

However, Mr. Lambert was even now driving them all in chase of Chantal! No, she must not forget that she was nothing to him. She was female and she was close at hand and he was a healthy male with a bit more charisma than was good for his character. When Mr. Lambert thought of love, he clearly thought of Chantal. She, Pru, was simply in range.

These truths helped steady her resolve. The fact that Mr. Lambert was out of sight helped to steady the thrumming of her nerves. She would be mistress of her actions! She might appreciate a finely made man but that did not mean she had to fall on her back the moment he noticed her in return!

When the carriage turned down the long drive to the Ardmore estate, Pru shifted Melody's limp form in order to peer from the little window. It was a grand house set in once formal gardens now gone a bit shabby. Not entirely untended, but Pru could see that the design was meant for crisp formality, not rangy overgrowth.

The carriage rolled into the graveled circle before the house and a young man in livery ran out promptly. He took Hector's reins and steadied him while Mr. Lambert jumped down to open the carriage door.

"Miss Filby, I would like it if you accompanied me. Evan, you can look after Mellie for a moment, can't you?"

Evan rolled his eyes, but nodded. Pru climbed out, curious.

"What do you need me for, sir?"

Colin ran his hand through his hair. He shrugged unevenly. "It isn't that I need you, precisely . . ."

Miss Filby narrowed her eyes. "You ain't seen her in a long time, have you?"

"Er . . . no. Not for a few years."

Miss Filby gazed at him for a long moment. Then she let out a long breath. "Well, I got a few things I'd like to say to her, so I'll come in w' you, at any road."

Colin was glad. He didn't really think it was all that important to ask himself why. He was here, finally, to present himself to Chantal, to offer her everything she could ever want. Himself, his wealth, his rank, and her daughter. Yes, he came with hands full. There was no reason to worry.

As it turned out, there was plenty of reason to worry.

"Miss Marchant is no longer in the house, sir."

The words hit Colin like a missed step on the stairs. He could only gaze at the liveried butler in surprise. "But, she must be here. She came only a few days ago with Lord Bertram—"

"Who is it, Petrie?"

The wavering voice came from behind the manservant. Colin peered past the fellow to see a very disheveled Lord Bertram lurching drunkenly down the hall. "Purty Bertie" wasn't looking quite so dapper this afternoon.

Lord Bertram peered at them through reddened eyes. "What do you want with Chantal?"

Colin drew back discreetly but the unfortunate Petrie was in full range of his lordship's whisky-soaked breath. The butler made no sound but his complexion took a turn for the greener.

"I'm trying to find her," Colin replied. "I have something important to ask her." That was about as much of his business as he was willing to advertise.

Bertram's face crumpled. "I had something important to ask her, too. Then my bloody brother beat me to it!"

"What?"

But Bertram had already turned around and was making his way back down the hall with one hand braced on the paneling. Colin shoved past Petrie and followed Bertram, scarcely noticing Miss Filby trotting in his wake.

They found the young lord in a study, pouring himself another glass of liquid consolation. He tossed it back as they entered.

Colin grabbed him by the arm and took the decanter away. "Lord Bertram! Where is Chantal?"

Bertram gazed at him blearily. "He took her." He extended his arm and pointed to the great portrait that hung over the fireplace. "Him! Baldwin! My elder brother, the Earl of Ardmore!"

"Oh, you poor man," breathed Miss Filby behind them.

Bertram mooned into his empty glass. "She needs *me*," he muttered. "She needs looking after."

Miss Filby looked highly doubtful of that. Colin ignored her. "Er, Lord Bertram, can you tell me where she went?"

"To Gretna Green, I suppose. Where else do people run off to get married?"

Colin went cold. "Married?"

Bertram hiccupped, then pulled a sheet of paper from his pocket and held it out. Colin took it but could make out very little. The ink had become muddled with dampness. One hoped it was only from tears.

"It says she's sorry but she can't resist him," Bertram explained mournfully. "It says she's going to marry him. It says to wish her happy and that it simply ruins her to let me go."

Miss Filby made a noise. It sounded something like, "Oh, please!"

Colin glared at her. "Please excuse Miss Filby, Lord Bertram. She's a bit biased on the topic of Miss Marchant."

Bertram blinked at Miss Filby. "Oh, hullo, Pru. Didn't see you. You're looking well."

Miss Filby dipped a curtsy and smiled. "Hello, milord. How are you farin'?"

Bertram seemed to fold in on himself. He dropped to sit upon the footstool before the sofa. "She up and left me, Pru."

"Yes, milord. She does that."

Bertram shook his head. "Not to me. We've a special bond, she and I."

Miss Filby bit her lip. Colin feared he was unable to keep the doubt from his own expression, for Bertram sniffed mightily and straightened his spine.

"I know what people say about me," he protested, his pale blue eyes glaring from the redness about them. "It's not my fault I'm pretty. I am a man, nonetheless. I love Chantal. And she loves me. She's just afraid, you see. She's afraid I can't protect her."

"Protect her?" Colin frowned. "From what?"

Bertram glanced away. "Debt, if you must know. A rather large one." His face crumpled once more. "I tried to tell her that Baldwin was a lout, that he'd never look after her properly. She's so fragile, so delicate—"

Miss Filby snorted. "About as delicate as a cast-iron cat."

Her words were too low for the befuddled Bertram to hear, but Colin glared her into silence.

Bertram began to weep openly. Discomfited by Bertram's raw emotion, Colin turned to gaze up at the portrait on the wall, the study of a handsome, broad-shouldered fellow with a lantern jaw and piercing blue eyes. "I remember Baldwin. He's a cad and a poor loser, but he can be charming when he likes."

"And he has the title and all the lands," muttered Bertie miserably. "There's never been a woman born who could resist my brother. Poor Chantal. What chance did she have? He blinded her with promises! He swept her off her feet!"

There was a time when Colin would have believed that. Now such gullibility on Chantal's part disturbed him deeply. Not that it would stop him from his pursuit. He was after more than simply a bride, after all.

He slid a glance toward Miss Filby, who stood next to him gazing at Baldwin's portrait. She appeared visibly unimpressed. She flicked her gray gaze toward him. "He looks a right piker to me," she murmured.

It seemed there *had* been a woman born who would not be swayed by such a fine face and a finer fortune.

"Chantal was seduced," Colin said firmly, despite his reservations. "This is not her fault."

He heard Miss Filby let out a long sigh. "Aye, sir. Whatever you say, sir."

"Right then. Time to move on. We must catch up to them and stop her from wedding him."

She frowned at him. "In a pony cart? With two little ones?"

"Look in every public house en route," Bertie offered with a sniff. "Baldwin's never been one to pass up a pint."

Colin nodded. "There, you see?" He turned to Bertie. "I'm sorry for your loss, Lord Bertram, but you may take comfort in knowing your brother will not have her." With a brisk bow, he turned on his heel. "Miss Filby, if you please."

There were a few daylight hours left. He had every intention of using them to his advantage. As he left the house to see the mumsy pony cart sitting on the drive, with one of the Ardmore grooms holding Hector's reins at the ready, he hardened his resolve.

Miss Filby and the children were simply going to have to bear with it. Chantal must be stopped from making the greatest error of her life.

Melody's future *must* be secured!

CHAPTER 17

As she followed Mr. Lambert from the Ardmore manor house, Pru sighed in resignation at the thought of further journeying. *Damn you, Chantal!*

No, wait. She was glad they hadn't found Chantal! Wasn't she?

"Did you get it?" Evan looked up eagerly when she opened the carriage door. "Did you get your pay from her?"

Pru climbed into the carriage and shook her head sharply. "She's not there. She's run off with another man."

Evan's thin face twisted. "Another one? Ain't she gettin' tired?" He sat back in his seat, an angry boy-lump. "She's nothing but a rotten, worthless wh—"

"Evan!" When he shot her a resentful glare, she indicated Melody with her chin. "Monkey see, monkey do."

Evan's already thunderous expression grew disdainful. "What should I care 'bout that? They got nothin' to do w' us! Posh toff and his posh brat, chasin' around after the likes of *her*!"

Melody looked up from her nest of odd playthings. "What's a brat?"

Pru glared at her brother. "At this moment, Evan is exhibiting a few of the classic symptoms."

Evan narrowed his eyes. "Best watch it, *Prudence*. Soundin' a mite posh there yourself."

Pru took a deep breath. She was only sister, not mother,

and Evan was beginning to realize that. To Evan, her own helplessness in the face of Chantal's betrayal must seem like yet another example of an unjust world. He was fast losing faith in anything but what he saw before him. And why wouldn't he? He remembered nothing of the charity, of the culture, of the noble and honorable side of the gentry. She was beginning to have trouble remembering such things herself!

With a sigh, she turned her attention to her job. "Come here, Melody. Let's take Pomme's feather and make a hat for Gordy Ann."

Melody readily climbed into her lap, always willing to shower attention and devotion on the tatty bit of rag that was her doll. Evan sneered. "Why don't he buy her a nice doll? He can afford it."

Melody clutched the knotted thing in her chubby little arms and gave Evan a glare that made even the boy blink. "Don't want a new doll. *Want Gordy Ann.*"

Evan held up both hands in defense. "Cor!" He shook his head. "Don't let's be takin' Princess Melody's nasty old doll!"

"I'm not a princess," Melody informed him absently, her fury already faded as she fussed with the feather. "I'm a lady. Lady Melody."

Evan scowled. "You ain't."

"I am so. Uncle Colin said so. And Uncle Aidan. And Grampapa Lord Aldrich. And Lady Blank'ship. And Billy-wick. He calls me 'little milady.'" Melody looked up at Pru seriously. "I like that." She turned back to her doll, humming happily.

The feather waved majestically, sticking somewhat sideways from the knot that formed the head. It looked a bit as though it had been impaled through the temple by a very impolite quill pen. "Doesn't Gordy Ann look nice?"

"Beau'iful." Pru smoothed the shining curls thoughtfully. *Little milady.* She and Evan shared a look, once again united in their feeling of being outsiders.

There must be complicated doings afoot in Mr. Lambert's life. Unfortunately, he wasn't likely to explain himself to a servant girl without the application of due force. Sadly, Pru was short an impolite quill pen of her own.

As Melody gradually turned limp in her lap, destined for another nap, Pru felt herself wearily following suit. Keeping one arm snug about the round little tummy in case of deeper potholes, she let her head fall back on the seat and closed her eyes. Sleep had come slowly last night after the . . . er, encounter, so now it slipped back upon her uninvited.

The road, the carriage, Evan, Melody, Mr. Lambert, and even the stolid Hector swirled about in her half-conscious mind, saying and doing outrageous things that made perfect sense in that moment.

Part of her was aware of Evan sorting through their things and she wanted to remind him not to disturb Mr. Lambert's things but her mind was too far from her body and the command to speak did not reach her lips. Besides, Evan knew to leave that be.

Evan knew better . . .

Up front, in the driver's seat, Colin was beginning to regret his impulse to dash off after Chantal without more of a rest. To be precise, it was his arse that was regretting it. The bumps and jolts inside were as nothing to the battering his buttocks were getting on the hard, enameled bench seat. He decided that when he returned to take over his own estate—as soon as this current matter was cleared up and, of course, as soon as he had followed up his previous publication with something even more astounding and therefore truly earned his knighthood—he would order all the carriage seats to be upholstered, even the driver's.

Especially the driver's. Thinking on it now, he was ashamed to think how many hours he'd ridden in carriages in his life and never given a single thought to the comfort of those who had driven them. He'd only thought of his own boredom and irritation at the lack of speed compared to a few hours on a swift horse.

At least there was really only one road to the Scottish border and the village of Gretna Green, where a couple could be married quickly with no questions asked. If he kept them on this country lane, which Bertie had said cut northeast across the farms to the nearest large village, then he was bound to catch up with Lord Ardmore before he connected with the Great North Road.

He bent forward, urging Hector to more speed. He had to get as many miles under those hooves as he could before—

The little trapdoor behind his seat opened. Colin ignored it. Come on, Hector!

"Uncle Colin, I gotta go!"

When the carriage stopped, both of the children were out of it as if shot from twin cannons. Pru followed Melody dutifully into a field. She spread her skirts wide for Melody's privacy, then had Melody hold up her shawl for her own.

She was in no hurry to go back to the carriage, where Mr. Lambert was stamping about in irritation at the delay. Mr. Lambert could fuss all he liked, but he wasn't the one bottled up in the carriage with two restless youngsters, was he?

Furthermore, Pru was dead sick of Chantal and Chantal's many lovers. Mr. Lambert was obsessed, despite the fact that he apparently kissed anyone in reach and then promptly forgot about it!

It was time to go but Evan was nowhere in sight. With a sigh, Pru set out to look for him.

She spotted his shock of red hair barely showing above the tall grass and grinned. Dropping low, she stepped carefully, easing her way closer. If she had the rest of her life to play, she would still never be able to pay him back for all the pranks he'd pulled on her in the last few years.

Seen clearly now, Evan was standing facing away from

the carriage, gazing intently at something he held in his cupped hands. Pru would wager that it was something either slimy or with too many legs.

It must have been fascinating indeed, for his inattention allowed her to completely creep up on him.

With a sick feeling of horror, Pru gazed down over his shoulder at the diamond ring sparkling in the nest of Evan's cupped and grubby hands.

"Where did that come from?"

He whirled, his gray eyes wide and guilty. "It's ours! It ain't right she should have it!"

"Oh, Evan," she breathed. "You *stole*?"

He flinched at the word but raised his chin defiantly. "Lambert's goin' to give it to Chantal. I figure Chantal owes us for treatin' you so!" His gray eyes flashed in his pale face.

Nauseated, Pru thought of all the times she'd railed against Chantal in Evan's hearing. She'd never considered what protective fury she'd been igniting in Evan's heart.

And now she'd prompted an act that could destroy Evan's future. Stealing from a man like Mr. Lambert, especially something so valuable, could land Evan in prison, even at his age! The thought of her sensitive young brother lost to such a place made her head swim with fear.

She held out a shaking hand. "Give it to me. I'll find a way to give it back."

Evan closed his hands over the ring and held it to his thin chest. "No! We need it!"

Not even trying to struggle for the ring, Pru reached her hands to his dear little face and brushed away the moisture from his hot eyes. He was so afraid, not just now but always. It tore at her heart. She let her speech return to the world they'd been born to. "My love, you know that it is wrong to steal. You must remember the things Papa would read to us after dinner."

She went down on her knees in the dirt and gazed into the eyes so like hers, so like their mother's. "Don't you remember how it was? Mama would sit close to the fire and sew while Papa would stand with his elbow on the mantel and read aloud. You and I would snuggle up on the settee and listen. The whole world would go away, remember? It was just us, just our little family, wrapped in Papa's deep voice like a blanket, safe and warm. Papa had the most wonderful voice."

A shudder went through Evan's thin shoulders. His lips pressed together to keep them from trembling. "I'm forgettin'," he whispered. "Half the time I don't know if it's me remembering or just you telling me."

She kissed his smeary cheek. "I know, my darling. Maybe that's enough, that I can remember for you. Maybe I can remember all the things that Papa said and tell them to you, so that you can be the man he'd want you to be."

He looked down at his fists clenched around the ring. "Papa wouldn't want me to steal."

Pru smiled softly. "Of that I'm sure. He'd tell you to cherish your honor and do right."

Confusion chased anger through his expressive eyes. "But you worked hard and Chantal cheated you. That's not right."

Pru sighed. "No, it isn't. Chantal took from us. But if we, in turn, take from Mr. Lambert, then we are just like Chantal."

He drew back, obviously not liking the sound of that. "I hate Chantal!"

"So do—" No, that was what got them into this mess. "I hate no one. I only wish to be fairly paid and then to never see Chantal again." She smiled at him tenderly. "You have a good heart, Evan. What does your heart tell you to do?"

He looked back down at his hands for a moment, then slowly reached them out to her. "Take it," he whispered. "I'm sorry, Pru."

It wasn't until the lovely thing dropped warm and heavy into Pru's palm, shining with luxurious promise, that it occurred to her that Mr. Lambert wasn't just pining for Chantal.

He meant to marry her!

CHAPTER 18

As Pru walked slowly back to the carriage, she saw that Melody was balancing on the placid Hector's wide back, her little legs stuck straight out to each side, Gordy Ann riding pillion. Mr. Lambert was halfway into the carriage, pulling their things from it one by one.

It looked very much like a search. Pru's heart fell. Any hope of slipping the ring back where Evan had found it died within her. Yet even that would not have satisfied her. She had survived this long while retaining her integrity and she didn't intend to begin lying now!

At least, not about anything more vital than her identity.

Feeling a bit queasy, she wrapped her fingers about the ring in her pocket and stepped forward. "Mr. Lambert, sir . . ."

He didn't turn. "In a moment, Miss Filby."

She moved closer and put her hand on his arm. "Sir, I must speak with you."

He went very still at her touch and looked up from his search. "Miss Filby, I'm afraid I . . ."

Raising her closed fist, she opened her hand before his eyes. ". . . lost something important." His gaze fixed on the gleaming diamond in her hand. "Oh."

He straightened, still gazing at the ring in her hand. "Where did you find this?"

Pru raised her gaze to his face. He was trying to give her a way out. He was going to let her say she found it rattling about the carriage, or in Melody's shoe, or some such nonsense. His kindness made it all the more difficult to do the right thing—yet at the same time, it made it easier as well. She had not trusted anyone in so long.

Perhaps, just perhaps, she could trust him.

Shaking just a bit, she reached for his hand. He gave it to her unresisting while she raised it, turned it upward, and dropped the ring into it. She closed his fingers around, relieved to see the last of it. "I apologize, sir. Evan took it from your things while I slept in the carriage."

His gaze met hers at last. His green eyes were confused, but not angry. "Why would he do such a thing?"

Pru swallowed. She'd avoided speaking badly of Chantal—or at least she'd tried mightily—but she saw no reason to spare him this truth. "Miss Marchant left Brighton without payin' me, sir. I'm owed several weeks' wages. Evan worried that we'd never find her, I think." She stopped there, further words stuck in her throat as she awaited his reaction.

Mr. Lambert gazed very intently at her. "I see. I shall correct that oversight at once, of course. You ought to have informed me sooner."

"Yes, sir." *Please, don't let it be a mistake to have told him.* Her belly shook with worry. *Please let him understand.*

"Well, since the ring has scarcely been gone long enough to be missed, I think we need say no more about it."

She couldn't believe her ears. "Sir?"

He tucked the ring into his weskit pocket and tilted his head at her. "Miss Filby, I am not a monster, you know. I have spent enough time with Melody to know that children sometimes get very skewed notions. I would never punish Evan for making a mistake."

Pru frowned. "Oh, I intend to punish him, sir!"

He grinned down at her. "You won't beat him and you know it."

"But—" This man was so confusing! "Are you saying I should just let it be?"

"No. Stealing is wrong, of course. I think an appropriate consequence might be . . . oh, brushing Hector every night until journey's end."

Pru would have laughed if she hadn't been so near crying with relief. "That's not a punishment for Evan!"

"Nonetheless, it is honest work and will give him time to think on what he did. Isn't that really the point of punishment?"

It was so much like something Pru's father might have said that she couldn't answer at all. She could only nod quickly and gaze at the ground, though it blurred before her eyes. *Chantal, you are the luckiest woman in the world.*

"The question remains of course, what am I to do with you?"

Startled, she looked up to see his eyes—so green they fair to faded the spring day!—gazing at her with a strange solemn expression. "What—what d'ye mean by that, sir?"

"You were very frightened when you gave me the ring. Did you truly think I would toss you and Evan into the nearest dungeon?"

She looked down at her hands, twisting her fingers together. "It could happen, sir."

Warm fingers cupped her chin and her gaze was lifted to his. She hoped he couldn't feel the shiver that went through her at his touch.

His gaze was warm and approving. The corners of his eyes crinkled though he did not smile. "Then, Miss Filby, what you did proved not only that you are honest," he said softly, "but that you are brave as well. Thank you for trusting me. I give you my absolute trust in return."

Then he turned away, moving to the front of the carriage to scoop Melody from Hector's back. Pru stayed rooted to the ground, for something very, very strange had just happened. The world had changed.

It was no longer entirely against her.

She only wished she could truly enjoy the sensation. Shame for something completely new rose within her.

What would be his reaction if he ever found out she was not who she said she was?

A group of riders trotted down the country lane. Vast fields stretched out on either side of the road, flat, green, and featureless but for the dotting of white sheep and lines of old stone walls.

These men did not pass their gazes appreciatively across the pastoral view. Focused and purposeful, they kept their eyes on the road ahead. The sooner they found the wayward woman, the sooner they could get back to business.

Only one man gazed about him, the one who rode last, just far enough behind the others that their dust did not affect him. His eyes moved constantly, though he seemed still. Watchful and sharp, like the predator he was.

He could have taken the fore and the other men would not have objected. Simply put, he preferred not to expose his back, even to his own men.

Perhaps especially not to his own men. They were a rough bunch, prone to violent reactions to the simplest of offenses. A useful trait in business, perhaps, but not likely to make for an enjoyable day of travel.

The sound of crisply clopping hooves slowed and the last man slowed instantly, alert to signs of disturbance in the dust ahead. A cross-breeze swept the view clean, revealing the group still mounted, their horses standing on the road ahead, clustered around something. A flash of bright fabric, a protesting feminine cry—the last man grimaced. Best let the rotters have their play. It wouldn't take long.

The last man turned his horse away from the road and the beast easily took the low stone wall nearest. A hundred yards into the field, the man halted his horse, turned, and waited.

From this vantage point he could see that there were three women trapped on the road. They were clad in colorful skirts and blouses, but they did not have the sharp-faced wariness of the Gypsy clans. Not farmwives either. Prostitutes, possibly, or perhaps part of a carnival.

Or both.

A hint of curiosity tantalized him, but not enough to investigate. He had no time to dawdle with other women when only one consumed his thoughts. Impatience made him twitch slightly and his horse responded with a start.

Thunder rolled across the landscape while he soothed his mount. Then, looking up, the man saw that the thunder was nothing more than a rather large horse racing up the road.

As the horse grew closer to the group ahead of it, it became clear that the horse was in fact gigantic. The illusion was furthered by the fact that the rider was also enormous, making the great white beast look somewhat normal until compared to the other mounts.

Then the horse hit his own clustered men with such impact that the man could not help but be reminded of a large rock thrown into a duck pond. He watched the resulting turmoil with disgusted dismay. Now there would be a fight. Someone would undoubtedly get himself wounded and then there would be further delay.

With a flick of his whip, the man raced his horse toward the road. At the last moment he reined to the side, sweeping his men up with him to gallop swiftly away from the temptation of felling the giant who had so rudely knocked them away from their pleasurable harassment of the women.

This time he kept point, leading his men at a pace too

furious to allow them to do anything but keep their seats. No more delays.

Nothing would keep him from *her*.

Big John Bailiwick, the largest bloke on staff at Brown's Club for Distinguished Gentlemen, was the one everyone called upon whenever something heavy needed putting in the attic—or when Little Milady was underfoot and needing a playmate. He was the fellow who'd never been afraid of anything or anyone—excepting Mr. Wilberforce, of course.

Big John Bailiwick closed his eyes and prayed for his life.

It was the horse that was the problem. The gelding was the only one Mr. Wilberforce could find that was big enough to carry Bailiwick, the one the hosteler called Balthazar. " 'E's the best 'orse in the world, 'e is!" It took a little while, but even Bailiwick eventually figured out that Balthazar meant "demon."

He was a monster, he was, like a shining white ghost horse from hell . . . with pink ribbons in his mane. The hosteler's daughter had put the ribbons in and Bailiwick had left them, thinking that Little Milady might like to see them when he caught up to her and Sir Colin.

Now the ribbons whipped his face like a punishment as the tears streamed from his eyes. He wasn't crying, of course. Never that. It was the speed that was doing it.

Balthazar didn't seem to have any speeds other than trudging walk and battle charge. When he was doing one, there was no persuading him to do the other until he bloody well felt like it. He'd trudged most of the day, despite Bailiwick's diffident urgings. Then, just when Bailiwick had decided to give it up and look for an inn for the night, suddenly the giant destrier had lifted his nose, trumpeted a noise that sounded a lot more like a battle cry than a whinny, and the monstrous dinner-plate hooves had begun to tear up the road.

Literally. Clods of dirt and gravel flew up and over Bailiwick, occasionally striking him in the face.

Up hills and through dales. Past farms and stone-walled fields filled with sheep. There was one horrifying bit where they'd crossed a footbridge so narrow that Bailiwick hadn't even been able to see it beneath the wide body of the horse, but that had been as brief as it had been terrifying.

He supposed, when he could think at all, that he was lucky Balthazar had decided to run in the direction Bailiwick had wished to go. The mad thing could just as easily have turned about and run back to London.

They'd be there by now if he had. The full gallop had been going on for some time—hours it felt like, but that couldn't be, could it?—and Bailiwick was becoming dismally sure that they had already passed the crossroads that would have taken them to Basingstoke and the Ardmore estate. Basingstoke was the only clue he had, from the manager at the theater Sir Colin had gone to. Lucky thing, Mr. Wilberforce knowing about that actress and all. Then again, Mr. Wilberforce knew everything, didn't he?

Except, quite possibly, that Bailiwick had been exaggerating a bit when he'd said he could ride. What he should have told the head of staff was that he *had* ridden. Twice, to be exact. Of course, that was long ago, before he'd grown so big that most horses would lie down and give up rather than carry him more than two steps. He'd simply assumed that no such horse could be found and that eventually Mr. Wilberforce would put him on a coach instead.

He had plenty of time to regret that fib as the miles flew by and Balthazar showed no sign of tiring. A few villages flashed past but the horse managed to dodge everything but the mud puddles. Most of which landed on Bailiwick, of course. If he hadn't been afraid for his life, the ride would have been almost boring.

Until, that is, they topped a hill and began to race down the other side.

Even Balthazar couldn't have meant to hit the group of mounted men standing in the road. His big bony head flew up, nearly colliding with Bailiwick's nose. The great haunches dropped nearly to the ground as he attempted to brake but size and momentum were against them. The enormous gelding went through the other horses like a bowling ball through pins. There was chaos and shouting and horsey sounds of alarm. Then Balthazar finally came to a halt amid a cloud of dust.

Bailiwick choked and flapped a paw before his face but it was a long moment before he could make anything out.

When he did, his jaw dropped. The horsemen were gone as if by magic and in their place stood three of the most beautiful women Bailiwick had ever seen.

And they were smiling at him as if he were a storybook hero come to life!

"You saved us!"

"Those bandits ran from you like leaves before the wind!"

The prettiest one, a dark-haired, dark-eyed creature with hints of faraway places in her gaze—perhaps even as far away as Wales!—approached him in silence, swaying seductively as she came even with his booted leg. She shot a warning glare at the other two girls, then slid her hand up Bailiwick's thigh. "May I have a ride, good knight?"

Balthazar was either tired—impossible!—or just as impressed as Bailiwick by the exotic beauty, for when Bailiwick obediently pulled the girl up behind him, Balthazar obediently set out at a prancing walk that a military parade mount would have been proud of.

Slim arms wrapped themselves around Bailiwick's waist. Fascinating soft bits pressed up against his back. "My name is Fiona. You must sup with our troupe tonight, kind sir."

Her voice was like warm honey in his ear. "Do you fancy the theater?"

She could have asked if he fancied being boiled in oil and he would have nodded eagerly, so swept away was he by the way she felt against him. The other two girls watched them ride away with open envy.

No one had ever envied Bailiwick. And definitely, no one had ever envied any person who was *with* Bailiwick.

Balthazar was the best horse in the world, he was!

CHAPTER 19

The country lane led Colin and his companions onto a more established road, just as Lord Bertram had promised. Though Melody's bladder grew no more tolerant, still they managed to make good time.

As they traveled on, they began to see more traffic on the road. Colin began to look for a place to stop, rest Hector, and ask questions of fellow travelers, though he hardly knew what to ask.

Have you seen a beautiful actress eloping with a handsome but obnoxious lord? They're off to Gretna Green and I must stop them because I have the lady's illegitimate child and must convince her to marry me instead.

No, he must continue to keep Melody's origins as private as possible. So far the gossips had not learned of her existence or her questionable birth. He didn't believe the secret could be repressed forever but Society would be much more inclined to ignore a "natural" birth if the wedding took place later. Even three years later, if the couple in question had wealth and standing enough. Minor gossip only, swiftly forgotten.

When at last they pulled into an inn, Colin was twitching with urgency. Turning Hector over to a sullen stableman, he helped Miss Filby get the children from the carriage.

"We'll stop for a bit and let Hector rest, shall we?"

Evan ran off after the horse boy, eager to begin his punishment." Miss Filby stretched discreetly, then swept Melody into her arms. "I'm for a glass of cold milk. Would you like to join me, Miss Melody?"

Colin was about to turn her loose with a pile of coin in hand, but then he took a closer look at the inn. It wasn't a true coaching inn, like the ones on the popular coach lines radiating from London. Those were large, clean establishments where ladies were looked after and children could run free.

This place was elderly and in poor repair. There was some sign of effort to keep up appearances, like flowers in the window boxes and clean sheets hanging on the lines, but the only other vehicles in the yard were farm carts and freight wagons. This was not a place frequented by the gentry.

Hoping that the public room would be clean and the food would be fresh, Colin accompanied Miss Filby.

It wasn't so bad inside, though there must have been something wrong with the flue because the public room was smoky and dim. Colin could make out the shapes of several men—no women and certainly no ladies—seated on the benches before the fire.

There was one table with chairs and there sat a large man whose face was buried in a tankard. Colin squinted against the smoke. The man's clothing was different than that of the rough farmers. He wore a good blue surcoat of superfine wool, a properly tied ascot, and a silk weskit chased in gold. The buttons alone could purchase the entire inn.

Miss Filby sidled up against him. "Who is that?"

The man drained his tankard with a last gulp, then waved it in the air before banging it demandingly on the table. "Alewife!"

The rough farmers and teamsters glared at the noise but no one said a word as the landlord's plump wife hurried to the table with a pitcher of ale. The well-dressed man grabbed it from her hands and began to guzzle directly from the pitcher, allowing ale to dribble down his costly clothing.

Colin's lip curled. "That," he said, "is Lord Ardmore, Purty Bertie's elder brother."

Miss Filby peered through the smoky dimness. "I was right. He is a piker."

Colin didn't bother to correct her disrespect. She was only stating the obvious. He gave the room another sweeping glance. "I don't see Chantal."

"Well, you wouldn't. She'd be in the best room, getting waited on hand and foot, probably for free."

He slid a warning gaze sideways at her. She shrugged unrepentantly. "Well, she would."

Again, undeniable.

He reached for Miss Filby's hand and pressed a coin into it. "See to Melody. Over there, where the alewife awaits. Stay in sight but out of the way. And when Evan comes in, keep him with you."

He didn't want to fight Baldwin, but if the man didn't see reason, Colin wanted Pru and the children safe.

Approaching the table, Colin had to resist the impulse to smooth his hair and straighten his weskit, simply in reaction to the slovenly appearance of Lord Ardmore. No daily bath with mint leaves for him!

Placing his palms on the table, Colin leaned forward. "Where is Miss Chantal Marchant?"

Baldwin jerked back, blinking in surprise. "What?"

Up close, Colin could see the damage done by such over-indulgence. The man before him was a pasty, bloated version of the portrait back at Ardmore. The reddened features of a habitual drunkard surrounded the piercing blue eyes, now gone vague and bleary.

Colin tried again, this time smacking his hand on the table to get the man's attention. *"Where is Chantal?"*

Ardmore belched. "She's gone."

Colin drew back as much from the man's disgusting breath as he did from shock. "Where has she gone? With whom? When?"

Baldwin waggled a finger in the air. "That way . . . or maybe that way. What's it to you?"

Colin narrowed his eyes. "Explain yourself, my lord! You were in charge of the lady!"

Baldwin snorted. "Lady?"

"Lady enough for you to propose marriage!"

"Oh, that." Baldwin flapped a hand. "I was just winding Bertie up. I couldn't marry an actress. Think of my standing. Besides, she's not as pretty as she used to be."

"Your standing would have been hers as well, once you'd wed," Colin pointed out, somewhat defensively. "Worse matches have been made."

Wait, what was he doing? He ought to be relieved. He'd come here to stop the marriage, remember? Yet he was furious at Baldwin's cavalier treatment of Chantal. "At the very least, you ought to have seen her properly returned to Ardmore. You sent her away alone?"

"Sent her? The bitch stole my curricle and my horse!" He hiccupped. "Didn't even know she could drive. She did, though, galloped out of here in racing form!" He gulped another draft and wiped his arm across his mouth. For the first time he seemed to actually see Colin. "I know you." He blinked slowly. "You and those other two. Always three of you." He peered across the room. "Where are they?"

"Elsewhere." Colin's voice was clipped. "Lord Ardmore, are you going to tell me where Chantal went or not?"

Baldwin's muddled gaze turned mean. "Why should I? I'm quite happy here. I've got good ale and plenty of coin. I might sit right here for the rest of the week and not give a tinker's damn about you and bloody damned Chantal!" He buried his face in the pitcher again, his next words distorted by his greedy slurping. "Thieving whore."

Colin felt a pull at his sleeve.

"What you doin', just standin' there?" It was Evan at his elbow. "I thought you were all lovey-dovey with old Teeth 'n' Tits. I thought I were goin' to see a duel!"

Colin stared down at the boy. "Evan, a gentleman does not refer to a lady as 'old Teeth 'n' Tits.'"

Evan scowled but also flushed with embarrassment. "What do I care 'bout gents and ladies?" he muttered. "Want to see you shoot his ear off at twenty paces!"

Colin sighed and looked back at Lord Ardmore in disgust. "Evan, violence isn't the answer to anything. Yes, I am very angry at his behavior, but even if I beat the tar out of Lord Baldwin, all that would accomplish would be to produce a black and blue version of the same man. Besides, then I'd have to bathe."

Evan rolled his eyes. "You can't fight, can you?" He walked back toward his sister, shaking his head. "Spineless, through and through."

No, just sensible. I am a scholarly, logical man. I don't act on impulse and I don't brawl in alehouses. An uneducated boy could not truly understand the notion of a civilized manhood.

Baldwin belched loudly as Colin turned and walked away.

Once Pru had Melody settled with a clay mug of milk and Evan was tearing into a chunk of remarkably fresh bread, she had a moment to breathe. Straightening and smoothing her hair, she smiled at the landlord's wife standing nearby. The woman had been most eager to serve the children.

Pru handed her the coin. "Those are your flowers out front, aren't they? You've done a right job sprucin' up the place."

The woman blushed, pleased. "I've only just got me start. Mr. Rugg and me ain't been married long." She was a well-padded woman of middle years with a touch of gray at the temples, but she blushed like the bride she was. "He said he needed a hand w' the inn and I said I had me a right good brewing recipe, so we met up with vicar last month and did it up right and proper."

Pru laughed. "That sounds perfect." She held out her hand. "I'm Pru Filby. This here's me brother, Evan. And this young lady is Miss Melody, Mr. Lambert's ward."

The woman smiled. "I be Olive. Olive Rugg, now."

Further demanding banging came from the one table in the room. Both women turned to glare at Lord Ardmore.

"Lord or no, I wouldn't feed that man to me pigs. He's pure poison." Olive plunked her fists on her wide hips and scowled at Lord Ardmore. "If he don't pay for all the ale what's spilled, he'll be leavin' that fancy weskit w' me."

Pru believed her.

Her husband emerged from the back room. "Ollie! Stop yer yakkin' and get out there." He grinned at his wife and smacked her on the buttocks as she passed. "Lazy cow."

Olive gave her ample rear an extra wag just for him and he barked a laugh before he disappeared into the back again. Pru smiled. Olive might have described a practical arrangement, but it was clear her husband thought the world of her.

Fortunate woman.

Mr. Lambert joined her where she sat with Melody and Evan. She turned to him, still smiling. He blinked as if surprised to see it. Was she being inappropriate? She reeled herself in a bit, letting the smile fade.

Something flashed across his expression. Now what? Disappointment? Men were so bloody confusing. She gave up and simply asked, "Did you find out what room Miss Marchant is in?"

He sat down next to her on the bench. Still he towered over her. The man was like a great tree.

And wouldn't you like to climb those branches? Well, any woman would.

He folded his arms and fixed Lord Ardmore with a flat

gaze. "She left him. He must have done something reprehensible to cause her to flee all alone, but I can get nothing out of him at the moment. Perhaps when he sobers up."

Thinking of the fresh pitcher of ale that Olive had just taken out to the man, Pru doubted that would be any time soon.

Just then, a crash of shattered crockery startled everyone in the room. Benches scraped as the other customers rose to their feet in alarm. Pru looked up to see Olive gazing down at a mess of shards and ale on the scrubbed boards of the floor and Lord Ardmore, standing over her, red-faced with fury.

Mr. Lambert took a step forward, but Pru was faster. In a flash she was at Olive's side, pushing the woman slightly behind her. She smiled at Lord Ardmore. "Sorry 'bout that, milord. We'll get you cleaned up in a jiffy."

Olive was near tears. "That were me best pitcher," she whispered sadly. "It were a weddin' present. I only took it out 'cause his lordship come."

Pru patted her on the shoulder. "Go get his lordship another one, quick now." She gave Olive a bit of a push, taking the woman's towel from where it hung from her apron. "I'll start w' the cleanin'."

Moving closer to the drunk and furious Lord Ardmore wasn't particularly appealing, but she grimly set to swabbing the ale from the front of his coat and weskit. In her opinion, he could have done with a more thorough drenching. *Oh, look, now I've made a clean spot.*

He grunted, sending a wave of putrid breath her way. "Lower down."

Pru gritted her teeth and moved to the front of his breeches. He gave a phlegmy laugh. Pru dabbed, staying away from the hazardous region. If it wasn't for the fact that she'd not have Ollie suffer for it, she'd clean his lap for him all right! *Would you like the mop shoved down your throat or up your—*

A big sweaty palm closed over her breast. She jerked

backward but the cad had her collar in his grip. He squeezed her flesh painfully.

"Keep rubbing, girl!"

And then Lord Ardmore learned to fly.

From her vantage point kneeling on the floor, Pru saw a green-coated blur hit Lord Ardmore from the side, taking him off his feet and sending him halfway across the room to barrel into the benches occupied by the other customers.

Pru scrambled backward out of the ale puddles and pottery shards. She stood, ready to rush to Mr. Lambert's side.

Colin sprang to his feet, in much better form than the heavyset lord. Unfortunately, when Colin pulled the fallen bench off the man he found his opponent lay still, freshly soaked in the other men's ale.

"Oy! What're you about?"

Colin looked up in alarm, the red haze of rage fading abruptly as he realized he was surrounded by rough, angry drovers. The largest—hell, he was big!—advanced on Colin, shoving him back. This wasn't good. This wasn't good at all. He held up his hands. "Now, my good man—"

"Sick o' your lot, I am!" the man roared. He shoved Colin again. "Comin' in 'ere w' yer fancy clothes and yer fancy women, spillin' the best ale in three counties!"

Colin braced himself and licked his lips uneasily. The fellow was right. It really was excellent ale. Top-notch.

He saw a meaty fist coming for his face. Pity he wasn't going to have the time to enjoy a tankard of his own.

CHAPTER 20

When Mr. Lambert took the first blow, Pru was ready to rush into the fray. There was nothing to hand but broken pottery but perhaps she could throw shards—

Olive pulled at her arm. "That's no good, dearie!" The woman tugged her back toward the bar. "Best stay out of the way until the dust settles. Besides, we got to defend the ale!"

Mr. Lambert's first attacker went flying backward. For a brief moment, Pru caught sight of Colin's face. "Oh! He's bleeding!"

Olive was much more matter-of-fact. She shook her head in disgust as she reached into a cupboard beside the kegs. "Another brawl. And I just got the blood scrubbed off me floor from the last one."

Turning, she hefted two brooms, then discarded the lesser one as unlikely to do adequate damage. "Get me rolling pin, dearie. Makes a handy truncheon, it does."

Mr. Rugg burst out of the back room, red-faced and furious. "Oy!" He strode into the fracas like a mad giant, tossing men away indiscriminately. The black rag he wore to keep his hair out of his face gave him a rakish air.

"Pirates!" cried Melody. "Raise the mains'l!"

One of the drovers atop Mr. Lambert flew across the floor and smashed a chair into splinters that peppered the room. Pru gave a yip of dismay and tucked Melody behind her. "The children!"

"Put the little ones in the back room." Olive indicated the door with her chin. "Then take up that rolling pin!" Olive swung her broom into battle position before the stacked kegs. "We got to protect the ale!"

It might have seemed silly but Pru realized that without their ale, Olive and Rugg would be ruined. Pru shepherded Melody and Evan through the door. It was a heavy oak panel, sure to withstand flying tankards by the look of the scars in the wood.

"Stay here!" She expected argument from her brother but Evan scrambled in, then held out his arms for Melody.

"I have her, Pru! Go protect the ale!"

Pru's lips twitched. Evan realized the value of good ale, even at his age. Were men born with that priority?

Then she picked up the massive rolling pin and joined Olive before the bar, ready to thump skulls.

In the back room, Melody snuggled close to Evan. She liked Evan. He was funny and he had pretty eyes. He wasn't looking at her right now. His face was pressed to where light shone through a crack in the door. She turned around, scrambling over Evan. "A peek-hole! I want to see!"

Evan turned and grinned. "It's a right scuffle, it is!" He let Melody peek.

The room was a sea of flailing fists and flying tankards. It looked as though in the smoke and confusion, some of the men had forgotten precisely who they were fighting.

Or perhaps they'd simply decided time was ripe for a fracas.

The smoky air gave the heaving pile of bodies a hazy unreality, as if ancient beasts fought a mythic battle.

A drunken drover slithered across the floor, thrown before the children's wide eyes. He grinned toothlessly in his sleep and began to snore.

Perhaps "mythic" was a bit of a stretch. Still, it was a bloody good show!

Melody squealed with excitement. "It's a pirate mutiny!"

Evan grinned. "I'll say it is."

"Keelhaul 'em, Uncle Colin!"

Uncle Colin had his hands full not having his face used to mop the floor. Rugg fought near him, apparently on his side. At least, Colin thought so until the large man picked him up and tossed him aside as well. He landed atop a pile of semiconscious men. At the very bottom, he recognized the gold-trimmed sleeve of Lord Ardmore.

"Bloody hell!" He began to dig the man out. If Baldwin died, Colin would never track down Chantal!

Without Colin to beat on, there was only the fury of the mighty Rugg to face. This made things difficult for the remaining brawlers, for without Rugg, there would be no place to drink and brawl. The final straw came when a washtub of icy water splashed over them, thrown by Pru and Olive. Then the humiliation of being smacked by broomstick and rolling pin—"Oy! Get off me, woman!"—took the last of the starch from their spines.

There was a general call to retreat and soon the taproom was empty but for the wreckage, two dismayed innkeepers, one panting seamstress, and Colin, gazing with dismay at the richly clad man who lay unmoving in the ale, splinters, and shards.

"He's out cold."

Pru brushed her fallen hair out of her face with the back of her forearm. "Good riddance."

Colin turned to gaze at her. For a moment he was distracted by her becoming disarray. How pretty she looked all pink-cheeked and mussed, with her rich auburn hair falling down and the neckline of her dress pulled awry and those generous breasts heaving . . . the way her flush descended all the way down . . . how far did it go?

"Ah." *Wake up, man!* He shook off his trance. What had she said? "No, no, it isn't good riddance. I've no way to find Miss Marchant until he awakens."

Olive gave Lord Ardmore the toe of her boot. "Well, he ain't dead, more's the pity. I've seen this afore. He won't be roused till tomorrow mornin'." She grinned at Pru. "You lot can stay the night and help tidy up this mess."

Miss Filby nodded. "O' course."

Colin twitched at the delay, but what else could he do? There were four possible directions Chantal could have driven from here. If he chose the wrong one, he could lose her forever.

Miss Filby came to him and laid a sympathetic hand on his arm. "Come on, guv. One more night won't matter that much, will it?"

Colin looked at her. She didn't comprehend the delicate situation.

So tell her. He opened his mouth but weeks of secrecy to protect Melody kept the words tightly locked away. Besides, now was not the time. He looked over his shoulder to see Melody and Evan emerging from their hiding place. Melody ran to Colin on chubby little legs and he picked her up, automatically hefting her to his hip. Melody leaned back to examine his face.

"You got hit, Uncle Colin." She pointed a tiny finger at his reddening jaw. "Cap'n Jack never gets hit."

Colin sighed. "Cap'n Jack ducks faster than I do."

Evan sidled up, his hands in his pockets. "I kept Miss Mellie safe, guv."

Colin put a hand on that thin shoulder. "I thank you for that," he said seriously.

Evan shrugged and glanced away, but Colin could see the boy was pleased. Then Evan slid a knowing glance back his way.

"Funny thing, that."

Distracted, Colin worked his jaw. Not broken. "What's that, Evan?"

"You said violence ain't the answer to anythin' when it was old Tee—"

Colin raised a brow.

Evan changed tack. "When it were Miss Marchant what got offended." Evan grinned. "Then you hit him like a speedin' alecart when it were Pru he put his paws on." Evan tilted his head and gazed at them both. "That were beau'iful, that."

He wandered off, a jaunty roll to his walk, while Colin and Miss Filby very carefully didn't look at each other. Colin resolved not to consider the ludicrous implications of such a notion.

He didn't succeed.

With nothing to do but wait for Lord Ardmore to recover from the brawl, Pru and Mr. Lambert took the children upstairs to the best room in the inn. The walls were unplastered boards and there were gaps around the warped frame of the single small window, but it had a fireplace and it was painfully clean.

"It ain't much, sir," Olive had told them, "but it has a lock on the door."

Pru set about soothing an overstimulated Melody and preparing her for bed, while Mr. Lambert and Evan made up pallets on the floor for themselves.

"I think we should all share the room this evening," Mr. Lambert had said. "Rugg is a good man, but this is not the sort of place a lady should stay alone."

Pru let it pass that he absentmindedly continued to treat her as a lady, for the truth was she didn't look forward to sleeping in the rough room alone with the children.

With herself and Melody in the bed and Mr. Lambert and Evan on the floor before the fire, it was quite cozy. She hadn't bothered to protest being given the bed, only snuggled gratefully into the deep straw fill. The ticking was coarse but smelled of soap and sun-drying and the blankets were old but clean and plentiful.

Melody insisted on a story and Mr. Lambert complied. As he spoke in his deep, rumbling voice, Pru held Melody in the curve of her body and watched as the brawl-inspired agitation melted away from the sleepy, soft baby features.

What a beautiful child. She was a brave little thing, too. Little on this journey had overwhelmed her good-natured liveliness. Pru smiled fondly. Give Melody a quick nap and she was ready to face anything.

I could love her.

I think perhaps I already do.

Mr. Lambert was bent on wedding Chantal. Would that make her Melody's mother?

God, what a notion!

Unable to bear the thought of saying good-bye to Melody at the end of the journey, Pru dropped her face to hide it in Melody's soft curls.

Mr. Lambert was still telling the story, for Evan was still wide awake and enraptured. "So of course, the princess of Spain fell madly in love with Captain Jack. After all, he was the only man she'd ever met who understood her love of climbing trees. But regretfully, Captain Jack could not marry her."

"Why not?" Evan's awe-filled whisper made Pru smile into her pillow.

"Because if he were to get married, he would have to stop sailing and he could never bear to give up the sea, not for anyone, not even a princess.

"But since she'd been such a model prisoner and a very fine cook, and she'd brought him such a very fine ransom, he told her he would take her anywhere she wanted to go in the world.

"Did she want to go home to Spain and the father who wouldn't allow her to climb trees? Of course not. She told Captain Jack that she'd once heard of an island where the trees grew so tall and covered so much of the land that the people had simply given up trying to cut them down to make room for houses and had decided to live high in the trees, so high that they could live from birth to old age and never touch a toe to the soil. Well, Captain Jack had sailed the world . . ."

Ten times over, Pru thought, listening with her eyes closed.

"Ten times over." Evan's voice was getting sleepier.

"Ten times over," Mr. Lambert went on. "So he knew of this mysterious and magical island of trees. He turned the *Dishonor's Plunder* about and after a minor hurricane or two, they dropped anchor off a perfect lagoon . . ." His voice faded away to silence.

Pru opened her eyes to see Mr. Lambert tucking Evan's covers more closely about him. He looked up to see her watching and smiled.

"He's a tough nut," he said softly. "Melody never lasts that long."

She rose from the bed, tucking the covers around Melody to keep her warm, then padded across the floor in her bare feet to see her brother's face. All trace of hardened, cynical street rat was gone, leaving only a tired little boy. "He hasn't gone to bed with a story for years. That was Papa's task."

Mr. Lambert stepped back as she approached. "Aren't you tired?"

She smiled crookedly. "Too many beheadings for me. But your stories are wonderful."

"Hardly that. High body count, low vocabulary."

"But they're so exciting! They please people."

He shrugged it off but he couldn't hide his flattered expression. "Hardly the sort of thing the Bathgate Scholars expect to hear from me."

"Scholars have their place, I suppose," she said without interest. "Yet what's so valuable about writing words that only a few people can understand? Isn't there something to be said for bringing happiness to many?"

He blinked. "I . . . I never thought of it that way." His

brows went up. "My father certainly thought that there was nothing more important than writing words only a few people could understand. The fewer the better, really."

Pru let out a sigh as she looked at Evan. "I told him stories every night for a while," she said, as she bent to brush Evan's overlong hair from his brow. "But what with working all day and evening . . ." She shrugged.

A warm, gentle hand fell upon her shoulder.

"You've done your best and I, for one, think you've done a wonderful job. He's a good boy."

No, she wanted to cry out. He's a good commoner boy, he's a good errand-runner, a good scrounger, a dab hand at picking through the grocer's leavings—but he's not a good gentleman's son.

He's not who he is supposed to be.

And neither am I.

If I could be a lady again . . . I might just be the lady who makes you forget Chantal.

The thought took her breath away. Dare she?

I could try.

Yet to reveal herself now, after years of pretending? Furthermore, it wasn't only herself she would be revealing. If Evan's whereabouts became known to the Trotters—no, it didn't bear thinking about.

I could try . . . as Pru. To make sure of him first, to be truly, truly sure . . .

CHAPTER 21

Miss Filby went completely still when Colin touched her. He became aware that they were virtually alone in the quiet night. The last time they had been thus, he had not been able to keep from ravaging her to the limits of her permission.

With great force of will he slid his hand from her shoulder and stepped back. *Look at me. I'm so proper and respectable. Only I'm not nearly so decent in my mind, am I?*

In his imagination, the plain nightgown was sheer and clinging and the firelight showed him every luxuriant curve. In the privacy of his own mind, Miss Prudence Filby was not frozen in dismay, but burning with a lust of her own, ready to press herself to him passionately once more. In the bedchamber of his fantasy, they were not master and servant but man and woman, equal and eager, two people without responsibilities or ties.

Or clothing.

She lifted her chin and met his gaze. Her gray eyes were almost silver in the firelight and he thought he saw something new shining in them. Was that . . . longing?

If it was, it was impossible longing. He would not be that man—the one who took advantage of a woman, knowing full well he intended to wed another.

Miss Prudence Filby, seamstress. With her quick mind and her clear honesty, she could be so much more. He admired her, which was odd considering that he'd never been one to like his women so tartly outspoken.

Nothing at all like Chantal.

Yes, remember Chantal. Remember how she made your heart thud, how she made your blood hot, yet how her delicacy and her vulnerability made you feel strong, her powerful protector.

That wasn't how Miss Filby made him feel. She was no fainting wisp. He reckoned he wouldn't mind having her at his back with a rolling pin in any fight. Yet, she also set his body afire.

And more. The way she saw into him, as if she understood what lay beneath the insouciant façade that most people never looked past. Being with her was like being with Jack, or Aidan.

Miss Prudence Filby, saucy and common, felt like . . . a friend. A friend who set him afire. What was a man supposed to do with a woman like that?

He heard Jack's voice in his head, the old Jack, the one who could laugh and point out the single obvious thing that Colin had never considered.

What do you do with a woman like that? You marry her, you idiot!

Oh, God.

"Chantal can only be a day ahead of us," he blurted, apropos of nothing. "Perhaps less."

Miss Filby drew back and the silvery gleam of yearning disappeared from her eyes, if indeed it had ever lived there. Colin's jaw clenched at the loss of it, though he'd killed it intentionally.

She bent to gather up Evan's discarded outer clothing, shaking his things out and folding them neatly. Her domestic motions made her old thin gown tighten about some very interesting portions of her anatomy. Colin bit down hard on the inside of his cheek and riveted his gaze on the smoke-tinted rafters.

Think about Chantal. Difficult, for he was beginning to think very little of his former lover. "She's not accustomed to travel. She spends all of her time in the theater, working." Or in some man's bed, apparently.

"Aye," Miss Filby said, with the barest hint of dryness in her tone. "It's that hard strollin' around the stage for three whole hours of the evenin'."

The thought of Miss Filby's work-worn hands mocked him. "Well, you can't deny that acting can be difficult . . . er, emotionally."

"Oh, aye." Miss Filby turned her back on him to gaze through the small bare window into the night. "She emotes all over the bloomin' place."

Thinking uncomfortably of the few tantrums he'd witnessed himself—that vase had come very close to striking his head—he changed tack once again.

"It's very late. We must leave as soon as I can pry Chantal's direction out of Lord Ardmore."

Miss Filby leaned her head against the window frame. "Hmm."

"It's been a very long day." He waited for a response. She said nothing for a long moment. He had the sudden sensation that the entire world was asleep except for the two of them. The feeling intensified, lonely and intimate at the same time.

Then, she let out a long, slow breath. "Do you ever wish," she said softly, "that you could wave your hand and change one thing, just one moment of your past?"

"Yes," he said instantly. "I do."

She turned, wearily rolling her head on the window frame as she leaned her back against it. "What do you wish to change?"

"I wish I'd stopped my friend Jack from going to war. He

didn't have to go. He didn't go to be a hero. He went to protect his idiot cousin."

She tilted her head and gazed at him. "How odd. Your answer had nothing to do with . . . well, never mind. I wish you could have stopped him, as well. Did he die in battle?"

Colin looked at the coals. "He might as well have. He's been a ghost of himself ever since." He let out a breath. Then he raised his gaze to hers. "What is your wish?"

She let her eyes drop to where Evan lay sprawled boyishly in his bed on the floor. Colin followed her gaze. One skinny ankle, attached to an astonishingly large foot, stuck out of the blankets.

"I wish I could have stopped my parents from going boating that day," she said softly. "It was lovely out and they'd been invited by friends, but a squall came in the afternoon. The boat never returned to the docks at Brighton."

Colin nodded. "It seems like it should have been obvious that something bad was going to happen. It seems as if we ought to have known that it wasn't just a quick jaunt to Spain to quash Napoleon."

"And we ought to have foreseen that there would be a storm on a beautiful day."

He approached her slowly. She stayed where she was, not shying away. She simply waited as he came close enough to gaze into her eyes. Her chin came up as he reached her and she gazed back at him.

"I'm sorry you lost your parents," he whispered. "You haven't had it easy, you and Evan."

She raised her hand slightly. "I'm sorry your friend suffered. I hope he comes back to you someday."

He realized just then that she'd been speaking like a lady for several minutes. He opened his mouth to comment upon it, but the look in her eyes swept the thought from his mind.

I comprehend, her gaze said.

The room seemed to disappear as he gazed into those

silvery eyes. Their breath mingled. He could feel the warmth coming from her body. The faintest hint of mint teased his senses.

She understands. She would never reject me for devoting my time to a friend.

Her hand rose a little higher, almost resting on his lapel. She'd never been the one to touch. He'd been the one to reach for her, the one to kiss first, the one to watch her when she didn't realize.

Touch me.

Her fingertips traced the outline of the bruise on his jaw. Then, so lightly, so tentatively that he could scarcely feel them, they slipped to the corner of his mouth and began to trace his lips. Her gray eyes fixed on his mouth with such an expression of longing that he had to close his eyes against it.

He would not touch her. He would not. It would be dishonorable. It would be disastrous.

It would be heaven. It would be devastating.

Because if he touched her again, he knew, with every throb of his speeding pulse, that he would never, ever stop.

Although he was resolved, he'd apparently used up every ounce of will simply to keep his own hands off her. He found himself absolutely unable to move away from her curious hands.

So he stood and let himself be touched. He closed his eyes against that beautiful gray gaze that saw through his every act, that revealed him to himself, that could laugh and speak and remonstrate with him without a word need be spoken.

Another cool hand joined the first, framing his jaw lightly, smoothing his brow, teasing at his hairline, testing the roughness of his unshaven cheeks. Growing braver, slim fingers ventured into his hair, ruffling it slowly and sensuously, making his entire body tingle with pleasure.

They moved down, those hands, down his neck, into the

open throat of his shirt. Her touch had warmed now, but it was no match for the heat emanating from his fevered skin. She stroked the neck of his shirt apart, spreading her fingers outward over his collarbones. He wished he dared strip it off so that she might have her way with his chest and shoulders.

Don't move. Don't even breathe.

Her hands slid out from under his shirt and stroked across his shoulders, measuring, testing, digging in slightly to feel his body. Then they swept slowly back together to rest upon his chest, directly over his thudding heart.

Pru's hands seemed to almost shimmer in the dimness, so possessed of tingling power were they. He stood there, offering himself to her touch, sanctioning her to explore him, giving her license to do as she wished.

If I could do anything with him—to him—what would that be?

She knew at once. Before she could even entertain an objection, she'd stepped closer to him.

So close, yet she moved closer still. She moved her body into his taller one and, closing her eyes, pressed her ear to his chest and closed her eyes.

His heart pounded like a racing horse.

For her.

Pru couldn't bear it. Here he was, everything she'd ever thought admirable in a man, yet what would such a man think of her lies?

He would understand.

Would he? How could she be absolutely sure? From where she stood between worlds, she'd seen the worst of both. It was becoming very hard to believe anymore.

She'd lived a rough and grimy existence, alone and unprotected. Though she'd defended her virtue with vehemence and a pair of pinking shears on more than one occasion, she still bore the taint of a wild, unsupervised life. Who would believe that she'd tried to remain a lady through it all?

Lady? When your skirts were rucked up behind the wagon, that was you remaining a lady?

Yet it became harder and harder to pretend she was less than she was. As she grew to know Mr. Lambert more, there was more inside her she wished to share with him, to say to him—things a common little seamstress would never say.

So she said nothing, only remained there, pressed to him, listening, willing herself to banish her distrust and believe— *believe*—in that pounding heart.

He stirred then for the first time, but it was only to enfold her in his arms, loosely, without demand. The moment stretched on and Pru imagined she could feel herself expanding in that protected circle of his hold. She could feel her soul reaching out, like wisps of candle smoke trailing from her, from him, wisps of need and longing and hope twining about them both, knotting them together, threads of soul and heart and mind . . . together.

Silent. In the dark. Bound as one.

Colin didn't tighten his hold, didn't bring her hard against him, didn't shatter the delicate harmony of having her in his arms. He only breathed her in, savoring the warmth of her, the wild, spring scent of her, her breath, her hair. Her.

He felt the pull of invisible threads tying them together and he mourned their breaking. Temptation teased.

Have her. Keep her. Wed her and teach her and show her the world and let her teach you. Let her show you the world anew through her eyes. Let her show you yourself.

Love her.

And ruin Melody's life.

Pain jolted through him. Guilt and loss whirled in his gut. *I've gone too far already. I cannot help but hurt her now. I must stop, before the damage grows deeper.*

He cleared his throat and stepped back. Then, because all he wanted in the world was to step closer and take her into his arms, he stepped back again.

She opened her eyes, blinking, gazing at him as if from somewhere far away.

"Miss Filby, I know that you don't approve of my search for Miss Marchant. You should know that I have my reasons. Chantal is—"

Melody shifted in her sleep, rolling over with a tiny mew of restlessness. Pru glanced at the child, but Melody found Gordy Ann with eyes still closed and stuck a corner of dingy fabric into her mouth and became still once more.

Mr. Lambert stopped and rubbed a hand over his face. "Well, perhaps now is not the time or the place."

Pru nodded sadly. The moment of empathy had passed. She was just a servant girl, not privy to his secrets, not a woman of his world.

Tell him.

Perhaps. Perhaps I will.

Tomorrow.

CHAPTER 22

The next morning Pru awoke early and dressed before the other occupants of the room rose. She set out Melody's clothing, then gently shook Evan's shoulder.

"Hector will be wanting his breakfast," she whispered. "Why don't you get up and help that groom?"

Evan rubbed his eyes and rose slowly but willingly. "That's Seth," he whispered back. "He's a bad 'un. I'll see to Hector meself."

Pru very carefully didn't look at the sleeping Mr. Lambert. Well, other than a quick glance to make sure they hadn't woken him. All right, she lingered a bit, but it was only because he looked rather appealing with his light hair falling over his forehead like that and she'd never realized that he had a sprinkling of boyish freckles across his nose. It made her feel a bit better about her own.

At any rate, they were downstairs to help Rugg and Olive long before the others. When Pru saw that Lord Ardmore still lay stretched out on the floor of the taproom, she contemplated the justice of that and decided that it was just the place for him.

"I couldn't carry him up," Rugg offered as he hefted a bench to his vast shoulder. "Me back, ye know."

"Oh, no. Of course not." She turned to Olive. "What can I do?"

Olive set her to picking up the worst of the shards while

Evan toted out the bits of shattered benches after he'd returned from visiting Hector in the stable.

They all worked in companionable silence until they saw Lord Ardmore stir.

"Argh . . ." He raised his head, blinking. "What happened?"

Olive swept on next to him, unconcerned. "I think ye had a bit much of my fine ale, milord."

Lord Ardmore sat up shakily, holding his head. "And you simply left me on the floor, woman?"

Olive continued to work around him, not trying terribly hard to avoid sending the sweepings his way. "Oh, did ye wish a room, milord? Ye didn't say."

Lord Ardmore had little option but to curse expertly and attempt to rise. He made it to his hands and knees and stayed there, breathing heavily.

Melody came nimbly down the stairs just then, a little skip in her step. She began to sing a sailor's song about "seeking buried treasure south of the navel isle."

Pru bit the smile from her lips and hurried to hush the song. Olive smiled appreciatively at the piping little soprano but Lord Ardmore groaned and clutched his head. "Somebody shut her up."

Pru stopped in her tracks and let Melody sing on. Furthermore, the battered lord received a faceful of dust from Olive's broom for his comment.

"Pardon me, milord, but ye might want to get off me floor. I'll be moppin' next. Unless ye intend to help scrub, that is."

Pru saw the man's face redden with fury, but how could he shout without adding to his own headache? She shared a vengeful grimace with a grinning Evan, who began to clomp about the room in his oversized boots, making a most satisfying racket.

Rugg entered with a bang of his swinging door and began to drag the few functional benches back into place. With each screeching scrape, Lord Ardmore paled further. It was a veritable orchestra of sound. Pru contemplated finding a few pots and banging them in time. She satisfied herself with making sure her broken crockery cracked together as much as possible.

Mr. Lambert came down the stairs carrying his bag. Pru smiled shyly at him but he turned away, grimacing at the noise. "Good Lord, it's a cacophony!"

Rugg and Olive grinned sheepishly and Evan laughed out loud. Only Melody kept on with her shrill little voice, singing sweetly of "longing for that home port."

Mr. Lambert's eyes widened. He turned to Pru. "Did you teach her that song?"

She shook her head, laughing. "I thought you did."

"Well, it has to stop!" He started forward, well furnished with fatherly disapproval, when Lord Ardmore found his growl again.

"Shut that little urchin up!"

Mr. Lambert's lips twisted. He scooped Melody up into his arms. "You have a lovely voice, pet. Can you sing me another song? Perhaps the one about the pony?"

Melody nodded enthusiastically. Mr. Lambert set her on her little booted feet and she began to skip in a circle and sing gustily. "If I had a little pony I would take him for a ride . . ."

Lord Ardmore clutched his head.

"I would visit all the neighbors, ride around the countryside . . ."

Colin approached Baldwin and knelt at his side. "I want to know what happened to Chantal."

"Bugger off!"

"If I had a little pony, if my little dream came true . . ."

Ardmore grimaced in agony. "Shut her up!"

"Tell me what happened. Where is Chantal?"

"If I had a little pony, I'd dream you a pony, too . . ."

"Oh, damn," Ardmore groaned miserably. "Shut her up and I'll tell you everything."

Colin considered the man for a long moment. "Melody," he called without turning his head. "I can't hear your pretty voice."

The song began again, louder. *"If I had a little pony I would take him for a ride . . ."*

Colin saw Miss Filby flinch at the volume. Rugg and Olive openly grinned.

"Oh, God. Stop her," Ardmore whimpered. "Please?"

"That's better," Colin said briskly. "Melody, go outside with Evan, will you? Miss Olive needs some wildflowers to brighten the place up."

"Aye, that I do, little one," Olive said seriously. "I'd take it as a right kindness."

Melody happily skipped out, hand in hand with a resigned Evan. Colin helped Ardmore none too gently into a chair. "Now talk," he ordered Baldwin, "or we'll all break into song! And you bloody well don't want to hear me sing!"

Baldwin brushed a hand over his face. "Chantal was all right at first. She didn't really want to marry me, despite what we let Bertie think. She simply wanted to get as far away from Brighton as she could. I told her I'd take her up north." He subsided, rubbing his temples. "God, the pounding . . ."

Colin gave the chair a shove with his booted foot. "Go on."

Baldwin winced and snarled. "She isn't a very amusing traveling companion, turns out. If she wasn't complaining about the jostling from my speed then she was whining about how slowly we traveled. I told her that I was going to stop for an ale while she made up her bloody mind."

He stopped to press his fingertips to his eyeballs. "Ale?" It was hardly more than a whisper of longing, but Olive was always ready with her pitcher. A chipped tankard was plunked onto the table and filled with an efficient splash. Baldwin reached for it with shaking hands, but Colin swept it out of reach.

"So you stopped for an ale?"

Baldwin gulped, eyeing the imprisoned fragrant brown brew with reddened gaze. "I got down and tossed my bag to that man-ape in the yard . . ."

"That'd be Seth," Olive offered. "He is full hairy. Always has been, since he were a boy."

Baldwin continued, fixated as he was on the shimmering dream of sweet ale sliding down his throat. ". . . and as soon as I started to walk around the curricle, she'd pulled up the reins into her own hands and snapped them, hard. Nearly bloody ran me down, me and the ape."

Colin slid the tankard a little closer. Baldwin licked his lips. "She took off like the hounds of hell were after her, leaving me standing in the yard like a fool. I came inside and ordered an ale while I considered my options."

"You didn't try to go after her?"

He shrugged. "It was Bertie's gig. Bertie's horse, too, now that I think about it." He grinned, a nasty, vengeful expression. "Poor Bertie lost his woman, his curricle, and his horse. I found the best ale in three counties. Not a bad day, all in all."

"Thank ye, milord," Olive said promptly. "We do try."

Colin snapped his fingers in front of Baldwin's bleary eyes. "What made her take off like that?"

"Couldn't say, but by the look on her face, she was nigh scared to death. Stupid cow."

Colin rubbed a hand over his face. "Did it occur to you, you great, irredeemable ass, that she might have had a good reason to be frightened? Did you ever think to ask her why she wanted to get away from Brighton? Do you even care that she is out there now, a woman alone, unprotected?"

Baldwin met his furious gaze with flat, uncaring eyes. "Not in the least. She is Chantal Marchant, stage actress. In my book, that's only about two guineas up from a common street whore. Why the hell should I give a toss? Now give me the bloody ale!"

Colin slid the tankard across the table with such force that half the liquid spilled before it reached Baldwin's hand. Then he stalked away from the man, sickened by his callousness.

He ignored Pru's gently reaching hand when he passed her. Instead he headed for the innkeeper. "Mr. Rugg, a word if you please."

Outside in the yard, Evan kept one eye on the door to the inn even as he set Melody free to scamper in the weedy drive. Not that Pru would ever leave him but he trusted old Lambert about as far as he could throw him.

So Evan was the only one to notice that Seth, the sour-faced brute who kept the stables for the Ruggs, lingered outside the inn door, listening. Evan wished he knew what the man heard, for it wasn't long before the fellow strode off to the stables, nearly at a run. Since Evan hadn't yet seen the bloke move faster than a resentful sloth, that was surprising in itself.

The fact that Seth emerged on horseback a few minutes later seemed entirely suspicious. Could it be he was just off on some errand for the Ruggs?

No. By the wary glance he cast over his shoulder as he rode the horse from the yard, Seth was trying to get away without notice.

Evan hurried Melody off to the side of the lane. "Look at these blue ones, Miss Mellie." He made sure they were both bent over, facing away from the inn, when Seth turned into the lane and began to gallop off.

Evan stood and watched him go. Best not to say anything to anyone. What the old gorilla was up to wasn't his business. He'd learned his lesson well on the streets. *If you mind your own, you're a lot less likely to lose it.*

He took Melody by the hand once more and led her back to the inn, her other hand full of wilting weeds with stems far too short for a vase. It didn't matter. The flowers had simply been an excuse. He knew when he was being used for a baby minder. At least Melody wasn't one of the bratty ones that cried all the time.

Her sticky little paw squeezed his as she hummed happily, eager to return to Olive with her prize.

Evan squeezed back.

Just a little.

CHAPTER 23

Peace was restored to the inn. Arrangements had been made. It was the right decision, Colin was sure of it.

Except that it was going to look like something completely different. He didn't like to think what Miss Filby was going to think of it.

Or Melody.

Oh, God. *Melody.*

His gut roiled at his own chosen path, but he refused to be swayed from it. The morning was passing and he and Hector had miles to make up. There was no time for argument.

Miss Filby sauntered over to where he was going through his valise on the taproom bar, removing only what he might need for a swift day's journey. He wanted nothing to slow him down.

She looked at him with a smile in her eyes. "I think we can clean the worst of it," she announced. "Mr. Rugg has gone to the next village for the carpenter. He needs new benches and more tankards from the potter."

"I know," Colin replied without looking at her. "I made compensation for the brawl, since I started it." And then some, but that was between him and Rugg, at least for now.

The smile grew to reach her lips. "That were kind o' you."

He shrugged. "I pay my debts."

"Lord Ardmore disappeared somewhere between sweeping and mopping," she informed him with her eyes full of vengeful glee. "Assuming he's headed back to his estate, he's got a long walk ahead of him."

Colin grunted. "Good riddance." He leaned over to pick up the saddlebag he'd found in the stable.

Miss Filby blinked when she saw it. "You're packin'." The storm began to gather in those gray eyes. "You're leaving us?"

That phrase hit home, for both of them. Colin looked away as he shoved the wrapped food into the saddlebag. "I'm only riding ahead to catch up with Chantal. I'll bring her straight back here when I find her."

"I'll believe it when I see it." She folded her arms. "Always Chantal. Don't you ever get sick of yourself?"

He had to look up at that. "Don't be impertinent!"

"I'm fairly certain I have nothing to lose by it." She narrowed her eyes. "No one can slow you down, can they? You're obsessed! You'll leave behind people who need you, a child who loves you, just to chase that petty alley cat across the countryside!"

He straightened, looming over her. He couldn't allow anyone to denigrate Melody's mother, despite his own growing misgivings. "You'll keep a civil tongue in your head while I'm gone, do you understand me? You are never to repeat that sort of talk around Melody!"

She paled with fury. "Who do you think I am? *Some of us* think a great deal of children. *Some of us* stick it out when it gets hard!"

He didn't back down. "And some of us take action to solve the problem instead of simply flailing about, getting nowhere!"

Her head came up and her stormy eyes flashed lightning. If she had her way, he didn't doubt he'd be struck dead. "Go on then," she snarled. "Walk away. Or better yet, run!"

She turned away from him sharply, her skirts whirling. In the breeze of her wake he smelled mint. Damn it! This was a simple journey, hardly more than a quick errand! She insisted on equating it with his actions before . . . well, he'd prove her wrong, that was all there was to it. He'd catch up to Chantal in a matter of hours and return here with her by nightfall.

Whereupon Chantal would clap eyes on Melody and Colin's masterful plan would succeed. Chantal would marry him, Melody would have her parents and her legitimacy—

And Miss Prudence Filby would go her own way.

There was a hollow feeling in the pit of his stomach. He would have thought he was hungry if it wasn't for the fact that his gut was atwist. Hefting his bag of supplies, he crossed the taproom to kneel beside Melody where she played with her rag doll. She was twisting the "arm" of the doll about a large stick. Colin slid his hand over her shining curls. "Does Gordy Ann have a fishing pole?"

"It's a rolling pin," Melody informed him. "For rolling heads."

Dear God, what had he done to this sweet baby? He was right to go on alone. There would be no more involving her in any more suspect activities. He slid his hands under her arms and picked her up. She settled onto his knee without thought, without even stopping her work.

He laid his cheek on her hair, breathing deeply of that sun-kissed baby sweetness. "Mellie?"

"Mm."

"Mellie, look at me."

The little round face turned up to his. Big eyes blinked and tiny rosebud mouth pursed expectantly. Little Mellie, always ready to smile.

This wasn't going to go well. One by one, she was losing everyone. They had all died, or left her, or ridden away. The fact that he was doing this in order to bring her a respectable future wasn't going to matter to her childish heart. "Mellie, I have to go away for a while. I'm sorry, but I cannot take you with me."

Gordy Ann dropped to the floor, forgotten. Big eyes

became bigger, pools of light blue that seemed to swim with doubt. "No."

"Yes, Mellie. I'm sorry." He was so sorry that he almost couldn't bear it. "I'll come back as soon as I can."

"I'll come, too. And Evan. And Pru."

"I can't take you all. I have to get somewhere very fast. If I ride Hector, I can get there right away. If he has to pull the carriage with everyone in it, then we have to go much slower so he won't hurt himself."

It was a dirty bit of business, bringing Hector's welfare into it, but he had to make her understand.

"You wouldn't want to hurt Hector, would you?"

"No . . ." The pools of blue began to flood. "Don't go. Stay here. Olive has good ale."

His throat went tight. "Olive has wonderful ale. I'm coming back soon to have some more. And to kiss you good night and tuck you in." Desperately he brought out his heaviest weapon. "I've got a new story for you. The pirate princess gets married."

The flood spilled over. Tiny arms twined hard about his neck as she wailed. "Nooooo!"

It hurt to pry those little hands free and to hand her over to Olive, kicking and shrieking. "I'm sorry, Mellie. I'll be back soon." *Don't do it. Don't say it.* He couldn't help it. "I'll be back in time to tuck you in. I promise."

He tore himself away and bent to take up his saddlebag. Rugg had saddled Hector and there was no further reason for delay.

Chantal was ahead of him. He'd set out to make her his wife and nothing was going to move him from that path. Not even his own heart.

The inn door closed on the pitiful wails coming from within, but Colin continued to hear them long after he'd put miles behind him.

I'll be back in time to tuck you in. I promise.

* * *

Big Johnny Bailiwick rode his very fine horse down the road, whistling in contentment. Even Balthazar, his horse, seemed unusually content. The huge pointed ears stayed forward and the mile-devouring trot remained steady.

That was odd. "I know why I'm happy," Bailiwick said out loud. "But since yer a geldin', I can't imagine why yer so happy."

One ear flicked back in a friendly way. Bailiwick regarded it suspiciously. "It ain't like ye to be so jolly. What're ye up to, ye great flatulent beastie?"

Balthazar whickered pleasantly and bobbed his head up and down. This was worrisome, indeed.

"No, I ain't buyin' it. Ye can put on pretty manners all day if ye like, but ye and I both know what a hell-creature ye really are."

If ever a horse laughed, it was then. Bailiwick began to scowl, his bright day clouding. "I'm ready for it, just so's ye know. No matter what manner o' trouble ye throw me way, I'll be ready!"

It was enough to rack a bloke's nerves, it was! Bailiwick tensed, prepared for anything the changeable beast could throw at him. He stayed that way, waiting for disaster, for the next eight miles.

When he finally arrived at the Ardmore estate, he was exhausted from his vigilance. Dismounting stiffly, he tossed the reins to Ardmore's groom. "Watch yerself, man. 'E's a right devil, 'e is."

The groom looked from Bailiwick to the placid gelding, then back again. "If ye say so."

Bailiwick watched warily as Balthazar plodded easily behind the groom as he was led away. Out to make him for a fool, damned fiend!

When Pomme's troupe had told him where Sir Colin was headed, Bailiwick had thought he'd have trouble gaining audience with the elusive Lord Bertram. He was only a footman, after all.

However, it seemed Lord Bertram was starved for any news of this Marchant female, even secondhand yesterday's news. When Bailiwick was led before his lordship, he found the young man draped across a wing-backed chair in the study, the very picture of melancholy.

Lord Bertram looked up. "Have you seen her? Have you seen my Chantal?"

"No, milord. I'm tryin' to find Sir Colin, I am. I heard he came this way, lookin' for Miss Marchant."

"I sent him on. She took off on the north road with my elder brother." Lord Bertram's reddened eyes filled. "I miss her. I want her to come back to me."

Bailiwick shuffled his feet. He knew a bit about love, he did, after kissing for hours last night with the winning Fiona, but this moping-about business . . . well, it just didn't seem manly, that's what!

"I shouldn't have let her go with Baldwin," Lord Bertram continued. "He won't look after her properly. I shouldn't have . . . let . . . her . . ." It wasn't quite sobbing. It was more like choking. The sheer dampness of it set Bailiwick's teeth on edge.

"Fat lot o' good yer doin' 'er, then!" he blurted. "What ye need to do is to stop cryin' into yer lemonade and strap yer balls back on!"

The outburst had the advantage of shocking Lord Bertram out of his sogginess. "How dare you!" Lord Bertram sat up straight. "What is this impertinence?"

"It's a bit o' cold, hard truth," Bailiwick insisted. "What ye been needin' a fat dose of, by the looks o' things!" He smacked his riding gloves against his thigh in irritation. "I don't blame Miss Marchant for lookin' elsewhere for a man! She sure as 'ell wouldn't be findin' one 'ere!"

Lord Bertram rose to his feet, shaking with anger. "I'll have you sacked, you insolent goon!"

Bailiwick shook his head. "I don't work for ye. I work for real men, men who know a bit about keepin' their women happy!"

Bertram blinked at that. "What? What do they know?"

"They know plenty!" Now he was talking out of his arse, but it was too late to stop now. "If a real man wants a woman, he gets off his packet and he goes after her! A real man sets his sights on a likely girl and he doesn't quit till he's claimed her!"

It was true, Bailiwick realized. It was how Lord Blankenship got his lady and even how elderly Lord Aldrich got his.

Lord Bertram sniffed again, but this time it was a thoughtful sound, not a mournful one. "Claimed her, eh? I don't think I ever got around to that . . ."

Bailiwick refrained from rolling his eyes. After all, his lordship was young yet. He'd learn. "That's the ticket, lad." The fact that Lord Bertram was older than his own nineteen years escaped him completely.

Bertram looked up, a new light gleaming in his watery blue eyes. "I could do it. I could try to find her and make her accept me!"

"That's right! Get some courage, man! Go get her if you want her!"

Bertram straightened, tugging his cravat into place. "By God, I will!"

Bailiwick clapped him on the back. "Good luck, milord!" Then he turned to stride manfully out of the house and back to his bloody-minded horse.

It wasn't until he was nearly a mile down the road that he realized that he had just encouraged Lord Bertram to pursue the very woman that Sir Colin was hell-bent on claiming.

"Oh, hell."

Balthazar laughed and trotted happily on.

CHAPTER 24

It took the better part of the day to return the inn to a state meeting Olive's stringent standards. Of course, everything took longer with Melody "helping," but Olive and Pru simply worked around and through Melody's messes. There was no mention of Colin and not a word about pirates. No one wanted to spoil Melody's fragile mood, for Colin's foolhardy promise to return in time for a bedtime story was the only thing keeping Melody from complete disintegration.

Even Evan was uncommonly kind to her. When Pru took pity on Olive and decided to remove Melody from the inn, it was Evan who suggested a picnic. Olive gratefully packed a basket with bread and cheese and pointed them in the direction of a pleasant meadow where the gooseberries were ripening.

"There's plenty o' bushes near the old abbey, and the little one will enjoy a fine day out," Olive told them.

The ruined abbey was nothing but spires and stone arches standing free in the meadow of wildflowers. Vines crept and twined upward, glossy green in the sunlight. The old stone gleamed white as bone, as if some graceful beast had once chosen this beautiful place to lie down and breathe its last.

Melody ran through the enchanted forest of stone, her little legs pumping high to keep up with Evan's longer ones. Her tiny hands stretched to the sides to brush the blooms of larkspur and poppy and yellow snapdragon that had naturalized from some garden of decades past.

They found a cozy corner where the sunlight reflected warmly from the pale stone. There was a section of the old structure there, small and sturdy enough to retain its roof. Some sheepherder must have been using it, for there was a ring of firestones and pile of sacking for a bed.

It was a measure of Evan's pity for Melody that he submitted to playing house. As she watched over them, Pru tried to keep her expression bright and happy, but there was a pall on the lovely day. Someone was missing and they all three felt it.

As they walked back to the inn in the deepening dusk, Pru had the feeling it wouldn't be the last wonderful moment Colin missed because of Chantal.

A band of men gathered about a fire, a ring of light in the growing dusk. Some tended their weapons, some tended their whisky flasks. A few of them compared stories of their recent run-in with a huge, white fire-breathing horse and the giant who rode him.

Apart from the group, half in shadow, half in flickering firelight, stood a man alone. A dark dangerous man. The form was fine, the face handsome. The eyes, however, held the inward-turned gaze of a man lost in obsession.

A shout came from outside the ring. The circle of men stood instantly, hands on weapons. A sentry appeared, pushing a bound man before him. Without a word, one of the men by the fire slipped into the darkness to take the sentry's place.

The bound man was shoved to his knees before the shadowy man. Panting, the prisoner lifted his head to look at his captor.

The shadowy man tilted his head as he gazed back. "Hello, Seth. I hardly recognized you with your face beaten to a pulp." The leader smiled gently. "It's all the hair that gave it away."

"Mr. Gaffin, sir—" Seth croaked.

Gaffin shook his head. "Shut it, Seth. And don't call me 'sir.' You aren't one of my men anymore. You left our life, remember? You went back to your puny village and now you shovel horse apples."

Seth licked his split lips and spat blood. "That's right, s— Mr. Gaffin. But I heard you was near. I come because I've news for you."

"What news could you possibly have for me, you worm?" Gaffin's disgust was all the more evident by his gentle tone. "Is the world running out of horse piss?"

Rough laughter rumbled through the group until Gaffin held up a hand for silence. "Spit it out, Seth, before I decide to use you for target practice."

Seth cleared his dry throat. "I got news 'bout that woman ye been lookin' for, that actress."

Gaffin straightened. His sudden stillness made him seem even more dangerous. "Chantal," he breathed.

Seth began to babble. It was pathetic coming from a great hairy brute like him. "She come to the inn with Lord Ardmore but she weren't there long. She knew me the minute she clapped eyes on me. Took off like a shot, she did. Stole his lordship's gig and all!"

The chill coming off Gaffin was enough to make the flames falter. "Ardmore said she were runnin' from Brighton. That's when I knew she were runnin' from you." Seth gulped a harsh swallow of fear and babbled on. "There's a bloke, a gent, back at Rugg's inn. He's on her trail, he's lookin' for her, too. Wants her bad, he does. Beat the hell out of his lordship just to find out where she were headed!"

Gaffin narrowed his eyes. "Did he now?" He lifted his chin sharply. Without a word his men began to dismantle the camp and saddle their horses.

Gaffin walked to the fire and gazed into the flames. All around him, efficient flurry made the camp disappear in minutes. Gaffin didn't move, didn't bark orders, didn't even look at his men.

His gaze was somewhere else, some when else. "No one touches Chantal," he whispered to the flames. "No one but me."

Colin was still riding. The sliver of moon gave enough light to easily see the pale chalk road before him and he didn't want to stop just yet. It was after dark and he hadn't made nearly as much progress as he'd expected.

His journey had been slow because he hadn't dared pass up any opportunity to stop and confirm Chantal's path. A few people thought they might remember a pretty woman driving a sleek curricle, but it was not enough to reassure Colin.

If the little information he'd come across was correct, Chantal was a full day ahead at least. Possibly two. It was surprising progress. Miss Filby was right. Chantal was not as helpless as he used to think.

Now he was going to be gone much longer than he'd planned. He'd been unwise, in such a hurry to leave that he hadn't given any thought to what would happen if he couldn't find Chantal immediately.

He shouldn't have left. He'd left Melody and he'd left Pru. He ached to remember the look in two pairs of gray eyes and one pair of blue ones as he walked out of the inn.

An image flashed across his mind, a single moment of the past. A small boy, short legs pumping fast, running down the country lane after the carriage that was leaving him behind. "Papa! Don't leave me here! Papa, come back! Papa!"

Melody's incoherent wail. *Noooo!*

He'd sworn he'd never be that man. He'd disdained his father for his failures and he'd vowed that when he had a family he would never abandon them so.

And yet he had. His reasons were sound, but no doubt his

father thought his reasons were sound as well. Reasons didn't matter to a child. They hadn't mattered to him. They certainly didn't matter to Melody.

The pain that he'd caused his tiny daughter made him draw a harsh breath. *What the hell am I doing?*

Just then he saw a light in the darkness ahead. Slowing Hector, he realized that a man stood in the road, waving a lantern. It was a common signal for help, so despite his sense of urgency Colin pulled back on the reins and slowed Hector to a stop.

"What is it?" He squinted into the circle of light. "Is there an emergency? Are you injured, sir?"

The man approached. His face was bruised and battered and his lips bled when his mouth stretched into a welcoming smile.

Then recognition flashed. Colin blinked. "It's Seth, isn't it?"

"Aye, sir, that it is." The hairy groom nodded and smiled, his face gruesome in the lantern's light. How unfortunate it was the last sight Colin saw before something heavy struck him on the back of the head.

CHAPTER 25

Back at the inn, Pru had to put a weepy Melody to bed without her promised story from her uncle Colin. Pru tried. "Once upon a time on the high seas, there sailed a mighty pirate ship. Upon the prow were letters etched in the blood of honest men and they read—" She waited.

Melody only chewed Gordy Ann's arm as two fat tears leaked from her big blue eyes. Pru ached for her.

I'm going to kill him when he gets back.

Her anger helped disguise her worry, for a short time anyway. When Melody finally drifted off, her pillow damp from her sorrow, Pru kissed a drowsy Evan on the brow and left the room.

Downstairs in the public room, Olive was polishing things that already shone. There was a plate of cold chicken waiting for Pru on the bar, but she could only pick at it restlessly.

She smiled her thanks to Olive anyway. "It's delicious but I'm simply tired, I suppose."

Olive nodded, avoiding her gaze. "Hmm."

The landlady's disquiet finally caught Pru's attention. Her gaze sharpened on Olive. "You've already cleaned that table twice," she pointed out. "If you're not careful you'll clean a hole right through it."

Olive pursed her lips and kept rubbing.

Pru tilted her head. "Are you worried because Mr. Rugg is not yet back from the next village?"

Olive blew out a breath. "No, miss. His brother lives there and he often stays over on a visit." She shot Pru a strange glance. "These roads ain't always safe at night, miss."

Pru walked slowly across the room, gazing closely at the woman. "Olive, something is bothering you. What is it?"

Olive turned away but Pru saw her hands, her knuckles white as she twisted the cloth in her grasp. She put her hand on the woman's arm. "Olive, talk to me." She let a little Prudence into her voice. "I insist that you tell me at once!"

Olive turned to look at her and chewed her lip. "It's Seth, miss. He's run off, he has."

Pru blinked, confused. "Seth? The stable hand? That's a shame. Will it mean a great deal more work for Mr. Rugg?"

Olive's shoulders rose. "It ain't that, miss. Seth . . . well, Seth wouldn't have nowhere to go, y'see, unless he were goin' back to that gang o' his."

A chill went through Pru. "Gang?"

Olive nodded miserably. "Seth's done some bad things in the past. I tried to give him a chance. I knew him when we were children. 'E weren't a bad boy, just had no one to look after 'im."

Pru nodded but she didn't truly understand why this was her concern.

Olive wrung her hands and went on. "It's that man and his lot—he turned Seth bad. He used to stop here on his way north and south . . ."

Pru waited, her gut chilled. Olive wouldn't be this upset if it weren't important. "What man, Olive?"

Olive looked left and right before uttering the name in a hoarse whisper. "Gaffin."

"Gaffin?" There had been a man of that name in Brighton, a man Chantal had taken up with for a while.

Olive nodded miserably. "It's opium. That's what he does. He runs opium up the North Road." She knotted her apron with her reddened hands. "That . . . and a bit o' kid-nappin'."

Kidnapping. Pru's stomach turned to ice. Oh, God. *Colin!*

After Olive's frightening revelation about Seth, Pru couldn't bear to go to sleep. She remained with Olive in the kitchen, drinking cup after cup of tea. Every so often she would jump up compulsively to check on the children in the room upstairs.

She kept the key in her pocket and unlocked the door silently, opening it just enough to wave her candle into the opening and light the room slightly. Once again, her worried gaze was met with two children, tucked safely in bed, peacefully asleep—if one didn't count Evan's manful snores. Evan didn't seem to mind having a chance at the bed, not even when it meant that he spent the night with Gordy Ann shoved into his side. Pru was fairly sure that the only reason Melody was asleep at all was because Evan was there with her. The little girl's baby face was still flushed with crying, her lashes still spiky with all the tears she had shed.

Just as silently, Pru withdrew her candle and shut the door. She locked it carefully and dropped the key into her pocket once more. When she reached the top of the stairs, she blew out her candle out of thrifty habit and began to descend toward the lighted public room.

"I know it's wasteful when no one's about," Olive had told her nervously. "But I just can't bear to sit in the dark tonight."

Pru sighed and rolled her neck against the tension in her spine. She'd known Colin's promise to return by nightfall had been ill thought and unlikely, yet she couldn't help worrying. Worrying had kept her and Evan alive more than once. Learning when to listen to their fears and instincts had helped them flee any number of unsavory characters in the past.

So when a fearful pounding came on the door of the inn, Pru shrank back up the steps into the shadow above and listened as Olive scurried across the public room to answer it.

Don't. Don't answer.

She didn't call the warning out to Olive, despite the chilling jolt that went up her spine. This was an inn. It was how Olive and Rugg made their living, letting strangers into the place.

Then she heard Olive shriek in fear. Then a harsh exhalation of pain.

In seconds, she was back at the door of their room, unlocking the door with shaking hands. Once inside, she turned back and locked it again as silently as she could. Then she flung herself to her knees beside Evan's sleeping form.

"Evan! Evan!" He grunted in protest.

"Time to run, Evan!"

His eyes flew open then and he sat up in the dimness. She shoved his boots at him and then felt her way to the other side of the bed. "Melody? Melody, sweetheart, wake up now. Shh."

Melody woke quickly. "Is Uncle Colin home?"

Pru hushed her piping little voice with one finger. "We must be very quiet, pet. Get dressed, quickly."

It seemed like hours getting Melody into her clothing and buttoning up her little boots, but it must have been only minutes. Evan was swiftly gathering up their things and shoving them willy-nilly into whatever carriers were handy, regardless of ownership. "We can't carry all this," he told her.

Rough voices raised in anger came from downstairs. Pru fought back her fear and tried to think. "Hide it, then. We'll come back for it." *If we can.*

Evan looked about the room for a moment, then got down on his knees and began shoving the valises far beneath the bed, up against the wall under the headboard.

"Clever lad," Pru said as she buttoned Melody into her coat. "Now, quickly, make up the bedding so it looks like no one used the room."

They did it quickly and none too neatly, but it wasn't that sort of inn anyway. Then Pru faced the part she'd been dreading. She opened the window and looked down. "Oh, sweet heaven."

Evan wedged his head out beside hers. "It ain't too bad. I've climbed worser."

Pru couldn't breathe. "How are we going to get Melody down?"

Evan clicked his tongue for a moment. "There's a bit of a ledge and then there's a drainpipe. We ain't all that high up, this being the uphill side."

"She can't climb down that! She's only a baby!"

Evan snorted. "Baby monkey, maybe. 'Sides, she can ride on your back down the pipe. Won't take but a minute to slide down that."

Pru withdrew her head back into the room. "I can't. I can't leave Olive alone."

Evan stared at her. "What d'you mean? You and me, we always run together."

She hadn't wanted to say it out loud, hadn't wanted to admit it to herself at all. Turning to Evan, she gazed into her brother's eyes and made her choice. "I can't leave. The intruders . . . they have Mr. Lambert."

When Colin was pushed to his knees and the hood taken off his head, he felt fear as he'd never known before.

They'd brought him back to the inn.

Oh, God. Melody.

Oh, God. Pru and Evan.

Olive cowered back from the rough group crowding into the inn. Her eyes met his for a second, then flicked away. Good woman. *You don't know me.*

He looked around covertly. No sign of Pru or the children. They must be asleep upstairs. Would they hear the noise? Would they know to hide or would they come downstairs and stumble into danger? Fear skittered madly in his mind. *Melody.*

Pru would take care of her. Pru never let anything stop her.

But who was going to take care of Pru?

The leader, the man with shadows of madness in his eyes, advanced on Olive. "Where is your man?"

Olive began to weep. " 'E's gone . . . to the next village. We needed . . . tankards."

"Don't lie to me, woman!" The leader raised his fist high. Olive shrieked in fear.

Colin rose to his feet in protest, starting for the man. Something hard hit him in the stomach and he collapsed with a groan.

Upstairs, Pru let herself quietly out of the room and waited in silence for a moment, listening. There were voices and the sound of heavy boots and coarse laughter downstairs, but no one seemed to be on their way upstairs. Not yet anyway.

A crude lantern hung on a hook in the hallway, right where she'd remembered it. It was the sort of thing one might find in a stable, not an inn, but for once Pru blessed the rustic surroundings. Quickly she unhooked the lantern and let herself back into the room. Kneeling before the coals, she used a piece of straw to light the candle within the glass and iron box. Light warmed Evan's worried scowl and Melody's excited eyes.

"Melody, Evan is going to help you climb down. You must be very, very quiet."

"Are the pirates back?"

Pirates. "Oh, yes, kitten—"

"Mousie. Maddie calls me 'mousie.' "

Pru inhaled. "Yes. Of course. Mousie. The pirates are back and Olive and I have to get our rolling pins out. Time for you and Evan to hide again."

"I want to watch."

"Not this time," Pru said firmly. "This time you go far away to hide."

She turned to Evan. "Take this lantern and tie it to your braces. Climb down and go back down the lane. Stay behind the hedgerows. We passed a farm when we came that way. Stay there until I come for you."

Evan nodded, his sharp little face very adult. "I'll take care of Mellic."

Yes, Evan was taking the danger very seriously. He knew a little something about dangerous people. Pru pulled them both close for a quick hug.

She helped Evan out the window and then lifted Melody to his back. He shot Pru a pained look when Melody clasped her hands across his throat, but quickly managed the ledge and then the drainpipe. They both took a spill at the bottom but Melody gave a single squeak of surprise and then remained silent. Evan waved up at Pru and took Melody by the hand. In a moment, they disappeared behind the hedgerows lining the road, the lantern light no more than a firefly's spark.

Swallowing her fear for them, Pru reminded herself that the night held less danger than the inn did. Then turning, she smoothed her fear-dampened palms on her skirts and let herself out of the room.

This time she left it unlocked. It was only an empty inn room now. Nothing suspicious about that.

Evan tugged Melody along the road, thinking. He'd lived in many different boardinghouses in Brighton. Enough to know never to trust strangers, not even if they lived close by. He remembered the night that he and Pru had run from the

Trotters. He remembered going to that man, the solicitor, and how the man had tricked them into going back into danger.

Stopping, he pondered the road that led to some stranger's farm. He didn't need some farmer. He didn't need anyone. He could take care of himself and Melody just fine on his own.

"Come on, Mellie. Let's go on another picnic."

Pru stepped slowly down the stairs, listening. Rough voices, crude laughter, the sound of tankards clinking on the tables. Olive was serving the "guests." Good idea. Olive's ale was enough to warm the hearts of even the most heartless men.

Was it Gaffin and his gang? She hadn't known about Gaffin's gang in Brighton, only that he was a dangerous sort and that, inexplicably, Chantal found him exciting. Pru cursed Chantal's one-track mind, for although Pru knew more than she cared to about Gaffin's sexual preferences, she knew nothing remotely useful.

Would he know her? Probably not. She'd seen him lurking about the theater, though only from a distance. She'd kept that distance on purpose, for Chantal wasn't one to share a man's attention, not even with her seamstress. When Chantal had a caller, Pru stayed in the costume room.

Besides, Gaffin had given her a chill down her spine, even from a distance. He was tall and very handsome, in a sharp-featured way. His hair was as blue-black as Chantal's own and his gaze flat and alarming. No-color eyes. Rather like a predator, with hunting eyes and prowling stillness. That predatory gaze had been fixed on Chantal and Chantal alone.

What sort of idiot woman sought out dangerous men? Pru would never comprehend it. Give her a warm, affectionate family man any day. A man like Colin.

Worry for him wound through her like a cold, slimy worm. She hadn't heard him again after that one sound of pain.

They won't kill him. He's no good for ransom if they kill him.

She only wished she could be more sure of that.

Finally, she was at the last few steps, where she would become visible to the public room in general.

There was no point in trying to sneak about. She really only had one option. Tugging her cap lower over her face and making sure her distinctive hair was completely hidden, she drew a deep breath. Then she trotted down the remaining steps, rubbing at her eyes and faking a yawn.

"We got guests, missus? Ye should o' woke me."

Half a dozen dark bearded faces turned her way and not a few knives and pistols as well. She didn't have to fake the shock that leached the color from her face.

Olive cleared her throat nervously. "'Bout time ye woke up, ye lazy cow. Get ye to the pourin'!"

"Aye, missus." Then, because Colin was gazing at her with ashen horror and more questions in his eyes than he ought to have, she added, "Good thing I cleaned out the best room, missus. All's ready upstairs."

Olive's eyes widened but she nodded shortly. Colin's color improved and he looked away from Pru just as Gaffin turned to gaze at him curiously.

"You came with people, Seth told me. A woman and two children. Where are they?"

Seth. Pru froze. She'd forgotten the hairy stable hand. Surely he would know her!

But Seth wasn't in the room. It seemed that the man had placed his loyalties in the wrong hands, for he'd not been included in the gang's activities tonight.

She wondered if he was dead. Poor Olive. She'd tried to save him. Personally, Pru felt a bit more bloodthirsty toward the man who'd endangered them all.

Olive handed her a thick crockery pitcher and gave her a shove toward the "guests." Pru bobbed her head at the "missus" and began to make the rounds, filling tankards as full as possible. These men looked like they could drink like fish and still win a knife fight blindfolded, but any little advantage would help. Generous helpings of Olive's fine ale might at least take the edge off their reactions.

It was all she could think to do. How in heaven's name was she supposed to help free Colin from the clutches of seven ruthless bandits?

To be truthful she was beginning to wonder how she was even going to free herself!

CHAPTER 26

Gaffin had Colin and himself seated at the good table in the only remaining chairs, positioning them in the best spot before the fire. The rest of the gang took up what was left of the trestle tables and benches, distributed more or less evenly on either side of the leader's table.

Gaffin called for a tankard for Colin and watched it be filled. Colin's hands were tied before him. He could have managed the ale well enough but he didn't touch it. Gaffin took a deep draught of his own ale and then wiped his mouth on his sleeve. He gazed at Colin for a long moment before speaking. When he did, it was as if he were simply continuing a previous conversation.

Colin didn't mind. He wasn't in the mood for pleasantries at the moment.

"See," Gaffin began, "it's like this, mate. Chantal's been workin' for me for near a year now. Always out of money, that's my Chantal. Shoppin', gamblin', she's a right menace when it comes to a bloke's wallet." Gaffin favored him with a chilling ghost of a smile. "I'll bet she made a dent in yours, eh?"

Colin made no response. He had no interest in masculine bonding with Gaffin and he certainly had nothing to say in defense of his own idiocy. For Chantal, he had been one of many, a fact that he'd known but chosen to ignore. He'd seen what she was and had chosen to believe the illusion instead.

It was a very beautiful illusion, magnificent in every detail, but somehow he'd known all along she was a daydream.

It wasn't just a folly of his youth, either. He'd continued the fantasy all this time in his mind, using the memory of Chantal to push away any possibility of another love.

He'd even brought along his child to chase her down—to use her to plead his case, for God's sake! Now Melody was in danger, as were Pru and Evan, all because he'd allowed himself to be guided by his cock rather than his mind!

Remembering the romantic drivel he'd written to Chantal, dozens of letters, made him cringe inside. He hoped she'd thrown them out, or used them to line her shoes or light her coals.

Now here he sat, the prisoner of yet another of Chantal's follies.

Gaffin ticked a fingernail against his tankard. In seconds, Pru slipped up beside him to refill it. She didn't look at Colin and Colin tried very hard not to look at her—only a glance, to make sure she was well. She was pale and nervous, but any barmaid would be in this situation. Utterly convincing.

Gaffin went on. "She used her position at the theater to find me buyers, y'see. Lots of coin loiterin' about theaters. Toffs are bored, lookin' for excitement, slummin' with the cast, pickin' out mistresses like they pick out a new 'orse. No one thinks nothin' of the toffs visiting the beau'iful actress after the show. She'd pass the goods on to the marks and then she'd pass the coin on to me."

From the corner of his eye, Colin watched Pru pouring ale nearby. She poured slowly and moved around the table at a snail's pace. Listening. *Be careful, my valiant treasure!*

"Opium. Good business." Gaffin pointed a finger at Colin. "Ain't even illegal, though there's some that are pushin' for a law. Still, the toffs don't like it gettin' public that they're stuck on the stuff. Fear of scandal makes for good profits, especially w' a bit o' blackmail thrown in."

Gaffin leaned back in his chair, his eyes colder than ever. "But she started skimmin' off the top, she did. Silly bitch. Like I wouldn't know—like I couldn't count! At first it was just a bit of the goods. Samples, she told me, just to get the marks started. But she was using it 'erself, she was. Got 'erself right stuck on it."

He paused to take another long gulp of his ale. He swirled the remaining liquid in the tankard as he watched Colin for reaction. "I didn't mind that so much. Opium made her easy to control. She ain't quite the she-devil between the sheets that she used to be, but no more is she like to throw things at a bloke anymore."

Sadness grew in Colin. Chantal was an addict? How terrible and, yet, how like Chantal. She was always looking toward the next thrill, the new excitement. Self-restraint had never been part of her makeup, not even in his fantasy version of her. That had been part of the appeal, as Gaffin had so crudely pointed out.

Colin, you are such an idiot. What the hell were you thinking?

I wasn't, obviously.

"Like I said, usin' a bit o' the goods wasn't so bad. But then she started skimmin' the profits!" Gaffin seemed honestly offended.

Colin didn't bother pointing out the irony in that. He was sitting there with half a dozen pistols primed and pointed in his general direction, after all. If Gaffin wanted to think of himself as a simple businessman cheated by a dishonest employee, well, who was Colin to poke holes in someone else's fantasy?

"She got stupid," Gaffin said with cold anger. "She took too much. She knew I couldn't ignore that, not even for her!" Gaffin's voice climbed, tinged in pain. It was no longer a betrayed employer talking. It was a betrayed lover!

Colin felt his brows climb. Dear God, Gaffin was madly in love with Chantal!

Poor bastard. Even armed and backed by half a dozen ruffians, even violent and murderous, even remorselessly criminal, Gaffin at that moment was the most pitiful creature on earth—a man in love with a heartless woman.

"I'm sorry," Colin said softly.

Pru nearly dropped her pitcher. Colin was continually surprising her, but to offer sympathy to his brutal, opium-running captor? She waited for Gaffin to shoot him or beat him or something equally violent, but to her stunned surprise, the gang leader simply nodded a sort of assent, acknowledging the sympathy without answering it.

As she dashed back to the casks to fill her pitcher, then poured another round and dodged increasingly groping hands, she thought furiously.

If Chantal was an addict, it explained a great deal. She'd missed so many performances, even leaving them unfinished for her understudy to stumble through in an ill-fitting costume. Pru had put it down to laziness or sheer spite. Yet now that she thought about it, Chantal had been growing thinner for months. Of course, Pru had noticed it. She had had to take the costumes in, after all. Still, she'd put it down to foolish vanity on Chantal's part, a shallow conviction that being thinner made her more attractive.

Pru had even attributed Chantal's pallor and weariness to that slimming regimen and had urged her to eat on several occasions—advice which went ignored, of course.

Stupid indeed. Unfortunately, the revelation did nothing to help them in their current situation.

Gaffin was speaking again. Pru tried to aim her pitcher and move closer.

"I told 'er she had to pay me back, every farthing, or I was goin' to 'ave to make an example of 'er. I gave her two weeks to talk the coin out o' one o' 'er lovers. When I come back, she'd gone off, run away from me w' someone called 'Bertie.'"

Gaffin leaned forward and gazed menacingly at Colin. "I think ye know who Bertie is and where I can find 'im."

Colin shrugged easily. "Of course I can, but it won't help. She left him behind days ago."

Gaffin blinked in surprise. Evidently he'd expected to have to beat it out of Colin. Then his brows rose as another thought apparently struck him.

"She didn't love 'im, then?"

His relief was so evident that it was all Pru could do not to roll her eyes. The fool actually wanted her back!

Colin, Bertie, Gaffin. What was it about Chantal? How could one woman turn so many men into slavering fools?

Pru would have given anything to have one of those men slavering after her. Really, what did it take? She had two eyes, two hands, two breasts, same as Chantal! She felt a hand on her backside and slipped away, reminded of her surroundings. Now was not the time to rant against Chantal!

Some of Gaffin's men had been listening in. There was a grumble.

"We ain't here to find yer woman, Gaffin."

Gaffin turned his cold gaze toward the men closest to him. "You'll be doin' as yer told!"

One bearded giant gazed back without fear. "There's no profit in chasin' birds. I'm for ransomin' this posh bastard and gettin' paid in actual coin!"

There was a deep and dangerous mumble of agreement. Pru couldn't decide if it was a good thing that there was dissension within the ranks or if it only made matters more dangerous.

"I have coin," Colin said clearly into the rising dissent. "Enough for the ransom and Chantal's debt as well."

Pru could have sworn that the bearded giant's ears actually perked. He shoved her aside to get a better look at Colin. "Now yer talkin', mate."

"You stay out o' this, Manx." Gaffin eyed Colin narrowly. "Hundred pounds."

"Done."

Pru flinched. He'd answered too quickly, making Gaffin look weak in front of his men. Bargain! Make him feel powerful and in control! Don't pick now to be the haughty toff!

Gaffin narrowed his eyes, clearly displeased. "Each. Hundred for you. Hundred for Chantal."

Colin leaned back. "Done."

Gaffin tilted his head, really looking at Colin for the first time. "Ye'd pay a hundred pounds for 'er, even knowin' what ye know now?"

Colin leaned forward and planted both elbows on the table. He gazed directly into Gaffin's eyes. "Yes."

There was a small spate of derisive laughter among the ruffians, until Gaffin silenced them with a glance.

He turned back to Colin, matching his pose. Nose to nose, eye to eye, they silently challenged each other to back down. Neither did.

God, they were like two dogs sniffing around a steak!

Gaffin examined Colin with icy eyes. "Yer a toff."

Colin didn't blink. "Not really. Not a blue-blood. Simply wealthy."

"Wealthy, 'e says," Gaffin murmured as if to himself. "What's a wealthy, not-blue-blood bloke like you goin' to do with a woman like Chantal, anyway? Marry 'er? Put 'er up in your big posh 'ouse like a lady?"

More laughter broke out in the ranks. Gaffin raised one finger. Quiet descended instantly.

Colin gazed evenly back at Gaffin. "Yes, that's precisely what I'm going to do."

Ale sloshed over the edge of the pitcher as Pru's heart cracked right down the center. He still meant to wed Chantal? Even now? Even after all this? Even now when there was no doubt she was bad? Even now when there wasn't a shred of anything good left to believe in?

"Oy!" The bearded man, Manx, leaped out of his seat. Pru stumbled backward.

Horrified, Pru realized that she'd sloshed ale over the man's shoulder and down his front. Every eye in the room turned toward her once more. Furthermore, her disguising cap had become dislodged when Manx had collided with her. Her red hair slipped its pins and fell as well, drawing attention like a beacon.

Terrified, she tried to duck her head, hiding her face away. "Sorry, sir! I'll get ye a bit o' towelin'—" Her attempt to rush off to the kitchen was halted by a single word from Gaffin.

"You!"

Pru froze. Through the pounding of her heart, Pru heard a sound of protest from Colin.

"Gaffin, we're in the middle of a deal here!"

Then Pru felt hard hands on her shoulders, spinning her about. Gaffin gazed down at her from his great height, his predator's gaze ice-cold, trapping her like a rabbit in a snare.

"You," he said again. Pru's heart thudded as his sharp gaze went over her, down and then back up. She could almost hear the gears turning in his mind as he tried to place her in his memory.

"You. I *know* you."

CHAPTER 27

Gaffin held Pru tightly. Her shoulders ached in the grip of his large hands. He peered into her face as if she held some secret he could divine merely by studying her.

"I know you," he said slowly. "How do I know you?"

Pru looked down, trying to hide behind her hair. "Couldn't say, sir."

He gave her a little shake, forcing her to meet his gaze. His eyes narrowed. "You." He smiled, a nasty stretch of grin across his handsome face. "You're the little sewing girl from the theater. You're the one Chantal's always complainin' about, the stuck-up one who can't sew a lick."

Since the game was up, Pru tossed back her hair and glared up into Gaffin's face. "And you're the bloke she was always complainin' about, the one who couldn't raise the mast."

Gaffin gave her another shake, this one harsh.

Colin growled. "I wouldn't do that if I were you."

Since most of her weight was being held by Gaffin, Pru felt that now was a good time to use her feet. She did so, kicking out with all her might, striking the ruffian's shins and knees again and again.

"Ow!" Gaffin flung her away from him, grimacing in pain.

Colin laughed, a low bitter sound. "Never underestimate a woman in pointy little boots, my friend."

Gaffin howled in rage and moved to where Pru had fallen. He wrenched her to her feet by one arm. "I'll set you straight, you little vixen!" He raised his arm and backhanded her hard across the face. Pru dropped without a sound to fall limply to the floor. Limp was wise, in these situations. It also helped with the graying wooziness Gaffin's blow had brought on.

"You blackguard!" Colin threw off his captors with a roar and made for Gaffin.

It took four men to bring him down this time.

"Keep 'im quiet!" ordered Gaffin. "I got things to see to here."

Dragging Pru upright once more, Gaffin peered into her face. "You ain't a-cryin'."

Pru was light-headed and her face felt as though fireworks had gone off in her cheekbone, but she was much too furious to cry. Snarling suited the moment much more nicely. "I wouldn't dream of giving you the satisfaction."

"Ooh. Fancy lady now, puttin' on airs." He grinned. "Just like Chantal, guttersnipe though she be." He let his eyes travel up and down Pru's body and his grin widened.

"Yer not so pretty but ye got a figure to make up for it. Is that what Himself sees in ye, then? Feels the same when the lights are doused, eh?" He snorted derisively. "Don't tell me, yer just like Chantal. Ye think a man like that means to wed ye in the end. Ye see yerself living in the toff's house, whelpin' the toff's pups, orderin' the toff's servants around, and spendin' the toff's coin, am I right?"

He spun her around and forced her to face where Colin lay beneath several sprawled men. "Did ye think that was his dream, too, then? Him . . . and *you*? And all the time he was dreamin' o' Chantal!"

He threw back his head and laughed. The rough truth of his mockery hit Pru in the raw, secret part of herself, the one she'd hidden even from her own awareness. Ever since that first blasted kiss onstage, some small spring of just such a hope had welled up unbidden. Just a wisp of a fancy, not even a fully realized dream, yet still humiliation stole her breath away.

She waited for Gaffin to spot it, to mock her further. To her surprise, he released her, tossing her aside like a rag he was done with. Instead, he strode into the fray, pulling men off Colin, shouting in rage.

"What ye done 'ere?" He dug into one man's hand and held up a clod of what looked like sticky brown soil. "Ye stuffed 'im with opium?"

Pru gasped. Opium was dangerous! Too much could kill. Rumors abounded in the theater of actors who had drowned their failure in the stuff, only to die from overuse!

Gaffin's men protested. "What? You said to keep him quiet. He's quiet, ain't he?"

"I said, quiet him, don't kill him! The law doesn't look aside when a toff gets killed, you idiot! Besides, I want this one to tell me where Chantal is!"

The other men grumbled at this. Manx spat in disdain. "Yer too worried about that 'ore and not about business. Gold can be split seven ways. Yer woman can't."

Gaffin advanced on the man slowly. "Ye challengin' me, Manx? 'Cause I'll take you on right here, right now. What you think? Knives?"

Pru heard Olive moan. "Oh, me floors."

Pru took advantage of the ruffians' distraction to rush to Colin's side. He was trying to sit up, his hand pressed to his ribs, already growing groggy.

"Spit it out," Pru whispered urgently. "Spit out as much as you can!"

He tried, clearing his mouth and throat again and again. "I swallowed . . . quite a bit . . . I fear . . ."

Pru looked at him closely. Even as she watched, his pupils grew huge, his irises only a thin line of green around the black. He grinned crookedly at her. "At least my ribs . . . don't hurt anymore . . ."

Taking hold of his face with both hands, Pru fought to stay in his wavering line of vision. "We must get out before it takes full effect," she urged him. "We can slip out while they're fighting."

Abruptly, a hand came down to drag her up by her collar.

"Ah, but we'll not be fightin' just now." Gaffin grinned at her where she hung from Manx's thick fist, as helpless as a kitten in his grip. "Me and Manx worked ourselves out a right nice compromise. We take the ransom and the debt, and I get to keep Chantal as my profit in the bargain. I always say, compromise is the art of a gentleman."

On the floor, Colin snickered. "A gentleman!"

Gaffin's eyes narrowed. "Yer slippin' into an opium fog, so I'll be forgivin' that remark. Furthermore, I'll prove it to ye."

He gestured to his men, then pointed at Colin. "Bring him."

Then he strode behind the bar and into the kitchen. At the back of the kitchen was a low door, just as there was in nearly every kitchen in the land.

The cellar, Pru thought with hope. A cellar might have a way out.

Then she saw Olive's worried face as they were dragged past her. Suddenly the cellar didn't seem like a hopeful destination.

Opening the door with a flourish, Gaffin indicated Colin's fate with a tilt of his head. The three men dragging Colin hefted him into the darkness beyond the door with a combined grunt. Pru winced as she heard his body hit hard somewhere in the dark.

Then Gaffin smiled at Pru. Stepping close, he stroked a strand of hair out of her face. Then he bent his head and kissed her, using considerable skill on her frozen lips.

When he pulled away, he laughed aloud at the revolted expression on her face. "Now, little sewin' girl, a true brigand would let 'is men take ye for a bit o' play." His smile widened when she paled further. "But ye see, I ain't like that. A businessman, I am. A gent, like. Don't you want to 'elp me find Chantal?"

Really, there wasn't any fit reply other than a curled lip.

Gaffin tilted his head. "Well, there's time for you to think it over. So . . ."

He nodded to Manx, who flung Pru into the cellar with a violent twist to her collar.

With a cry, Pru flew into the blackness with no way to know how far she would fall.

Evan shivered, though the night wasn't all that cold. The abbey ruin was eerie enough in the dark, when the white granite arches shimmered in the faint starlight like ghostly gateways. When the storm clouds blew in and filled the night with the rolling promise of thunder and rain, Evan found himself shutting his eyes against the view of the arches towering over them like a giant, reaching bone-white fingers to the earth.

Maybe the farmhouse had been a better idea after all.

Melody wasn't frightened in the slightest. She snuggled into Evan's side and whispered a constant story into Gordy Ann's alleged ear.

Evan was glad she was too little to think of things like giant bony hands. For a moment he wished he was.

No. He had to be strong, the way Pru was always strong. Pru hadn't been much older than he was now when they'd had to run away from the Trotters. He only remembered Pru's fear, Pru's command to run, Pru's assurance that life outside their world was better than life inside it would be from then on.

He'd believed her then and he believed her now. Pru always told him the truth.

So when she'd pushed him out of the window and run back downstairs to be with old Lambert, Evan had been shocked to his core.

Pru never chose anyone over him, not even herself!

Evan thought about what he'd seen the night before. He'd been sleeping before the fire and he'd rolled over and blinked sleepily, surprised to see Pru and Mr. Lambert standing in front of the window.

Hugging.

Well, Mr. Lambert was hugging Pru. Pru was mostly just standing there, only she was standing really close to Mr. Lambert and not slapping him or anything like she did when the lads at the theater tried to hug her.

Evan had just about decided that he didn't mind old Lambert too much. He was a decent bloke who looked after Hector real well. Hector liked him more than anyone. Hector's opinion mattered to Evan.

And Melody's, although she was just a baby and thought everyone was her new best friend. Still, Melody thought her uncle Colin had hung the moon and the stars, too.

Even Pomme had liked old Lambert in the end, and Pomme had set out to punish him but good. Still, the thought that Pru might like old Lambert better than she liked him, Evan, made Evan feel kind of hot in his middle.

What if Pru left? What if she went off with Lambert and Melody and Hector and left him behind?

She wouldn't, that's what. She just wouldn't.

It had been an awfully long hug.

Melody snuggled closer into his side and smiled up at him, Gordy Ann's story all finished.

"I like this game," she said. "I play this game at Brown's."

"What game?"

"Hiding. I'm good at hiding," she chattered brightly, raising her little voice over the growing noise of the storm outside. "I can be quiet and hide and no one can find me except for Billy-wick. He's really smart." She leaned her head on his shoulder. "You're smart, too. I bet you could find me."

"Not hard," Evan said brusquely. "All I'd have to do is listen."

"Oh, no, I'm quiet as quiet can be. And then sometimes I fall asleep and then everyone is cross with me and says they were worried. I don't know why. I like naps."

"Couldn't talk you into one now, could I?"

"No. I'm not sleepy."

"Yeah. Me either."

The little shelter was little more than a stone box. It was like a shed added on the outside of the original abbey wall, too short and squat to fall into rubble like the rest. The roof was slate and mostly whole, though cracked. He and Melody had made a sort of bed in the most sheltered corner out of leaves and straw that had accumulated on the floor. It was dry and dusty and crackled when they moved, but they were dry and even a bit snug. When lightning began to flash, it showed through the cracks in the slates and through the low, square door.

Even stalwart Melody started loudly every time the flashes came. When the thunder began to roll in earnest, Evan felt her begin to shiver.

"Don't be scared, Mellie. It's just like fireworks over the quay, like on Prinny's birthday."

"Fireworks?"

She'd been in London on Prinny's last birthday. She'd never seen how the entire city stood on the rooftops to see the display hanging in the air over the Brighton Pavilion.

"It's like a show, where they send fire up into the sky and it explodes, and little stars sprinkle down. It bangs and it pops and the bigger the bang, the more stars you get—all silver and gold and glittery, falling like rain."

"I like stars," she said, entranced. "I like gold and glittery."

"Well, that's what we got here. We got our own fireworks show, just for us."

Lightning flashed then, blinding and fierce, a double, crackling light, followed a second later by heavy thunder. Evan whooped and clapped his hands. "That was a good one! Wasn't that a good one, Mellie?"

Melody, wide-eyed and nearly in tears from the startling crack, clapped her little hands weakly.

"That's not the way," Evan said. "Come on!"

He stood them both up and brushed off the straw, then towed her to sit just inside the doorway, with a perfect view of the sky and the windswept fields outside.

"Now get ready, 'cause we're gonna get a right good show now!"

Melody chewed on her lip, but held her clap-ready hands up and watched the sky. When the next blinding flash came, Evan whooped and danced and clapped approval at the sky. Melody giggled uncertainly at his antics, but by the next flash she was on her feet, ready to hop up and down.

"That was a good one, Evan! Wasn't that a good one?"

Evan grinned down at her. "That was a right smart one, Mellie." She wasn't scared anymore.

And now that he thought about it, neither was he.

CHAPTER 28

Pru managed not to tumble down the narrow steps by an agility gained over years of dodging rough hands. Still, she scrambled down as quickly as possible to reach Colin.

He sprawled limp and lifeless on the earthen floor of the cellar, a still body in the rectangle of light coming from the door at the top of the steps.

Then the door slammed, shutting out the light and leaving Pru to find her way to Colin by feel and memory. She touched a firm body part, covered in cloth. His calf. Fumbling her way up his body, she found his head. A quick, light examination revealed no obvious bumps or bruises.

He stirred beneath her touch, then pushed himself up on his hands and knees. "I can't see."

She let out a breath of relief. "We're in the cellar."

"I hear rain." His words were beginning to slur.

"Yes," she told him soothingly. "That's the storm outside."

A hand, cold and gritty with dirt, came to rest on her arm, then slid down to her hand. "Pru?"

"Yes, yes, it is I."

He grunted a dissent. "No, you're posh Pru. Where's my Pru?"

She laughed damply. "Right here, guv."

He drew her down and whispered urgently, if a little blurrily. "Pru, there's bandits!"

"I know, guv." She smoothed a hand over his brow. "How do you feel?"

"I'm floating. Or maybe sinking. It feels beautiful. I don't like it."

"Good. Remember that." She stood, tugging at his arm. "Can you stand?"

He tried to move upright, but only got as far as his knees. "Pru?"

"Yes?"

"Say 'yes, guv.' "

She gasped a laugh. "Yes, guv."

"There's bandits, Pru."

"I know, guv."

"I'm going to lie down now." He slithered out of her grasp to fall bonelessly to the floor.

She supposed it was as good a spot as any. The ground was dry and dusty and cold, but at least it wasn't damp.

Leaving him there for the moment, she began a blind, fumbling search of the cellar. Following the walls by touch, she made the circuit in a depressingly short amount of time. The space was tiny, hardly more than a closet, most of which was taken up by bushels of potatoes and parsnips.

No outer door. No window.

No way out.

Her path led her back to Colin. Dusting her hands off, she knelt beside him.

"Roll over, then, guv." If he lay on his back at least he wouldn't breathe in the soil. He rolled obediently, but he did not let go of her arm so she rolled down with him, landing on his chest, face-to-face.

She felt his breath gust on her face, the sickly-sweet smell of the opium still scenting it.

"I can feel your breasts," he said conversationally. "You have magnif'cent breasts."

"Er . . . thank you."

" 'Thank you, guv.' I love it when you call me 'guv.' " He hummed weirdly to himself for a moment. "Call me 'guv.' "

"Yes, guv." Should she try to keep him awake or should she let him sleep it off? She had the notion that if he went to sleep he might never wake up, so she shook his shoulder hard. "Wake up, Colin. Wake up, guv!"

His arms came about her, pulling her down close to him. "Mm." He nuzzled her neck. "You smell so good. Always smell so good."

She put her hands on his chest and tried to push herself away. His hold did not give. In fact, it tightened, pressing her body into him, face-to-face, toe-to-toe. She felt a flush of heat run through her. Lust. How inappropriate.

Then again, it was one way to keep warm. And, perhaps, to keep him from falling asleep.

Oh, well done! Excusing lust with such rational argument. Bravo!

Yes, I thought it was rather good.

The dark was playing tricks on her. She'd never feared it. In fact, she rather liked the way darkness hid her, set her free from prying eyes and relieved her need to keep her mask on.

Now, that sense of freedom combined with the danger they were in to stimulate her imagination. Colin swinging a great hammer, sweating in the sunshine. Colin behind the stage wagon, all hot hands and hotter mouth, sucking her nipples, slipping his finger into her. Colin, beneath her right now, holding her hard to his granite chest, his breath hot on her cheek and ear.

Unable to stop herself, she wriggled her body on his.

"Mm." He spread his warm hands over her back. "Breasts."

She kissed him. His lips were warm and a little slack, though after a moment, he did his best to join in. She raised her head, gusting a sigh. "Not your best work, guv."

"Your mouth . . ."

Encouraged, she shook him. "Yes? What about my mouth?"

"Beau . . . ful mouth."

She smiled, flattered.

"I could do things . . . with that mouth . . ."

Her brow furrowed. Was that still flattering?

"Pru?"

"Yes?" She smiled. "Yes, guv?"

"I hear rain."

Pru sighed. "Yes, guv. We're in the middle of a storm."

A storm there was no apparent way of getting out of.

Colin floated. Rain fell all about him but he could not feel it. Pru appeared before him as a wavering vision. She raised her arms and tipped her head back, surrendering herself to the torrent. Wild, buffeting drops hit her in such a cascade that she could scarcely draw breath between them. The thrilling power of it made her gasp with laughter.

Then, in a flash of lightning, he saw her clearly. He felt the cold slap of rain, smelled the electric edge of the storm. Pru stood in the open, face tilted up into the torrent, arms wide, looking for all the world like a pagan sacrifice to the tempest.

He rushed toward her, his feet slithering in the instant mud. He couldn't reach her. She didn't respond to him at all, but only lifted her hands to her hair, shaking it out long and dark down her back.

"Pru!"

She straightened at last, turning to watch as he ran toward her. At last his feet took purchase on the ground. When he caught her shoulders in his hands, she smiled.

It was a wild, free, half-mad smile that stopped him in his tracks. It transformed her plain sharpness into fairy delicacy, making her large gray eyes gleam silver like portals to another world. For an instant he felt as though he'd inadvertently captured a creature from a story in his hands.

"Isn't it wonderful?" she cried. She placed a cold, wet hand upon each side of his jaw. "Can you feel the power?"

For an instant, he felt what she felt. He felt the whipping of the trees and believed that they were about to shake free their roots and dance away. He felt the wind and the sideways pelting of the rain and felt that if he flung his arms wide he could fly away upon it.

Then he felt the hairs on the back of his neck rise up and he heard a strange sizzling sound that screeched primal alarms in his mind. Without thought he wrapped his arms about Pru and flung them both to one side of the road, rolling down into the rushing rivulet of rainwater at the bottom of the ditch, just as a deafening crack ripped open the world.

Then, he lay upon her. Dazed and blinking, he realized that her arms were about him, her fingers digging into the back of his coat. She opened her hands and smoothed them down over him slowly.

The throbbing in his hearing eased and he became aware of a soft rasping sound in his ear. Hot breath warmed the side of his face. He lay upon her, one knee between hers. He could feel the heat of her center on his thigh. Where had her skirts gone? Rucked up between them, he supposed without much concern.

Half of him was cold, very cold, but the other half, the front of him, basked in the heat of her, letting her warmth sink right through their soaked clothing as if it wasn't there at all.

And then, in the manner of dreams, it wasn't. It was wet, slippery skin on skin. She was a soaked nymph on silken sheets, undulating beneath him, opening her thighs wider, thrusting her pelvis up into his.

Her breasts were in his hands, in his mouth, ripe and heavy. Her nipples went hard with desire as he sucked them, moving back and forth, tasting each.

Wet hands twined through his hair, tugging his head

close as she writhed beneath him. He moved down, leaving her breasts with the promise to return soon. He kissed her taut, wet belly and drank the rain from her navel. Then he parted the silken lips of her with his tongue.

She went mad as he teased and tasted, her body bucking and trembling as she gasped his name.

"Colin . . . Colin, I want you now. Please . . . please!"

He moved above her, gazing down at his beautiful, wet, slippery nymph. Water fell from his hair and dripped down her face, pebbling her panting lips with dew.

He drank it as he plunged within her, from chill to heat, from wet to wetter. She screamed his name and wrapped her thighs about his hips, her hands still tangled in his hair.

She was hot and tight and perfect. Every touch, every taste, every panting, begging word drove him higher until he spent himself in her, in his delicious, succulent Pru.

He smiled in his drugged sleep, lost in the sweet impossible dream of the woman he loved.

Pru lay pressed to Colin's body in the dark, chill cellar. It had been hours since he'd spoken or responded to her at all, but she could hear his heart beating strongly against her ear. She was forced to satisfy herself with that.

This left her nothing to do in the dark but worry and run Gaffin's words through her mind.

Colin had baldly told the bandit that he meant to wed Chantal. Of course, he might have been trying some sort of trickery. Unfortunately, she could not think of what.

No, she might as well face it. He had the ring. As soon as Chantal was within arm's reach, he truly intended to propose.

Rising up on one elbow, Pru indulged herself in a single, halfhearted punch to his shoulder. Cad.

Only he wasn't a cad. He really wasn't.

He simply wanted Chantal more than he wanted her. Shallow, petty Chantal! Gorgeous, exquisite Chantal.

What was she to do about that, for pity's sake?

Her wayward imagination now began to paint images of Colin, sweating and perfect, with Chantal.

Sighing deeply, she tucked herself back into Colin's warm side and wrapped her arms about him.

Bloody Chantal.

Chantal, with her eyes bright and her cheeks perfectly pink, describing her latest lover in regrettable detail. Chantal, lounging on her chaise, snarling about some imagined slight from another actor.

Chantal, drooping at her dressing table, going on about how she was overworked and underappreciated and how it would serve everyone right if she simply walked away.

Rousing slightly, Pru tried to focus her weary mind on that last memory. It had been just before Chantal had disappeared. What had she said?

Sleep took her, even as she managed to pull the memory from her mind, mingling it into a dream, a dream where Chantal told her she was going to swim away from them all. Swimming in the water . . . in the pool of water . . .

Evan sat on the floor of the shelter with Melody on his lap, the leaves and straw gathered around them for warmth. Melody apparently only feared the storm when she couldn't watch it firsthand. Unfortunately, it still raged too loudly and powerfully for either one of them to get any sleep.

Evan blinked wearily at the slashing rain outside, then shrugged one shoulder against a chill drip that landed inside his collar and ran down his back. Both of them were a bit wet and Melody was developing a proper sniffle by now.

Then, between one lightning flash and the next, a sight appeared on the crest of the hill that shocked Evan into full wakefulness.

A giant. A giant on a giant white horse. Blimey!

Even as he watched in horror, the rider turned the massive mount toward the abbey and started down the hill toward them.

He jiggled Melody fully awake. "Mellie, quick—we got to hide!"

Melody blinked at him. "Hide? Why?" Then another flash of lightning revealed the oncoming rider, a devil astride a red-eyed snorting demon!

Evan shrank back, hoping that the light had not reached into their dark shelter. "Come on, before he spots us!"

But Melody, mad little thing that she was, ran into the doorway and waved excitedly. "Hi! Hi!"

Evan scooped her up and carried her into the darkest corner, hoping the giant hadn't seen the tiny girl or heard her piping cry over the sound of the storm.

No such luck. The next time the lightning flared, it was to reveal a great black silhouette, blocking the low doorway.

Evan pushed Melody behind him. He didn't have anything! Not a stick or a rock or anything! Remembering the iron-and-glass lantern, whose candle had burned out long ago, he hefted it. He might get a swing or two in, maybe beat him off long enough for Mellie to run for it—

Melody ran forward, slamming her body into the thick legs of the giant, shrieking in . . . fear?

The massive intruder swept her up and swung her about. "Little Milady!"

Melody's shrieks were, in fact, glee. "Billy-billy-billy-wick! You have a lightning horse!"

Evan lowered the lantern and frowned. "Billy-wick? He's real? I thought you made him up."

The demon was now revealed by a flash of lightning to be a blond young man with a funny, lopsided grin. He seemed to be as glad to see them as Melody was to see him. He stepped forward and held out his hand to Evan. "I be Bailiwick, young master. Now, how did you find yerself out in the storm with Lady Melody, sir?"

"We're hiding from pirates," Melody stated with authority.

Bailiwick shot Evan a look. Evan shrugged. "More or less. What're you doin' here?"

The big horse chose that moment to push his head into the shelter. A great snort sent up a shower of leaves and dust and horse snot, making Melody giggle.

Bailiwick let out a sigh. "That monster brought me."

Evan frowned. "Ain't horses s'posed to do what the rider says?"

"Well, someone forgot to tell 'im that!" Bailiwick scratched his head. "I'm dead lost, I am. Goin' in circles out in that storm, lookin' for some inn I heard about this mornin'. I think there might be some bad blokes on Sir Colin's trail."

"Pirates," Melody said knowingly.

CHAPTER 29

In the darkened public room, six men slept. Stretched out on benches and tables and even the rickety bar, they snored and snorted and scratched in drunken repose.

Slowly, carefully, Olive Rugg picked her way across the room. Stepping lightly, shielding her small candle flame with her hand to keep it from falling across anyone's eyes, Olive maneuvered her way across the wooden floor without triggering a single squeaking board.

Well, it was her floor, wasn't it? Hadn't she scrubbed and sanded and waxed it back into gleaming condition with her own hands?

At the door, she quickly slipped out, not wanting a rain-soaked breeze to chill anyone's nose. Once outside, she stood beneath the brief overhang and sent a quick, uneasy prayer heavenward.

Don't let Rugg come home unaware.

Then, with a deep breath, she pulled her shawl up over her head and plunged out into the rain.

The first cottage door she banged on belonged to the farmer nearest, the one Miss Pru had whispered that she'd sent the children to.

After what seemed like hours of knocking, the door finally creaked open to reveal a man with a candle and a very peeved expression.

"What ye knockin' for, ye crazed cow?" He peered at her, then snarled. "Oh, it's ye, alewife."

Olive pushed at the door, letting herself in. "Are the children all right?"

The man scratched his head. "Me brats are up in the loft, sleepin' like they orta be. What d'ye care?"

Olive stared at him. "Your children? What about the two little ones, Evan and Melody? Did not a boy and a girl come knockin' at yer door this night?"

The farmer, who had been none too pleased at the re-opening of the inn in the first place, for he claimed the customers would trespass into his fields and frighten his sheep, scowled at her.

"What ye playin' at, woman? No one's broken down me door tonight but yeself."

Behind him, Olive saw the fellow's thin, shy wife peering from another room. "Missus! Did you not take in two children tonight?"

The woman's eyes widened to be addressed, but she shook her head quickly. "No, alewife. None here but ourn own."

Olive bit her lip. She must have got it wrong from Miss Pru.

Turning to the farmer, she waved her hands. "I'm that sorry to wake ye, but there's bandits takin' over me inn! I need to gather folk to fight them off!"

The farmer laughed in her face. "I knew that sin house o' yours would bring ye evil luck! Fight 'em off yeself!"

Olive eyed the man coldly. "Sin house, is it? And what would ye be doin' there on a Wednesday ever' week, sir?"

The man slid an uneasy glance toward his wife. "Need a bit o' warmin' up, I do, after a day at market."

"Hm. I know what you want. I brew the best ale in three counties and ye know it." Olive folded her arms. "So ye might care to know that them bandits are in me inn right now. *Drinkin'. All. Me. Ale!*"

The farmer's brows went up and his jaw dropped in horror. "All of it?"

Olive nodded. "Ever' drop. Won't be another cask ready for weeks yet."

The farmer straightened then, resolve evident in every inch of him. "Wife, fetch me pitchfork!" He slung on his heavy wool coat and tugged a woven cap down over his eyes. When his scurrying wife returned, he armed himself and turned to Olive.

"Well, what ye waitin' for, woman! Let's rouse the village!"

Attack began at dawn. When the first barrage of fist-sized rocks struck the front door of the inn, six burly fellows scrambled to their feet in the public room, gazing about them in hungover panic.

"The 'ouse is fallin' in!"

Manx rubbed at his aching head. "Fetch Gaffin!" He gave another man a push toward the stairs.

Gaffin was already on his way down, alert and fully dressed. "Oy, shut it, ye bunch o' little girls!" Striding into the room, he looked around at them all. "Some idiot let the ale-wife get out and now she's brought down the village on us."

Manx went to the window and blinked at the frightening assemblage of hodgepodge weaponry. "Pitchforks? Torches? What're they huntin', werewolves?"

"Pitchfork'll gut ye without the man ever comin' into reach." Another man pressed his face against the glass. "Cor, that's a big 'orse!"

Manx's eyes widened. At the front of the attacking horde, like the point of a spear, loomed a nightmarish sight. A giant, holding a three-tined hayfork like a lance, sat mounted on a great, snorting dragon of a horse, a colossal creature as pale as death itself. Even through the wavy glass, one could see the grim countenance of the giant. Like a merciless spirit, he seemed prepared to trample them all in his vengeance. "I know that 'orse!"

"Fools!" Gaffin pulled them away from the window. "It's naught but alewives and farmers! We're in no danger from them!"

Still, he couldn't resist another look at the giant on the horse. "Blimey," he whispered.

Then he turned to face his men. They looked confused and hungover and thoroughly rumbled. Bloody hell. You simply couldn't hire good criminals anymore.

Seven pistols. Seven shots and then no more until everyone had reloaded and tamped their powder. Plenty of time for a crazed horde to charge the inn and take them all down in a wave of pitchforks and axes and God-knows-what-else.

Outnumbered and outgunned, so to speak.

Another barrage of rocks struck the front door. Gaffin narrowed his eyes, noting that none of the missiles broke a window. The villagers obviously wanted their inn and their ale intact. He'd never used a cask of ale as a point of negotiation before, but there was always a first time.

Then a call came from outside. "Throw out yer 'ostages!"

Hostages? Ale casks? Then Gaffin remembered that he did indeed hold at least one very valuable hostage.

"Get those two up out o' the cellar," he ordered, striding to the center of the room. "We're about to get out o' here with our skins intact!"

When Gaffin's men came to drag Pru and Colin out of the damp and chill of the root cellar, Pru had made up her mind. She avoided the men's hands with a grimace of disdain and stalked out of the darkness under her own power. Blinking in the dawn light that wasn't much brighter, she picked Gaffin out of the group and strode up to him, her hands clenched into fists at her side.

Despite the grimness on the faces of his men, Gaffin smiled and tilted his head to gaze at her approach with approval. "You got somethin' to say to me, then, pretty Pru?"

Pru fixed her furious gaze at his middle weskit button. "I been thinkin'." She wiped her dusty face with one hand and lifted her baleful gaze to meet his amused one. "I been thinkin' that bitch ain't my burden. I been thinkin' that she'd be laughin' at how I had me eye on his highness over there."

She shot a resentful glance to where Colin stood, awake and blinking in the dimness but still groggy enough to need the support of two of Gaffin's men. He turned his head in time to meet her eyes, then he frowned when he realized that she was talking to Gaffin—and that no one was restraining her as they did him.

He pulled weakly against the hands that held him. "Pru . . . what is this?"

She turned her back on him and folded her arms, tucking her fists in hard, her shoulders high. "I got me pride, you know," she told Gaffin, her voice flat. "I got blokes what want me. I don't need him." Then she lifted her chin, letting her hot eyes fill with the shine of betrayal. "But I don't want her to get him, neither!"

Gaffin nodded, pleased understanding on his face. "Yer doin' the right thing. You got no place with the likes of 'im. Posh bastard don't deserve you or Chantal. Tell me where she is and I'll make sure Master Collie don't get to drink at that well again."

Behind her, she heard Colin struggle against his captors. "Pru, don't do it, please! You don't underst—"

The sound of a thick fist hitting something came and Colin's protest subsided.

Don't turn around. Don't falter. It must be done. Pru sniffed mightily and then let out a long breath. "She's on her way to her mum's," she told Gaffin. "In Black—"

"Blackpool!" Gaffin's eyes lit. "O' course! She told me she was done w' that town forever, but—"

Pru nodded grimly. "But where's a woman to go when she got no one else?"

Gaffin's second in command approached. "There be more folk outside the yard." He looked frazzled. "It's like a forest o' pitchforks out there!"

A long, slow smile took over Gaffin's handsome face—a carnivorous smile that made Pru's spine twitch in alarm. For the first time she felt a flicker of sympathy for foolish, selfish Chantal. What a dangerous man for any woman to become involved with!

Gaffin turned to his men. "Hold 'em here. I got an appointment with an alewife."

Pru watched as Gaffin went to the door and opened it carefully. Her eyes widened as he ducked back to avoid a rain of flying rocks. What in heaven's name?

Gaffin pulled out a handkerchief and waved it through the partially open door. "Truce!"

When no more rocks flew, he cast a bitter smile back at Pru and then exited the inn with his hands in the air.

"What is going on?"

Manx growled at her. "Village's gone mad. Like rabid dogs out there. Pitchforks and giants and what-not. We just want to get out o' this hellhole."

Giants? "Mad, indeed," she murmured.

In a moment, Gaffin had reappeared. "I got 'em to back off a bit. Manx, you and another man take Himself and Pretty Pru here out in the yard and hold 'em there where the village idiots can see 'em right plain. The rest o' you, go to the stable and get the 'orses ready."

He turned to Pru and smiled. "Ye got me what we both wanted anyway. I'll take Chantal away from this blighter and ye'll get out in one piece." Though his eyes were cold and glinting, his smile widened. "I've had worse days."

Outside in the yard, Pru stumbled along with her hands high and Manx's meaty fist around her arm. It took two men to keep Colin on his feet. They stood facing an unimaginable army.

It was a forest of pitchforks and axes and shovels, lighted by torches and furious faces, led by a demon on a monstrous steed.

Beside her, Manx let out a breath. "Blimey, this lot likes their ale."

"Best ale in three counties," Pru said proudly.

The rest of them brought out the saddled horses and packed them hurriedly. Gaffin approached Pru and Colin.

"Toss 'em," he ordered. "We got somewhere else to be." He strode to his horse and mounted. As he rode past Pru he put a fingertip to his hat brim and gave her a gentlemanly nod. "Good mornin', Miss Filby."

Colin did not enjoy such a thoughtful farewell. Gaffin's men tossed him, just as they were ordered—tossed him into the pigsty. Then they mounted their horses, laughing, and rode out after Gaffin.

Pru ran to where Colin sprawled in the muck and leaned over the low rough-hewn fence of the pen. "Give me your hand."

He only glared at her as he attempted to get on all fours. His knees slid out from underneath him and he went back down into the filth with a nauseating squelch. "Bloody hell!"

"Colin, take my hand," Pru ordered.

His head whipped around and he fixed her with such a furious gaze that she drew back. "How could you . . . tell that hyena that she went to Blackpool?"

He awkwardly made it back onto his hands and knees, cursing. "I should have thought of it. She told me . . . of her life there . . . how she was mistreated, how she fled to London with a traveling theater troupe—" He went down with another squelch. This time he stayed down and simply rolled over onto his back so he could look at her with accusation. "If you knew . . . why didn't you tell *me*?"

Pru rested her elbows on the fence and dropped her chin onto her laced fingers. "Because Chantal isn't on her way to Blackpool." She smiled at the confusion on his face. It was over and he was awake and unharmed and her relief was so great she could have taken wing with the lightness in her heart.

"She isn't?"

The opium was obviously still at work in his system, for his anger disappeared in an instant, to be replaced by a rather loopy expression of hope. Such continued eagerness to find Chantal even in the face of the truth dampened Pru's joy slightly. She straightened to stand with her hands resting on top of the fence. The fact that her knuckles were white with the strength of her grip on the old wood bypassed Colin completely.

"No, she isn't. Chantal Marchant is precisely where she told me she was going nearly a week ago. I simply wasn't listening." She gazed at the handsome, wealthy, kind, and generous man who lay covered in pig shit before her. Bloody undeserving Chantal was going to win again, because Pru couldn't lie to Colin Lambert, not even to save him from himself.

She took a deep breath. "Chantal has gone to take the waters in Bath."

CHAPTER 30

The situation, which would undoubtedly be forever known to the locals as the Battle of the Ale, was over. The villagers mingled, comparing pitchforks and tall tales, which were growing taller by the second.

Pru pushed through the crowd in the inn and spotted Olive, who hurried over at her urgent signal. Her second-best pitcher sloshed happily and there was a triumphant glow on her round face.

Pru had no time for mutual congratulations. "Have you found the children? I sent them to the cottage down the lane!"

The giant young man who had led the charge stepped forward. "I got Lady Melody and the lad. Found 'em in the old abbey last night during the storm." He jutted his chin toward Olive. "Left 'em with the lady's old mum. She says to save 'er a pint."

Pru's spine melted in relief and she found herself sitting in a hastily procured chair. The fellow hovered worriedly.

"You all right, miss? You look right pale, you do."

She smiled up at him weakly. "Thank you." Then she blinked. Lady Melody? Her brow furrowed as she realized that he was dressed differently than the people of the village. "Who are you, sir?"

He puffed up a bit. "I'm Bailiwick, miss. Third under-footman of Brown's Club for Distinguished Gents in London, I am."

Billy-wick. "Heavens," she breathed. "The very best service, indeed!"

Dropping her head into her hands, Pru started to giggle. She was still shaking with weak half-laughter when Colin passed her, supported by a burly villager.

"Oh, Bailiwick. Good to see you, lad," Colin said cheerfully. "Did you know I was captured by opium runners? It was very exciting."

"Yes, Sir Colin, it were a right adventure," Bailiwick replied.

Pru went very still. *Lady Melody. Sir Colin.*

"Could you go fetch the children, Bailiwick? I don't like to have Mellie out of my sight."

Bailiwick nodded. "Yes, sir, but they only just nodded off two hours ago. I'll go and watch over them while they get a bit o' rest, all right?"

Colin waved a hand. "Yes, thank you." Then he seemed to see Pru for the first time. "Miss Filby! You need a bath."

His cheerful accusation made Pru grimace. "As does yerself, Mr. Lam—Sir Colin."

The big man supporting Colin boomed a laugh. "I'm gettin' a bit mucky meself. Pig shit is contagious-like."

"Hot baths all around, then!" Colin dug into his weskit for a coin, then frowned. "Bailiwick, did Wilberforce send you with pence or three? I appear to have been robbed."

"I've two guineas, sir," Bailiwick said proudly. "One for you and one for Lady Melody."

"Good man." He grinned foolishly down at Pru. "Miss Filby, I order you to have a bath." A dreamy glaze passed over his eyes. "You like baths. I remember when I caught you bathing by the stream—"

"Bailiwick! See to the children!" Pru jumped to her feet and glared at the two men flanking the rambling Colin. "You there, take Sir Colin to a room and order up baths for us."

Bailiwick jumped to obey, as did the village man.

"Isn't it droll when she talks posh like that? One would almost think she'd been speaking so all her life . . ." Colin's cheerful rambling faded with distance. Pru closed her eyes and ordered the always ready blush on her cheeks to fade.

It was hard to be ginger.

Pru bathed quickly and efficiently, though she longed to dawdle in the warm water. The children would be returning soon. There would be carefully edited explanations to give and heaven knew when Mr.—when Sir Colin would be fit to give them.

The fact that she was dying for a few explanations of her own didn't signify, she thought bitterly. She was no one, after all.

She donned her nightgown to wear while she dried the greater part of the water from her hair. After she'd pulled her damp hair back in a quick twist, she dug out her second-to-last clean gown. Again it was a simple dark dress with no real shape. A servant's dress.

It was becoming harder and harder to clothe herself in such things. It was becoming harder to remember why she should.

A crash and a curse came from the next room. She waited for someone to respond but she heard nothing but slow and steady profanity in a deep, familiar voice. Setting her gown aside, she went to the door. Biting her lip, she peeked into the hallway, but there was no one there. Slipping out of her room, she went to the next door and tapped lightly.

"Mr.—" Blast it! Would she never remember? "Sir Colin? Is everything all right?"

"Bloody mumble-mumble. Damn it all to mumble-mumble."

Pru pressed the latch and opened the door just a crack. "Sir?"

"Pru? Come in! Come in!"

She entered, then realized that she ought not to have. Sir Colin was sprawled on the floor next to the tub, entirely naked but for a drugged grin and an advantageously draped piece of toweling.

And the towel was slipping.

CHAPTER 31

On the floor, Colin flopped over onto his back and looked up at Pru. "Now I know how Gordy Ann feels."

"Gordy Ann," Pru muttered as she bent to help him, "is far too intelligent to get herself into such a pickle." *Do not look. Do not.*

"Pickle? Ambushed by opium runners is a pickle?"

"If you'd stayed with us where you belong, you and the opium runners would never have met."

He shook his head. The motion was a little wobbly. "We would have, you know. All Chantal's lovers are converging in this chase."

Bloody Chantal. "She is a one-woman disaster on wheels."

"Shiny spinning curricle wheels," Colin said dreamily.

Chantal was shiny, all right. A bright and shiny toy mesmerizing men all over England. "You reek."

"I scraped off the worst of it."

Pru looked at the wreckage of poor Olive's best linens. "I see that."

He shrugged. "What's the point of bathing if the water is filthy?"

"And will you replace what you've ruined in the process?"

His dreamy eyes fixed on her face. "You're quite pretty, you know. Even when you're angry with me . . ." He laughed. "No, *especially* when you're angry with me . . ."

Her heart flipped over in her chest. *You're pretty.*

I covet you.

"Now is hardly the time, sir." Taking a muscular arm in both her hands, she helped him to his feet. The towel around his waist slipped. He grabbed for it but it fell to the floor. "Oops." He gave her an embarrassed grin.

I will not look down. I will not look down.

She glanced down, then yanked her gaze right back up. Her palms went damp . . . and that wasn't all. *Oh, my.*

I hope he didn't see me do that.

Fortunately, Colin was still too dreamy to notice much. With her help he climbed into the tub and slid beneath the concealing soapsuds.

Pru straightened and wiped her damp palms on her night-gown. Looking down at herself, she realized that her old, thin gown was no match for the way his nearness affected her nipples.

Next time, she would dress before getting close to him.

Crossing her arms over her chest, she backed away from the tub as he closed his eyes and lay back with a sigh.

And nearly went under.

"Sir Colin!" Stepping forward quickly, she plunged both hands into the water and grabbed him by the shoulders. "Wake up!"

He came up blinking and sputtering, then clumsily pressed her away. "I'm fine, I'm fine. It's just rather remarkable . . . every time I close my eyes . . ."

Pru took a deep breath. "I think I'd best stay with you."

He smiled at her. "That's nice. I like it when you're with me." He leered happily at the front of her nightdress. "Especially when you're wet."

"Oh, for pity's sake!" She grabbed up his discarded towel and threw it over her shoulders like a shawl, hiding her dampened bosom.

His brow crinkled. "What a shame. Such a magnificent pair of—"

She tossed the sponge into the water, splashing his face. "Time to get the pig off you."

He dutifully tried, but the soap eluded his fumbling grasp and he had the tendency to fall asleep in the middle of scrubbing. Finally, Pru had had enough.

"Give me that." She knelt by the tub and took the sponge from his hand. "Where's the bar of soap?"

He blinked at her innocently. "I dropped it."

She stared him down. "Then find it."

He snickered and began to feel around the bottom of the tub. "It was worth a try, don't you think?" He found it and handed it to her.

She bit her lip. Laughing would only reward him. She soaped the sponge well. "Lean forward." His shoulders ought to be a safe enough area to begin.

Except for the fact that she happened to be particularly fond of his wide, muscled shoulders. Except for the fact that she couldn't resist using her hands as well as the sponge, stroking over and over his slippery skin to remove the black stain of the mud.

He sat quietly with his hands braced on the sides of the tub and his head bent, submitting to her touch once again. There wasn't a sound in the room but the small splashes of the bath and their own breaths.

Pru's mouth went dry and her body began to hum with an unfamiliar vibration—unfamiliar until she'd encountered this man. Now it seemed that she was always in some state of excitation when he was in the room. Here, now, spreading her hands wide over his hard back, feeling the muscles shift under his skin, seeing the way the light moved and rippled with his every breath, outlining every hard ridge and flexing fiber . . .

Her body tightened, squeezing her thighs together involuntarily. This strange state, this awakening to senses she hadn't known she had, what was she to do with all of this . . . his *power*?

She swallowed hard and leaned back, dragging her hands from his skin with effort. "I have to wash your hair." Was that her voice, all husky and shaking? "Sit up and tilt your head back."

When he lifted his head, the expression blazing in his hot green gaze made her look away.

"Close your eyes," she ordered as she picked up the tin pitcher and plunged it into the water to fill it. She used one hand to shield his eyes while she poured the water over his scalp. Then she rubbed her hands full of lather and began to work it into his thick hair.

The suds turned dark as his hair turned fair once more. She rinsed it and then lathered it again. This time she rubbed slowly to get all the grit free . . . and also because she loved running her hands through his hair. She itched to since the first moment she'd seen him holding Melody on that stage in Brighton. He'd been like a golden god standing there, except he'd been so real and solid in that place of lies and fantasy.

He'd offered her everything she'd thought she wanted and had delivered it as well.

Why now did she want more? Why couldn't she simply take his pay and watch his child and then go on her way?

I don't want to part from him.

You'll have to tell him the truth.

He won't understand why I've lied.

You'll have to trust him to.

She rinsed his hair once more and sat back. "Can you manage the rest?" *I cannot do this any longer. I can't sit here in this steamy intimacy and be his servant girl.*

So tell him. Trust him.

Perhaps . . . perhaps I can.

Perhaps I will.

He opened his eyes and ran wet hands through his hair. "I'm clean. How wonderful." He smiled at her, his grin a little off center. "You saved me."

She lifted her chin. "Don't worry, guv, it won't happen again," she retorted saucily.

He reached out and took her hand, splashing her in the process. "Pru, I mean it. You saved me." He blinked and shook his head, trying to focus his vision. "In the inn last night, on the road here, in Brighton." His words tumbled over each other a bit, but he pressed on. "You keep saving me, again and again. Why do you do that?"

His hand was large and hot wrapped around hers. She stared at it so that she wouldn't have to meet his eyes. "That's what you're payin' me for, guv."

"Since when is such a valiant heart for hire?"

When no one wants it for free.

She tried to slip her hand from inside his. His grip tightened, not harshly but not yielding, either. "Why won't you talk to me, Pru? What secrets are you keeping? What is going on behind those impossible eyes of yours?"

She lifted her head then, snapping her gaze to meet his. "You're a fine one to talk, *Sir Colin*!"

He blinked. "Sir Colin. Yes."

"You never mentioned it."

He shrugged. "It's a bit new. I'm still getting used to it."

"You were knighted. By the Prince Regent himself."

He nodded. "Prinny, yes. With a sword and everything. It felt very odd."

"So you're Sir Colin and Melody is Lady Melody."

He blinked rapidly. "Well, yes. No matter who her father is really, she would be Lady Melody, wouldn't she?"

Pru narrowed her eyes. "Are you her father?"

"I think so, yes." He lifted his brows and smiled. "That's a bit new as well."

Nanny Pruitt took me to Brown's to meet my papa.

"So you've recently discovered you have a child."

He nodded, a few times too many.

Pru hesitated. It seemed in this state she could ask him

anything and he would tell her the truth. It was a heady power but she ought to take care. Knowing too much could be dangerous.

Yet she had to know. "Who is Melody's mother?"

Don't say it. Don't say—

"Chantal. Chantal is Melody's mother." He shook his head. "At least . . . I need to be . . . I need to find Chantal." He held her hand and gazed into her eyes, trying mightily to focus his pupils. "Do you understand why it's so important to find her?"

Pru nodded slowly. "To ask her about Melody."

"Yes, and to wed her."

Pru drew back. "Are you using Melody to get Chantal to marry you?"

"Yes." He blinked. "I mean . . . there's more, don't you see? I need Chantal!"

Pru stiffened. "You've made that very clear. You're mad for her."

"No, no, not anymore. I see now that she's . . . she's not the woman I thought she was."

"Then why?"

He let his head fall back in frustration. "I can't . . . words aren't coming . . ." Lifting his gaze to hers, he held her hand and drew her closer. The intensity in his green eyes made her breathless.

"Melody is a b . . . a bastard." He said it as if he could scarcely bear to use the word. "I can fix that. I can make her part of Society, make her my own in truth . . ."

Ah. Pru's heart broke a little as the fog cleared. "You can legitimize her birth if you wed Chantal."

"I must. I *must* wed Chantal."

There it was. It had been right in front of her the entire time. His drive, his compulsion, his burning desire to find the woman he'd once loved—it was all to save little Melody from a life of being snubbed and ridiculed. If he didn't, no matter how powerful her father might be and no matter how openly he might claim her, the shadow of illegitimacy would follow that sweet child forever.

She would always be on the outside, looking in.

Pru's chest tightened. A wave of protectiveness swept her. No. Not that, not for brave Melody, with her passion for bloody pirate tales and her silly little knot doll.

And Colin, desperate to become the father Melody needed, was willing to wed an amoral woman who was bound to make him unhappy for the rest of his life, just to give Melody the future she deserved.

He was still watching her, blinking in his effort to fix his eyes upon her. "Do you understand now?"

She nodded, for she did not trust herself to words. *I understand and now I understand that I can never have you and that's really, truly too bad because I just realized that I am in love with you, entirely and completely.*

No, best not to speak just now.

Or ever.

After she'd helped a clean and naked Colin to bed in the best room, Pru slowly descended the stairs to find Olive nearly had the public room back to rights.

Pru smiled wearily at her new friend. "Don't you ever stop?"

"Rugg is due back this mornin' and I don't want 'im to worry too much. He'll hear the tales right enough, can't help that. Still, if he comes back to a shambles, he'll never dare ride out again!"

Pru fell into a chair. "You were up all night. Stop before I sit on you."

Olive gazed about her domain and declared herself satisfied. "Once Rugg gets them new benches and all, it'll be right nice." She pulled up the last chair and sat with Pru.

"When I saw 'em throw you in the cellar, I was that worried. Didn't know if they'd ever let you out again."

Pru shook her head. "It wasn't so bad. I don't mind the dark."

"Ye got rid o' that snake, Gaffin." Olive gazed at her keenly. "That were right clever. How did you think o' that so quickly?"

Pru shrugged listlessly. "I was too terrified to do anything else." As the fear and fury and tension of the last twenty-four hours began to leak away, it left her empty and weary to her bones.

"You ain't no servant girl, I can tell ye that."

Pru let out a long sigh. "No, I'm not. I'm not anything. Neither fur nor fowl." Abruptly she put her head down on her folded arms. Gentle work-roughened hands fell upon her shoulders.

"It's all over now, pet. Ye can let it go."

Pru sniffled. "But what about next time? What if I can't think of anything brilliant next time? Or the time after that? What if something terrible happens to Evan? Or Melody?" *Or Colin?*

People died every day. Mothers and fathers and children and even strong powerful men. Sometimes she felt as though storm and evil and accident waited around every corner, ready to steal away the people she loved.

Olive chuckled. "Nothin's going to happen to 'em. They're fine. Come here. I got somethin t'show ye."

Olive tugged her into the kitchen. There sat the children by the fire. Evan was proudly showing Melody a scrape on his knee. Melody bent to peer closely at it, awe and admiration etched into her round little face.

Pru gave a damp little laugh. They were fine. They were beautiful.

They had all survived the night. Now if she could just survive the rest of her journey with Colin.

* * *

Colin woke with a foul taste in his mouth and new bruises all over his body. Memory swept into his mind.

Gaffin's band. Pru in danger.

He remembered part of the night very clearly. After he'd been pinned down and stuffed with opium, everything was a smeary mix of images and sensation, smoke and dreams.

The dark chill of the cellar.

Pru in the rain. Pru wrapped around his cock, shivering in orgasm.

Oh, surely not. An opium dream. Unfortunately.

The smell of pig.

He lifted one arm and sniffed it. A trace of swine remained, nearly wiped out by the smell of soap.

Pru's hands roaming over his wet, naked body.

Her bodice soaked, her nipples rosy and evident.

No. Another dream.

Then the bathtub full of grimy water and the piles of soaked toweling by the fire caught his eye.

Perhaps not a dream, after all.

He dressed, moving his sore body carefully. His ribs ached with every motion. He'd had a few beatings in his time. The ribs didn't feel broken. He'd be fine in a few days. All in all, he'd come out fairly unscathed.

Which meant that he had no reason not to resume the search for Chantal at once.

He went down the stairs to see the inn looking as though nothing had happened. How long had he been asleep?

He smelled a meat stew and pushed open the door to the kitchen. Olive stood at the stove, stirring, while Pru sat at the table peeling potatoes. On the floor by the fire, Melody watched Evan play a game involving a handful of stones and a small India rubber ball while she chewed on a corner of Gordy Ann.

It was a blissful domestic scene. Oddly, it saddened Colin to his core.

What was he to do with Pru? She was too good for her position, too clever and brave by half to be a servant all her life. She glowed with honor and character, more beautiful than women with perfect faces.

Like Chantal's. He was finally convinced of Chantal's wickedness, but he had to carry on. He owed it to Melody to find the truth.

Pru looked up then and saw him. The smile she sent him was wry and knowing and a little sad. *Aren't we in a pickle?*

Indeed.

How could he do the right thing without losing the best friend he'd ever had?

CHAPTER 32

That afternoon, they left for Bath. Colin rode with Pru, Evan, and Melody inside the mumsy carriage while Bailiwick drove Balthazar in the traces. Hector trotted along behind, tied to the rear.

In the carriage, Colin held Melody in his lap, despite her pointy little knees and elbows digging into his bruised body. He'd been so worried the previous night that he couldn't bear to part with her now, not even to place her in the opposite seat.

Pru and Evan rode facing forward. They both fell asleep almost as soon as the ride began. At first Colin suspected that Pru was feigning sleep so that she would not have to converse with him, but false or not, sleep soon took her over for real.

She was obviously exhausted. Rightly so. She'd dealt with bandits and drugged men and pig shit and had still helped prepare dinner afterward.

She was quite a woman.

Colin couldn't take his eyes off her. In sleep her face was so sweet, so exotic and otherworldly. Her eyes were always so extraordinary that he sometimes saw little else. Yet her heart-shaped, delicate face was very pleasing. Thick russet lashes lay upon her cheeks. Freckles sprinkled across her nose. Her mouth was pink and soft and relaxed, free of her wry humor and terse retorts for once.

I should like to wake up to that sleepy face. Every morning for the rest of my life.

Yet how could it be so?

Feelings warred with obligations as the hours and miles passed. Melody finally slept as well, draped limply across his lap, Gordy Ann tucked beneath her chin in a gray little ball.

How could it be that he was probably going to spend the rest of his life with a woman he didn't love, and lose the one he did?

Love.

Oh, God. It was true. He loved mad, brave Miss Prudence Filby, seamstress. He loved her completely, trusted her utterly, accepted her—nay, cherished her!—precisely as she was.

Outspoken, outrageous, fierce, slightly vengeful Pru!

Colin passed a hand over his eyes, not denying the moisture there. Losing Pru was going to hurt, dear God, it was going to nearly kill him!

His fingers felt for his handkerchief but instead came in contact with crisp paper. Jack's letter.

Bailiwick had given it to him that afternoon, but Colin had not had an opportunity to read it. Now he broke the wax seal and unfolded the battered missive. It looked as though it had traveled halfway around the world.

"I will come back to Brown's."

At last. Of course, when Jack returned, Colin would be a married man, living in his own house and not the club.

Had Jack received any of their letters regarding Melody? Did he think he was returning to a daughter even now?

Sorry, old man. Life just doesn't turn out how you expect sometimes.

In front of the carriage, hearty Balthazar trotted on through the night, not stopping even when Bailiwick dozed at the reins.

Balthazar scarcely ever bothered to mind the reins anyway.

At dawn they reached the outskirts of Bath. Bailiwick stopped the carriage on the crest of the hill above the city and they all stumbled wearily out.

Freshly woken, Pru swept a strand of hair from before her eyes. "So this is Bath," she said flatly.

Evan came to stand beside her, his hands stuffed into his pockets. "Looks like Brighton, w'out the seagulls. Or the sea."

Melody clung to Pru's skirts. "I don't see a bath."

Colin swung her into his arms. "They'll be all around you, pet. The water comes bubbling up out of the ground boiling hot and all the people bob around in it like potatoes in the pot!"

Pru stepped out of the way of Colin's heartiness and turned back to the carriage. He was doing his best for Melody, she knew, but that didn't mean she had to like the idea of finding Chantal.

Damn you, Chantal.

She had always wanted to see Bath. Even in the midst of her gloom, the drive along the Crescent pierced her with the elegance of the architecture, the lovely houses gleaming like ivory in the morning sunlight. This was a place for the wealthy and the wish-they-were to play.

That wasn't her life. As soon as Colin found Chantal and released Pru from the duty of caring for Melody, she would begin searching for work. She took a deep breath and lifted her chin.

Hearing her name, she looked up to see Colin looking at her expectantly. The carriage was paused at a corner and Bailiwick was asking for direction through the little trap-door behind him. Pru realized that Colin had just asked her a question.

"Sorry, sir. What was it?"

He drew his brows together. "I asked you where Chantal might be staying while she is here. Do you have any ideas?"

Chantal, Chantal, Chantal. Pru sighed. "She only mentioned it in passing. I don't know . . ." But she did know Chantal, didn't she? She knew precisely where her previous employer's priorities lay. "The dressmaker, of course," she murmured aloud.

Colin blinked at her. "Truly?"

Pru shrugged wearily. "It's as good a place to start as any. Miss Marchant won't like the other ladies bein' ahead of her in style."

Colin chewed the inside of his lip. "No, I suppose she wouldn't. But Baldwin claimed she hadn't much money. How would she pay for dresses?"

Pru gazed at him in disbelief. "How does Chantal pay for anything?"

Evan snickered. She elbowed him on the sly without breaking her gaze with Colin. She watched him color slightly, then he glanced away.

He cleared his throat. "Right. Dressmakers. They'll be on Bartlett Street." Bailiwick snapped the reins and the carriage jolted into motion once more.

Another advantage to this matter being over soon. She'd never have to sit in this bloody conveyance ever again. Feet would be her carriage, nice, steady, slow feet. Back to a simpler life, just she and Evan.

Oh, yes, the simple life—a life of barest survival, of hunger and cold and the occasional bout of sheer terror.

Can't wait.

When they reached Bartlett Street, there was only one sign Colin needed to look for.

When he saw it, he pounded on the trapdoor. Bailiwick pulled over instantly. Balthazar snorted at such decisiveness, but Colin was tired of playing about.

He leaped lightly to the sidewalk. "We're here."

Pru blinked at him. "But we don't know which dressmaker she—"

Colin gave her a twist of his lips. "Shall we begin at the top?"

Pru gazed at him quizzically, then looked past him at the shopfront. Her eyes widened. "Lementeur? He'd be more'n Chantal could talk her way up to."

"Ah, but he knows everyone who is everyone and precisely what everyone is up to. I met him when he dressed Maddie and Melody for the wedding." Colin collected a drowsy Melody from where she'd been draped over Pru's lap. Pru glanced away when the back of his hand passed over her thigh.

Colin seemed not to notice. "Come on, Mellie. We've stopped. There's someone you'll like to see."

Evan seemed glad enough to jump down. "Naught but dresses," he muttered in disgust.

"Then you can tend Hector, Milord Finicky. He's been trotting back there all night." Pru stepped down smartly before Colin could offer his hand. Taking Melody from him and setting the child on her feet, she shook out her skirts and raised a brow. "Who'd have thought I'd ever go to Lementeur?"

As they entered the shop, Colin smiled at the young man who approached them. "Hello, Cabot. Is His Majesty about?"

Pru was gazing about her in curiosity, the girlish part of her sighing in pleasure at the luxurious, stylish surroundings. The room was elegantly furnished, almost like a parlor but for lengths of fine fabrics draped about, part function, part décor. Silks and satins and velvets. Hair bobs and ribbons and lacy jabots. Pru thrust her work-worn hands behind her, unwilling to sully any of the beautiful things.

Melody felt no such compunction. "Pretty!"

Then the man himself emerged. Small of stature, famous of name, trim and dapper and screamingly stylish, London's premier dressmaker emerged from somewhere, popping into view as if by magic.

"Sir Colin! What a lovely surprise!"

"Button!" Melody shrieked and ran for the small man. Lementeur laughed and unselfconsciously dropped to one knee to receive a Melody death-grip hug about his neck. Then he set her back upon her feet and bowed properly to her.

"Lady Melody, I am very pleased to see you again. How is Miss Gordy Ann this fine morning?"

Melody grinned and dropped a babyish curtsy of her own. "Gordy Ann needs a new dress to get merry."

"Ah." Lementeur tapped a finger to his lips thoughtfully. Then he whipped a silk handkerchief from his pocket and draped it across his arm as if he showed a rich damask to a duchess. "A fine Chinese silk, madam, dyed by aristocratic maidens in a perfumed garden. The very thing for such an esteemed client."

Melody giggled and accepted the handkerchief with a regal nod. "Thank you, Button." Then she dropped into a squat on the floor to tie the silk about Gordy Ann then and there.

Pru mentally applauded the man. He'd pleased Melody and gotten her out of the adults' way in a matter of seconds.

"Masterful," she murmured.

Lementeur's quick eyes flickered over her, assessing her from tip to toe. Pru oddly felt as though the man had measured her with entire accuracy.

Inside and out.

It turned out that Lementeur did indeed know of Miss Chantal Marchant. "She tends to make an impression. I don't know with whom she is staying, but she is oft accompanied by a Dr. Bennett to the finest parties in town. I don't doubt that she shall make an appearance at Lady Beverley's ball this evening. Dr. Bennett is a favorite of Lady Beverley's."

Colin nodded grimly. "If she is attending that ball, then so are we."

Pru felt a jolt of surprise. "We?"

Colin slid an unreadable glance at her. "We," he said, in a tone that brooked no argument. "You can do it. You mimic upper-class speech perfectly."

Lementeur's eyes danced. "Yes, I imagine she does."

Pru opened her mouth to protest, but Lementeur held up one hand. "Do not fret, my dear. I have the very thing. Lady Carlton turned up at her last fitting with a little passenger. I had to replan her entire summer wardrobe. One of her ball gowns was already finished. It will look admirable with your stunning hair."

"But—"

It was no use. Colin and Lementeur closed ranks against her and had the entire matter planned out before she could even form a protest.

Perhaps she didn't try as hard as she might have. She'd never been to a ball. She'd missed her coming out, her presentation, her first Season—all the things she and her mother had planned so dreamily so long ago.

I'm going to a ball, Mama.

With Sir Colin Lambert.

However, Pru knew perfectly well that it took days to prepare for an evening like this, if not weeks. She tried to convince her captors of this, but they only stared at her blankly.

Finally, Lementeur shook his head. "My dear, it is entirely possible to prepare for a ball in one day—if one is very rich." He smiled approvingly at Colin. "Very, very rich."

Pru narrowed her eyes at Colin. "Very, very? But you dress like an accountant! And you were going to fob me off with five pounds?"

He smiled at her grimly. "Always negotiate."

Swine. Pru folded her arms across her chest. "As you wish, guv. It'll cost you ten pounds to get me to go to this shindig and not a farthing less."

Colin's expression was priceless, but Lementeur only smiled.

"You should have asked for twenty, my dear. As I said, very, *very*."

CHAPTER 33

This time it was no rustic inn they checked into. Colin guided them all into an establishment that made Lementeur's shop seem almost monastic.

Pru followed Colin through the hushed and gilded lobby of the hotel in a daze. Liveried boys came to take her battered valise from her hand. Even Bailiwick was reduced to having his saddlebags carried for him.

And not once, not for a single moment, did any of the hotel staff look twice at their rumpled and worn appearance. They were treated with utmost respect and deference.

Very, *very* indeed.

Bloody hell!

Pru was shown to a room she would share with Melody, while Evan followed Colin and Bailiwick to the suite next door. A pretty chambermaid ordered her a bath and offered to help her undress. When Pru demurred, the girl curtsied deeply and left her with a steaming tub, a dish of scented soap, and a pile of toweling so luxurious it made Pru throb with acquisitive desire.

Though she'd bathed the day before, she didn't hesitate to submerge herself into the steaming decadence of the vast tub. Scented soap!

Melody helped her wash her hair and Pru surreptitiously made sure that Gordy Ann "fell" into the tub as well. All in all, the three of them had a lovely girlish time of it.

Afterward, Pru donned the satin dressing gown supplied by the chambermaid and sat down before the mirrored dressing table. Goodness, was that her? She hadn't had a moment to examine herself in a glass for years.

Well. She wasn't as plain as she remembered, which was nice to know. Rather more freckles than she'd like. Her mother had recommended lemon juice. With her pockets full of Sir Colin's very-very, she mused that she just might indulge in a lemon now and then.

She took up the silver bristle brush and began to work it through her hair. As it dried she brushed it smooth and shining over her shoulders.

When a knock came at her door, she jumped up to answer. The borrowed gown was due any moment.

To her surprise, she opened the door on Lementeur himself. He tilted his head and regarded her with open pleasure. "Oh, my. Yes, indeed."

In he came, followed by several of the hotel staff toting a large box, a small box, several paper-wrapped parcels, and a leather-strapped case.

"Thank you, thank you." Lementeur clapped his hands and the minions departed, filing out in the same order in which they had entered. In moments, he had shooed Melody off to Bailiwick next door, where her supper awaited her. "Off with you, Lady Melody. A party with your own personal guard giant. You and Gordy Ann will enjoy yourselves immensely."

Unbelievably, Melody scuttled off without the tiniest protest.

This is a dream. A very odd, very nice dream. A dream which I am shamelessly going to enjoy to its fullest.

After all, it was only a dream.

Then Lementeur took over and it was all Pru could do to breathe at her own pace. First, he plunked her down at the dressing table and did mysterious things to her hair, which he would not let her see.

Then it became truly strange. Though entirely polite and gentle, Lementeur would brook no demur as he stripped her naked and dressed her from the skin out.

Silk pantalets. Silk chemise. A corset so light and well made that it lifted her bust and refined her waist without restricting her breath or movement in the slightest. Clocked stockings with blue silk garters. An underskirt of cotton batiste so fine that it might as well have been silk.

Then he ordered her to close her eyes. She heard him open the large box. Raising her arms obediently when ordered, she felt him lower a gown over her head and settle it down over her body.

She tried to peek but he would have none of it until he'd done up every last button and even then he insisted on sliding perfectly fitted dancing slippers onto her feet first.

Then he turned her and positioned her carefully.

"Now you may look."

Pru opened her eyes. At first she couldn't grasp that the figure she saw in the oval standing mirror was not some priceless portrait decorating her room.

Then she realized that the flame-haired goddess in the glass was herself.

The gown was blue. Yet to say it so simply was to insult the radiant, iridescent azure silk. With her every tiny movement, it shimmered like moonlight on a pool of water.

The cut was deceptively simple. A graceful Grecian-style bodice appeared to be loosely draped and gathered, but her breasts were supported and displayed with no chance of some unfortunate neckline mishap. However, to the outside observer, her bosom looked as though it was considering its very own debut. The tiny cap sleeves only emphasized her natural assets.

She'd never realized she owned such a lot of creamy, seductive real estate!

Where most gowns hung from a high waist and concealed the lower body, this one clung to every curve as if it were wet. It wasn't tight in the slightest, yet every time Pru angled her body to see it in the mirror, a new part of her anatomy was briefly and seductively outlined before the silk fell away again. This magnetic effect collaborated with the elegance of the fabric to make one think one was imagining such a shameless display.

The gown, bosom included, was the largest bit of theater. The rest of her appearance was uncomplicated, even plain, yet screamed expensive elegance.

Her hair was wound simply about her head with tiny, curled tendrils "escaping" at her brow and a surprising fall of loosely curling locks down her back. With no ornament save a single blue ribbon, her auburn hair shone like a crown of dark fire.

Her face looked entirely bare of embellishment, except for the divine fact that her freckles had gone missing, yet her eyes had never been so large and darkly mysterious.

Incredible.

She couldn't help herself. "Bloody hell!"

Lementeur laughed out loud. "Most gratifying, if a tad on the vulgar side. Still, I shall take credit where credit is due. I am a genius. However, you, my dear, are a true beauty."

Pru twisted and turned in the glass, trying to see herself from all sides. A true beauty?

"I don't look half nice and that's a fact, sir, but this is all your doin'."

Lementeur took her hand and smiled gently at her in the mirror. "Don't you think it's time you left that charming but unsuitable accent behind you? Do you truly need it any longer?"

Pru froze. Yet, what had she to fear from this man?

She smiled back then, a little shyly, not accustomed to being herself. "How did you find me out, sir?"

Lementeur regarded her with a slight tilt to his head. "Perfect posture. Refined grace. A voice like an angel. And when you forget yourself in a moment of temper, you hold your chin at such a haughty angle that I dare Princess Charlotte to do better."

Pru blinked. "You are most observant, sir. I pray Sir Colin does not follow your example."

He shook his head. "Why not simply tell him? Whatever difficulty forces this charade, he would help you out of it. He is a very admirable fellow."

Pru sighed. It was only a soft exhalation, but Lementeur's brows shot skyward.

"Ah. You love him. And he seeks another."

Pru blinked away the heat behind her eyes. "It is not his fault. He only wishes to legitimize Melody."

She clapped her fingers over her wayward mouth and gazed at Lementeur in alarm.

He only smiled, his eyes crinkling at the corners. "My dear, I am well acquainted with Lady Melody's . . . er, parental mysteries. Is Sir Colin so very sure of this Miss Marchant, then? You worked for her. Is she truly Melody's mother?"

Pru shrugged miserably. "I could not say. I did not know her at that time. It is possible, I suppose. She is not very . . . self-restrained."

Lementeur quirked a brow. "How polite. I think I preferred you before."

She couldn't help quirking a grin at him. "Whatever you say, guv. It bein' your dress and all."

He smiled back. "Delightful." Turning, he retrieved a deep midnight-blue cloak from yet another box and swung it into a great circle over her shoulders. Then he slipped the hood carefully over her hair, so that her entire costume was concealed. "Keep that on until you've arrived at the ball." He squinted playfully at her. "Mystery is *everything*."

Then he stood back and regarded her with pride. "Off with you, Princess Prudence. Your prince awaits you in the carriage."

CHAPTER 34

They arrived at the ball in a fine rented coach.

"We don't have an invitation, so we need to look as though we belong," Colin told her. It was almost the only thing he said to her. Of course, she remained silent, concealed in her cloak, trying her best to portray "mystery."

Colin looked rather mysterious himself, clad in a black evening cape from Lementeur. Pru was almost as eager for his unveiling as she was for her own!

Their lack of invitation did not cause them grief, although Pru noted that the footman's hand did go to his pocket after he allowed them entrance.

"Is there anyone you cannot bribe?"

"My family fortune is finally good for something." Colin lifted one shoulder in a disinterested shrug. "Don't forget to speak carefully."

Pru nodded silently. Sir Colin had a surprise in store. She smoothed the ribbon tie of her cloak and took a deep breath as a footman approached to take their things. This was her chance to see if Colin would be attracted to the real Miss Prudence Filby!

She slipped off the cloak in a single graceful move, handed it to the waiting footman, then turned to see Colin's reaction.

Colin froze in the act of removing his hat and cape, leaving the footman reaching for nothing at all.

She shimmered. Her gown was a clinging confection of

blue silk, and the perfect counterpoint to the russet hair that tumbled from an intricate knot high on her head, flowing down her back in a mad silken cloud. There was something different about her eyes. He couldn't decipher the mystery of feminine cosmetics, but her eyes were huge and shining.

And then there was her bosom. He'd seen those breasts in a damp shift and in a damp nightdress—God, he loved it when Pru got wet!—but he'd never seen them displayed thus, with a barely functioning neckline not quite containing them, served up for a man's enjoyment like sumptuous pastries on a platter.

She was entirely elegant and refined—and yet she was also more nearly naked than he'd ever seen her!

He nearly choked. "Put that cloak back on!"

She grinned at him then, much like she had grinned at him in his opium-soaked dream, like a wild pirate girl. "That's the nicest compliment you've ever paid me." She held out her arm. "Shall we dance?"

When he silently and grimly took her arm, Pru had to turn away to hide her laughter. Mystery, indeed!

The gown felt delicious, clinging sensuously to her legs as she walked into the ballroom. It had been a long time since she had felt anything but the most utilitarian fabrics against her skin. Even the fine lawn shift beneath seemed to stroke her flesh with every movement of her body. By the time she had made her way into the ballroom at Colin's side, the heat was already rising in her blood.

It didn't help that Colin looked magnificent. Clad in perfectly tailored black, he seemed darker and more dashing than before. He seemed to tower over lesser men and the brilliance from the chandeliers turned his fair hair to gold. He looked like a pirate prince surrounded by his minions. Then he turned to someone and smiled. The flash of white teeth against his sun-darkened skin made Pru's heart stutter.

Even his stance was different, with a haughty tilt to his head that told everyone he was a man of substance here.

Pru faltered in her steps, suddenly unsure of herself. She'd known he was a gentleman. She'd realized he had a certain amount of wealth and status . . . but it was something else to see it with her own eyes.

Then he turned and his gaze locked on hers. He smiled as he bowed. "My apologies. I do not believe we have been introduced. Sir Colin Lambert. And you are? If I am not too forward?"

He was being silly, and bold, and far too flirtatious—an aspect of him she had never before seen.

Throwing caution and the past and even the future to the winds, she curtsied deeply in response. "You are bold, but all great adventurers are, are they not?" She gave him a dimpled smile when he took her hand to help her rise. "Introductions are for people who worry too much about the morrow."

You are not the only one who can be too bold!

The flash of humor in his green eyes was reward enough. He swept her into his arms and they began to dance.

With Pru swaying gracefully in his arms, Colin enjoyed dancing more than he ever had before. She was a good dancer, moving to the precise steps as if she'd been born to them.

It wasn't long until other men began to appear to beg an introduction. Pru greeted them gravely and politely thanked them for their thoughtfulness, but would dance with no one but Colin.

He knew it was only so that her ruse would not be penetrated, but her obvious preference made him want to beat his chest! Dance after dance, they whirled about the floor, ostensibly searching for Chantal, yet unable to take their eyes from each other.

Abruptly, Colin was no longer in a hurry to find Chantal. This was the last time he would be with Pru like this, he realized.

Just one night. Just this moment, I want to believe that it is she who awaits me in bed tonight. Tomorrow. Forever.

She seemed more than willing to play along with his fantasy. She danced, she laughed, she sipped champagne and fended off suitors as if she'd been training for this night her entire life.

And then it finally penetrated his dream state. She was very good at such mimicry.

Too good.

Even Chantal wasn't that good.

He halted in mid-turn and stared down at her. Pru smiled up at him, her eyes laughing. "Did you forget the steps, Sir Colin?"

He shook his head slightly. "Who are you?"

She drew back, her brow crinkling. "What?"

He looked down at them both, at how her hands were placed perfectly, at how her head was lifted at just the right angle, remembering that not once, not even one single time, had she stepped on his foot.

"Who the bloody hell are you?"

She backed slowly out of his hold, her eyes wide and her lips parted. Then she turned without a word and slipped off into the whirling dancers.

Pru didn't stop running until she had run from the crowd and even from the house itself. She took refuge in the dark gardens, fleeing down the gravel paths until the fine corset took its toll on her ability to breathe.

There was a stone bench nearby. Pru sank down onto it. Her lungs were nearly bursting and her brain buzzed with champagne. She didn't hear the footsteps crunching on the gravel until far too late.

It wasn't until she raised her head from her hands that she realized that he stood directly before her. Sitting up straight, she lifted her chin to glare at him. "You needn't loom so, Mr. Lambert. Even a weed needs a bit o' sun to grow."

He didn't smile as she'd thought he might. His expression as he gazed at her was harder than she'd ever seen on him before. She edged backward warily on the bench.

"It is night. No sun." His voice was clipped.

She looked away. "Now you're just bein' particular."

"Yes. Particular."

The gravel on the path crunched beneath his feet as he took a step closer. If she wished to look at him now she would have to tilt her head all the way back. This was not a problem, for she most assuredly did not want to look at him. She looked at his boots, gleaming in the moonlight. Fascinating . . . and much easier to bear than the strange, considering expression upon his face.

He stood so close she could hear the rasp of his inhalation. "Miss Filby, how is it that you happen to know how to dance the quadrille?"

"Even servants dance, sir. Belowstairs, if we can 'ear the music."

He was silent for a moment. "How did you know just the perfect depth to curtsy to the Duke of Clements?"

Blast. She ought to have fumbled that. "Did I? I just did what I seen Chant—Miss Marchant do on stage, sir."

The silence stretched out this time. Blue shine, silver flickers. Stars pasted on the void. The chill in her belly grew.

"When you speak, Miss Filby, why is there not the slightest hint of commoner in your speech—not even a fragment of a hint?"

"I'm a right good mimic, I am."

"Indeed. My question is, which speech is the mimicry and which is the tongue you were born to?"

The soles of his shoes grated on the pebbles again. His boots disappeared beneath the hem of her skirts, his toes just barely contacting hers.

She raised her gaze now, for she had no shiny leather on which to fix her eyes. Lifting her head slowly, she followed those black-clad legs up. Perhaps she could meet his eyes and not give anything away, perhaps she could keep her wits about her long enough to—

She gasped aloud. Oh, heavens.

Even in the dimness she could see that his trousers were tight about his enormous erection.

I covet you.

Her body sounded a responding chord. *Yes. Here. Now.*

She turned her face away with a jerk and then went so still that she could hear her own pulse pound in her ears. Had he heard her gasp? Did he know what she'd seen?

If she touched it would it feel like flesh or steel?

As the thought ran through her mind like a sneak thief in flight, slipping in and out of the dark places, her body gave a deep shudder in response.

"Are you chilled?" His voice was raspy now. He sounded nearly as breathless as she was.

She shook her head quickly, not trusting herself to speak, not trusting her voice not to give her away as his did.

An instant of contact, feather light. His fingertips pushing back a wisp of her hair that had fallen awry. Her heart nearly stopped its furious pounding. *Oh, God, don't let him touch me. If he touches me I shall leap upon him and devour him whole.*

Please touch me.

CHAPTER 35

Pru's champagne-glamoured thoughts bubbled in her mind. While her mind was busy, it seemed her hand decided to act on its own. She watched, as if from a distance, as her hand, white in the dimness, moved outward toward him, not stopping—oh, my, where was this leading?—until it found its home covering the bulge in his breeches.

Too far.

Or was it? Had he not touched her there, touched her and more?

"Fair is fair," she whispered to herself. She heard a gasp from him, a sort of desperate laughing sound, but she ignored it. This was between her hand and his groin.

He was hard and hot, even through the fabric she touched. Her head tilted to one side in bemusement as her rogue hand traced the outline of his swollen shape. It grew even as her fingers stroked it lightly. A deep groan from him seemed to wake her other hand to action. It floated through the air to join the first one, pressing and stroking and—

What was this? Buttons? Yes, on either side of his trapped organ, there were two rows of buttons.

Let's see what happens . . .

The buttons were no work at all. Nor was the drawstring of the drawers beneath. Then, like a gift given with a deep heartfelt gasp, his erection sprang into her hands.

Cock, Chantal had named it. Cock, indeed. Proud and strong and so absolutely part of *him*.

A marvelous development, all told.

Her wayward fingers enfolded him, both hands, yet there was more. He was so rigid, so hard yet sensuous, like a sword wrapped in silk. His long finger had delved into her and driven her mad. What would this mighty weapon do to her?

A deep shudder traveled her body, starting in that very center place.

Cunt, Chantal had called it.

Cock and Cunt. Sword and Sheath. Meant for one another. *Oh, yes.*

Her entire body now seemed to be under the tutelage of her rogue hands, for she observed that she was now leaning forward.

She kissed the tip of him. He gasped and jerked in her hands, but she would not free him until she was done with him. Not that he seemed truly interested in pulling away.

She kissed him again, this time with her lips soft and parted. The tip of him was damp. She licked him from her lips. As she did so, her tongue accidentally rolled over the blunt end of him. His hand landed in her hair, warm and pleading but not forcing her closer. No, she did that on her own, falling closer to him until the rounded head of him slipped between her wetted lips and into her mouth.

He tasted of salt and something new, something she'd never tasted before. Sharp and stimulating, like a spice. She drew on the head of him experimentally, sucking gently as her tongue explored the blunt end, the edges of the rounded cap, the curious slit at the tip.

"Oh, sweet heaven . . ." His voice was guttural, deep and groaning and helpless.

Was he helpless before her? Truly? How *marvelous*.

Testing this theory, she wrapped her hands tightly around

the base of him and guided more of his length into her mouth. How deep could she take him? He filled her mouth until he pressed nearly into her throat, yet there was still more of him left outside. Reluctantly, she began to withdraw from the experiment.

He cried out, a sound of surprise and ecstasy combined. She'd forgotten to release the suction, she realized. Did that give him pleasure?

She drove him deep into her mouth again, then pulled very slowly away, sucking. As she drew near the end of him, she let her tongue free to slide over and around him, tasting that sharp flavor once more.

He made that sound again. Out loud, as if he had no care or awareness of being heard. Curious, she looked up at him to see that his head was thrown back. One hand was tangled in her hair and the other was fisted at his side.

Wanting to make him cry out for her more, she sucked him again and again, sliding him in and out of her mouth, tasting him, tasting power, making him gasp and moan and beg. The great slippery size of him in her mouth and in her hands made her grind her own body down into the bench. The noises coming from him made her feel hungry and helpless as well.

He moaned. "Oh, yes . . . Oh, Pru!" Abruptly, his hand fisted in her hair and his entire body spasmed as his cock jumped and throbbed inside her mouth. The taste of him flowed over her tongue, strong and thick and creamy. She swallowed out of instinct, swallowed while he remained inside her mouth, making him gasp once more. He stood there, shuddering and gasping, his hand in her hair, for a long moment. Then he seemed to catch his breath. One warm hand wrapped around her jaw and he pulled himself from her mouth.

Still a bit lost in the dark and the heat and the taste of him, it took Pru a moment to realize that it was over.

Bloody hell. She was still thrumming with heat and ache and want.

Colin put himself away and rebuttoned his breeches, trying to still his own spinning thoughts. So good, so damned good—the hot wetness of her mouth, her sweet tongue, her intent to give him pleasure—

But wrong. He ought to have stopped her. He never should have allowed it.

When he'd put himself together again, he turned back to her. She sat on the bench, her hands braced on either side of her, her eyes wide as she gazed back at him.

Then she absently licked her lips.

His cock throbbed in response, as if she'd called it by name. She'd swallowed him. How flattering.

I never even kissed her. How rude of me.

In one step, he was down on his knees in the gravel where he'd stood before and his mouth was on hers. A simple thank-you kiss, soft and sweet.

Until she moaned into his mouth.

Oh, no. No. Absolutely not.

Oh, yes.

His hands came up to wrap around her jaw, holding her still as he thrust his tongue deep into her mouth, finding the hot depths. His cock had known those depths. The knowledge drove him wild.

He felt her hands fist in his weskit, pulling him close. Fighting for sense, he lifted his mouth from hers and dropped his face into her neck, panting. *Think. For God's sake, think!*

"Pru . . . I can't."

She was breathing hard, every exhalation almost a whimper of need in his ear. "I . . . I need . . ."

God, she was sweet. So passionate, so intense, and yet so innocent. She had not even the words to ask for what she wanted.

He knew, however. He knew what her body was doing to her. He knew how to save her from it.

Honor forbade him from going further. Basic good manners decreed that he not leave her like this.

Perhaps . . . perhaps there was a way . . .

He moved, standing then straddling the bench facing her. She turned toward him, moonlit eyes confused. "Shh," he said. Then he kissed her, wrapping one arm about her and pulling her sideways into him. She crooked one arm over his neck and kissed him back, eager and heated and lost.

Oh, my sweet Pru.

Reaching down with his other hand, he slid it beneath her hem and up her calf and over her knee. Her thighs parted easily as she gasped into his mouth. She was damp and hot and tender, for she jumped at his slightest touch.

Easy. Slow and easy.

Pru nearly cried with gratitude as she felt his fingers flick softly over her. He deepened his kiss, parting her lips with his tongue even as his fingertip entered her. He penetrated deeply, leaning her back in his hold. His thumb found the nerve-filled button of her clitoris and stroked it gently, round and round.

The combined sensation of his exploring tongue, his thrusting finger, and his clever, clever thumb made her tense with aching pleasure. Yes. Yes, finally—

Then a second long finger joined the first inside her, slipping into her tightness, pressing deep, thrusting slowly in, then pulling slowly out. She recognized the rhythm from her own oral adventures even as her hips rocked in instinctive response.

Knowing him, trusting him, she released all thought and fell into the pleasure. She hooked one arm around his neck and let the rest of her body go, melting wax in his hands. She moaned into his mouth, she quivered and she rocked and her body burned like hot ice. Fingers rubbing, thrusting, teasing, tormenting, driving her up, toward something new. She followed mindlessly, entirely his creature, submitting to every stroke, every thrust.

Yes . . . yes . . . closer . . .

She whimpered in her need. He responded by increasing the speed of his penetration, of his slippery thumb. He pulled her tight to his body as he impaled her again and again, a sweet invasion, a tender violation, a hot, wet, mad, plunging race to somewhere—

She ached, she throbbed, she rocked into every thrust, reaching, reaching. *Oh, yes. Please!*

She spasmed tight around his fingers. Shock resounded through her, echoing shocks undulating outward like shimmering ripples in a fiery pond!

She clutched at him, she cried out and gasped and didn't bloody care—

Oh, sweet heaven!

Flying, flinging, floating, spinning—it was like nothing she'd ever known and yet she knew it was right, oh, yes, so very right—

When her heart had slowed its desperate pounding and her breath was actually filling her lungs adequately, she became dimly aware that he'd smoothed her skirts down and now held her quite sedately in his arms.

I just did something scandalous in Lady Beverley's garden! She turned her face into Colin's chest and began to gasp.

His arms tightened about her. "Don't weep, sweet Pru."

Helpless giggles bubbled up from within her, spilling into the night air. She buried her face in his weskit and laughed and laughed, every embarrassing, titillating detail coming back to her.

"Somehow, you never do quite the expected, do you?" he commented dryly. "I can't decide whether to be flattered or insulted."

"Hmm . . . flattered," she managed. "Very flattered . . . not that I've anything to compare it to."

"Again with the faint praise," he mused. "Pru, you do know how to keep a man humble."

At that moment they heard voices approaching. A man and a woman. Quickly they straightened and composed themselves and sat completely nonchalantly. Around the corner of the path came a couple. The woman was elegant and black-haired and beautiful.

Colin jumped to his feet. "Chantal!"

Chantal halted with a gasp of horror, then stepped backward, stumbling slightly. Then she turned and picked up her skirts and ran back down the path. Her companion followed her with a cry of protest. Colin ran as well, leaving Pru sitting wide-eyed and stunned on the bench.

"Chantal. Of bloody course."

Taking a deep breath, she stood, forcing her rubbery knees to behave. More sedately than anyone else, thank you, she walked down the path, following the others back toward the great house.

CHAPTER 36

When Pru reached the ballroom, it was just in time to see Chantal, still pursued by the two men, stagger to a halt in the middle of the dance floor and then swoon elegantly and very publicly into Colin's arms. Pru couldn't hold back a bitter little laugh. Of course, because if Chantal had swooned a moment earlier in the garden, she wouldn't have had an audience.

The entire ballroom was enraptured with the dramatics. When Chantal swooned, there was a great united gasp of alarm. When Colin swept Chantal up into his arms like a rescuing hero, a sigh of romantic satisfaction swept the circling crowd. It was one of Chantal's finest performances. Too bad she'd missed it.

Pru now had to push through the gathered elite to reach the others. Chantal's companion, a stocky fellow of middle years, gestured urgently and guided Colin, who bore Chantal as lightly as a feather, off to a side chamber.

Don't follow. He has found her at last. You know what is about to happen. Really, really, don't.

I might as well see this through to the end.

Then you're a fool!

Oh, yes. That I know.

Pru followed the three of them into the retiring room, pausing in the doorway to observe the two men bending over the elegant figure draped becomingly over a chaise longue. It truly couldn't have been better staged. The small antechamber was luxurious in cream and gold. Chantal wore a vibrant purple, the one that matched her famous "twilight eyes." The contrast was striking and attractive, so that the woman in the center of the room captured one's eye entirely.

Pru wondered sourly if the scheming creature had investigated the very colors decorating the great house and had dressed accordingly.

Taking a deep breath, she entered the room, circling the two men until she stood at Chantal's head. Chantal lay on her back on the chaise, exquisitely posed, one slender wrist upturned above her head, her long neck arched back and her perfect face perfectly turned to capture the perfect light.

Pru bit back a snarl.

Still so beautiful, even wasted by addiction. Nonetheless, as Pru looked closer, it was clear that however elegantly coiffed and superbly dressed, Chantal was not the woman she had been. Always pale, the actress's skin was now very nearly transparent. She was thinner than Pru had ever seen her, her once bounteous figure now wasted away. The most alarming development was the bluish tint to her faultless lips.

Pru looked at Colin. "Is this because of her addiction?"

Colin shook his head. "I don't know. We need a physician."

The other man shot them both a scathing glare. "I *am* Miss Marchant's physician! I am Dr. Bennett." He knelt next to the chaise and took Chantal's wrist in his fingers, checking her pulse. "Fools! Making her run from you, in her condition! I think you should leave—you've done more than enough damage this evening!"

Colin ignored the demand. "We were told that Chantal is addicted to opium. Is she suffering from that now?"

The doctor grimaced disdainfully and looked as though he'd like to disregard Colin entirely, but he answered. "It is true that Miss Marchant has developed a dependence on opium, but only because of the great pain that she suffers every moment of every day."

Colin frowned. "Pain?" he asked urgently. "What is this pain?"

Even as she watched, Pru could see the sympathy and regret grow in Colin's beautiful eyes. He was slipping farther away from her with every moment.

How can you lose what was never truly yours?

Dr. Bennett finished his examination and stood, turning to face Colin with fury on his face. "Miss Marchant suffers from damage to her heart, you idiot! She is constantly weary and unable to handle great excitement." He glared at them both. "Something that the two of you seem determined to cause!"

Her heart? *I didn't know she had one.*

Pru was instantly ashamed. Chantal was obviously ill. Thinking back, Pru realized that she had been for some time. *I am terrible.* She'd been so busy resenting Chantal that she'd never realized the woman wasn't well.

Yet how could she know? Chantal, however indolent, was never without the energy to snipe or backstab. Chantal always had the strength to be unfailingly vain and shallow and unkind. Now Pru's mind's eye showed her a clearer memory of Chantal, growing gradually more pale and listless.

However, she'd not complained of any ailment—and since when did Chantal not complain?

Since she thought her career would end when people discovered she was ill.

On the chaise, Chantal stirred. When her eyes opened, she gasped. "Gaffin!"

Colin turned toward her immediately, bending over her. "No, Chantal. Gaffin is not here."

Chantal's panicked eyes searched the room. "I saw him! In the garden! He found me!"

Colin took her hand gently. "Chantal, you saw me in the garden. Gaffin is on his way to Blackpool—where he thinks you have fled to avoid him."

Chantal blinked up at Colin. For a moment, it seemed to Pru that she didn't recognize him—a notion that went a long way to cheering Pru up—but then Chantal reached a pale, languid hand to touch Colin's face. "Is it you? Are you my darling Colin Lambert?"

Colin laid his hand over hers, pressing it to his cheek. "It is I, Chantal. I found you. You are safe from Gaffin now."

Limpid blue-violet eyes, ringed in thick lashes, glazed in just the right amount of tears, gazed up at him. "You saved me! My darling clever man! I owe you my eternal gratitude!"

"Actually, it was I who was clever," Pru pointed out under her breath. "Sir Colin was playing with the pigs just then."

Chantal noticed Pru then, but simply scoffed prettily and looked away again. Colin shot Pru a quelling glance, making her feel instantly ashamed of herself. Why did she allow Chantal to bring out the worst in her?

"Sir Colin?" Chantal clutched at Colin. "My love, it is all such a terrible misunderstanding! I had to flee Brighton to avoid him! This . . . little problem . . . of mine has made me quite desperate, I'm afraid. Gaffin has somehow acquired the notion that I took something from him. You don't believe I'm a thief, do you, my darling?"

Colin patted her hands and eased her back on the chaise. "You have nothing to worry about, Chantal. Don't upset yourself. You've been very ill."

"Ill." Chantal sighed, a sweet, long-suffering exhalation. "Yes. I am dying."

Colin lifted his head in surprise, shooting a questioning glance at the doctor.

Dr. Bennett nodded shortly. "I must fetch my bag," he said. "See that she remains quiet." He left the room.

Dying? Stricken, Pru knelt next to Chantal's chaise longue. "You ought to have said something. I could have helped you."

Chantal fixed her with a look of irritated scorn. "You? You couldn't sew a flea onto a dog."

Pru backed away, fighting back the urge to retort. What did it matter now?

Limpid eyes turned back to Colin. "I can't believe you came for me, my darling. Of all my many—of the few gentlemen I've become acquainted with, you are clearly the most worthy."

"Chantal." Colin's voice was husky. His intimate tone struck Pru deep in her belly like a knife. If she'd been alone she would have doubled over from the pain of it.

Colin knelt next to the chaise where Pru had just been, but Chantal did not push him away. When he leaned close, her pose softened invitingly and her face rose to meet his.

"Chantal, I must ask you a very important question. When you turned me away three years ago, did I leave you with my child?"

Colin felt Chantal's body stiffen and his cheek warmed from the long sigh she gave. "Your . . . child."

"It's all right, Chantal," he said gently. "I have her in my care. I only want to legitimize her and bring her mother home to my estate."

"Oh." It was a long soft sound. A sigh of relief at truth finally told? He saw her beautiful eyes were filled with tears of happiness and she was nodding. "Yes. Yes, my dearest. Bring me home."

Yes.

That was that, then. Somewhere inside him, a hope he hadn't realized he nurtured died with a faint and futile gasp. He sent the pain someplace deep and cleared his throat. When he spoke the words, they came out louder than he'd intended. "Chantal, will you be my wife?"

Behind him he heard a faint noise of protest. A noise that Pru quickly stifled.

I'm sorry, my love.

"Oh, my darling!" Chantal's pale cheeks flushed in eager patches of pink. "I cannot believe it! I am the most fortunate of women! I have dreamed of this moment for so very long!"

Then she cast a triumphant look over his shoulder. "Filby, must you gawk? Isn't there something useful you could be doing someplace else? Someone must want a crooked bodice or a bunchy hem!"

There was a sudden rustle of skirts and Colin turned just in time to see the aforementioned skirts disappearing through the chamber door. He started to rise.

Chantal pulled him back by the hand. The desperation of her grip was surprising in its strength.

She smiled up at him enticingly. "My love, my darling, we must talk. There is so much to do—to plan!"

CHAPTER 37

Late that night, Colin finally entered his room at the hotel. It had taken hours to convince Chantal that the best thing for everyone was a quiet ceremony, as soon as possible. Perhaps he shouldn't have been surprised that she carried fantasies of a full-blown, theatrical production of a wedding. Chantal never did anything by halves.

Moving quietly, he took a candle from the fireplace mantel and lighted it from a glowing coal. He glanced at the sofa by the fire, expecting to find Bailiwick awkwardly cramped upon it and possibly Evan as well, long asleep.

Instead, he saw a woman poised just outside the circle of light cast by the candle. Frowning, he peered toward the shadowy figure. "Pru?"

A familiar voice came from the dimness, beautiful and familiar yet new. "I have something to say to you, Sir Colin." Gone was any attempt to sound like a simple servant girl.

Colin tossed his hat and gloves down onto the table by the door. "I have much to say to you, as well. We did not finish our conversation in the garden."

A low laugh came. "We might have, but you do tend to forget what you're about sometimes."

Colin felt himself blush as he remembered the pleasure she'd given him. He thrust his hands behind his back, for he truly didn't know what else to do with them. Reaching for her would be a very bad idea. Unfortunately, it was an idea that would not leave him be.

Then she stepped forward into the light. His Pru . . . except not his Pru at all. Not the devastating coquette of the ball, either. This Pru wore a simple sprigged muslin gown instead of her gabardine servant's dress. A gentlewoman's gown. It was a little out of date and a tad small in the bodice, but he was never one to object to a little emphasis on the bosom. He'd never before seen her in anything like it.

"You look like . . ."

"A lady?" She smiled and stepped a little closer. He could see that she wore her beautiful hair loose and long, bound back only by a single ribbon, a river of dark fire down her back.

"Yes."

"I am a lady, Sir Colin."

When he gazed at her without comprehension, she went on. "I am Miss Prudence Filby, daughter of Mr. Atticus Filby, a gentleman and a philanthropist, and Adele Spencer Filby. Very old families both." A flash of the old irreverent Pru appeared in a quick grin. "I'm a toff!"

A lady. It shouldn't be possible . . . and yet, he'd known. Her mimicry was too good, the manners too deeply bred, even the way she danced, whirling with the ease that only thorough tutoring gave.

He rubbed a hand over his face. A lady. "Pru, how can this be? You were living out in the world, working at the theater—you were starving!"

Smoothing her gown a little self-consciously, she nodded. "Our parents died five years ago. Evan and I had to make our own way. I was too young and without friends—I could not find respectable employment. Folk are more willing to hire a common girl."

"Which you are not." Abruptly, he found he was offended. "You lied. You lied to *me*."

"Yes." She gazed at him gravely. "I am sorry about that. At first it was simply because I didn't know you. There was too much at stake to trust a stranger. Later, well . . . I almost told you so many times."

"And yet you didn't."

"Neither did you," she retorted with some asperity. "Melody is your child and Chantal is her mother. Facts you neglected to mention when we first met!"

"I . . . I almost told you, so many times." He rubbed his neck. Then another thought struck him with horror. "You're a lady! I—oh, my God, the things I've done to you!"

Honor dictated that he wed a young lady he had compromised so. Honor also dictated that he wed the mother of his child. He gazed at Pru, making no effort to hide his pain. "Chantal and I are now engaged." Shame swept him. He felt as though he'd been unfaithful, as if it were Pru who was his bride and Chantal who was his mistress.

Pru's eyes were luminous. "Yes, I know. I heard you propose."

"It isn't . . ." What could he say? "I only want . . ."

"You want to make Melody legitimate, of course. Completely understandable. Admirable, even. You would do anything for Melody. As would I."

Colin shook his head, confused. "If you know all of this, then why, tonight in the garden—"

She moved forward, graceful and serene. Her eyes gleamed silver in the candlelight. "Sir Colin, don't be an idiot. Tonight in the garden was because I love you, of course."

His heart thudded. *She loves me!*

She mustn't.

Yet I love her, too!

He mustn't.

"Oh." *Idiot! Say something better than that! Say what you truly want to say!* Ache and longing welled up from so deep inside him, his throat was almost too tight to speak. His vision blurred. "I—"

In one rustling step, she darted close enough to press a finger to his lips.

"Don't," she whispered, her eyes burning into his, her beautiful voice thick with grief. "Don't *ever*." Then she stepped back, visibly drawing herself together once more.

Pru lifted her chin and tried to smile at him. "You wished to know who I am. That is who I am."

He nodded. "I see now. You and Evan were orphaned and left penniless—"

Pru shook her head, her smile growing. "Not penniless. Not in the slightest."

Colin frowned at her. "Not? But you—the theater—five pounds—your *boots*!"

She blinked at him in surprise. "What's wrong with my boots? They come in very handy when a fellow gets too . . . handy."

Colin closed his eyes. "I have had a very long day," he said tightly. "I would like to know more about this 'not penniless' situation, if you don't mind."

Pru smiled at him fondly through the mist of tears she would not shed. Such a darling man. Even when disoriented and exasperated, he never lost his temper. She should be ashamed of herself, but she'd never been able to resist winding him up a bit.

Lucky, lucky Chantal.

"Colin," she said softly. He opened his beautiful green eyes. They were so filled with pain she ached doubly for him. "In six years, Evan will be eighteen years of age. When that day comes, he will inherit my father's fortune."

Moving slowly, she began to circle him as if idly wandering the room. "Until then, his fate was given into the hands of people my parents trusted. They revealed themselves to be vile, evil schemers and we fled them. Since that day, I have worked to keep us safe and mostly fed."

He shook his head. "Miss Prudence Filby. Lady gone rogue."

"I believe the inheritance totals more than four thousand pounds. Enough to live a gentleman's life, enough to buy a small manor—"

Colin interrupted. "Enough to provide his sister with a tempting dowry."

Pru ignored the point, taking a few more steps. Colin turned with her, unaware. "He will no longer need me."

Frowning, Colin held up a finger. "With you two gone, what's to keep these people from simply declaring you both dead and taking the money?"

Pru smiled. It wasn't a nice smile. "No, if they have Evan declared dead, they get nothing. The entire trust goes to a charitable house, my mother's work." She laughed a small, ironic sound. "An orphanage."

"So, you are a lady. Someday you will be a rich woman." He gazed at her for a long moment. "Why tell me this now?"

She stopped moving and tilted her head, facing him. "Because I don't want you to worry about us when we go." She took a deep breath. Don't hesitate. Don't contemplate. Life must amount to more than mere survival! "And because I want you to know who you're making love to tonight."

Colin felt his entire body tingle with shock. "I cannot!"

Pru gazed at him with something frightening and a little thrilling shining in her beautiful eyes. "You can," she said softly. "You will."

"I cannot." He rubbed a hand across his face. "You will marry someday! You must be pure!"

Pru gazed at him with that same unbreakable concentration. "I will never marry, Sir Colin Lambert. I will not lack for means or independence—"

"You cannot say that for sure. You might change your mind in the future!"

"That is a someday and a perhaps. I will not bank my happiness upon it."

"What do you mean?"

"I mean that this is not a someday. This is now. Now and here and *you*. Loving *you*. That will bring me happiness—or at the very least consolation and solace in the days ahead."

She took a step toward him. Then another. It wasn't until that moment that Colin realized that somehow she'd placed herself between him and the door. Panic jangled through him—panic and eagerness and horror at his endangered honor. He knew Prudence Filby a little too well to think he might get out of this one easily. His cock was already thickening in his breeches, merely from the intoxicating look in her eyes. *I'm going to have you*.

"Which do you think you would regret more, loving me or not loving me?" Her voice was husky and low. *Sex and velvet*.

Oh, God, he was in for it now. "I am eng—engaged!"

She was close now, close enough to reach for, close enough for him to see the longing and sadness behind the lust in her eyes. That only made it harder to resist her.

Lifting her hands, she reached for the ribbon that caught back her hair and slowly pulled the bow undone. The rich, russet fall of her hair fell forward over her shoulders. A thick curl dropped over one eye, turning her instantly from sweet to wanton.

That hair streaming across his pillow, flowing over his chest. Burying his hands in that hair as he thrust hard into her, making her cry out and toss her head.

She twined the ribbon idly through her fingers. "Sir Colin Lambert, you may be engaged *tomorrow*. That will be soon enough."

"Pru, stop this at once!"

She only smiled at him slowly. "I don't work for you any

longer, guv." Reaching behind her neck, she began to undo the buttons of her dress.

Colin backed away hastily, stumbling a step as he ran into the arm of the sofa. She followed him mercilessly, making quick work of her buttons. The gown sagged, then slipped away. Clad only in a thigh-length chemise and gartered stockings, she stepped out of the pile of muslin and kept coming.

God, her figure was stunning. The silken chemise clung to her bountiful breasts—*I touched those!*—and shimmered revealingly over the rigid points of her nipples—*I sucked those!*—and floated lightly over the mound between her thighs—*I stroked her there until she came apart in my arms!*

The blood abruptly abandoned his brain and made a race for more rewarding areas. His rigid cock stretched his breeches and robbed his mind of sense.

Touch her.

Hold her.

Claim her.

He closed his eyes, fighting for sanity. *Save her, from you and from herself!*

The sofa struck him in the back of the knees but he did not fall. Instead, he pushed off and, twisting, flung himself over the back of it, putting it between him and the advancing goddess.

She raised her brows at his antics. "That was impressive," she said. Then challenge lit her eyes and her hands went to the hem of her chemise. "Watch this." In one motion she lifted it up and over her head, throwing it down between them like a gauntlet.

She stood there, clad in nothing but rippling red hair and lacy white stockings and a pitiless glinting dare in her eyes. Her pale skin shimmered like ivory in the candlelight and her hair glowed with all the fire that had always been contained within her. She was ripe and rich and powerful. He wanted to worship her. He wanted to conquer her. He wanted to pull her down onto the carpet and spill her hair across his arms and take her until she clung and quivered and screamed his name.

Colin gasped for air. "Pru, I *can't*."

For the first time, she truly seemed to listen. A tiny crease appeared between her brows. "You can't?" A quick glance at his groin seemed to convince her otherwise.

Trying very hard not to feel insulted, Colin clarified himself. "I *can*. But I *mustn't*."

She crossed her arms before her, more in irritation than in a belated effort of concealment, but a voice inside him cried out in protest anyway.

"I see. You *can*, but you *won't*."

He held up both hands in placation. "I want to, I really, really"—*her triangle below is as fiery as her hair. Her thighs are like sugar and cream and I've never been so hungry in my life!*—"*really* want to." He had to take a breath and force his gaze to meet hers. "But I simply, absolutely, entirely *cannot*."

Her eyes widened. "Oh." She looked down at herself. Bending quickly, Colin picked up the chemise and held it out to her. She took it and draped it over her front, hiding herself from him at last. Then she looked up at him with sad eyes. "I suppose that if you can't, then you can't."

He breathed a sigh of relief. He hammered at the wall between them in a rage—but that was only on the inside. Outside, he smiled hopefully at her. "I'm glad you understand." *I hate my own existence.* "I wouldn't want to part unhappily from you." *It will kill me to part from you.* "I should go now." *I need to find a brawl. It is time to get beaten senseless.*

He took a step toward the door.

"Wait." She lifted her chin, defiance giving her cheeks color. "I think that before you go, you owe me something."

"What is it?" *Other than my heart, my life, my home, my everything?*

"You owe me," she said as her lips turned up in a smile both prim and evil. "You owe me *an apology.*"

Oh, no. Swallowing, he gazed at her, desperate and pleading. Yet, in all truth, he could not deny that he did, indeed, owe her the great ancestor of all apologies.

I can do this. His throat dry, his heart pounding, he opened his mouth. "I'm . . . sorry." The breath left him in a whoosh. He'd done it!

Yet she merely tilted her head. "Sorry for what?"

Diabolical! Nonetheless, it had hardly been a proper apology. She had every right to ask for better. Grimly steeling himself, he inhaled.

She dropped the chemise.

It took every scrap of will he had not to look at her sweet, inviting body. He gazed directly into her eyes. "I'm sorry that I kissed you. I'm sorry that I touched you. I'm sorry I allowed you to . . ."

Pru watched his green eyes glaze at the memory of what she'd done to him in the garden. "Allowed me to what?" she asked huskily.

He swallowed hard. She lifted her chin and threw her shoulders back, tilting one hip forward in an enticement as old as Eve. She was shaking inside but this was not a battle she intended to lose. Not this man. Not this night.

"Allowed me to take you with my mouth, Sir Colin?"

A harsh growl erupted from deep in his chest. In less than a second, the civilized veneer fell away and the inner man filled his gaze. Hot, male lust centered on her and focused. The intensity of his gaze took her breath.

In two strides he was upon her like a starving beast.

CHAPTER 38

Even as Colin gave in to his lust and his need, he hated himself. Love and honor warred within him, not quite drowned out by the pounding of his heart.

You will walk away tomorrow. Forever.

I know.

Then stop!

I cannot.

Not yet. Not this woman. Not this night.

Then she was in his arms at last. He pulled her tightly to him, pressing her soft naked body close, lifting her to meet his descending mouth, filling his hands with warm, thick hair. He whirled her and fell with her onto the sofa, her softness pressed beneath him.

Pru gasped and shivered to feel his weight and hardness upon her at last. She was naked and vulnerable beneath his clothed body. The contrast seemed naughty and wicked and enticing. She could feel the buttons of his weskit cold against her skin and her nipples rose in response to the silk weskit rubbing against them.

His groin pressed into hers, hard against her soft, his trapped, hers liberated. The pressure made her squirm beneath him. He groaned and dropped his face into her neck. Hot hands roved over her, sliding, rubbing, pressing, squeezing. Hot mouth on her neck, her breasts, kissing, nibbling, *sucking.*

Oh, yes, please!

Hot man pressing her deep into the cushions, pinning her, conquering her, claiming her at last.

He slid one hand down her thigh and pulled it high up against his hip, opening her to his grinding pressure. She wrapped her arms about his clothed body and held tight to him as he touched and tasted and teased. He was wild, out of control, a fearsome male animal she'd released from a cage of his own making.

Just for one night.

He found her wrists and pinned her hands on either side of her head. "Oh, my God, Pru . . ." For a long moment, he kept his face in her neck, breathing heavily. He was fighting for control, she could tell.

Experimentally, she ground her hips upward into him. He groaned but did not release her, nor did he return to the ravishing in progress.

When he lifted his head at last, she was afraid to meet his eyes. If he rejected her now—

"Pru," he whispered, his voice achingly gentle. "There is no possibility that I am going to make love to you on the sofa."

The battle was over. She'd lost. Biting her lip, fighting off tears, she nodded. "I know. I'm sorry."

"So you had better undress me so that we can get into bed."

What? Her gaze rose to meet his. His green eyes were filled with tenderness and want. A tiny smile played at the corner of his mouth. He knew he'd gotten her, but she knew she'd deserved it.

In answer, she merely tugged deftly at his cravat, untying it like a speeding valet. "Sir Colin," she informed him as she began to swiftly and systematically relieve him of his clothing. "I am the fastest dresser in the entire theater." His surcoat flopped over the arm of the sofa. "I can strip an actor out of his costume"—his weskit flipped across the room—"in the time it takes a curtain to close and then open again."

His shirt was ripped up and away, leaving him clad only in his breeches and boots.

Warm hands caught at her wrists again. His eyes were wide and shocked. "*His* costume? You stripped *men*?"

She sent him a saucy smile. "It's a living."

Now he pinned her back onto the cushions so he could lift his body high and look down at her, the heat back in his eyes. "Well, my Lady Rogue, as much as I appreciate your asistance, I think I'll take it from here." With that, he levered himself off her and stood, pulling her up with him to stand pressed chest to chest to him.

He pushed her wild hair from her face with both hands, then kissed her so sweetly that tears welled up in her eyes. "If I release you," he whispered, "will you behave for two entire minutes?"

She nodded, her throat tight. This man, this marvelous, gentle, strong man, was hers. Yes, hers for one night, yet also hers forever. He would always be the first man she'd loved, the first man she'd kissed, the first man she'd given herself to.

He stepped away from her and retrieved his surcoat from the arm of the sofa. He draped it over her for warmth, tucking it closed with a smile. "Keep that warm. I'll be right back."

Bare-chested, he moved quickly about the room. He took the pillows and the coverlet from the bed and spread them in a luxurious bed on the carpet before the fire. He dove one hand into his valise and took something from it. Then he pulled off his boots and stripped off his breeches. His brief drawers followed right before Pru's fascinated eyes.

He straightened and moved to the edge of the freshly made love nest. Turning to her with a smile, he held out his hand.

Pru couldn't move. She couldn't speak. She'd seen him bare this and bare that, but the entirety was a completely different kettle of fish!

Broad shoulders tapered to narrow hips. Muscled chest, rippled belly, hard tight buttocks, long strong legs—Pru nearly inhaled her tongue!

And then there was his . . . cock. That brief glimpse in the dim garden had not done it justice. It was strange and thick and beautiful and rigid, a darkened sword jutting out from the nest of brown hair, waiting for *her,* wanting *her.* Between her thighs, her own sheath answered that need with a rush of wet heat.

Stepping shyly toward him, she let his coat drop to the floor as she took his hand. He pulled her slowly into his arms. His cock prodded into her belly. With one tentative touch she gently tilted it up to lie between them as she moved closer still.

He pressed something into her hand. "What is this?" she whispered. Waxy paper crackled in her fingers. She unwrapped it to reveal a strange soft tube of a translucent substance. One end was open, the other was tied closed in a tiny knot.

"It is a sheath, to hold back my seed. It will prevent pregnancy."

She blinked at him. "You carry this always?"

"I was not assuming . . ." He shrugged, a little abashed. "When Melody came along, I realized that I had been very careless and selfish. I resolved not to be any longer."

Pru looked down at the sheath. This thing was for her benefit, so that he would leave her no bastard.

His child, green-eyed and thoughtful, but with a ready smile.

Not for you.

No. I know that.

This is a wise and kind thing. Say thank you.

She raised her gaze to meet his and smiled. "How do I put it on?"

He showed her how to roll it like a stocking and unroll it

onto him. He hardened further in her hands, filling the sheath until it was stretched so thin she could barely tell it was there.

He took her back into his arms then, holding her close. The room was warm but she shivered as she felt his cock jump as her body pressed into it. Skin to skin they stood as she slipped her hands up behind his neck to pull him down for her kiss. "Thank you," she whispered just before their lips met.

They had kissed before. They had never kissed thus—lips soft and gentle, warm tongues slipping and greeting, arms tightening about each other as they made a simple vow without words. *This night is ours. This is our forever.*

Lost in his mouth, in his promise, Pru was surprised to find her back meeting the piled pillows and silk. He laid her down beneath him and then rolled closer to the fire, so that she was above him.

"Straddle me," he commanded softly.

She spread her thighs apart and felt his cock lie rigid and thick, pointing along her wet slit, parting her lips and pressing its thick head against her small, sensitive clitoris.

He put his big hands on her hips and held her still on him as he flexed his buttocks. Hard flesh slid across soft, slippery places. She gasped aloud at the sensation. Then he flexed back and pulled the length of his cock down again.

Pleasure. Hot, wet, slick *bliss.*

Tilting one big hand across her belly, he laid the tip of his thumb upon her clitoris and circled it ever so gently. Her body quivered in shock at the sensation but he was careful and very, very skilled.

Slide and circle, circle and slide. He did it again and again, sliding and rubbing and making her writhe and pant and beg, until she dug her fingers into the muscles of his chest to hold on, his big hands ruthlessly holding her in place as he rubbed and rubbed and—

She cried out, tossing her head back and panting out her orgasm in sharp, high cries.

He drew back very far then and, gripping her hips firmly, thrust into her, *hard*.

Her moans ended in a tight, pained shriek.

"I'm sorry." He caught her quickly to his chest and held her there, cradling her as she trembled. "I'm so sorry, love, shh." He pushed the hair back from her face, looking anxiously into her shocked eyes. "Shh. Just breathe. It was better quickly done, when you were at the height of pleasure and had not time to tighten in resistance."

She curled upon his broad chest and blinked back tears. She still lay straddling him, impaled upon him, aching and tight and full inside—yet it was already easing, already dying back to a burning throb, then a painful twinge.

She lifted her head and blinked down at his face, seeing that his brow was creased in worry for her. "I don't want to do this anymore."

His jaw worked but he nodded. "That is your choice, always."

He was so kind. How could any man be so large and strong and brave and yet so very gentle? "I'm sorry," she whispered. "I thought I'd like it."

"I understand." His green eyes were bright in the firelight. "However, if you wish to stop, you will have to move first."

She nodded, resignedly. "Right." Lifting herself with her hands on his chest, she bit her lip against the oncoming pain and slowly began to rise off him.

Pleasure. Her eyes widened and she gasped, gazing down at him in surprise.

He broke out into a laugh, his eyes alight. "Oops. Did I forget to mention that it only hurts once?"

Her eyes narrowed and she drove herself back down on him. He caught his breath at the rush of sensation, but her trick only backfired on her as she gasped aloud at the wicked, deep *pleasure*.

Big hands roamed up her body, framing her waist, lifting and cupping her breasts, slipping into her hair. He looked deeply into her eyes, heat and pride and love flowing from his bright gaze. "Ride on, Lady Rogue," he whispered.

She rode. Rising, she let him nearly withdraw until she ached for him, then falling, drove him into her until she nearly burst from him. Pressing her hands on his muscled chest for balance, she set the pace, filling herself again and again.

He cried out and arched his head back, straining beneath her, wild and wicked, the muscles of his torso rippling in the firelight, a great, untamed beast, leashed to her will.

Her pleasure was twofold. Her body loved the slippery, wonderful, wicked sensations. Her heart loved his freely offered abandon, his release of power to her hands. He gave himself to her, an instrument for her pleasure, holding himself back as she rode him to higher and higher peaks.

The moment came, the rippling, sparkling, shimmering moment and she threw her head back and cried out his name as she spasmed around his jutting cock.

Finally, she fell upon him, damp and weary and spent. Warm arms came about her, supporting her, holding her as she gasped and quivered and pulsed around his still rigid erection.

When she caught her breath, she lifted her head and kissed him softly. "I want your pleasure now."

He shuddered, his self-control straining at the seams. "We . . . had better not. You are too new," he gasped.

She slid her hands up his big body, feeling his vibrating need. "I want you to."

"I . . . don't think I can be gentle now. I don't want to . . . hurt you."

He wasn't listening again, so she bit him, once, sharply on the chest.

With a throaty growl, he flipped her beneath him and plunged *deep*—oh, sweet heaven, she'd thought she'd done deep but it was nothing, *nothing* like this wild invasion! He groaned above her, her beautiful, wonderful, gentle man, as he drove into her again and again, the beast unleashed, the civilized man gone wild. He pulled her thighs high to grip his hips, opening her to his forceful penetration, his big body bucking and sweating and pounding into her as she hung desperately on with her arms about him and her head thrown back on the pillows, lost in the whirlwind of his naked, gasping *need*. It did hurt, a little, but his turbulent passion re-whetted her own, giving her body the slippery ease it needed to take on this powerful onslaught.

Then giving a guttural roar, his entire body went rigid and his arms held her so tightly she lost her breath and she felt him pulsating deep inside her.

It was the end, like when she'd taken him in her mouth and he'd throbbed his seed into her. Smoothing her hands up his back, she kissed his damp neck and whispered calming things as he trembled and gasped on top of her.

She'd wanted all of him. She'd certainly gotten her wish!

CHAPTER 39

After a long moment, Colin's tight grasp on Pru eased and he slid his weight from her, going onto one elbow so he could peer into her face.

"I'm sorry," he said softly. "That was . . . unforgivable. Are you all right?"

She smiled at his worry. "Me? Look at you. You can scarcely breathe and your heart is pounding like a coach team." She touched one finger to the faint bite mark on his chest. "Oh, dear. Did I do that?" She shook her head regretfully. "I think I used you very ill."

He blinked. "But I—that was not how I should have—"

She rolled her eyes. "Really, Sir Colin, I know you're a man of honor and all things gentlemanly, but may I please have a bit of blame for my own aches and pains? You never stood a chance."

The regret left his green eyes as his teasing grin reappeared. "I feel so cheap."

Her mission accomplished, she shed her saucy mien and smiled shyly at him. "I did like it. I liked it very much."

He raised a brow in doubt. "All of it?"

"Every moment but one, and that was necessary." She wriggled closer into his big, warm body. With him at rest and her own urgency quenched, she let her fingertips explore his nakedness in tender curiosity. The thick planes of his muscular chest, the startling dips and swells of his biceps, the curious flatness of his nipples, like copper coins. "Men are so very different," she mused.

"Men are very straightforward. We are like horses or cattle. Women are the strange beings. All those soft bits and secret places. So very sensitive."

"What about this?" She let her hands roam down. He jerked and gasped slightly. "This seems entirely sensitive to me."

He gently pried her fingers from his still tumescent cock. "This needs a few moments to recover." He rolled away from her and tossed something into the fire. The sheath. Then he turned back and scooped her into the curve of his body. She hooked her knees over his bent thighs and used his brawny arm for her pillow. She was naked with a naked man. She ought to be horrified and shamed and weeping at her ruin.

No regrets. Not now. Not ever. No shame, not even embarrassment. She loved this man, all of this man. From his big, shapely feet to the oddly vulnerable curls at the nape of his neck. Being naked with him was the most natural thing in the world.

She toyed with the wiry brown hair that filled his chest between his flat nipples. "So . . . how many is a few?"

He kissed her ear softly. "Hmm?"

She shivered as his deep murmur vibrated through her. "How many moments is 'a few moments to recover'?"

His long fingers wrapped around her chin and tilted her face up to meet his kiss. "Not as many as you will need, my sweet."

She brightened at that. "I'm fine! Right now!"

"Oh, really?" His wide palm slid down her body. She purred with pleasure at his touch—until he probed gently into her slit. "Ow!"

He stopped instantly and covered her mound soothingly with his warm hand. "Tender?"

She frowned, disgruntled. "I didn't know—I thought—bloody hell!"

"Tut-tut." He laughed softly. "Such language."

Looking away, she blinked back abrupt tears. He saw and kissed her temple, pulling her closer still.

"What is it?"

Feeling like an idiot, she swiped at her face and blew out a disappointed breath. "I didn't know I'd only have the once," she whispered brokenly. "I thought we'd have all night."

Once. Once to make love to him, to make memories that were supposed to last for her entire life. Once!

Colin's heart ached at the sadness in her voice. One night was bad enough. Just once seemed so unfair. He sat up and pulled her limp body to sit in his lap, turning them both to face into the fire for warmth. He pushed back her beautiful hair and tenderly kissed her damp eyes, one then the other. "Don't weep."

"I'm not. I don't weep. I'm just . . . leaking."

He chuckled. "Then don't leak."

"But I ruined everything. You tried to warn me and I didn't listen—"

"And you're still not listening. Nothing is ruined. You are here, warm and sweet and naked in my arms. I lost myself in you the way I have never lost myself in anyone before. I am replete. Satisfied."

She sniffled, just once. "Never? It isn't always like that for you?"

He dropped his face into her neck and laughed, a short, broken noise. "No, my fiery Prudence, it has *never* been like that for me. No woman has ever made me lose my senses or turned me into a slavering, rutting beast."

"Oh," she said in a pleased and awed tone. "Well, all right then." Exploring fingertips slid over his belly, testing the ridges. He sucked in a breath and she stopped. "Are you ticklish, Sir Colin?"

He knew that innocent voice. "Don't you dare, Miss Filby, or I shall be forced to do this." He rolled the tip of his tongue around the shell of her ear. She shivered in his arms but desisted in her restless play.

A contented silence fell. It was a full sort of quiet, with small kisses and gentle touches and soft, warm sweetness between them.

Colin felt the seconds ticking away like the threat of an enemy at his door. Time was against them. Morning would come.

Mourning would come.

He dropped his head and breathed her in. She smelled sweet and female, like some luxurious soap, but he missed the wild, sharp smell of mint.

She tilted her head back and gazed up at him. Her eyes were like silvery pools reflecting the firelight. "I love you," she whispered. "Always."

I love you. He tightened his hold and tried to make her feel the words she would not let him say. *Always.* His throat tightened until he thought he might stop breathing entirely. What was he to do without his outspoken dearest friend, his open and honest lover, his fierce and valiant cohort?

How am I to go on without my Pru?

His life before her seemed like time wasted, foolish spendthrift years squandered away without her. "Where were you when I was twenty?" he murmured.

After a moment of silence she turned to him with a frown. "I believe I was learning to spell 'cat.'"

"What?" He drew back and gazed at her in horror. "How old are you?"

She blinked and gazed into the distance, a little crease between her brows. "You know, I'm not sure. Time sort of ran together. I was born in August. I was fifteen when my parents died and Evan was eight—"

Somewhere in his mind he must have been practicing his

mathematics, for he suddenly went cold. "Oh, my god. You're only nineteen!"

She tilted her head and quirked her lips. "You're a quick'un, ain't ye?"

Saucy Pru was back and he'd missed her terribly, but now was no time to reminisce. "I've ravaged a *girl*." Dismay laced through him. Some men might pursue maidens fresh from the schoolroom, but he'd found the practice appalling.

"How tedious." She rolled her eyes to the ceiling and sighed. "Am I obligated to make you feel better now, Sir Colin, or can we simply accept that I am mature for my years and continue on?"

He swallowed. She was right, of course. There was nothing to be done about it now and any histrionics on his part would be purely selfish. Still, he repressed a groan at what Aidan would have to say about it.

Aidan will never know. He will never meet Pru. She will never be friends with Madeleine. After tonight, she will never be with you again.

It was unimaginable. It was inevitable.

As if she knew what he was thinking—and she probably did—she turned and abruptly flung her arms about his neck, pressing her face into his chest and holding on as if invading pirates threatened to tear her away.

He lifted her to sit facing him, her legs wrapped about him, breast to chest, heart to heart, and he held her, simply held her while she sobbed, broken, dry-eyed, and trembling. He felt the same.

After several minutes she raised her eyes to look into his. "I have so much to say to you. We've had so little time. There is so much I want to ask."

He kissed his way from her forehead to the end of her nose. "What do you wish to know?"

She blew out a breath that only hitched once. "Tell me about Sir Colin. Tell me how that came about."

He shrugged. "I published something of my father's. It was recognized as worthy work. I suppose since he was dead, Prinny thought he might as well knight me."

She frowned. "That cannot be all. Tell me the truth."

He looked away. "I don't discuss my father."

"Your father made you the way you are. You cannot ever leave him behind entirely. So tell me how it was your father managed to have you knighted with absolutely no effort from you. And then tell me the truth."

He blew out a breath and slid his gaze to meet hers. "Miss Prudence Filby, grand inquisitor."

"You're stalling."

"Yes, guv." Colin tipped her head down onto his shoulder so he wouldn't have to see himself in those moonlit eyes. He'd thought he was naked before!

"I didn't truly know my father. He sent me away after my mother died and I was raised by my aunt."

"With all the cousins. Yes, I know this part."

"As a young man, I was a disappointment. Believe it or not, I was prone to causing trouble with my good friend Jack. My father did not approve of my lack of serious study and completely dismissed me from his mind. I stayed away from Tamsinwood and him and he did his best to pretend I had never existed."

She squeezed him but said nothing.

Colin went on. "After my father died, I decided to shut the manor up for a while. I preferred the liveliness of London. The staff took care of everything else, but I thought I ought to handle his study myself. I gathered all his papers and research. I'd thought I might box them up and deliver them to the Bathgate Scholars, with whom my father associated. At least they would know what to do with them all. I was shoving it all into a trunk when I looked down at a page in my hand and saw my father's handwriting, so perfect and precise yet sort of cramped and hurried, as if he couldn't get his thoughts down fast enough . . .

"I began to read, and it was as though I could hear his voice in my mind. It struck me at last that he was never going to walk through that door again, that he would never sit at his desk, with his cold pipe held in his hand, arrested in thoughts that made him forget his tobacco, his dinner, and sometimes even his bed. I realized that he would never look at me the way he used to, with mystification and disappointment. Yet I held part of him in my hands. He might be dead and gone, but on those pages he still lived. I stayed in his study for nearly a month, reading every single word he'd written."

He shook his head in wonder even now. "My father was a very interesting man. What a pity I didn't realize it until it was too late."

"What did the papers say?" Her voice was a whisper, her body a warm comfort.

"At first I simply read, without judgment or discernment. Then I began to sort out what I'd read, spreading the pages out all over the room, dividing them into factual records, or random thoughts, or discarded theories. When I ran out of room, I moved everything into the ballroom, with the staff banned from disturbing me on pain of death. As I sorted and read and sorted again, I began to see the pattern of my father's thoughts, of what he'd been trying to prove with all that information."

He dropped his face into her hair and breathed. "And then I saw where he went wrong."

Her arms tightened about him.

"It wasn't a dramatic error. He'd simply gone a bit to the left when he ought to have focused on the right. I was merely a fresh pair of eyes. It was something he likely would have realized had he lived long enough."

He let out a long breath. "So I finished it. It wasn't difficult, for my father had done all the work. Under his name, with mine only on the manuscript by way of explanation, I sent it to the Bathgate Scholars for review. The next thing I know, they're clamoring to publish it and the Prince Regent is sending me congratulatory messages and suddenly I'm Sir Colin Lambert, knighted scholar!" His voice broke abruptly. "What an enormous cauldron of shite!"

She leaned her head back and looked at him, forcing him to meet her knowing gaze. "You don't want to be a scholar."

He drew back, startled. "It isn't a matter of wanting. It simply is. My father always expected it. Now the world expects something more, some brilliant new work to top the last."

"You expect it." She shook her head. "You're clever and you saw his mistake, but your heart is not in it. To you it's a chore, isn't it? Like sewing is to me. I can do it, but I despise it so that I do not do it well."

He gazed down at her, about to explain that it was nothing like that, that sewing costumes in the dank cellar of a tawdry theater was nothing at all like blazing a new trail in the statistical social sciences.

Sitting at a desk. Totting up research numbers. Counting and rearranging and counting again. And again. And again.

While all along he knew that his latest theory was nothing but the most godawful rubbish—and that he was clever enough that he could likely shove it down the Bathgate Scholars' collective throat and make them like it.

"I loathe it," he heard himself say out loud. "It makes me want to run screaming down Pall Mall, foaming at the mouth." His startled gaze met hers. "I don't know why I said that."

She smiled. "Because I ordered you to tell me the truth."

"Now tell me the truth."

She blinked at him. "I already did. You know all about me."

"Your past, but not your future." He held her gaze, not releasing her so easily. "You are about to disappear, aren't you? You and Evan are going to slip away again, forever."

She met his gaze and did not falter. "In six years Evan will have what is rightfully his. He will not need me anymore. I do not plan to stay in London or Brighton or anywhere that will—"

"That will remind you of me."

She lifted her chin. "Can you blame me? Would you wish that pain on me? Am I to spot you in Covent Garden and feel your loss anew, like a knife in my heart? And what would you do if you saw me on Bond Street as you walked with your wife and daughter? You would look away and then you would keep walking."

I would die inside. And then I would keep walking.

She cupped his jaw in her hands and pinned him with those beautiful eyes. "That is how it *should* be. How it *must* be. I must go and live another life so that it *can* be."

"What of me? Am I to wonder forever what became of you? Am I to hear of a fire in a house two counties off and worry that you were in it? Am I to read of a ship sinking off the coast and fear for your drowning? Am I to stare at every auburn-haired woman that crosses my path for the rest of my life and wonder, 'Is that she?' "

She smiled, a sad little tilt of her lips. "I promise not to burn or drown. I'd rather not change my hair, thank you."

Abruptly he could not bear it. He could not play this civilized game of letting her go. He pulled her close and rolled into the pillows with her, kissing her desperately, pressing her down, pinning her, *keeping* her.

I will not let this happen. I will not.

She gave in to him, submitting to his will, refusing him nothing, not even when his now rigid erection probed her tender slit. Her only protest was a tiny flinch.

He knew what to do. Hurrying, he kissed his way down her body, stroking her thighs apart with his palms, gently spreading her inner lips with his tongue. Ignoring her dismayed cry, he immobilized her with his hands as he licked her.

At first he soothed and stroked and eased her, softly laving at her soreness and helping her relax. Then he caught at her clitoris with the tip of his tongue and began to tease. He knew what he was about and he meant to make her beg, to make her need, to make her want to stay near him forever.

Pru could not bear the conflict between the pleasure in her body and the pain in her heart. She could feel his need. She could hear the question unasked, the proposal undared.

Stay with me. Be mine, outside my marriage, outside my vows. Love me in the dark and secret and hidden moments and then kiss me good-bye to return to my family.

She knew that he wanted to trap her, to trick her, to bind her to a life without hope or honor. She would not let him do that to her, nor to himself. He was not a man who could live with that sort of betrayal, not without becoming a different man altogether.

And that she could never, ever allow.

So she took his tongue and his need and his silent, begging question and she came again at the demands of his mouth. And when he moved up her body to wrap his arms about her and bury his face in her hair and penetrate her again to thrust slowly and skillfully until she quivered and cried out in his grasp, she took him into her arms and into her aching body and into her broken, mourning heart.

And all the while, in her heart she knew she would leave him in the morning.

CHAPTER 40

When Colin woke the next morning it was to find Pru gone and Bailiwick in the room doing his best to lay out some sort of decent suit from the clothing Colin had carried in his valise for a week.

The big footman was red-faced with frustration. "I'm that sorry, Sir Colin, but I ain't a real valet."

Wearily, Colin only clapped a hand on the fellow's shoulder. "It doesn't matter how I look today, Bailiwick."

"But it's yer weddin' day! Mr. Wilberforce wouldn't want ye to go about such an important day lookin' like a ragman!"

Colin felt lower than that, actually. He'd thrown all honor out the window last night for the simple selfish joy of possessing the woman he loved, just for a few sweet hours. The fact that he would never, ever regret it made him think even less of himself, if that were possible.

He dressed in the least wrinkled of his clothing and allowed Bailiwick to fuss clumsily over his appearance for only a few minutes. Then he left the fellow to pack up their belongings and let himself out of the hotel room into the hall.

The sight of Pru leaving her room at the same instant brought him up short. He watched her as she ushered the children from the room and as she spent a moment trying to tame Evan's rebellious hair and futilely trying to improve the appearance of Gordy Ann by the application of a little spit on a handkerchief.

As Colin stood there, the ever-expanding hole in his heart grew fresh and dreadful depths. These three might have been his family for the rest of his life. He might have become father to Evan, or at least elder brother, helping to guide him into his future as a gentleman. Melody might have had a mother worthy of her, a mother who would encourage her bravery and educate her spirit. He might have had more children with Pru, enough to fill the silent halls of Tamsinwood with shrieks and giggles and running feet. Playmates for Melody and fond nuisances for Evan.

Then Pru lifted her gaze and saw him standing there. Surprised, her first expression was one of startled joy, swiftly darkened. She turned to Evan and whispered something to him.

Evan turned a gaze of burning betrayal on Colin.

He knows. He hates me.

Quite right, too.

He nodded acknowledgment of Evan's rage, unwilling to deny the boy his due fury. Evan had evidently been told to bring Melody to Colin, for he walked the little girl forward, gray eyes flashing.

Colin knelt before his tiny daughter. She blinked big blue eyes at him expectantly.

"Mellie, Bailiwick is going to take you back to Brown's. You'll be home tomorrow, with Wilberforce and Grampapa Aldrich and everyone."

Melody, already cheerful, widened her eyes in ecstasy. "Wibbly-force! And Maddie and Uncle Aidan!"

Colin smoothed her gleaming dark curls. "They'll be there very soon as well." How much should he tell her now? How much could she even understand?

"Mellie, my love, you'll be riding with Bailiwick and Pru and Evan back to London. I can't come with you today, but I'll be following very soon. Is that all right?"

"And then you'll tell me a story?"

He smiled. "Always."

She considered his offer for a moment, then nodded decisively. "All right. You follow fast."

"As quickly as I can, milady."

She threw her arms around his neck, slapping Gordy Ann into his spine, and planted a smeary kiss on his cheek. "Byebye!"

Holding her close, he apologized to her silently. He was a coward for not telling her more, but why not let her have the next few days with Pru and Evan and a happy journey? There would be plenty of time to break her heart later.

At Colin's nod, Evan took Melody's hand and marched her away down the hall, oversized feet clomping even on the carpeted floor as Melody danced lightly alongside, already beginning her day's chatter, Gordy Ann swinging from her other hand. Pru watched them go and only faced Colin when the children had turned the corner.

As she walked toward him, her features lighted by the window behind him, he wondered that he'd ever thought her plain. Her elfin face was now softened by a healthy diet, which only made it a perfect canvas for her lustrous eyes. Her shimmering auburn hair was pinned up in the manner of a lady, not capped and hidden like a servant's. She wore her good gown. Colin had the impression that the servant disguise had been abandoned forever.

Her steps faltered as she came closer and she stopped a bit farther away than he would have liked, but he made no move to close the distance. It stretched between them, a lasting and forever distance.

Quite right, too.

Her hands were clasped before her, her knuckles whitened, but when she spoke her beautiful voice was smooth and controlled. "How are you today, Sir Colin?"

He gave her a very correct nod. "I am completely undone, Miss Filby. And you?"

She blinked and her storm-gray gaze dampened. "Entirely, sir."

Colin swallowed. "Bailiwick will take you and Evan to London as promised. I would ask you to remain with Melody until you reach Brown's."

"Of course. Bailiwick is a miracle, but even he cannot mind a child and drive at the same time."

Colin's lips twitched. "Wait until you meet Wilberforce."

Her mouth quirked sadly. "I look forward to it. After Melody's tales, I shall not be surprised if that man takes wing before my eyes."

Colin ached to reach for her. "I am saying nothing I really wish to say."

She tilted her head. "I would thank you not to. Did we not say everything last night?"

"You would not allow it."

I love you. I want to say it every day for the rest of my life. Her eyes saw it all. *I know.*

"There is something I wish you to have." He reached into his breast pocket and removed a sheaf of foolscap, folded in half. He handed it to her.

She took a bare step forward, just enough to reach the papers with her arm extended. When she had them, she stepped back once more.

I am not a wild animal.

Agony raged in his heart, shaking the bars of its cage. *Then again perhaps I am.*

She opened the fold and gazed down at the top sheet. "Once upon a time on the high seas . . ." she read, then glanced up at him in surprise. "You wrote it down!"

"Just the story about Captain Jack and the Spanish princess. I don't think Evan ever managed to stay up until the end."

A short sound escaped her, a lost little laugh. Tenderly, she folded the story again and pressed it to her bosom, her hands crossed protectively over it. When her gaze lifted to his, her eyes shone like silver. "I shall read it to him every night."

"I think he might rather you burned it."

She shook her head. "He will understand. Someday."

Really? Then perhaps he can explain it to me. "On the last sheet, I wrote the names of several solicitors in London. They are all trustworthy fellows who could help your case against the Trotters."

She lifted her chin. "I have not made a decision about that yet."

"Stubborn woman." He would not smile at her independence. It was too hard-won. "At the very least, they might know of appropriate employment for you. I've included a letter of reference as well."

She nodded. "For that I thank you."

He thought about asking her to wait for him. Chantal was not well. He might very well be a widower before the year was out.

Then a year of mourning. Then another of half-mourning. And what if Chantal lived on? The doctor had said there was no way to predict her health.

How long will you make Pru wait, hanging on when she could make a new life for herself? How ghoulish are you, to wish your own wife a speedy death?

Not selfish or ghoulish enough, apparently, for he could not ask it.

The door behind him opened and Bailiwick came out, ducking his great height apologetically. "Pardon me, Sir Colin, but I could see outside that the carriage is ready and the children are waitin' inside."

"Thank you, Bailiwick. Please take Miss Filby's things down to the carriage and wait for her there."

"Yes, sir."

Bailiwick lifted the valises without effort and trotted down the hall, obviously eager to be out of the way.

Colin couldn't take his gaze from Pru. *She is going to leave now and you will never see her again.*

Kiss her. If he did, he would never stop.

Hold her. He dared not, for fear he'd never let go.

Ask her to stay with you anyway. He would not, for it would only dishonor her.

Pru shifted uncomfortably beneath the intensity of his gaze.

Kiss me.

She had to leave at once.

Hold me.

If he so much as touched her, she would throw everything away and beg him to keep her forever.

Ask me to stay.

Stay? As what?

Mistress, whore, bedwarmer—sounds good to me, guv!

His beautiful face was set like stone. His body held straight as a soldier. Only his green eyes, those laughing eyes that no longer laughed, swam with a sea's worth of anguish.

He loves me. No one will ever love me like this again.

Then love him enough to let him go.

With jerky movements, for her body had gone stiff with pain, she turned her back on the only man she could ever love. Take a step. Now take another.

The silvery threads broke, one by one, as she slowly walked away, each sending a jolt of agony through her heart.

"Pru!"

She should not stop, she should not turn. Yet the harsh misery uttered in the single syllable of her name halted her in her tracks. She looked back at him, so tall and golden and handsome. So alone.

His shoulders heaved as if he'd run a great distance. "On this day, every year for the rest of my life, I shall remember you. I will not forget a moment. Every year, on this day, I swear to it."

Oh, my love, I will remember every second. I will polish them daily, like jewels in my heart.

But she only said, "This is your wedding day, sir. You must think of your wife on this day."

Then, because she could not leave him thus, she cast him one last flashing smile. "You may remember me *yesterday*."

Then she picked up her skirts and ran down the hall, as fast as she could with her throat closed in pain and her eyes swimming in tears. Her ears were clear enough to hear his single gasp of damp laughter as she turned the corner and left him forever.

The mumsy carriage pulled away from the hotel entrance and into Brighton traffic, Bailiwick at the reins, driving his enormous white horse. However, the city was not large and they were soon traveling through the rolling green hills of the Avon Valley. Pru sat facing forward with Melody on her lap. Opposite, Evan looked out the window with his chin on his folded arms, pointedly ignoring them both.

"Ev."

He turned to give her a filthy look over his shoulder, then turned back to the view outside. "Don't want t'talk to you," he said shortly.

"Ev, I know you're upset. It's been an upsetting time all round, but—"

He flung himself back on his seat opposite to glare at her full on. "Ain't *upset*. Girls get *upset*."

She lifted a brow. "What are you, then?"

"It's *him*. Rotten old Lambert."

Pru saw it coming and clapped her hands over Melody's ears just in time.

"Bastard!"

Melody perked up and tugged Pru's hands away. "What did Evan say?" Eager curiosity blazed. "Evan, what did you say?"

Pru reached into her pocket and pulled out an old hair

ribbon she'd kept for just such emergencies. "Melody, look what I have for Gordy Ann!"

Melody was soon absorbed in fashioning a noose for her poor little rag doll. Pru slid her gaze to meet Evan's rebellious one. "He isn't, you know," she said softly. "It is I who left him behind."

"I heard Bailiwick. He's gettin' married! To her!"

"Yes, he is. He was always going to. I knew that."

Evan gaped. "You knew? All the time? Then what did you go and start huggin' and kissin' him for?"

Yes, tell. We all want to know the answer to that one.

Instead, she decided to invoke her rights as elder sister. "I shall tell you someday when you're old enough to understand."

"I understand. You're just a—"

Pru held up one hand sharply. "Evan Filby, if you finish that sentence you'll find your mouth washed out with soap. Is that entirely clear?"

Evan blinked in surprise. "You wouldn't!"

"I certainly will. It is high time you began to behave like the gentleman you were born to be. From this moment onward you will cease cursing entirely, or the soap will appear instantly!"

Evan stared at her as if he'd never seen her before. However, she saw some old tension leave his shoulders as he gazed at her with new respect. For the first time in his memory, there was an adult in the room and it was Pru. She shook her head as she smiled at him with fond exasperation. "You and I will be fine. I am going to find respectable employment in London now that I have such an excellent reference. We will take a nice room this time. No more starving and no more running mad through the streets. You will study and I will work and when you are eighteen we will descend upon the Trotters with a solicitor of our own in tow."

Evan's expression lightened with grim enjoyment of that image. "We'll squash 'em, won't we?"

Pru folded her arms. "Try that sentence again, if you please."

Evan blinked. "We shall squash them, shall we not?"

Pru grinned nastily. "Like insects on the sidewalk."

Melody looked up from where she was stringing up Gordy Ann. "Don't squash the bugs, Evan!"

Evan grinned at Melody. "Just pretend bugs, sillykins. Come here. I'll show you how to make a proper noose, sliding knot and all."

Melody crawled obediently across to the opposite seat, happy to have an ally in her merry mayhem.

Pru leaned back in her own seat and watched them, her fierce determination flagging as she realized once more that by tomorrow she would be bidding farewell to Melody.

Forever.

My sweet baby girl. How can I let you go as well?

Because it was best. Melody needed her mother, and as much as Pru disliked Chantal, she would not rob her of her last months with her child. Unfortunately, knowing that she did the right thing gave her no consolation whatsoever.

Melancholy descended upon her like a stifling blanket. Her shining new life simply refused to glow in her mind. She would be better off than she had been in years and yet the future loomed like a gallows, dark and dreary.

She turned away from the children to stare out of the window as helpless tears rolled down her cheeks. *Oh, my love. How am I to wake every day and brave the opening of my eyes, knowing that you shall not be there?*

How am I to go on?

Colin walked out of the hotel with only his valise in his hand. He felt strangely light, traveling only with himself. Light and empty, as if he didn't walk in the same world as everyone else. People passed him, striding quickly, their faces wreathed in smiles or scowls or puzzlement—emotions he vaguely remembered but that seemed to have nothing to do with him.

The awful numbness was worse than the pain, for it didn't ease the loss at all. He only felt more bereft than ever, as if he'd lost himself as well.

Pru, my love, you took my heart with you. There is nothing beating in my chest now. I am hollow.

Yet he knew she'd left him because she loved him. It burned, deep down beneath the ice, like snowcaps on a dormant volcano. For the first time, Colin truly understood Jack's shadows. How could one continue to walk normally in the world without a heart?

Yet, he carried on. Numbly, he arranged a special license with the bishop in the arching halls of the Bath cathedral. Numbly, he rented a suitable carriage, comfortable and well sprung, the better for Chantal to travel back to London. Numbly, he entered Lementeur's establishment, only to emerge pressed and resplendent and still entirely, completely numb.

Numbly, he climbed the steps of the church on his wedding day, prepared to marry a woman he would never love.

CHAPTER 41

At the altar, Colin waited with his single witness at his side. Chantal's physician, Dr. Bennett, had been designated to give the bride away. Colin was still trying to decide quite what that symbolized.

Next to him, Lementeur brushed at Colin's sleeve with a frown. "Lint," the smaller man informed him in a whisper.

Was there really a world in which people worried about such things? It seemed bizarre, but then this day already had such an unreal quality to it.

The bishop cleared his throat and Colin looked up to see Chantal coming down the aisle on Dr. Bennett's arm. She wore a gown of pale peach. It looked odd on her. Colin had only ever seen her in dramatic jewel tones.

She was wan but still so lovely. The picture of a delicate, nervous bride. When had he become immune to such obvious beauty? Chantal had once seemed to be all that was exquisite and precious and beautiful in women. She was even more striking now that she was ill—languid, misty-eyed perfection.

Her faultless face left him cold.

Regularity of features was an accident of birth. Chantal depended solely upon her ability to attract and did nothing to improve her chances of keeping. She did nothing to improve her mind or her personality. Traits that he would insist upon in a male companion—truthfulness, honor, courage, and intelligence—were entirely lacking in this perfect caricature of a woman!

Her blue eyes glowed like the evening sky as she met his gaze. Her smile, however, was the one she used on men she wished to avoid.

This marriage was not going to go well.

Yet, what did it matter? In mere moments, Melody would be nearly as legitimate as if she'd been born in the next year, which was quite good enough for Society's standards. All the doors of the world were swinging open for his daughter even now.

Worth every moment of the coming hell.

Chantal came even with Colin and took her place by his side. Dr. Bennett and Lementeur took a step back as Colin and Chantal turned to face the bishop.

As the bishop began to intone the words of the ceremony, Colin spurned regret. That was useless now. He'd made this bed years ago and he'd done it with glee, thoughtless cad that he'd been. He took Chantal's hand in his and opened his mouth. "I vow—"

"What?" Melody's cry was practically a shriek, making Button cringe at her noise and lean away from her on the sofa where they sat.

"He married Chantal? How could he? What about Pru? What about Evan? What about *me*?"

Button gazed at her. "I can see that this particular story might not be the best way to calm your wedding nerves. Perhaps it's time we got you dressed."

"No! No, please, Button. I need to know. Really. I'm calm." She smoothed her wrapper where she'd been clutching it tightly with both hands and plastered a serene expression on her face. "See. Very calm."

"Hmm." His gaze was skeptical but he returned to his

spot next to her and allowed her to wrap his arm over her shoulders once again.

"Very well, then. Let's see . . . where were we?"

"Colin and Chantal are just wed."

"Are they? Well, let us see . . ."

Colin inhaled deeply. "I vow—"

A commotion at the church door drowned out his words. All faces turned to the back of the church to see a slender man lurching up the aisle, waving madly.

Colin squinted against the light streaming in from the open doors. "Purty Bertie?"

Lementeur made a humming noise. "Oh, my. Such an elegant fit . . ."

Chantal outright shrieked. "Bertie!"

With that, Colin's bride shoved her bouquet into Lementeur's hands and flung herself back up the aisle she'd so recently come down—

And into Lord Bertram's eager arms. Dr. Bennett rushed after her.

"Miss Marchant, you must take care not to excite yourself!"

Colin realized he'd never seen Chantal so excited in his recollection. She was kissing old Bertie as if he had the only supply of air in the room. Bertie kissed her right back, his arms tight about her.

One elegant hand was planted firmly on Chantal's arse.

Colin shook his head. "You truly shouldn't believe everything you hear."

Lementeur watched the amorous couple with raised brows. "Even I might have called that one wrong, sir."

Dr. Bennett finally persuaded Chantal to come up for air. Colin waited for the three of them to meet him at the top of the aisle. Really, he didn't dare move for fear that his boots would begin to speak or something equally bizarre.

The bishop was fuming. "Sir," he snarled at Bertie, "this is a house of worship."

"Be nice," Colin murmured in an aside. "He's even richer than I am."

The bishop stepped forward, his arms open to welcome the happy couple. "Sirs and madam, I can see that there are matters to discuss. If we might all step into my retiring room . . ."

In a matter of moments, they were all seated in the bishop's quarters. Chantal had a death grip on Bertie's hand. Dr. Bennett had her other one, ostensibly checking her pulse although Colin suspected he was simply loath to let go of his favorite patient.

Lementeur remained standing at the back of the room.

"All the better to watch the proceedings," he'd confessed to Colin a moment ago. "I am going to dine out on this story for years."

"Dirty gossip."

"Oh, I'll make you out nicely, sir, don't you worry. The shining knight, coming to the rescue of the beautiful, ill actress even though he loves another."

Colin had glanced at him sharply. "How did you know?"

Lementeur smiled. "Miss Filby is a very unusual young lady, sir. You have admirable taste."

The reminder of Pru made Colin ache. "Oh, all right, then." He sighed wearily. What did a bit of gossip matter? He was going to have to pry Chantal away from Bertie and marry her anyway. He had no doubt that his entire life was going to be gossip when Chantal got through with her likely vengeance.

Now, the bishop could hardly get a word in edgewise, for Bertie and Chantal were breathlessly avowing their devotion to one another.

"I had to leave you behind!" Chantal was saying piteously. "Gaffin would have killed you!"

Bertie shot Colin a resentful glance. "But you said yes to wedding *him*!"

Colin frowned at that. "Yes, you said yes to wedding me. I suppose it is all right if Gaffin kills me?"

Chantal ignored him. "I had to agree to Sir Colin's proposal. Here I was, stuck in Bath with nothing and no one—"

Dr. Bennett looked as though he wanted to interrupt, but Colin put a hand on the man's shoulder. "It's no use, man. She only wanted you for one thing."

Dr. Bennett subsided mournfully. Colin wagered that Chantal's free medical attention had just come to an end.

Chantal went on. "I couldn't send for you then, because I didn't think you could ever forgive me!"

The unbelievable thing was that Colin didn't think Chantal was acting, not for a moment. Gone were the practiced looks of longing, the seductive tones, the calculated displays of bosom and fluttering lashes. This was a Chantal he'd never seen before.

Bertie clutched her hands in his own, pressing them dramatically to his heart. "Oh, my darling, my forever love, there is nothing I would not forgive you!"

"Well, that's a relief," Colin murmured. After all, Chantal's list was rather a long one.

The bishop rather obviously dropped a large volume of hymns to the floor. The well-calculated *bang* echoed painfully through the chamber, halting the lovers' effusiveness at last.

The bishop smiled hopefully at Bertie. "My lord, it seems we have a bit of a kerfluffle. I provided Sir Colin with a special license only this morning in order for him to wed Miss Marchant. In the doctrine, this means that they have already entered into the marriage contract."

"But—" Chantal was horrified. "But we never spoke the vows! How can we be wed if we never spoke the vows?"

The bishop made a show of rubbing his chin thoughtfully. "That is true . . ."

Colin raised his hand. "Miss Marchant is forgetting one

thing in her excitement." He shot a look at his bride. "Our daughter?" he reminded her. "Melody?"

The bishop paled. "There is already a child of your union?"

Chantal fluttered a hand. "No, no, no. That was all a . . . a misunderstanding. I don't have a child." She had the grace to look ever so slightly ashamed of herself. "I wasn't being entirely honest about that."

Dr. Bennett cleared his throat. "How old a child, might I ask?"

"A scarce three years, perhaps."

Dr. Bennett shook his head. "Then I can vouch for Miss Marchant's innocence in that regard. The rheumatic fever she suffered nearly four years ago left her heart too damaged to withstand a pregnancy, if I might be excused for that indelicacy."

The bishop seemed relieved. "Well, that's settled, then . . ."

The air seemed to leave the room. The voices around him faded as Colin heard only one phrase echoed again and again. *I don't have a child.*

If Chantal didn't have a child, then . . .

Neither did he. Melody was not his daughter. Not his.

He'd thought he'd been in pain earlier today. He'd thought he could lose nothing more.

He'd been so damned wrong.

Oh, Mellie. Oh, my funny, sweet little Mellie.

He felt someone put a hand on his shoulder and squeeze. Lementeur.

"Sir Colin, all is not lost," the dressmaker whispered into his ear. "Remember Prudence."

Colin gulped air and shook his head. "I sent her away. I've lost her."

"You can find her again."

Slowly, through the dimness of his grief, Colin heard a thudding sound. The beat of his own heart, back in his chest where it belonged.

Ready to give away once more.

I can find her. I can have Pru.

And Melody was at Brown's, where she should be. Jack's daughter, after all. Chantal had no right to her.

Uncle, not father. Uncle Colin, forever.

Not as he'd wished it, yet not the worst of fates.

He stood abruptly. "I have to go."

It took a great deal of persuasion to keep him there, but eventually the bishop convinced him that it was better to manage the legal matters now, to finish them for good. However, Colin itched at the delay. Only Lementeur's soothing hand on his shoulder kept him in his seat.

Bertie leaned forward urgently. "If you could see your way clear to revoking the license, your grace, I would be most appreciative. Really, *most appreciative*."

As the bishop's eyes narrowed in calculation, Colin hid a sour smile. Bertie was going to pay a pretty penny for stealing his bride. Good. A man had his pride, even in such a twisty arrangement as this one.

When all was ironed out and the old special license burned and the new one made out, Colin was ready to make for the door. Hector had quite a gallop ahead of him tonight!

Just as he was impatiently making his polite good-byes, he heard Bertie make a comment to Lementeur.

"Thank you for sending me that message about the wedding, sir. Your courier found me on the road just outside of Bath. I shan't forget the kindness."

Colin turned to Lementeur with a frown. "You did that?"

Lementeur blinked. "Oh, my. Yes, I suppose I did," he said smugly. "Was that wrong of me?"

Colin stared at the smaller man, his thoughts tumbling over themselves. "You . . . you are a most unexpected fellow, Lementeur."

Lementeur smiled a puckish grin. "My friends," he said with a small bow, "call me Button." Then he gave Colin a playful push. "Get thee gone, sir knight. Your princess awaits."

"Button, I am not a knight." Colin gave the man a grin, joy bubbling up within him. "I'm a pirate."

With that, he strode from the church, his heart beating strong and eager in his chest.

Right where it belonged.

CHAPTER 42

When Colin finally rode into London proper, he and Hector were filthy and exhausted. It was a miracle that Hector wasn't lame as well, for Colin had not spared the speed, not even in the darkest, moonless portion of the night. However, good roads and a complete lack of baggage had made for fairly easy travel for the big gelding and Hector still trotted along, his head high and his tail waving like a black satin banner.

It was almost as if Hector could feel Colin's joy.

Beneath that joy scurried little monsters of worry. What if she had already disappeared? What if he couldn't find her? What if she couldn't forgive him when he did?

He tried to remind himself that a mumsy carriage carrying four could not have made such good time to town. He even tried to convince himself that he'd arrived first and could very well be the one awaiting them at Brown's.

Then again, Bailiwick's horse was a great strong beast who could likely pull that little carriage all night without noticing it. Pru might be in a tearing hurry to send Melody home and put all the pain behind her.

A gaggle of brightly dressed females crossed the street before Hector. Colin tried not to twitch with impatience, especially when he found himself forced to tip his hat and bow at the women, who turned out to be ladies of his acquaintance.

Giggles and fluttering lashes met his impatient overture and the entire group slowed to a crawl, all the better to assess his outrageous condition.

He was filthy of course, as was Hector. Road dust coated them both and Colin's suit might have been acceptable yesterday but a night's worth of hard travel and that one short bit of rain had left him most sincerely rumpled.

This only fueled the storm of giggles and gossip that kept the gaggle swirling in place directly in his path. Irritated at the delay, Colin glanced this way and that, hoping that his lack of interest would send them on their way.

A flash of light reflected from something, catching his eye in truth. He looked to his left to see a jeweler's window. Displayed upon velvet were a few pieces in gold and amber. The only brilliant thing in the display was a ring displayed upon a glove stuffed to present a hand.

Feeling Colin lean to one side, Hector obediently stepped closer.

The ring was a pretty thing. The diamond stone was not large, but it sparkled. The gold filigree work of the band was lovely in its simplicity. On either side of the diamond were set three gleaming moonstones, soft and shimmering counterpoints to the clarity of the diamond.

Moonstones. They reminded Colin of Pru's eyes in the firelight.

Before he realized what he was about, he had dismounted. Striding into the shop, he commanded the clerk's attention away from at least four customers and purchased the ring.

He left the shop, tucking the small box into his breast pocket. As he walked quickly back to Hector, who was obviously musing upon the idea of walking home to the mews where he was kept, Colin smelled something that stopped him in his tracks.

Turning swiftly, he realized that the shop next to the jeweler's had a flower box beneath the window. In this box grew several pinkish flowers and a spill of familiar, spicy-scented leaves.

Mint.

It was a sign. *She is here. She is waiting for you.* Colin sprang for Hector and mounted, then yelped the gelding into a breakneck pace, sending the great horse's hooves skittering on the cobbles like a puppy on a polished floor.

I'm coming, my rogue lady! Wait! Wait for me!

When Colin rode up to Brown's, his heart fell as he saw Bailiwick step forward, ready to take Hector's reins.

He swung his leg over Hector's back and dismounted. "Bailiwick, have you been long back? Did she leave at once? Did she say where they were going?"

Someone cleared his throat. Colin looked up to see Wilberforce standing at the top of the steps, gloved hands behind his back, gaze fixed in the middle distance.

"Sir Colin, Miss Melody requires your assistance."

Oh, God. Melody must be heartbroken to lose her beloved Evan! Colin strode up the steps, pulling off his gloves, hat, and riding coat. "I ought to have explained better," he told Wilberforce mournfully. "I can't seem to get that part right."

"Indeed, Sir Colin. If you would, please—no one seems to be able to assist Miss Melody as she requires."

"Good Lord, not even Bailiwick?" Melody must be shattered if her partner-in-crime Billy-wick couldn't distract her.

Wilberforce only raised a brow. "So it would seem, Sir Colin."

With a gust of worry, Colin headed for the stairs and the rooms above. He halted when Wilberforce cleared his throat once more. By God, the man had them all well trained, didn't he?

Wilberforce inclined his head regally. "Miss Melody is in the kitchens, Sir Colin."

"Kitchens?" Colin turned and followed the man. He'd

raided the kitchens a few times when they were still trying
to conceal Melody from the staff. They were cavernous
tiled rooms full of sinks and stoves and tables. He entered
the main kitchen right behind Wilberforce. It was hardly
the sort of place Melody would run to when she needed
comfort—

Melody stood on a chair at the stove under the supervi-
sion of the club's cook, enveloped in a gigantic apron, stirring a pot so briskly that the steaming contents slopped
enthusiastically over the rim to sizzle on the stove. Gordy
Ann peeked warily from the pocket of the oversized apron
that wrapped twice around Melody. Melody spotted Colin
and gave him a big, sticky smile and a spattering wave of her
spoon. "Uncle Colin!"

Colin blinked. His heartbroken little charge looked in
fine form. Happy as a pig in mud, actually. He turned toward
Wilberforce. "What is the meaning of thi—"

He saw her. *Pru.* She was standing at one of the tables, up
to her elbows in flour, rolling out pastry with a giant rolling
pin that made him have a sudden craving for ale. At least,
that was what she had been doing before he walked into the
room. Now she stood frozen, staring at him, the pastry
dough falling from the raised rolling pin in useless clumps.

Everything inside Colin abruptly settled into place. In that
moment, he knew precisely who he was and what his purpose
was in this world. Calmly he moved forward and rounded the
table. With one hand he took the rolling pin from her strength-
less grip and set it on the table. With the other hand, he took
his handkerchief from his pocket and began to wipe the flour
from her beautiful, delicate features.

Her eyes were fixed on him as if he had risen from the
grave. When he was done with her face, he started on her
hands, wiping and scrubbing at them until the handkerchief looked more like a glob of dough than a square of
linen.

Then he tugged at those hands until she followed him, pulling her from the room and into the hall that led to yet another kitchen. As they left, he heard Melody giggle excitedly. "I'm going to get merry again!"

Indeed you are, little mousie.

In the silent kitchen beyond, Colin turned a strangely compliant Pru so that the light from the window glowed on her face. "Miss Prudence Filby," he whispered. "I did not wed Chantal. Melody is not my daughter. Chantal lied."

Pru blinked at him. "Well, it's hardly the first time."

Colin smiled to hear her old asperity return. Pru without a ready retort wasn't Pru at all. "I have something to say to you, Miss Filby. Will you shut it and listen?"

Her lips quirked. "Sure, guv, it bein' your proposal and all."

He tipped her chin and gazed into those beautiful eyes. "Do you know why I left you behind that second day?"

Pru frowned at him. What was he about, reminding her of that horrible day now when she was so happy to see him? "Yes. Because we were in your way . . . your way to Chantal."

He smiled. "Exactly." He took her shoulders gently in his large hands. "You got in my way. I held you in my arms that first night and fed you broth sip by sip and watched you sleep and knew that if I didn't get you out of my way, I would lose sight of the most important thing in the world to me."

She relented. "I know how much you love Melody. You longed to believe she was yours."

"Yes . . . and no." He laughed at her puzzlement. "I love you. There, I said it. I love you. I fell in love with you . . . oh, probably when you called me a 'lout.' " He kissed her frown away. "When I had to leave you behind again—"

"Sir Colin, I'm beginning to remember why I don't like you!"

He pulled her close. "I'm sorry. I'm so sorry. I won't do it again!"

She began to laugh, the helpless laughter of one outsmarted by fate. She dropped her forehead against his neck and laughed herself limp in his arms.

"Now . . ." He went down on one knee, enjoying the thrilled uncertainty on her face. When he pulled the small box from his pocket he could hardly keep from laughing himself at the riot of emotions that crossed her expression.

He extended the box. She drew back from it. "I don't want Chantal's ring. I couldn't bear it."

Smiling, he opened the box. "I found this one earlier to-day. For you."

Her expression went rather blank. "But . . ."

"I didn't know where you had gone but I thought that if I started looking immediately, I might find you in time."

She sniffled. "In time for what?"

He took the beautiful, delicate moonstone and diamond ring from the box and slid it onto her finger. "In time to spend the rest of my life with you."

He stood and drew her into his arms again. "I love you, Miss Prudence Filby, rogue lady. I shall love you until your russet hair turns white and your freckles fade."

She laughed. "You're in for the long haul then, guv." She hugged him, then pulled back when a sharp scent bit at her nose. "What's this?" She reached into his breast pocket and pulled out a crushed green stem. "Why in the world are you carrying this about?"

He smiled easily but there was a hint of embarrassment in his face. "It reminded me of something, that's all."

She frowned at the sprig until he plucked it out of her fingers, tossed it over his shoulder, and swept her back into his arms.

"Where were we?" he murmured into her neck.

She took his hands and placed them firmly on her back-side. "About here, I think, guv."

EPILOGUE

Colin sat at a table in one of the unused card rooms at Brown's. He reached his right hand out and stretched his fingers from the cramped claw they'd fixed themselves into.

A knock sounded at the door. "Go away," he replied grumpily. "I have to finish this!"

The door opened anyway and Pru danced into the room, wearing one of the new gowns he'd purchased for her from Lementeur. It was a rich and shimmering emerald green and made her every inch the lady she truly was.

"What do you think?" she asked, twirling. "I wouldn't presume to criticize Lementeur, but I wonder if it isn't just a bit snug in the bust?"

Colin ignored that question. After all, he'd paid the dressmaker a good bit extra for just that purpose. "My lady, you look stunning."

She grinned. "You bet yer arse I do!" She spun, then landed in his lap. "Lementeur delivered them personally. Then he stayed for tea. We had the most wonderful chat. You never told me that Lady Madeleine was kidnapped! Imprisoned right here, in the club!"

Colin patted the manuscript that continued to grow on the desk. "The entire tale is in here . . . well, a fictional version of it, anyway."

She brightened. "Oh, wonderful. I do love a good kidnapping!" She eyed the book for a long moment. "You do realize that if—when!—your brilliant stories get published, it is entirely possible that Melody will read them someday."

Colin smiled. "Oh, I doubt she'll remember the true events. She's such a tiny thing. To her it's all a bedtime story."

"Speaking of which, Button brought her a new outfit as well."

Colin nodded without surprise. "That's nice. I'll wager she looks nearly as pretty as you."

"Well . . ." Pru tilted her head. "I don't—"

The door burst open and a tiny pirate ran through the room, clad in purple striped breeches, tiny high black boots, and waving a disturbingly real-looking sword. A filthy knotted rag dangled from the pirate's belt. It wore a tiny eye patch. "Avast, you swine! Black Jack will run you through!"

"Oh, bother," Colin said mildly. "And this is a new weskit."

One wide blue eye glared at him happily. The other was covered by a black silk patch. The little sword, which Colin was relieved to see was merely gilded wood, pointed at him with pirately ire.

"Keelhaul him! Make him walk the plank!"

Colin saluted. "Yes, Cap'n Melody! As soon as I've had my tea."

The sword dropped slightly. "Tea? With lemon seed cakes? Pirates love lemon seed cakes."

"Ah, then, I foresee a brief cease-fire," Pru said dryly, "for Cook did indeed bake lemon seed cakes this morning."

Colin brightened. "Really? Because novelists love lemon seed cakes as well."

Pru laughed. "Cap'n Mousie, please tell Evan it's teatime. I'm sure he's hungry."

"He's always hungry. *Evan!*" The tiny pirate dashed from the room, narrowly missing the legs of Wilberforce, who was just entering the study.

Wilberforce, of course, took the miniature marauder in

stride, as he did everything. He bowed. "Sir Colin, Lady Lambert, I am here to report that although Lord Aldrich's wedding is imminent, he is not quite ready to depart his rooms on the top floor. In fact, he has requested that he be allowed to keep them, 'should life with the Dowager Countess Blankenship occasionally prove overpowering.' I quote."

Pru smiled. "Of course. We're only planning to expand into two apartments, after all. And Lord Aldrich is on the other side of the hall." Then her brow clouded. "Oh, I see. That would be Aidan and Madeleine's side." She turned to her husband. "Colin, I daren't speak for them. I've never met them, after all."

Colin grinned. "Oh, I dare. I dare all the time. Wilberforce, tell Lord Aldrich that he is more than welcome to keep his rooms. No one will be more sympathetic to the need for occasional respite from Lady Blankenship than Aidan and Madeleine."

Wilberforce nodded. "Indeed, sir."

Pru smiled at the head of staff. "How was dining room etiquette with Evan, Wilberforce?"

"Master Evan is learning quickly, albeit reluctantly. At the moment he is taking his chess lesson with Lord Bartles and Sir James, while being instructed in the kings and queens of England. They speak highly of his scholarship. Lord Aldrich reports great progress in mathematics, as well. I daresay Master Evan will be caught up in no time. I shall be sorry to see him sent away to school. I find him very useful in wearing out Bailiwick."

"Oh, dear." Pru wrinkled her nose. "School. Melody won't like that."

Colin blinked. "Neither will I. I've only just got him." He frowned. "I've so enjoyed teaching him to ride every afternoon."

Pru smiled at him tenderly. "Don't worry. He worships Hector . . . and you, too. And he needn't go right away. Next year will be soon enough, or even the year after. Isn't that right, Wilberforce?"

"Oh, indeed, my lady. There is still much to do."

Pru patted Colin on the chest. "See? All better."

At that moment, noises rose in the entrance hall. Colin listened curiously for a moment, then smiled widely. "They're home!"

He lifted Pru from his lap and dropped a kiss on her nose. "Come and meet the rest of the family!" He rushed from the room.

Pru followed Colin into the entrance hall more slowly. There she saw her husband greeting a tall, dark-haired man by clasping his forearm and clapping him on the shoulder.

"You look like hell, you bastard."

Ah, yes. Man-speak for "I'm very glad to see you again."

Then her adoring, loving husband turned to sweep a stunning woman into his arms. Pru watched in shock as he planted a sound smack on someone else's beautiful lips.

"Madeleine!" Colin set her back at arm's length and grinned at her. "You've returned to me at last, you vixen! Are you done toying with this lout's emotions and ready to admit your true feelings for me?"

Pru folded her arms and cleared her throat loudly. She narrowed her eyes at Colin when he turned. "Darling." She smiled sweetly. "I have pointy boots and I know how to use them."

He laughed aloud. "Too bloody right, you do!" He held out his hand to her and she came to him, smiling up into his face. He brought her hand to his lips and kissed it, still smiling.

He turned them both to face the newcomers who were looking at her with great surprise. Colin laughed again at their expressions. "Aidan, Madeleine, I'd like you to meet my wife, Prudence."

The tall man, Aidan, blinked. "You work fast. We've only been gone a few weeks."

"What a lovely surprise!" Madeleine managed a graceful elbow to her husband's midsection, all the while smiling at Pru in a friendly way. "And how are you liking Brown's, Lady Lambert?"

I like her. I didn't know if I would but I do. Pru smiled back. "I love Brown's completely. However, I think perhaps that I am Pru and you are Maddie, so let's not waste another moment with that 'ladyship' rot."

Madeleine laughed, then patted Colin on the shoulder as she passed him. "Well done, you," she murmured.

Colin grabbed her hand and kissed it. "Glad you like her. We're your new neighbors upstairs."

"Oy," Aidan said wearily. "Paws off my bride."

"Maddieeeee!"

A gaudily clad pirate missile landed in their midst. Madeleine was down on her knees in an instant. "Oh, my mousie darling! I missed you so!" She picked Melody up and stood, holding her tightly, her eyes closed. "No more honeymoons, Aidan. I couldn't bear to go away again."

Aidan, tall, lordly sort that he was, looked rather misty-eyed as well. "You look well, Lady Melody."

Melody sprang across the short distance, landing on Aidan's chest with unerring accuracy. She didn't say a word, but simply twined her arms about his neck and laid her curly dark head upon his shoulder. He silently wrapped his big arms about her. Pru doubted he'd be letting go for a very long while.

Movement at the doorway caught her eye. She turned and gasped, making the others turn as well.

A dark silhouette of a man stood in the doorway, wearing a seaman's greatcoat and holding a small valise. He was tall and very thin, almost wasted, though one could see that he would be very handsome if he were fit. Pru swallowed at the hollow emptiness she saw in his dark eyes.

Aidan let Melody slither down him to stand on the carpet. He stepped forward. "Jack."

Pru felt Colin leave her side. The two men approached their old friend with a strange sort of care, as if he might bolt back out the door if startled.

He wasn't looking at them, however. He was gazing between them and down, his eyes locked on the tiny girl who had plucked her silk eye patch from her face in order to see him better.

He dropped his valise and moved toward her.

Colin cleared his throat. "Er, Jack, I don't know if you got our letters—"

Aidan stepped up. "Jack, we discovered her a few weeks ago—"

Madeleine smiled up at him gently. "Lord Jack, you don't know me, but may I present to you—"

Jack held up a hand and they all went very still. "I know who she is." He knelt on one knee in front of Melody. "You look just like your mother," he said softly.

Pru pressed a hand to her breastbone, her heart thudding. Out of the corner of her eye she saw Madeleine knot her hands together, her knuckles white. Neither dared utter a word.

Melody blinked her large blue eyes at the man before her, then reached out to stroke his thin face with her pudgy baby fingers. "You're Cap'n Jack."

He didn't smile but only nodded seriously. "And you are?"

She put her other hand on his face, framing his darkness with pink softness. "I'm Cap'n Melody."

"Hello, Melody. I am your father."

Melody tilted her head and gazed at him for a long moment. No one in the room dared breathe. "I like ships," she said finally. "Do you have a ship?"

He nodded again. "I have many ships."

"Can I see them?"

"Certainly." He stood and held out his hand. "I shall show you my flagship, *Honor's Thunder.*"

"All right." She took his hand and walked him to the

door, then turned to wave at the assembled pairs of wide eyes. "I'm going to go see Papa's ship. Bye!"

Wilberforce helped Melody into her little coat, then opened the door for them, bowing silently as the two passed from the club. Then he shut it behind them, the click of the latch sounding through the hall.

It was as though everyone exhaled at the same moment. Madeleine came to stand next to Pru. "Was that wise, do you think?" Her dark eyes were worried. "He's very odd. What does he know of children?"

Pru shook her head, more than a little concerned herself. "I don't know. But what right have we to say? He is her father."

Colin moved to stand with Aidan, who still gazed at the closed door where recently had passed a troubled man hand in hand with a tiny pirate. "Will it work, d'you think?"

Aidan shook his head slowly. "I don't know. He seems more remote than ever." He let out a long breath. "Still, if Melody can't reach him, I very much fear that no one ever will."

Melody leaned away from the circle of Button's arms and gazed at him in stunned surprise.

"I can't believe it. Everything happened just like Uncle Colin's second novel, *Bride of the Pirate,* when Captain Collins goes in search of his lost love Giselle and finds all those characters on the journey. And there really is a Pomme, just like in the book? And Giselle is the actress Chantal Marchant, the one who died? And the black pirate Gafferty, that was this Gaffin fellow? Gafferty always scared me to pieces. Did Aunt Pru really kick him?"

"Most assuredly." Button smiled with satisfaction. "Furthermore, she tricked him so thoroughly that he never did find Chantal, not unless it was her grave he visited. Dear Lord Bertram hid her away and took such wonderful care of her. She lived much longer than anyone expected her to, and they were deliriously happy, right to the end."

Melody shook her head in wonder. "I cannot believe it." Then she sat up. "Of course! Uncle Aidan and Aunt Maddie—that was Uncle Colin's first novel, *My Lady's Shadow*!" Laughing, she leaned back into Button's shoulder again. "Clever Uncle Colin!"

Button smiled. "Oh, yes. You know he wrote about your parents, as well."

Melody giggled. "Well, it certainly wasn't in his next book, *Queen in the Tower*!" She sighed. "I love that story the best of all of his books."

"I'm not surprised, since it happened to you." Button raised a brow.

Melody turned her head to stare at him in consternation. "But that book could never truly happen!"

"Is that right?"

Her puzzlement grew. "But . . . it had an *elf*!"

Button's smile became very mysterious indeed as he leaned back into the cushions and began again. "Once upon a time . . ."

Read on for an excerpt from
Celeste Bradley's next book

SCOUNDREL IN MY DREAMS

Coming soon from
St. Martin's Paperbacks

"Once upon a time there was a man
who had lost everything . . ."

"Papa! I can see the house! It's a big house!"

It was quite possible that no one in the world could be as excited as not-quite-four-year-old Melody could be excited. She jumped on the sprung carriage seat, she hung from the window, she even forgot her rather loathsome rag doll for two consecutive minutes.

Jack, or rather Lord John Redgrave, heir to the Marquis of Strickland, picked up his tiny daughter's doll from the floor of the carriage and put it back on Melody's seat. Gordy Ann looked like a tatty cravat tied into knots and then dragged behind a mule team for a year or so.

Yet Melody's love for her knew no bounds. Jack could hardly complain, for that expansive circle of love now included him as well.

I rank somewhere after Gordy Ann and before berry trifle. Well, perhaps I am tied even with berry trifle.

It was an acceptable place to stand. After all, he was rather partial to berry trifle himself.

Or rather, he had been long ago when the world had consisted of colors other than gray and tastes other than sand.

Beside him, Melody bounced on the seat and sent him a gleeful look over her shoulder. "Papa, I can see the door!" Her big baby-blue eyes sparkled.

Things were looking up. His world of gray now included the color blue.

They were her mother's eyes exactly. Eyes like morning sky, like blue topaz, like the egg of a robin. Amaryllis's eyes could tease and flash and twinkle, turning unwary fellows into brainless wax in her hands.

And those eyes could turn as cold as the shadows of a glacier, like the ones he'd seen in the north seas. Like the one he carried inside his chest.

Tiring of the unchanging view from the window, for they still drove slowly up the lengthy winding drive, Melody scrambled over to the other seat to fetch Gordy Ann and then returned to Jack. Without hesitation, Melody climbed into his lap and leaned contentedly against his chest. Looking down, Jack tried to decide if he ought to put his arm about her for safety. She looked secure enough, so he let her be.

Tirelessly affectionate, Melody was like a candle flame, trying to thaw that glacier inside him. Yet even a tiny thaw might become a summer, given time enough. He tucked his arm about her, just in case the carriage hit a pothole.

He was a little surprised that she wasn't intimidated by him. Most children were, as were most adults, now that he thought upon it. Melody, however, had simply adopted him as part of the strange and unlikely family of Brown's Club for Distinguished Gentlemen and had instantly accepted him as her very own Papa.

He'd known she was his at once, for she looked exactly like the only woman he'd ever loved. Even without such a reference point, Melody had seemed to simply know him.

She called him "Papa" to his face and "Cap'n Jack" to

everyone else. He was a captain, actually, for he held his uncle's fleet of ships—ships that would someday soon be his when the Marquis finally let go the tenuous thread of his existence.

Melody was his child and his responsibility, yet over the last three days she had become something much, much more than that. Melody was the first person in a very long time to make him feel anything at all.

Which made him doubly furious that Miss Amaryllis Clarke could abandon his child to half-hearted foster care and go on her merry way!

Anger was also something new to his gray world. Interesting thing, anger. Anger meant that he cared about something. Each new/old emotion unfolded before his numbed soul like a letter written by him but long forgotten. Familiar, yet entirely untried.

The carriage rolled to a smooth halt. Jack looked through the window to see a vast and luxurious house. His view was limited mostly to the semi-circle of costly marble steps that led to the richly carved front doors. A flurry of liveried grooms came forward to hold the horses and to open the carriage door.

Jack was unimpressed. Strickland was older but every bit as luxurious, with five times the estate of this place. Amaryllis had married well. She was a wealthy baroness. If she'd waited a little, she could have been an obnoxiously rich countess, who might or might not deign to notice a mere wealthy baroness.

Amaryllis had never been a patient sort.

Jack and Melody were admitted at once and installed in an ostentatiously formal parlor. The room was so grand and gilded and dripping with crystal that the usually irrepressible Melody clung to Jack's leg and stuck a corner of Gordy Ann into her mouth, gazing about her with wide eyes.

Jack didn't sit. He remembered that much about anger. Anger was done better standing.

In an almost-but-not-quite-rude amount of time, the door opened and Amaryllis drifted in. Tall and elegant, hair as dark as fine mink, eyes like cool blue pools. Perfect features, inviting figure, exacting fashion sense. Her gown was as black as a mourning gown, but the cut was perfection.

She was every bit as lovely as the last time he'd seen her, when she was furiously demanding that her father throw him from the house, but now her liveliness was replaced by a layer of acquired ennui.

She watched him closely for his reaction, though she pretended stylish lassitude. "Jack? Is that really you? Heavens, what in the world brings you to this dull old house?

Jack waited curiously, but the sight of Amaryllis left him entirely cold. Except for the anger.

"I've come to speak to you about our child."

Amaryllis flicked a bored glance in Melody's general direction, then focused on Jack with a calculating gleam. "I don't have children, darling. Everyone knows that."

Without another word, Jack turned and walked Melody to the door of the parlor. He pointed at the bottom step of the grand winding staircase. "Sit."

Melody sat, clutching Gordy Ann close. She gazed up at him with those eyes—couldn't Amaryllis recognize her own features in miniature?—and her bottom lip slowly emerged.

Jack gazed at her, nonplussed.

She thinks you're angry at her.

Oh.

"I'm not angry at you, Melody."

Big blue eyes blinked. And dampened.

Oh, God. Alarm was a new feeling. Definitely one for the list.

"Melody, I am angry, but I am angry at the lady in the parlor. I am going to say some rather rude things to her now and I don't want you to have to hear them. If you sit here with Gordy Ann, I will come out in a few moments to fetch you."

As he watched, the lower lip began to retreat and the eyes blinked back the moisture. "You're angry at the lady?"

"I am."

"Gordy Ann doesn't like the lady."

Oh damn. "Gordy Ann might like the lady better after a while."

Melody nodded, but Jack had to admit that Gordy Ann didn't look very forgiving.

"Will you stay here?"

Melody nodded again, this time seeming her usual self.

Jack left her sliding Gordy Ann up and down the polished banister at the bottom of the stairs and returned to the parlor.

Amaryllis had arranged herself attractively on a sofa. There was plenty of room for Jack to join her, but he remained standing.

"How can you deny you had my child?"

Amaryllis blew out a breath and abandoned her seductive pose, instead reaching for a chocolate from a box on the table next to her. "I don't have children, Jack. I'd never ruin my figure so."

Frowning, Jack sent an assessing glance over that figure. He was no expert, but Amaryllis looked exactly the same as she had four years ago. Possibly slimmer.

She was watching him look at her. "Do you like what you see, handsome Jack?" She ran a fingertip along her neckline, ending at her cleavage. "You used to like it quite a bit, if I recall."

"I don't recall, actually." He narrowed his eyes. "Amaryllis, no more games. Four years ago, you came to my bed. The next day you announced your engagement to another man. Nine months later, you deposited our child with a nurse and left her there. Two months ago, you ceased paying that nurse, whereupon she abandoned our child on the doorstep of my club. Go on, admit it!"

As he'd spoken, her face had undergone a journey from

amusement to surprise to outright confusion. Now she gazed
at him with her jaw frankly slack and her eyes blinking un-
comprehendingly.

Then she shut her jaw, opened her mouth to say something, closed it, blinked, and then laughed out loud. "God,
you've gotten so droll, Jack! It's a silly joke, but it has brightened an otherwise deadly day immeasurably." She chuckled.
"A secret baby! Good lord, what a thought!"

Jack gazed at her, his anger turning to furious bewilder-
ment. "Amaryllis, this is deadly serious! How could you do
such a thing? And why, of all things, did you stop paying the
nurse two months ago? You obviously have not suffered
from some sort of financial upheaval, unless all this is riding
on debt!"

At that, her eyes snapped. "Of course it isn't and I'll
thank you not to spread such rumors!" She stood, angry herself now, and advanced on him. "For your information, Lord
John, you are intruding on my mourning with your nonsense! I think it is high time you left—or shall I have you
tossed out on your arse, *again*?"

Mourning? The black gown. "Your husband?"

She rolled her eyes. "How I wish. No, it is my father. His
heart, eight weeks ago."

Jack reeled in his fresh, unaccustomed anger and took a
step back. He bowed. "My apologies. I shall go. Give my sym-
pathies to your mother and sister."

Amaryllis plunked back down on the sofa and took another chocolate. "Mother died a year ago. Laurel wasn't fond
of Papa anyway."

Jack turned and walked slowly from the room. Amaryllis
might be lying, yet her confusion had seemed entirely genuine. She sincerely had no idea what he was talking about!

Melody looked up from her little spot on the stairs and
blinked Amaryllis's blue eyes at him.

Could Amaryllis have *forgotten* that night?

That night . . . the night that he could not erase from his mind. No matter that she had refused his proposal the next day, no matter that she was quite thoroughly married now.

That one night still ranked as the only moment in the last few years that he'd felt even remotely human—that one night where the world was not cold and gray and grim.

Lost in his swirling thoughts, Jack took Melody's little hand and walked her down the hall toward the great doors.

Amaryllis had looked at Melody like some sort of unpleasant subspecies, as if at any moment the little girl might lunge at her with grubby paws extended, intent on soiling her gown.

No, Amaryllis was no one's mother.

Which meant that he, Jack, was no one's father. Then who was Melody?

Lost in thought, he passed a dark-clad woman in the hall without truly registering her presence. She dropped the book she carried as he passed. Quite automatically, he bent to retrieve it and pressed it back into her hands. "Pardon me, madam."

Melody waved at her, opening and closing her pudgy fingers in the manner in which tiny children wave.

How in the world was he going to break it to Aidan and Colin that the little girl they loved so much was of no connection to them whatsoever?

Miss Laurel Clarke, clad in black mourning—but not for the parents she'd despised!—never married, never asked, stood in the hallway of her wealthy sister's house and watched the man and child walk away from her to the door. Her shaking hands held a book with a grip that turned her knuckles white with strain.

The world had just spun wildly on its axis and had come down in an entirely different shape.

Memories. Fear. Pain. Then at last, the tiny furious wail.

The midwife who wouldn't meet her gaze. *Born dead. Poor little mite. It happens.*

Now, the man in the doorway, the man who couldn't be there, the man who had just walked past her as if she didn't exist. He knelt before the child at the open door. "It looks like rain," he said quietly. "Are you buttoned up?" He stood and extended his hand down. "Come along, Melody."

Blue eyes.

Melody.

Just like hers.

Melody.

Born dead.

"I heard her cry." The words slipped from her numb lips like a whisper, like a battle roar, like the last words of a defiant prisoner.

She'd heard that cry. She'd believed that cry. So she'd named her child, despite all the argument and disbelief.

Melody.